Power

The Girl in the Box
Book 10

Robert J. Crane

Power
The Girl in the Box
Book 10

Dedication

This one is for the readers, who have supported me en masse and given me the power to tell the stories I wanted to tell.

Chapter 1

Apiolae, Roman Empire
264 A.D.

She didn't know that today was going to be the day that she died, and even if she had, it wouldn't have mattered one bit.

The pains of labor were coming hard and fast upon Camilla now, and she was tilted back to minimize her discomfort. The smells in the small hut were overpowering—the sweat, the stink of childbirth made her nearly want to gag. She was perspiring, her skin clammy. She could hear the sound of her own straining. In her head, it sounded like wood being pushed to the snapping point. The pain between her legs heralded the baby's coming. That or her death, she figured.

"Camilla," came the voice from down there, down by the pain. She looked upon the darkened face of Aelia, the midwife. "Things are moving quickly now. I will have you push upon the next swelling of the pain."

"It is all pain," Camilla said between abruptly drawn breaths. They were like fire taken into her body, each of them.

Aelia smiled sweetly, the cow. "I see the top of a head. Do you have a name for the child?"

1

Camilla drew another ragged breath, trying to keep from screaming. "Marius, if it's a boy. Aureliana, if it's a girl."

Camilla did not miss the subtle flickering of Aelia's face as she glanced down, then back up to meet Camilla's eyes. "Is Marius the father's name?"

Camilla took another impatient breath. She'd kept the father's identity to herself. It didn't bear talking about, in her opinion, that she'd met a strange man and fallen prey to his charms. She'd woken up groggy, disoriented, and barely able to see straight the next morning.

She'd found out about the baby not too long after.

And for the life of her, she could not remember his damned *name*. She remembered his low words, but barely, the smooth lines of his face, the near-glow of his green eyes. His caress when he brushed her arm and shoulder had felt silky at first. She remembered him speaking to tell her his name, but it was as though the words themselves had been ripped from her mind with a touch.

A touch that had turned to fire.

Camilla had had lovers before, had been with men in dark places and felt their touch. Rough or gentle, she'd never met a man who made her feel a searing in her skin before, all pain and no pleasure.

And what in the skies of Jupiter was his name? It was gone. Just gone.

"The baby is crowning," Aelia said, her tone neutral. The cow sounded as though she were delivering nothing more important than a baby ... well, cow. She had helped deliver more than a few of those, Camilla supposed. "A few more good pushes and we'll have them out." She glanced up and smiled. "As I said, it is moving fast. Another few minutes at most and you'll be holding your baby."

"Oh, good," Camilla said. The pain was interminable, and hearing that there was a definite end to it was a comfort in itself. She could buttress herself against the torment for a few minutes more if that was all it would take. She could feel the agony rising within her for another wave and she pushed as furiously as she could.

Her nerves sang in pain, screamed in pain, and after a moment of resisting she added her own voice to the chorus because WHY NOT OH IT HURTS IT HURTS IT HURTS IT HURTS AIIIEEEEEEEEEEEEEEEE—

Camilla realized after a moment that she had started to scream along with the pain, had sung with it. The searing fire built to a crescendo and then began to subside, replaced by her own labored breathing. She sagged back on the bed, feeling the steady burning in her loins.

"Very close now, Camilla," Aelia said. "The head is out and I've very nearly got the shoulder clear." She sounded so calm, the cow. Like she was in the midst of something ordinary, as though there wasn't pain, pain, pain as far as the eye could see, the ear could hear, the skin could feel—

Camilla grunted. The pain she felt now was not like the other pain. It was a burning that was continuous, a searing that seemed to be rising in her groin, independent of the labor pains. This one sizzled inside, inside her like—

"It burns," she moaned and felt her face contort even as the other pain—the labor pain—rose again within her.

"It comes quickly now," Aelia said, her voice muffled, not looking up. "This will be the time—"

"*It burns!*" Camilla screamed as the crescendo of labor clashed with the screaming, burning fire against the skin of her insides where she could barely feel the baby lodged within her. Even with the pain she could tell there was something wrong, something different from the waves of agony that had come with the birthing. That was rising again, too, there was no stopping it now, but the other pain—

Oh, gods—

Camilla's scream tore free from her throat as though it had been ripped from her like a goat's skin from its meat. The pain of labor crashed in again and she found herself pushing involuntarily, against her will, mind howling about

ROBERT J. CRANE

how there was something terribly wrong even as the child began to slip from her. She could feel it against her, the writhing thing, could feel it *burning* her as it passed—

"Just a moment more," Aelia said, but she sounded so very, very far away.

Camilla's scream faded in her own ears as the fire reached its height, its zenith, and she felt rather than heard something pop loose. Her sight fled, the smells of the room faded, her pain dropped away into black as her own screams abruptly ceased. It was all darkness and then—

Fear.

The world came back in a rush of crying. Screaming and crying. It was short, sharp cries, cries born of need and ignorance and pain.

The cries of a child.

Camilla could hear them, had expected them at the outset of the labor. But they sounded … different … than ones she'd heard before, at other births she'd been at. They sounded—

Like she was hearing them from within her own head.

She saw nothing, just a faint light through unfocused eyes. "There, there," came Aelia's soothing voice. "It is a boy, Camilla. What was the name again?" There was a pause. "Marius?"

Yes, she tried to say, but her throat would not cooperate.

Her throat …

… was already crying …

… the cries of a baby.

There was something else with her, raw fear pushing against her. She could feel it, something squirming and afraid, something longing for warmth and darkness. Something scared of every raw, cutting sound, every rough touch of Aelia's hands. It pushed against her thoughts, and she pushed back roughly.

What … is … this …?

Camilla tried to give voice to the words, tried to push them past the screaming of her lips, but failed. The fear of the other was overcoming everything.

"Camilla?" Aelia's voice permeated her consciousness, broke through the screaming of the child using her voice. "Camilla?" She could hear Aelia's voice get higher. "Marcellina!" Aelia called, the panic obvious as she screamed out for the assistant she had left outside.

There was a surge of light—the door opening, Camilla dimly realized over the screaming and the fear from the other—and the sound of harsh footsteps on her floor. She could feel the rough sensation of a blanket being draped over her skin, wrapping completely around her, of a sense of warmth.

The other felt it, too, and a little of the fear subsided. Just a little, though.

"Take the child," Aelia said, and Camilla felt the world shift roughly, the balance tilt. A dim hint from that came to her, and she dismissed it as madness—

"Is she …?" Marcellina's voice came from above her, and a subtle rocking began, the bare motion of left to right.

"Dead," Aelia said. There was a pause. "She must have died during the last moments of the labor."

What …?

"And the child?" Marcellina asked. She was barely a girl herself, a thin, reedy little thing. There had been a reason she'd been waiting outside. Gossipmonger.

"We will take him with us, for now," Aelia said. "Camilla had no family left. The boy—Marius, she wanted him to be named—we will have to find him a home."

A silence filled the air. The cries had subsided, and only the faintest hint of light made it into Camilla's vision. But she could feel the blanket around her, strong arms beneath her. She could smell, could hear. *It is not possible*, she wanted to tell herself. And yet—

Somehow it was.

5

She pressed her thoughts against the other thing that was with her, the other ... mind? She felt it press back only gently, a deep weariness already falling over it. It was incomprehensible, nearly, especially for a woman who tried to think of herself as reasonable, tried not to indulge in fits of fancy—

It is like a story of the gods, a tale of punishment and madness and woe for those who go against them. What did I do to deserve this ...?

The other mind in her body slept, and she felt it drift away while she stayed awake, fighting the urge to sleep that came with it. She stayed, numb in her shock, the faint light still flooding through her eyes as she was rocked, back and forth, like the baby she now was.

Chapter 2

Sienna Nealon
Now

The door burst off the steel box with the fury of a succubus unleashed. It felt as if I'd been speaking to Adelaide in my head for hours, but I knew when I'd come back to myself that only minutes had passed. Minutes that I'd spent in that cramped metal box, the smell of blood and fear still trapped in the dark with me. The steady thrum of the aircraft's engines buzzed in the background, and I smiled as a slightly oily scent flooded into the open box along with the light of the cargo plane's hold.

"What's up, bros?" I snarled as I stood there, feeling the cool air run over my skin.

Two massive specimens stood in muted shock in front of me peering in, one to each side, a divide between them where I'd sent the door to the box that had been imprisoning me skittering across the metal grating of the deck. The guy on the left side had long, curly red hair and a red beard while the other had short dark hair and a clean-shaven face.

They both looked at me blankly. I could tell that their brains hadn't gotten the tray tables up and the seatbacks locked just yet. There was a boiling anger in me that wasn't entirely my own, something closer to the surface than usual that wanted to tear off their faces, shred the skin from their bodies in large chunks, expose their entrails to the sweet light of day—

Settle down, Wolfe.

But it will be so sweet, Little Doll, to taste their blood on the tip of the tongue, to—

"That's about enough of that," I said, letting my thoughts form out loud.

"Wh–what?" The red-haired one asked, and I could see the genuine surprise on his face. What was his name again? Grihm, that was it. Grihm was the redhead. Which made the clean-shaven one Frederick. I glanced at him; he looked just as stunned as his brother.

"I wasn't talking to you." I surged out of the metal enclosure with a speed greater than I'd ever had. I had tapped directly into the power of Wolfe, and of the many things he'd been—murderer, psychopath, serial killer—

Hey, the voice of Wolfe protested from within me.

Well, you were. Are. Still would be if you could be.

—he was also a lot stronger and faster than I'd ever been. I couldn't have hoped to break open the door to the box that his asshole brothers had trapped me in, but for Wolfe it was all, "Knock and the door shall be opened unto ye."

I was hoping his brothers' skulls operated under the same principle.

I slammed into Grihm with a punch to the midsection that he was just beginning to prepare for when I hit him. These two jerkoffs had done a number on me recently, busted open some of my internal organs, laid a hurting on me like I hadn't felt in a while.

All signs of it were gone now. Healed by the power of Wolfe, that creepy and sadistic and magnificent bastard. One of the souls that lingered in my head, and now my new BFF.

That probably should have been cause for concern.

Hey, he said again with a little bit of umbrage.

Sorry.

The blow to the midsection caught Grihm flat-footed. If he'd been surprised I'd broken down the door, he was almost completely unprepared for the world-ending blow to his gut that I struck him with. He grimaced in pain.

And flew into the ribbed steel hull of the plane twenty feet away.

The whole world shifted with the sudden impact of his body against the bulkhead, a tilt in gravity as though something heavy had just impacted the plane from the outside. I felt like I was on the bridge of the *U.S.S. Enterprise* during a space battle, and the world turned sideways while I lost my footing. I watched Frederick go tumbling with me as I scrambled to grab hold of the grating on the deck. My fingers caught hold while I watched that dark-haired bastard fall a few more feet before he managed to get a grip as well.

It took a moment for the plane to stabilize, and I returned to my feet before either of the other two, which was good. They still both had that look like they were shaking off surprise. Which was even better.

Because it made them prey.

Prey are unprepared, Wolfe said, lecturing me. *They wait, they react, they try to fight back after the hunter has made his move.*

Yes, thank you, I said. *Really helpful. And kind of scary.*

He was right about one thing, though, I reflected as I stooped into a low crouch and readied myself to spring.

They were prey.

My prey.

I launched myself at Frederick in a low run, my center of gravity closer to the deck than his. I was average height for a woman, after all, five foot four, and he was a mountainous, towering beast who looked like he should have been hitched to a wagon in the old west, lashes falling across his back as he pulled his burden along a dusty road.

I actually giggled at that image as I slammed iron knuckles into his back and heard him release his breath. I'd hit him in the kidney, just the place where he'd hit me not ten minutes earlier. It had hurt. A lot. And I carried a grudge.

I hit him again as he struggled with his balance. He threw back an elbow to try and knock my head off my neck, but I was short enough to duck it. It caused him to lose his balance, and I was nimble enough to let his momentum carry him to the ground. With a little help, maybe.

I knocked one of his legs out from beneath him at the most vulnerable moment. "Timber!" I cried gleefully. When I'd fought these two only a half hour before, they moved like lightning and hit like … well, also like lightning, I suppose. I'm fast, but I'm not *that* fast.

Or at least I hadn't been. Things had changed.

I landed on Frederick's back as his face hit the deck. I heard his roar of rage on impact and knew that it hadn't hurt him one bit. I planted another painful blow to his kidney and this time he howled. These creatures were on such a level of strength, their skins so resistant to damage, that they could shrug off bullets like they were BBs and brush aside punches from powerful metahumans like they were wet cardboard being slapped against them.

I drove another fist into Frederick's kidney and listened to the roar mingled with pain—real pain—and grinned. I was going to turn him into wet cardboard by the time I was done—

I saw a flash of movement out of the corner of my eye and it set my predator's instincts into motion. Grihm was charging at me, and he looked like a rhino loping its way across the plains. Huge. Powerful.

Well, if the plains were a confined cargo plane's hold, and the rhino was a subhuman beast barely a step above a wild dog on the evolutionary chart—

HEY.

Oh, hush up, Wolfe, we're busy here.

Grihm was coming at me without thought, without logic. He was all out on his run, uncaring about what he hit behind me, so long as he turned me into a greasy smear on the deck in the process.

Big and dumb, that's what these boys were. Just like—

HEY—

SHUT UP, WOLFE.

I propelled myself low, taking advantage of Grihm's absurd height advantage. He may have been charging at me, but his center of mass was still several feet off the ground. I greeted his left knee with a booted foot. His joint didn't give out—he was still obscenely tough, after all—but it didn't have to.

I knocked his damned leg right out from underneath him.

Grihm collapsed, coming down in an absurd triangle, with his ass making up the apex, his feet being one point, head being the other, and the deck making up the bottom of the shape. Well, sort of. I was beneath him, after all, so technically, I guess I was the bottom of the triangle. And since having one of these obtuse, moronic mules landing on me wasn't in my plans for the day—*Shut up, Wolfe, stop taking my insults to them so personally, you wuss*—I kicked up and landed a foot in Grihm's crotch and changed his downward trajectory back to up.

That dumb son of a bitch flipped ass-over-teakettle and hit the wall behind the metal box I'd been trapped in so hard that the plane rocked again. My fingers snapped into the grid on the deck and held fast, keeping me from sliding. Frederick was not so lucky, and I watched him face plant into a cargo pallet. I doubt it hurt him, but it was fun to watch.

A screeching of metal against metal greeted my ears as the plane leveled out. The door to the box that I'd broken open had skidded across the deck, and it came to rest only inches to my right. It was heavy, it was metal, and it was like getting an express delivery of awesome, right to my fingertips.

I watched the Wolfe brothers get to their feet as I stood waiting for them, watching to see which of them would get up first, which of them would be less wounded. Neither of them were significantly injured yet, and even if they had been, they healed fast. I mean, with Wolfe's power at my fingertips I was pretty sure I'd healed a ruptured liver and kidney in less than a minute. My meta healing was fast, but not that fast. These boys were absurd; not only could they take punishment like nothing else on earth, but even when they did get hurt, they healed from it faster than most people could have even imagined inflicting damage on them.

Fortunately, I was not "most people" when it came to imagining damage. And now I wasn't even "most people" when it came to actually inflicting it.

Just for kicks, I shouted, "Heads up!" at Frederick as he stumbled to his feet. He was wobbling a little, still holding onto his back like it hurt. I swung the door of the box like I was a WWE wrestler and it was a metal folding chair. I aimed for his face and I heard it hit solidly. I saw at least three teeth fly into the air above the door and Frederick smashed through the cargo pallet as if the wooden boxes stacked on it were Styrofoam packing peanuts. Pieces went everywhere.

And Frederick went through the hull of the plane with a crash that drove us sideways once more.

The lighting in the cargo hold went dim, flickering from the impact. The remains of the cargo pallet hammered into the hole in the side of the plane and wedged there, partially closing it off. There was a roar of air from outside as the pallet tried to work its way out the hole, but it remained lodged in place as the plane centered itself once more.

I could feel the plane descending, and I wondered when that had happened. If the pilot was smart, he'd have started the descent when we first began rocking around. If he was dumb, he'd have started it just now, I supposed.

I was back on my feet and I cast a look around for my other quarry. Grihm was behind the box, still working to get his balance. I think I might have disoriented him with all that flinging him around. Guy like that, his inner ear probably wasn't used to all the ups and downs. It's not like he got tossed around every day.

I hit him from behind with an epic sucker punch. It drove his face into the metal side of the plane and—I swear—left an imprint like an iron mask. I ripped him out of it and saw his lips were bleeding. A little cry of joy escaped me, and I punched him squarely in the face, watching the cut widen on his lip.

His long, red hair was blowing in the wind that was rushing around the cargo hold, and his eyes were glazed. He blinked at me, and I hit him again without mercy or remorse. I hit him so hard that his shirt ripped, pulling him free of my grasp and sending him flopping toward the back of the plane. He rolled head over ass twice, his limbs unresisting. He landed at the rear of the hold, where the decking rose in a forty-five degree angle to indicate the ramp where they loaded the cargo.

He came to rest splayed out, supine, a human body formed into an X. It didn't take much more than a gentle reminder in the form of memories of what he and his brothers had done to me to coax me forward again. Mercy was for the weak and stupid, so I ran up and stomped his groin as hard as I could. It produced the sort of reaction you might expect, complete with a scream that made him sound like he was about to burst into tears.

"Not so much fun when someone does it to you, is it?" I snarled. He was curled up into the fetal position, and I planted another kick to his lower back, aiming for kidneys again. It's a good place to hit, lots of pain involved. "How do *you* like it?"

I didn't even recognize my own voice as I asked him.

I was so focused on monologuing like some old-time movie villain, that I didn't even see the punch that downed me. I felt my face hit the deck, leaving an impression of my own there, and I hoped it wasn't quite as ugly as Grihm's had been. I heard metal grind and gravity shift once more. The

13

deck lurched beneath my feet and face, then lurched again. The faint howl of the hole in the side of the plane became a much closer—and much more frightening roar.

My hands grabbed instinctively for the metal grid. I opened my eyes and lifted my face to see that the impact of the blow that had sent me against the deck had broken open the rear cargo door of the plane. It dangled, bobbing gently, the wind ripping at me as I held tightly to the only purchase my fingers could find. I looked left and saw Grihm there, hanging on with one hand and up in a crouch. His lip was still covered in blood but there was no sign of a wound.

I glanced up the ramp and saw Frederick standing, just outside the reach of the wind that was whipping around his brother and I. He glared down at me with a fury that made my stomach go flip flop. Neither of them were injured anymore. Both of them were mad as hell—at me—

And to top it all off, I could feel the descent of the plane steepening and had a vague intuition—named Roberto Bastian—telling me that we were, without doubt, on an angle of descent so steep that we were certain to crash.

I kept one eye on each of the two beasts before me and steadily rose to my feet, watching my balance in the rapidly descending—sorry, crashing—plane. Not that it mattered for much longer.

"Little girl, all alone," Frederick said, and I could hear him over the roar of the wind. "No one to save you now."

I saw them both coming, charging at me. The impact would surely be bad, would guarantee injury, pain. It was not something I wanted to get hit with, not only because of the impact, but because I'd be close at hand with the two of them. Close enough to work their claws. Close enough to let them rip and tear.

Oh, and the plane was going to crash. Couldn't forget that.

I took two steps down the ramp and leaped backward, Grihm and Frederick behind me. I wrapped my arms around myself and turned my body like I was completing a graceful dive. I could see shadowed ground somewhere below, shapes of trees, and branches, and then a glint of light on water.

I twisted and brought my legs down as the wind rushed past me, the night air swallowed me up, and the darkness and gravity dragged me down, down to the earth.

I slammed into the hard ground with the fury of gravity—

Chapter 3

—and came right back to my feet like I'd stepped off a curb and not a falling airplane.

I can't say I didn't feel it, and I can't say it didn't hurt, but I can say I didn't care. I was still fuming over the beating that Grihm and Frederick and their boss had laid on me earlier in the evening, aided by a telepathic bitch named Claire. I don't think it was just the fury of Wolfe that made me want to push through any pain until I had flayed them all alive.

Okay, well, maybe it was Wolfe driving on the flaying bit. I was okay with just killing them with a modicum of pain and violence and terror.

I felt my joints popping and cracking as they realigned after the impact from my landing. I could see the outline of trees around me, could hear the lapping of water and the sounds of wildlife at night. Light glistened on a pond to my left, and I felt hard sand under my feet. The smell told me I was in a swamp, probably just south of Minneapolis and St. Paul, outside the city loop. Somewhere below Bloomington, I guessed, but I had no time to find evidence to support that hypothesis—

I heard two thumps close by and knew that the brothers Wolfe had joined me on the ground. I hoped they had landed on their stupid, ugly faces—

Grrrrrrrrr, Little Doll—

—but I doubted it, since they'd been around for a while longer than me, and I'd already gone out of a plane without a parachute once this year myself. Odds were good they'd done this before at some point in their millennia of experience.

"Little girl, all alone," came Frederick's voice out of the darkness.

My teeth grated as he said those words again, and my response was quick and to the point. "I haven't been alone since the day I killed your brother, asshat." Since the day I found out what I was.

"Sounds like the Wolfe is riding along in your head," Grihm's voice came from a different direction. My ears perked up, and I could feel newfound instincts that I hadn't developed listening hard, taking sniffs of the wind—

Searching for my prey with all my senses.

"It won't help you," Frederick took over, and I could tell he was somewhere behind me. "He was the least of us."

"He disagrees," I said, turning slowly. I had a suspicion— approved by Wolfe's instincts—that told me that they were going to come at me from two directions at once. This was the coyote approach, feinting and darting, getting a little piece of your prey at a time until they were too wounded and hobbled to fight back.

Coincidentally, it was the exact strategy I'd been trying to employ against Century, so I was well-versed in its application.

"We aren't going to kill you, you know," Grihm said from off to my left.

"Killing you would be too good for you," Frederick said from my right. I kept from wheeling about, staying steady and quiet in the center of their little circle. The attack was coming soon. Presumably after they were done boring me— *Grrrrrr*—sorry, intimidating me. Whatever.

"We have to break you, after all," Grihm said.

"Many have tried," I said. "None have survived."

"Ooh, she has spirit," Frederick said with glee.

"She'll make a good bride for Sovereign," Grihm agreed.

"I wouldn't go sending out any 'Save the Date' cards just yet," I quipped. I knew where both of them were now, and they knew where I was. Since they knew I was channeling Wolfe, it told me that now that they were aware of me, aware of my ability, they were overconfident again.

It's not many people who can get their ass squarely kicked, beaten all around a plane, and then think they've reestablished their dominance just because of a perceived numerical advantage. I'd been fighting longer odds than these clowns—*shut up, Wolfe, I'm not including you in this insult*—for a long damned while. This was as close to a fair fight as I got anymore.

And my power had just leveled up.

Anyone else care to join me and Wolfe in the fight of our lives? I asked inwardly.

Whatever I can do to help, I'm there, Zack said.

I don't know how much help I could be, Roberto Bastian said, *but ... yeah ... okay. I'm with you for this, since you've got your head out of your ass now.*

Bjorn? Gavrikov? Eve? I asked.

Pass, Bjorn said.

No, Gavrikov said.

Go f—, Eve began.

Got it, I said. *Well, Roberto, you weren't too shabby on strategy and tactics. Any ideas?*

There's a moment of distraction coming, Roberto said. *Use it.*

My eyes flashed as I realized what he was talking about. I could sense Grihm and Frederick coiling to spring. It was instinctive, the hint that their muscles were flexing just so, ready to leap upon me.

And they did so just as the plane exploded on the horizon.

I threw myself into a backward roll as flames lit the night sky in a mushroom cloud of orange fire. I saw the brothers Wolfe illuminated by it, springing to the place where I'd been only a second earlier, and I smiled. They narrowly missed hitting one another and each landed roughly, their anticipated target of soft flesh—me—having evaporated from beneath their feet.

I didn't wait for them to recover to move. Grihm had come down with his back to me and I had only a second or two to take advantage of it. I lunged, grabbing him with both hands in his long, red hair. I twisted it around my fingers, coiling it tight.

This motherfucker was about to know he was in a fight with a girl.

I yanked him off balance by ripping at his hair. I didn't pull it as hard as I could have, because to do so that abruptly would have torn it right out of his skull, and I wasn't ready for that quite yet. I kicked him in the gut and pulled him hard in a circle, using my strength to break his legs free of the ground—and any resistance they might offer to what I was going to do next.

Before he had a chance to stop me, I swung him around by his hair like he was an Olympic hammer. I did one orbit to build up some speed and chucked him before he had enough time to settle his inner ear enough to punch me in the face. Which would have been easy for him after all, being as he had at least three feet of height on me. I watched him arc about ten feet up before he vanished over a low line of trees. "Hasta luego, dipshit," I called after him. I'd see him later. I was planning on it.

I could hear Frederick coming at me from the side, but I was ready for him. He charged at me like these morons always do, and rather than reacting like Wolfe—like he doubtless thought I would—and meet him head on, I reacted like Sienna Nealon with enhanced reflexes and used my years of martial arts training.

Which is a fancy way of saying that now that I was as fast as he was. I grabbed his wrist and twisted it behind him as I let him charge past. I knocked a leg out from under him as he went, and a feeling of déjà vu—hadn't I just done this to one of these assholes? It's a classic for a reason, I suppose—came over me as I landed squarely on his back.

His whole body tensed, waiting for the blow to fall on his kidney. He thought he knew what was coming.

He had no idea.

"Hurt me all you want," he said as he grunted against my wristlock, "but you'll never stop us—"

I donkey punched him so hard in the back of the head that I could hear the vertebra snapping. I did it again for good measure, and then again. I could feel the flesh tearing against bone shards by then, his spinal column fragmented and ripping through the skin as I hammered him a fourth time.

Then I grabbed his head and twisted it back and forth at sickening angles to the left and right, up and down. I heard the popping of things that were never meant to pop, and I folded his head backward at a one-hundred-and-eighty-degree angle to the rest of his body before I twisted it three-hundred-and-sixty degrees around.

I did that three more times, ripping hard at it, a knee buried in his back, until his head popped off in my hands.

I heard movement in the brush behind me and turned. There was still a faint light of fire somewhere in the distance where the plane had come down, but I didn't need it to see Grihm stagger out of the bushes. He was soaking wet, and I assumed he'd landed in a pond somewhere nearby.

I tossed the head to him and he caught it instinctively. He looked down at it with unblinking eyes, like it wasn't registering what he was actually seeing.

"Question," I said, "can you boys survive decapitation?"

He looked up at me, face twisting in fury and disbelief. "I'll kill you," he said in a near-whisper. I would have expected something louder, more approaching a roar, but I suspected the fear was starting to settle in on him.

"You think so? I've now killed two out of the three of you bastards," I said, unconcerned. "I don't favor your odds."

His face changed into something feral, positively wolf-like (and Wolfe-like), and he let out a low growl like a dog that was warning someone off.

"Wow," I said, unruffled, just waiting for him to come at me, "such doge."

The faintest hint of confusion crept over his features. "Doje?" He sounded it out. "What the hell is that?"

"It's an internet meme," I said, matter-of-factly. "I'd tell you to Google it, but you've only got about five minutes to live and you're going to spend every one of those fighting for your life."

"You're going back in that box," Grihm snarled.

"I think we're heading for a Grihm finish," I said, smiling at my own pun. If I didn't, who would?

Not me, Zack said. *That was awful.*

Pawful? I sent back. *Because they're like dogs—*

There was a chorus of groans in my head.

"You better buckle up," I said to Grihm. "You bastards have done everything you can to make me fear you from day one." *Sorry, Wolfe, but it's true.* "It's about damned time you realized who has the power here."

I leapt at him before he had a chance to open his stupid mouth and respond. He saw me coming high, with a punch, but missed the low kick I whipped at him at the last second. It caught him in the knee while he struck me in the face with a clawed hand. I felt my cheek split wide, a gash three inches long running all the way up to my ear. It burned and made me want to cry out with pain …

… but I didn't.

I landed on my feet as Grihm stumbled back from my kick. I kept Wolfe front of mind the way Adelaide had taught me, and I could feel the cheek wound start to knit back together. I snarled and kept on toward Grihm, pushing forward, striking with another jumping kick and causing him to stumble back a few more steps. He was ready for my attacks, and they weren't having as much effect now that he wasn't off balance. He was parrying, countering, as best he could, and with thousands of years of vicious fighting experience, he was reasonably good at it.

My mother had once said to me that experience was a funny thing. I'd been slacking off in my training at the time, and she knew it. Rather than hammer at me about it, land on me with both feet and kick my ass into the box for defiance, she came about it a different way. "You can either have ten years of experience at something," she'd said, "or you can have the same year of experience ten times. One will make you a great fighter. The other will get you killed. You choose whether you want to take this seriously or not."

Okay, so even at her most delicate, she wasn't exactly cashmere soft. This is my mother we're talking about, not Molly Weasley.

The brothers Wolfe were some of the most feared predators in the world. They were stronger, they were faster, and they were more vicious, wicked and nasty than almost anyone else walking the world.

And as I'd discovered just a few months back in a museum in the heart of London—to my great surprise—thinking you're at the top of the food chain is a really good way for complacency to set in.

Grihm countered me, but he was slow. I kicked him again and he batted my kick away, but just barely, and he failed to exploit the opening I gave him. He felt slow. Strong, but slow. I could taste all the years of complacency settled around him. All the years of being invincible to the mooks he'd preyed upon. He'd been the alpha predator and hadn't gone up against anyone that was nearly a match for him—or his brother—in centuries.

All in all, it was a really good way to stay alive.

Until you met someone who was more of a predator than you were.

I feinted for the first time and he tried to block it. I'd gone high, leaving his leg exposed to a kick that made his knee go in the wrong direction. Grihm let out a sharp cry and fell to his good knee. I knew without doubt that he'd have it back to fixed in seconds and be right back to being on me.

Unfortunately for him, I was a predator who was constantly fighting bigger and badder nasties. I was at the top of my game.

Seconds were for pansies. Seconds were more than I needed.

I braced and hit him with a reverse side kick in less than a second. It's a spinning kick that gives you more chance to build momentum and force than a simple standing kick. It's the next best thing to a running, jumping one, or one in which I could have taken a few strides toward him. We were close, though, and this was what I could do with the space I had and the time I had.

More strength would have been better, but really, all the strength in the world was useless if you didn't aim it properly.

I hit that bastard right in the neck and listened to the sweet, popping sound of his throat crushed under explosive force.

His eyes went wide, fearful, and I heard him make a choking, gasping noise. His hands snapped up from his knee, which was still disjointed, and clawed at his throat.

While he did, I hit him with a reverse side kick again. Right in the face, as hard as I could.

His neck snapped like it was on a rubber band, back and then forward, whipping like he'd been jerked by the hand of a god. Goddess, I guess, technically.

Grihm's eyes rolled up in his head, and his body wavered there for another second, ready to tip and fall.

I hit him one last time for good measure, and his body just rolled end over end, limp. A silver light suddenly shone down on him, and I looked up to see a full moon shining down on me from where it had just come out from behind a cloud.

In the distance, I could see the metal structure of a bridge, a few hundred yards away, its dark outline over a river that was lit by the thousand sparkles of the shining moon. I listened and could faintly hear traffic on it, a car here and there. I sighed. I'd need to catch a ride back to the Agency. Rally the team.

I had a war to fight, and I'd just been handed a shiny new weapon. And a warning, something that I wasn't even sure if I wanted to share with the others. Not yet.

I looked back down at Grihm's unmoving figure and sighed again. First things first, though—this bastard wasn't going to rip off his own head, and it wasn't like I could leave him without making sure he was dead …

Chapter 4

There had been a really wide, swampy river channel between me and the road, and although I'd jumped with my newly found Wolfe strength, I hadn't quite cleared it. I'd say this was not my night, but frankly, this was the least bad thing that had happened to me this evening.

There were still worse things—much worse—that I didn't want to deal with yet.

My shoes were still sloshing as I walked through the doors to the lobby of headquarters. I could sense that I was being watched, but when I looked up I was greeted by an assload (technical term) of assault rifles and submachine guns pointed at me from all directions on the ground floor and the second floor balcony.

Reed, Scott, Zollers, Janus and Kat were standing just in front of the security checkpoint's metal detectors, and only Zollers and Janus looked relaxed. I figured they'd gotten the telepathic and empathic read on me while everyone else was still assuming the worst. I had blazed past the front gate guard without offering more than a cursory explanation, after all. Plus I had an unconscious body—the driver of the car who stopped to pick me up—in the passenger seat. I had suspected the guard would whistle for help as soon as I was through, which is what I would have told him to do if I'd been training him.

I should probably get him a raise, come to think of it.

"It's me," I said, raising my arms as if I were surrendering. "I promise. Pinky swear."

"You can't pinky swear with your hands up like that," Reed said, and his bravado almost masked the slight crack I heard in his voice.

"It's her," Zollers confirmed, and I felt the unease in the room drop, along with all the gun barrels. Which was a relief, because even with Wolfe powers, I wasn't sure my skin was conditioned to resist bullets like his had been. At least not yet.

Was it bad that I was already thinking ahead about that?

"How'd you get away?" Scott said, and his voice cracked too, big time. "I mean, you got dragged off by Weissman, didn't you? How did you—?"

"He stuck me on a plane," I said and caught a glimpse of red hair as Ariadne shouldered her way through the crowd, Agent Li a pace or two behind her. "With the brothers Grihm—and Frederick, hilariously enough."

"The what?" Scott asked.

"The big guys at Como Zoo," I said. "They were Wolfe's brothers."

"Holy shit," Reed breathed. "And did you …?"

"They're dead," I said. "I'd say it was sudden and tragic, but it took me a while. They, uh …" I swallowed hard, "… Weissman is still out there. He …" My voice trailed off and I felt a lump in my throat.

"No, he's not," Ariadne said, entering the conversation as she crossed the floor toward me in slow steps. "His body was found at the airfield in Crystal, north of Minneapolis. Along with …" She hesitated.

"My mom's," I said and felt a cool trickle of sadness run over me, causing a shiver down the back of my neck. "I saw him stab her, knew she was …" I blinked and the world got blurry. "We should … we should go to the conference room." I snapped my hands at the guard detail still filling the room, their black tactical gear a wall of ebony across the lobby. "Dismissed."

Security didn't waste time carrying out my orders, dispersing to their posts and filing away down the white hallways with military precision. Ariadne, Scott and Reed made their way toward me in the bustle of activity, and I watched them come with a reluctance born of the last ounces of denial I had in me.

My mother was dead.

And seeing the look in their eyes—Reed, my brother, Scott, the man who wanted to be my lover—that last ounce of doubt—of hope—was erased.

It wasn't either of them that took hold of me, though. They held their distance, the strong men they were, uncertain of what to say, of how to deal with the warring emotions I'm sure were raging across my face. It wasn't like I had them often. I could see the indecision.

There was none of that in Ariadne. She knew, just knew, and I felt her delicate arm find my shoulders as she steered me. I could smell the faint hint of her fragrance as I walked along numbly. I could sense Kat and Zollers and Janus around me as we stepped into the elevator, but I didn't even notice when it dinged and we stepped out on the top floor.

I let Ariadne steer. Let her guide me.

We stepped into my office and I noticed the squishing of my shoes, still wet from my plunge in the river. It was chilly, but I didn't care. I felt nauseous and strong bile threatened to burst out of me. My shirt was clinging, which I was pretty sure was the main reason that the guy who picked me up on the side of the road bothered to stop at all. It was also the reason I rendered him unconscious seconds after getting into the car. The shirt felt clammy against my skin.

"I got your suit dirty," I said to Ariadne, realizing that her pinstripe suit was sodden where she'd wrapped an arm around me.

"It's okay," she said as I sat on my couch.

"My mom," I said, and my face felt strangely paralyzed, like it wasn't capable of motion, "did she … was she the one … who … Weissman?"

"It looks that way," Ariadne said, and she sat down on the couch next to me. Reed was next to the door, and so was Scott. I saw Zollers there, too, barely in the frame.

"She took him out," I whispered. "How would she have …?" The suspicion came to me, and I glanced at my desk to see the bonsai tree that I'd left there, with a fresh envelope in front of it. "A debt repaid."

"Shhh," Ariadne said, shaking her head. "It doesn't matter now."

I leaned back against the soft cushions of my couch, and the weight of everything that had happened that evening hit me. My meeting with Akiyama, my fight with Weissman and the Wolfe brothers, my imprisonment, and my discussion with Adelaide … with Andromeda …

Remember.

My eyes felt weary. It had been a long day.

Mom.

I felt my eyes get heavy, again, and I fought back against their urge to water, fought back against the lump that threatened to rise in my throat. I pushed down on myself, flexed my inner muscles and thought of frigid cold until the heat of the emotion faded to a manageable level.

"Weissman's dead," I said. "Maybe … maybe without him running the program … maybe Sovereign will change his mind. Call the whole thing off. I'm not sure he has the stomach for doing what he'll have to now that his right-hand man is out of the game." I swallowed hard, the mere thought of what had been sacrificed to remove Weissman threatening to make me well up.

"Maybe," Ariadne conceded. "We don't have to think about that now. There's nothing more to be done at this moment."

"She's right," came Zollers's gentle voice from the doorway. "You should rest." His words carried the weight of wise suggestion, and I wondered if he'd suggested it with more than just his voice.

"I don't know if I can sleep," I said and put my head against the couch. The world tilted sideways.

"You should at least try," Zollers said and gestured toward the door. "You'll be right here in your office, and if anything happens, we'll wake you."

"I'll be right outside," Reed said with a sharp nod, his long, dark hair swaying in agreement with the Doctor's pronouncement.

"Me too," Scott said. I looked at him for just a moment, and in his flushed cheeks I saw none of the uncertainty that had plagued him so badly in the last few days. Washed away, I suppose, by the knowledge of what our enemies were doing—had done—to his family. "We'll keep an eye out and let you know if anything …" His voice trailed off.

"Thank you," I said, as he disappeared through the door. Zollers followed with a gentle smile, and I knew without him saying anything that we would talk later.

Later. When I could handle it.

"Just call if you need anything," Ariadne said as she stood, smoothing out the lines of her rumpled skirt. "I'll be in my office next door." She pointed a thumb, as though I were too discombobulated to recall where her office was.

"Thank you," I said, voice a whisper. "Ariadne …" She paused at the door. "Thank you for … everything. Everything since the day I met you. You've been … kind to me, even when I wasn't to you."

She flicked the light switch, and the scant illumination from the fluorescent bulbs shining through the door and in the cracks of the blinds of the window above the couch where I lay cast the entire office in faint light. She started to open her mouth to say something but stopped. Her face went from a hint of a smile to a moment's discomfort and settled into unease. "Just rest," she said, and closed the door as she left.

She'd acted like a mother to me since the day we'd met, protecting me more than once from the machinations of Erich Winter when she could. But she wasn't my mother.

My mother was dead.

I lay on the couch, and the tears I'd held back for so long came out in small, muffled sobs, hot liquid burning as it ran down my cheeks. I kept on that way until I had no more tears or sobs left inside, and some time after that I fell into a deep, restless sleep.

Chapter 5

No one touched him and no one wanted to be near him, and for Marius, that was just the way it was. By age six, he'd worn out his welcome nearly everywhere in town, and skeptical eyes followed him any time he was around. You could only engender extreme pain with your touch and talk to yourself so often before they got wary, and they were wary of him and more.

He'd been fortunate enough to have found a mean old man of the village who suffered him to live with the animals in the barn, always with a wary eye on him. He kept a stick to poke at Marius to keep him at length, but that was fine. It was rarely employed and never needed, because Marius had learned to keep his hands to himself at a very young age.

He lay in the fresh hay that he'd just placed in the bottom of the barn in his own little paddock that he'd claimed when he'd come here. He lay there and ate quietly, a meal of cheese that he'd made from goat's milk and honey he'd collected from the bees out near the cliff. The old man had taught him much, enough to survive if he had to.

The smell of the barn was strong, though not much stronger, in his opinion, than that of the old man's house, on the few occasions he'd had to go in there. The old man's musty stink was different than the animals and less palatable to Marius's nose. Here, things were familiar.

There was a rustle in the goat pen and he looked up. They were always a little restless around him. They could almost instinctively tell that his touch was not good for them and kept their distance. It wasn't as though he tried to touch them, and their fur protected their skin some even when he did.

Because you're a murderer, and they know it. You're a demon, a spawn of Pluto—

"No, I'm not," he said, almost casual about it. He nibbled on the piece of cheese in his blackened, calloused hand, tasted the sharp tang of it on his tongue. "You keep saying that, but I'm not."

Everybody thinks it. Everybody knows it. You're a dark child, a destroyer of everything you touch.

This was how it always was. Every day. Marius tried to ignore her, but he knew eventually she'd get through to him, provoke him.

She always did, somehow.

"The animals seem fine," he said, swallowing the piece of cheese. "I haven't destroyed them."

Yet.

He sighed and took another nibble. He was getting older, nearing his late teens. He was a man, by all rights, and should have been seeking his own fortunes, his own house. His own family—

You can't have a family. You'll destroy them, just like everything else. The voice was harsh, near-screeching, and so deep in his head that it felt as if his ears rattled with each low word spoken.

"I won't—" He felt a sharp surge of anger and then paused to let it subside. It was like this, always. Every day. He soothed himself and took a drink of the goat's milk in the skin next to him. It was refreshing on a hot day like this. It gave him a moment to compose himself before he ranted into the barn air. It wasn't as though the old man cared as if he were crazy, but the old man wasn't always the only one wandering around.

And it wouldn't do to give any more of the locals fodder for stories about him, more reasons to hate him. No, that wouldn't do at all. It wasn't like they needed the excuse.

You're a disgrace, the voice came again. Harsh and grating, filled with rough anger that flowed through every word and drove out any happiness. *A worthless beast, useless to anyone and so limited in your skills as to be nothing more than an animal yourself. You're a goat herder, and you'll never be more than that or a whelp of little aid to some poor old bastard so blind he can't afford to be picky about the help he gets.*

Marius felt the hard lump in his throat. "Well, at least I'm useful for something." He felt his eyes burn. "Unlike you. Unlike you, who dig at me and lash at me and do nothing but burn in my head like a low-ranging fire."

You destroy like fire, burn everything and everyone around you like fire. All you need do is show up at a place and—

"Shut up! Shut up! SHUT UP!" Marius was screaming, the rage taking over as he squinted his eyes closed. Every day it was like this, every day it happened, and it always built to this finale. He sat there shuddering, hands shaking in front of his eyes as he hoped against hope that this would be the day that she didn't come back. That this would be the day that the voice was gone forever from his thoughts.

Marius smacked his dry lips together and then licked them before taking up the piece of cheese again. He'd dropped it in his frenzy. His breathing had almost returned to normal, and he could swear he smelled the faint hint of smoke from the old man's fire.

Every day was like this.

See you tomorrow, the voice whispered in his ears, fading as though the speaker was going into the distance, walking over a hill toward the horizon. She'd be back, though. She always came back.

"Yes, Mother," Marius said, low enough that he hoped not even the animals could hear him.

She always came back. That was her defining characteristic. Mostly it seemed to happen when he was around people, this constant, grating sense in the back of his mind that she would be there. She would always be with him. She would continue to make him look mad, provoke him, drive him into scorn and scrutiny.

He looked around the barn, took a deep breath of the air of his home. "I need to leave," he whispered, and deep inside he knew the truth of it. Here he was unwelcome, in this small place, where everyone knew him and his madness. But perhaps somewhere else, where no one knew him …

The answer came to him, just like that. Somewhere big. Somewhere that no one would know him, no one would see him.

Rome.

Chapter 6

I drifted in dream, feeling heavy in thought and mind. It almost felt like I was experiencing fever dreams, as if an excess of thought was causing my head to spin and my body to break into the waking world every few minutes to turn over on my couch.

The world was dim around me, and that tired feeling just stretched over me. Everything held a familiar, dreamlike quality, and I pushed my toes against resistance beneath them and felt something grainy. It felt like dirt, and I looked down in the darkness to see that it was indeed dirt between my toes.

I realized with a shock that I was standing, and that there was an earthy aroma in my nose. I glanced down to see if I was having one of those naked dreams, but let out a sigh of relief when I realized I had on pajamas. I glanced up and saw darkness before me, only a few lights illuminating the place where I stood.

There were half-built walls all around, and I looked up to see a ceiling of latticed rebar above me. I was on a construction site, and it looked awfully familiar. It took me another second to place it, and only another second after that to realize exactly what was going on. "Come out," I told him, speaking into the darkness.

"Okay," he said, and he was suddenly there, as though the darkness had spit him out when I wasn't looking. "You catch on pretty quick; I was ready to wait a few minutes for you to acclimate, but boom! You figured it out seconds after coming in. What was the tip off?"

"It's the construction site where we last met," I said to Sovereign as he regarded me across the empty space between us. I folded my arms in front of me against my pajama shirt. The soft cotton felt good against my skin. "I don't remember wearing this, though. Did you get to dress me for this little meet-up?"

He gave me a slight nod. "It's the power of the dreamwalk, yeah. After a while, you figure out how to shape it to your advantage—location, the clothes your subject is wearing, how they perceive you. You, being a succubus, have more control in this situation than, say, a normal person would, but it's still in my hands at the outset."

"Oh, really?" I asked, and glanced down at the pajamas. They were ... fluffy. "What the hell, then?"

He shrugged. "I was aiming for comfortable."

I gave him a glare and looked him up and down. He was wearing jeans and a t-shirt, looking very Joshua Harding and not very Supervillain at the moment. "Then dress me normally—" I stopped and felt a flare of anger. "Actually, you know what? You shouldn't be dressing me at all, this is appalling—"

"I'm sorry," he said and held up his hands in surrender as he took a step closer to me. "I apologize for even coming into your dreams this way, but I needed to see you. Needed to talk to you." He looked genuinely contrite. "I need to ... to say I'm sorry for what's happening to you right now. I didn't know what Weissman was doing."

That rage that had been percolating in my skull? It came out. "You didn't know your sick friend was kidnapping me for a fun bout of torture with the two heads of Cerberus before delivering me to you in a mashed-up, quivering mess?"

"I had no idea," he said, and a flicker of rage crossed his face. "And if he wasn't dead, he'd be experiencing my full displeasure right now—"

"If he wasn't dead," I said, letting my voice lower into a rough whisper, "you wouldn't know yet."

He sighed and nodded, looking pained. "I promise you that as soon as I can find the plane you're on, I will make sure that you're freed—"

"I wouldn't worry about it," I said, letting a smile of satisfaction that was as hollow as any I've ever felt creep up. "I downed the plane and killed your guard dogs."

A ripple of shock across his face culminated in an eyebrow nearly creeping up his forehead. "You ..." He let out a breath. "Ahhh ... you figured it out. How to control your powers. I'd hoped you would." The look on his face became something I found deeply disquieting, something approaching satisfaction. "You truly are a worthy—"

"Shut up," I said, disgusted. "Your dogs got off the leash and killed my mother, and you're happy because one of the side effects is that I'm a better consort now? Truly, there are no words to describe how much I loathe you."

"Fair enough," he said, but I caught the disappointment as he looked down from my eyes. "I'd feel the same if someone had done to me what's happened to you tonight. I know it counts for less than nothing, but I want to give you my sincere condolences—"

"Less than nothing," I agreed. "So stop wasting your words and my time." I tried not to let the slow burn of emotion I was feeling splash him again because an idea suddenly came to me. If Weissman was dead, and what he'd told me before was true— "So ... what now?"

A veil of indifference fell over his features in the dark and shadow. "I don't know what you mean."

I paused and composed my thoughts. "Your top lieutenant, the big cog rolling this machine forward, is now dead. You told me that he was running the extermination because you didn't have the—" I stopped myself before throwing down on him by saying 'balls,' "stomach to do it yourself." I could tell by the mild flinch that he got my meaning even so. "So ... now what?"

The man I knew as Sovereign stared at me, not a hint of Joshua Harding's boyishness on display. He just looked tired. "Because you've killed almost all of our telepaths, we're having to start what you've so charmingly called 'phase two.'" He folded his arms in front of him to match my pose. "Why? What did you think was going to happen?"

I froze and tried to choose my words carefully. "I think a lot of us were hoping that with Weissman dead, you'd be hanging it up."

Sovereign looked at me, and I saw hints of intensity in his eyes even through the shadows that hung between us. "Weissman is hardly the only power at work in Century. There are a lot of committed people in our group, people who want to change the world for the better."

"By taking it over," I snarked.

"I believe in what we're doing, the world we're creating," he said, but he looked so tired he barely put any gusto into saying it. "Can you say the same about the one you're defending? I mean, the woman who killed Weissman tonight is the same one that used to lock you in a box."

"She was afraid," I said. "You—Century—made her afraid. And it feels like whatever this phase two is—you're basically doing the same thing to the whole world."

He looked at me levelly. "What makes you say that? You don't even know what we're doing yet."

"You're starting by destroying metas," I said. "If that's your phase one, then phase two, whatever it specifically is, involves eliminating the other threats to you. Disarming people to put them under your control." I caught a hint of emotion from his face. "Typically, good things don't come following behind mass exterminations and forcible disarmings. Whatever grand and fantastic scheme you've got in mind to solve the world's problems reeks of a desire to control the world, Evil Overlord-style."

He almost smiled. "What about a Benevolent Overlord?"

I shook my head. "You've got two motivators available to you—a carrot and a stick. So far you haven't had much use for the carrot, which rules you out of the benevolent camp entirely."

"I've offered you a few carrots," he said.

"I'm not a donkey," I replied crossly. "I don't want your carrots, and I intend to break your stick."

He paused as if thinking over what I'd just said. "Is that a thinly veiled castration metaphor?"

"God, you men and your—" I cut myself off before snarling at him. "It's about power. You want it, and that means you're willing to take it from everyone else in order to secure it for yourself. And I'm going to—"

"Stop me, I know," he said, almost resigned. He looked weary. "Same old argument, huh?"

"Same old story," I said. "Some douchebag wants to take over the world."

"It's a very different story," he said. "You don't know anything about me. Either that or you aren't listening."

"I'm listening very carefully," I said, "but your actions are screaming so loud I can't hear a word you're saying."

He gave me a hard look. "I just wanted to make sure you were all right. And to tell you … I'm sorry for what Weissman did."

"No, you're not," I said. "You're mistaken if you think you are. You're planning to do so much worse than what he's done so far. At least an Evil Overlord could admit it to himself."

"Good night, Sienna," Sovereign said, turning away from me. "See you soon."

"Not if I have anything to say about it, asshole," I muttered as the dream world faded around me.

Chapter 7

"Sovereign is going to phase two," I said, my knuckles cracking as I forced them against the cold surface of the conference room table.

"He's going to make weapons using the Tesseract?" Reed asked, a little light in his eyes and a quirk at the corner of his mouth.

"Hah hah," I said. "'Do I look to be in a gaming mood?'"

"Nice," Reed said, arching his eyebrows. "Though you going with a Thor quote seems a little out of place."

"Felt right to me since I've killed two of his brothers now," I said. "Back on subject, we seem to have deprived Sovereign of the ability to efficiently hunt metahumans to extinction the way he and Weissman were doing it, so he's decided to skip ahead to subjugating humanity."

That declaration sucked all the air out of the room. I was surrounded by Ariadne, Reed, Janus, Li, Scott, Kat and Zollers. It was a grim lot already, and my words took any happiness that might have been lingering completely out of the equation.

"Where's Senator Foreman? Shouldn't he be here for something as important as this?" Reed asked, breaking the silence while shifting in his chair, arms folded over his leather jacket.

Li shook his head. "He's busy."

"Doing what?" Reed asked, his eyebrow turned upward. "What could possibly be more important than stopping Sovereign from taking over the damned world?"

"Making sure the 'damned world' doesn't find out about Sovereign trying to take it over," Li said humorlessly.

"Great," Ariadne said, looking just as weary as she had for the last few weeks. "What do we do now?"

"How do you know about this? About this 'phase two' starting?" Kat asked, just a little guarded. I couldn't tell if she was holding back because she thought I was going to hit her or something.

"He told me himself last night in a dreamwalk," I said. I caught mixed reactions around the table, but they all denoted at least some surprise. "He stopped in to reassure me that he had nothing to do with Weissman's little play to kidnap and torture me."

"Yeah, right," Scott said, expression darkening, "he probably gave the order himself."

"Maybe, maybe not," I said, "but it doesn't matter because kidnapping me ranks pretty far below genocide in my estimation, and since he's already up to that, I don't really have a lot more disdain I can add to his personal pile."

"So, he's reached the point where you can't get any madder at him?" Reed asked, his lips again hinting at a smile. "I honestly didn't know such a thing was possible."

"That's because you're not there yet," I said, "though you seem to be rapidly heading that way. We need answers. We need insight. We need—" There was a knock at the door, "—a do not disturb sign, maybe?" I finished lamely. "Come in."

The door opened and a geeky, dark-haired guy with hipster glasses breezed in. "Oh, hi," J.J. said as he entered, as though there was no meeting going on.

"J.J.," I said, my voice at a pitch I reserved for warning people before I started to beat them senseless, "we're a little busy right now."

"Of course you are, chief … err … chiefette … err …" He paused in his circuit around the table, faltering before resuming his course and ending up next to Li's chair. "I'm just bringing in some data, as requested." He handed the FBI agent a closed manila folder.

I turned my gaze to Li. "I'm going to assume it's important."

Li gave me a look that was flecked with annoyance and contempt. Per usual for him. He opened it, gave it a glance and said, "You assume correctly. Remember that storage locker in Tulsa that Century had?"

"Yes," I said. "It was the weird thing on that list of safe houses we found for them."

"Yes." Li stared at the file in front of him. "The FBI raided it yesterday on my orders." I heard Scott draw a sharp breath and Li looked over at him without expression. "No casualties. No one there. Just some … peculiar equipment."

I waited for him to enlighten us, but he just kept looking at the folder. What an ass. "Such as?"

"Not sure," Li said, and pulled a photo from the file, a little 3 x 5 that he clutched between his fingers before putting it on the table and sliding it toward me. I caught it and lifted it, giving him a look as he kept reading. Janus, sitting directly at my right, caught a glimpse of it as I raised it to look for myself.

I felt a slight snap of surprise. I'd seen this before. It was a black cylinder that looked big enough to hold a person inside. "This looks like …"

"It is," Janus said, looking down at the smooth surface of the table. "It most assuredly is. Stripped down to the very core components, but … it is."

"Okay, for those of us not in the special club at the end of the table," Reed said, "what is it?"

I looked down at the photo again, taking in the smooth lines. "You tell them," I said to Janus. "I may know what it is, but I don't have a name for it."

"It is a piece of technology that Omega developed internally to preserve the body functions of metahumans in a sort of rough stasis," Janus said, with no enthusiasm.

"And how do you know what it is?" Reed said, giving me a frown. "From your five-second stint as the head of Omega?"

"No," I said, tearing my eyes away from the stasis chamber. There were chills running over my scalp and down my neck, like I was looking at something vitally important but just couldn't quite make the leap to how it mattered … yet. "It's what Andromeda was in when I found her."

Chapter 8

"Oh, yes," Reed said, waving his hand in the air. "The mystery of the dead girl that Omega was keeping. I swear, we deal with so many mysteries that I've forgotten all the ones I haven't had answered yet—"

"She was a succubus," I said, looking up from the picture. "Named Adelaide." I glanced at Janus and he looked startled. "Mentored by Wolfe. Ordered captured by the old Primus. And then … juiced with power by being forced to drain other metas at Omega's command." I kept my eyes on Janus. "Does that sound about right?"

He gave me a slow nod. "Missing a few details, but overall you have it, I'd say."

"Wow," Reed said. I saw a similar quality of shock in faces all around the table. "When were you going to mention that?"

"I have been in a coma for several months," Janus said with a faint air of irritability. "Forgive if I do not rush to offer information that seems completely useless at this juncture. The girl is dead, after all."

"On Weissman's orders," I said.

"So she was supposed to do what Sienna is doing?" Scott asked "Fight Sovereign?"

Janus hesitated. "If need be."

Scott narrowed his eyes. "I sense there's more to this than you're telling us."

"She was also kept as a possible bribe," I said. "An attempt to buy off Sovereign."

"That is what was called 'Plan B,'" Janus said warily.

"Ah, Omega," Reed said, blowing air between his lips in barely concealed fury. "You'd never find a more wretched hive of scum and villainy."

"Heh," J.J. said. "It's a Star Wars line." He glanced around the table. "It was a good line. Perfect placement."

Janus ignored him. "It was not my plan," he said to Reed. "It was originated by the old Primus, in the time when I was out of Omega's operational command. I argued most strenuously against it in favor of training a succubus to fight Sovereign instead, but the Primus wanted the truth about incubi and succubi kept secret because—"

"Because the moment the secret was out," I said sourly, "there was no putting that particular genie back in the bottle."

"Correct," Janus said, glancing sidelong at me. "In addition, he had reached a point where after so many attempts to ensnare you—Wolfe, Henderschott, Fries, Mormont, the vampires—he believed that even were I to bring you into the fold, your loyalty would always be suspect."

"Because it was predicated on one thing, right?" I asked him. "On a common enemy."

"And once that enemy was gone ..." Janus said with a slight nod. "He was not a man prone to solving one massive problem by unleashing another. He was very careful to protect his interests and those of the Ministers by finding solutions that would insulate them from additional fallout."

"Yeah, he was a real prince," I said acidly. "Unfortunately, the rest of us have to deal with the consequences of his failure to act." *And yours*, I didn't say.

"How did you know?" Janus asked after a moment's pause. "About Adelaide?"

"She's left a ghost in my head," I said, looking back at the photo of the stasis unit. "She's the one who told me how to use my powers." She'd told me a lot of things, actually. Showed me things. I felt a shudder and suppressed it.

Things I wasn't ready to talk about just yet. That I couldn't talk about.

Remember.

"How is that possible?" Scott asked, and his voice sounded a little hoarse. He cleared it, looking around the table self-consciously.

"She was the stronger succubus," Janus said, shaking his head very lightly.

"That doesn't make any sense," I said. "She touched me for a long time, like ... way longer than it would have taken for a succubus's power to work." I caught the hint of something in Janus's gaze, a flicker, and he looked away from me. "What are you not telling me?"

Janus paused, and when he answered it was with more than a hint of irritability. "Nothing that pertains to defeating Sovereign. Let us keep the focus on the matter at hand—"

"Whoa, whoa, whoa," Reed said, leaning forward on the table. "You don't just get to dish out and withdraw a little bit of info like that. You're saying there's a way to control a succubus—and assuming that's right, presumably an incubus's power, too, right?" He glanced around at all of us, his look somewhere between incredulity and relief. "This could be the thing that stops Sovereign."

"She could still use the powers of the metas she'd absorbed," I said with the shake of my head. "Whatever it is, it doesn't keep them—us—from being able to use what we've got already."

"Nor does it keep a succubus or incubus from being able to absorb fresh souls," Janus said with that same wary air, now flecked with the barest hint of indignation. "Should we apply this particular treatment to Sovereign, it would do precisely nothing. It is little more than a method for a succubus to voluntarily control their absorption powers."

I swallowed as I felt a rush of hope run through me. Control my powers? Make it so I could keep from absorbing someone's soul the moment I touched them?

Make it so I could live a normal life?

"I'd be interested in hearing about it even so," Scott said from his place down the table. I met his gaze for half a second and looked away.

"It is not relevant to the discussion at hand," Janus said, and the menace in his voice was unmistakable. There was a sudden, dark pall over the table, a palpable anger that made everyone lean back a little in their chairs.

"Whoa, there," Zollers said. "Restrain yourself, Janus."

"I apologize," Janus said after a moment more. He stood abruptly, and his chair clattered as he did so. "I'm afraid I must withdraw from this conversation. I have nothing more to add to the discussion at this time." He looked around the room once briefly, his eyes so low that he never met any of ours, and then he left the conference room as quickly as I'd ever seen him move.

"Wow," J.J. said. "That was super awkward. What do you think his secret was?"

Kat had a flushed look, slightly alarmed, and her gaze was rooted on the door. "I don't know. I've never seen him act this way before. But if he says he's got nothing more to contribute that would help, I believe him—"

"I don't," Reed said sourly. I wheeled my gaze to him. "I don't care what he says, he's still Omega in my view, and they're all filled to the brimming with secrets and lies."

No one said anything to that, but Kat flushed and left in nearly as much of a huff as Janus had. The rest of us sat there for a minute more in eerie silence, while I wondered if Reed was right.

Chapter 9

Scott lingered as the meeting broke up. So did Reed and Zollers, but they hung back. I sat in my chair, the smell of leather thick in my nose. My fingers danced over the surface of the leather covering the arms, soft, pliable material slick with the sweat on my fingertips. Just nerves, I hoped.

Nervous for the weakling? Wolfe asked.

I appreciate your assistance, I told him, *but unsolicited opinions aren't my favorite things ever.*

Since the Little Doll asked so nicely, he said, and I caught a glimpse of his fearsome smile in my mind's eye before he sauntered off to the back of my head. I could feel the press of the others in my head, too, now that I had let them out of their prisons. They seemed reticent to say anything, though, and that was just fine by me.

Reed and Zollers remained at the other end of the table, watching me with careful eyes. They didn't bother to pretend they weren't paying attention to everything I was doing, and I respected them for it. False discretion wasn't going to convince me they weren't eavesdropping; they were metas, and they'd have to at least leave the room in order to avoid hearing a conversation between Scott and me.

Scott shuffled up, hands in his pockets. He took a moment to meet my eyes, but when he did, I could see the emotion in them. "I just wanted to tell you … I'm in. All in. Whatever it takes to stop these bastards."

"Good," I said, a little more choked up than I would have thought I'd be. I looked up and saw Reed hide a wry smile by turning away from me. "That's … it's good to have you on the team." I wanted to smack myself for the excessive formality I was lapsing into, but let's face it, I didn't want to have a deeper, more private conversation with my brother and my therapist in the room. That's practically family counseling, and it was not something I was up for.

"Way to come off the bench at the buzzer, Arthur Curry," Reed said, and he turned back for just a second to smirk.

"Who the hell is Arthur Curry?" Scott asked, confusion stitching a downward line across his brow.

"Aquaman," I said with faint amusement. He looked at me and his forehead puckered further. "Arthur Curry is Aquaman."

"What the hell, Reed?" Scott gave him an insulted look, to which my brother just shrugged. He turned back to me. "And, uh … I'm sorry about your mom."

"Yeah, well, we'll, uh … deal with it later," I said and meant it. "No time for mourning at the moment."

"Can you and I talk later?" he asked. The annoyance on his face at Reed's jibe had faded, replaced with something else, something closer to concern.

I took a breath before answering. "Yeah. Though we might want to do what we'd talked about before everything hit the fan and just … wait until things settle out with Sovereign."

"Sure," he said, and I watched him swallow heavily. "Sure, we can do that. Wait until everything is, uh … over … before …"

"Thanks." I smiled faintly. Part of me didn't want to put it off. Part of me wanted to dig into it right now and get it out of the way. This wasn't the sort of thing I really wanted to leave open, like a wound, while I was heading into battle, but I wasn't sure it was the sort of thing that could be fixed with a couple stitches, like … a smaller wound, I suppose.

The truth was I didn't have any idea what to say. My feelings regarding Scott were immensely complicated, and I was still feeling exhausted from all the garbage that had been dumped on us in the last few days.

"Well, okay, then," Scott said, and he swung toward the door almost as though he were on a string, being pulled toward it. His movements were mechanical, shuffling, and reminded me a little of how he'd acted after Kat had lost all memory of him. He disappeared through the door without another word.

"You know that keeping him at a distance is going to come back to bite you in the ass sometime between now and the final battle, right?" Reed asked, and I turned my head to find him standing there, leaning on the back of one of the chairs, watching me.

"Everything comes back to bite me eventually," I said. "Leave my house, get drawn into a war. Kill Wolfe, piss off his brothers. Fail to kill Weissman when I had a chance, he comes back and kills my mom." I said it grimly, but I didn't feel sorry for myself about it. I didn't know many people who'd been left with the shitty choices I'd been given in the last year and a half. Any people, actually. All I had were shitty choices. And I didn't feel sorry for myself about it, not anymore. This was just reality. "I'll deal with Scott when I figure out *how* to deal with Scott," I said. To me, it had the ring of bracing honesty. I didn't know how my brother or Dr. Zollers took it, but their facial reactions didn't indicate they took it well. I looked to Reed. "Are we still in lockdown?"

"We're always in lockdown," he said, breaking a smile. "We live in a perpetual state of lockdown around here. It's all we do anymore."

"Good," I said. "We may not have much left, but better safe than—"

51

"Yeah, yeah," he said, waving me off as he started toward the door. "You should know that I'm 'all in,' too." He paused at the doorway. "In case you didn't already know."

"I knew," I said and felt the hint of a smile grace my lips. That took some doing at the moment, piercing through the shroud of numbness that felt like it had settled on my bones. "But I appreciate you saying it anyway, Hal Jordan."

Reed's eyes narrowed and his lips puckered in deepest betrayal. "Green Lantern? You consider me a Green Lantern?"

"You can kinda fly, but you're no Superman," I said with a shrug. "Just a touch of arrogance—"

"Ohhh, I am retracting my all-in," he said and slapped the doorframe with mock irritation. He smiled, rolled his eyes and started to sweep out. "We'll talk later, right?" His look turned to hesitancy, and I knew what he wanted to talk about—Mom.

"Yeah," I said and glanced at Zollers. "But I have a feeling I might be all talked out on the subject pretty soon."

"Maybe *I* won't be," he said quietly.

"Okay," I said and gave him a nod. He left without another word.

"So ..." Dr. Zollers said, completely unreadable.

"So," I said. "Therapy session, huh?"

"Not necessarily," he said, edging toward me quietly. His hands were folded in front of him, and he looked solemn. "Seems like everyone wants to talk to you now."

"Yeah," I said. "Gotta console the grieving, I suppose."

"Are you?" He raised an eyebrow at me. "Grieving, I mean?"

I felt that faint smile broaden. "You haven't changed a bit, have you? Psychiatrist to the last."

"Reminds me of a joke I heard," he said with a faint smile. "How many psychiatrists does it take to change a light bulb?"

"I don't know," I said, feeling a hint of impatience.

"Only one. But it has to really want to change."

I felt an absurd little laugh escape my lips at that. "That's … terrible."

"It truly is," he said, and the familiar light that had always been in his eyes twinkled. "Do you know why so many of them want to have a conversation with you like I am right now?"

"They're worried about me," I said. "Worried I'll … I don't know, go charging off the edge of a cliff or something. Worried I might drop the ball on running this war."

"They're worried about you," he agreed. "Not the war. I mean, Li is worried about the war. But Scott, Ariadne, Reed—none of them are worried about the war in relation to you. They're worried about you because … it's you."

"And what's Janus worried about?" I asked.

"No idea," Zollers said with a shake of his head. "I can't read him, not even a little. His empath powers blot mine out without him even having to try. I can't even read the others when he's around, he's so strong."

"To answer your question … I'm fine," I said without enthusiasm.

"I don't have to be a telepath to know that's not true."

"In relation to what happened with my mom, I'm fine," I corrected. "For now. It's not like I feel nothing, I just …" I sighed. "I hate to go all Scarlett O'Hara on this, but I'll think about it tomorrow."

He frowned, his lips compressing in a tight line. "If you'll forgive me for saying so … now that I can read you, mentally, you do not feel fine." He paused, as if he were stopping to take the temperature of the air, his eyes drifting into open space. "It's not about your mother, the distress I'm detecting. It's—"

"Yeah," I said, nodding, not meeting his eyes. "It's something else entirely."

I felt his eyes on me. "What aren't you telling us?"

I chewed my lower lip. "Things. You're a mind reader. Why not just take a look?"

"I could do that," he said, stopping a step away from me, "but ..." He squatted down, bringing his eyes level with mine. I avoided his gaze no longer, looking into his deep, mocha-colored eyes. "... I really don't care to invade your privacy if you don't want to share it."

"I'm sure it'll come out at some point," I said, and felt a tightness in my throat. "But not yet."

"All right," he said soothingly. As always. "Do you want to talk about your mom?"

I felt my throat tighten further. "I don't know what else to say. She never even saw it coming."

"Oh, she did," Zollers said with a nod, drawing my attention back to him. "She knew it was coming. My mind was with her, blocking Claire's ability to read her as she hitchhiked on the back bumper of Weissman's car with you. She was at peace, knowing that her end was coming. Most people don't have the level of serenity—"

"Oh, bullshit," I said, feeling impatience bubble out of me. "My mother was many things, but serene was not one of them."

"In this case, she was as close as one could get," Zollers said quietly. "Don't get me wrong, there was rage and anger and fear—for you, I might add—but she was as peaceful at the end as I have ever felt her. You were right, Akiyama was there. He allowed her to get the drop on Weissman, and the words they exchanged gave her a sense of peace before the end came." He shook his head. "Having been present for my share of deaths, I can tell you that it's more than most get."

I pushed my lips together hard and let them stay that way for a moment before speaking again. "We said a lot to each other just before she died. But ... it doesn't feel like enough."

"It would never be enough," he said quietly. "She has power over you and always will. Parents are like that. You'll always want her approval." His eyes glistened faintly. "Her love."

"She said she was sorry." I felt the lump in my throat. "For what she'd done. For how she'd failed. Like she knew ahead of time she was going to die."

"The life expectancy of people engaged in this particular endeavor is not very high," Zollers said, and he stood. I could hear his joints popping as he did so. "This is war, after all."

"And my mother is one of its casualties." Adelaide's voice came back to me again, soft and warning. *Remember.* "And not the last, either, if Sovereign has anything to say about it."

Zollers's eyes narrowed, just slightly, as if he caught my deeper meaning. It made me wonder if it was something he was reading from my thoughts or something from his own experience with Sovereign that made him react that way. "No. No, it won't be." He paused and took a breath. "Is there anything I can do for you?"

I pulled my eyes from Zollers and rested them on the photograph of the Omega stasis chamber, still sitting face up on the table, the glare of the overhead lights blotting out a portion of the picture. Just like my sense of Sovereign's plans, it looked utterly incomplete this way, unfinished, so much of it out of view. But I could still see a lot of it.

I took a breath, pulled my gaze from the photograph, looked Dr. Zollers in the eyes, and told him what I needed from him.

Chapter 10

I found Janus on the roof, which was the last place I would have looked. There was a helipad up there but it wasn't in regular use. We used the one on the grounds out of habit, I supposed. Those old habits, they're a real bitch to get rid of.

Suspicion was an old habit for me, though, and it wasn't going anywhere.

"Janus," I said quietly as I stepped out into the gentle breeze blowing across the rooftop. It was an overcast day, late summer, and not nearly as hot as it could have been. Part of me had trouble keeping track of the days. Why did it matter, after all? When the world is roaring to an end around you, who cares whether it's Tuesday or Saturday? It's not like I had any days off, after all.

"Sienna," he said, loud enough to be heard. "Dr. Zollers told you where to find me?"

"He pointed me in the direction of the giant black hole in his mind's coverage of the campus, yes," I said. Janus was standing a couple feet from the edge of the roof, staring off. We hadn't exactly followed safety regulations and installed railings or anything yet. There was nothing but a gaping, open space in front of him leading to the south lawn, and he stared across it as though he had a better view than a four-story building could provide. "You got pretty defensive in there."

"Yes," Janus said simply. He did not turn to look at me as I sidled up next to him.

"And then you run up here to … what? Think about your problems?" I stared out onto the lawn. I could still see each individual blade of grass from up here. That was meta eyesight for you.

"Think about how to handle my problem," Janus said, not stirring. The wind came through and rustled his tweed jacket. I wondered if Kat had packed that for him when she brought him over from England.

"I prefer head-on, personally," I said.

He rolled his head toward me, just enough to give me a sidelong look. "Yes, without doubt, that is how you handle things. I am uncertain that it will yield positive results in this instance, though."

"Couldn't hurt," I said.

"Oh, but it could," Janus said, staring back at the grounds. "It could very much hurt."

We stood there in silence, side by side, and I tried not to further invade the privacy of his thoughts by looking at him. "I don't believe that whatever you're hiding about what Omega did to Adelaide to reduce her powers will change the course of our war."

"Then you are the only one," he said tightly. "The benefit of being an empath is that you can feel the emotions of others. Their suspicion would be obvious even to the unskilled of my kind, let alone someone who has been dealing with this for several thousand years. They regard me as a liar. And perhaps they are right to." He laughed without mirth. "After all, before I was attacked by Weissman and—sidelined, I think you would call it—I had promised you the truth about everything."

"You told me the biggest truth," I said.

"But perhaps not all of it," he said, lowering his head. "Not every truth I know. Certainly, there are several thousand years of them to sort through, but I know things—

little details, here and there—that might be of some use in our current circumstances."

"We've been busy—" I said, starting to make excuses for him.

"There is no need," he said, waving his hand in the air in an abrupt cutting motion. "The problem with being me—with being who I am, with sitting in the seats of power the way I have for most of my life is that you learn to control information. And being an empath has made me even more careful with what I learn." He looked at me, and I saw a sadness in his eyes. "Controlling the flow of secrets, carefully spinning the truths I allowed out, making certain that they reached the correct ears—this has been part of my duty with Omega."

"When we met," I started, slowly, "I confronted you with your reputation for being two-faced. You told me that there were multiple variations of the truth."

"A lie I tell myself to soften the truth, I think," he said, and his shoulders slumped. "There are always multiple perspectives. What one person holds to be truth, another would dispute until the day they die. People are contrary, argumentative. In order to make someone 'see the light' and accept a truth, sometimes it must be presented in a different way. When someone believes something so strongly that it is almost conviction for them, depriving them of that falsehood and replacing it with the truth is not something done by simply shouting that truth at them. They will reject it out of hand. They will deny it at every juncture. They need to be smoothed. The way needs to be prepared. You must approach it … with a ready supply of half-truths to gradually move them to the position where their mind is open to the truth. The real truth."

I blinked. "Uhm … okay, you lost me."

He looked at me then sighed. "I am a liar who has spent most of his life in service of liars and thieves and murderers. I have lied to myself to justify my actions, and now I find myself in a most curious position, one I have not been in before, even when I was exiled from the good graces of the Primus and forced into retirement. I am no longer in the service of a liar and a murderer. Realizing that I am in a position where the truth is more than just a tool or a weapon is …" He sighed again. "… It is difficult to adjust to."

I went through what he'd said then replayed the words again. "In essence, you're saying that after a lifetime of hiding the truth from the evil people you worked for, you're stumbling at telling the whole truth, when you're working for …" I bobbed my head a little, trying to find a way to soften the words and finding none, "… the good guys?"

"That's … about it," he said, and nodded slowly. "You are not a monster, Sienna. I have told you this before, and I believe that to my very bones."

"Thank you," I said. "I think? I'm not sure what it has to do with the matters at hand, but—"

"It has nothing to do with the matters at hand," he said, "and everything to do with the reason I stormed out of the meeting just now." He looked at me, focused his eyes on mine, and I could see the weary lines of age around his eyes, crow's feet that had settled in the skin, making him look old, painfully old. "There is a way for you to be able to control your powers, of course. To make it so that your touch is innocuous to others, as harmless as the touch of anyone else."

I felt my spine stiffen involuntarily. "Okay." I felt myself quiver a little on the inside at the prospect of being able to live a normal life.

"But the price," Janus said, shaking his head. "It is …" He shook his head again.

"Look," I said, "this is, uhm … I mean, this is something that can maybe wait until after the war is over. I clearly don't *need* to touch people right now, since I've lived this long without—"

"It doesn't matter when you find out," Janus said, and another shake of his head followed the dry, scratchy pronouncement. "Let me explain the theory behind this."

I leaned in closer, afraid to miss a word of it now that he was explaining to me how I could potentially touch—hug—caress—kiss—and—and—everything—with another person.

"You know, of course, that your power comes from the marriage of Hades and Persephone, from the hybridization of her ability to heal with touch and his to steal souls from a distance." I saw him waiting for an acknowledgment and nodded. "Then you must understand that your power is truly the polar opposite of a Persephone. Their touch heals, yours kills."

"I have noticed that," I said, listening warily. I remembered telling Scott after meeting Kat for the first time that I was her opposite—she was life, I was death.

"Then you must realize that the only way to put the stopper in your deadly touch," Janus said, drawing out every word, "is to absorb a power that would be its equal and opposite. Something that would keep it from being able to act through your touch, something that would block its use."

I froze and remembered the touch of Adelaide's—Andromeda's—hand on mine as she had steered me out of the Omega facility where I'd found her. It had felt as though she was taking away my pain, gradually healing the wounds from the beatings I'd suffered before meeting her. "No," I said and shook my head.

"Yes," Janus said, nodding. There were bags under his eyes, I realized, the weight of his knowledge pulling on him. In that moment, his motives became clear to me and I knew why he'd rushed from the conference room earlier. I wasn't a monster, he said. Yet the thought of what I could do, right this minute, in order to have that power, in order to be able to live a normal life and touch like a normal person flashed through my mind—

I pictured myself kissing Scott, and realized … I wanted to. As aggravated as I'd been at him for all the ups and downs lately … I wanted to. I wanted to take his face in my hands and kiss him, long and deep, feel his fingers on my face and … elsewhere.

With a shock like a cold bucket of water dousing me, I cut off that thought. I could see the look on Janus's face and it did most of the work for me. He knew. He'd seen it in my eyes, in the way I'd reacted. "I am not a monster," I said, repeating it aloud almost as much for his benefit as mine.

"I should hope not," Janus said, and he looked tired beyond belief, as though he were ready to lapse into another coma, right there in front of me. "Which is why I told you."

I swallowed, hard, and broke away from his gaze. It was natural to think about it, wasn't it? It didn't make me evil for considering it, did it? For thinking that only a few stories below, there was an easy answer to my desire to live a normal life?

And all I'd have to do … was kill Kat by draining her dry.

Chapter 11

Playing a dangerous game, Little Doll, Wolfe whispered in my head. *And playing it close, out of sight of your friends.*

"Dangerous is all I know," I muttered as I opened the door into the bullpen on the fourth floor. There was a buzz of activity, and I could tell by the smell of melted cheese that someone had ordered pizza. I realized I was hungry, famished actually, having not really eaten since yesterday. I steered toward the smell and found an empty cubicle filled with a half dozen boxes of pizza. There were a lot of missing pieces and I could tell that they'd been hit hard in a first wave. A couple of empty boxes had already been bent in half and stuffed into a big black garbage bag that was sitting next to the table. A few two-liter containers of pop were spread out at the end of the table with paper plates and cups, and— oddly enough—plastic cutlery.

"Sienna," J.J. said, nodding to me as I drifted into the cubicle. He was munching on a slice of pepperoni and sausage, chewing and moving his head in rhythm.

"J.J.," I said, making my way over to the pizzas. I hovered over the Hawaiian one, and the fragrant scent of pineapple caught me like a fishhook. I grabbed a plate. "What's the word?" I asked him, more conversationally than anything.

"FBI raided the Century safe houses across the country a few minutes ago," he said, and I nearly dropped my plate.

"What. The. Hell?" I asked, correcting only a second before my piece of pizza went sliding to the floor. "Who authorized that?"

"Li, maybe?" He gave me a shrug of the shoulders. "I don't really know. I just know they did it, and they're finished now."

I stared at his unconcerned features as he took another nibble of his pizza. "I assume, based on your demeanor, the raids did not culminate in the mass deaths of all the FBI agents."

"Yeah, they're fine," J.J. said, struggling to cram half the piece in his mouth. I resisted slapping him so hard it would all fly out so he could get me a clear answer—but only barely. "Nobody was home at any of them. Looked like they'd been abandoned." Flecks of chewed cheese the size of pencil erasers flew out of his mouth as he spoke. "Score one for the good guys, huh?"

"Not really," I said. "Now they've gone underground." I put aside my annoyance with J.J. and chewed my own piece of pizza. A thought occurred to me and I spoke, managing to keep the food in my mouth from spraying out as I did so. "Did Weissman charter that plane or did Century own it?"

"Uhrm …" J.J. said, and he looked like he'd been caught by surprise. "I don't know. NTSB is investigating the crash, local police are on the hangar."

"I know what caused the plane to crash," I said.

"Might not want to tell the NTSB that," he said with a shrug. "Not sure how well they'll take it when you give working for a government agency that doesn't exist as an explanation for why you dropped it in the swamps outside the third most populous city in the state."

I frowned at him. "Confession may be good for the soul, but time in jail does nothing for my complexion." I waved one of my pale hands in front of my face. "I was just thinking that if we could trace the origin of the plane, either by following the money if it's a rental or by following its trail if it's owned by Century—"

"Yes!" His eyes lit up, and he got it. Finally. "Yes, I can do that. I'll just—" He made as if he was going to move, then hesitated when he remembered the pizza plate in his hands and took a staggering step, tried to keep from falling as he regained his balance. Then he stared at the plate like his mind had skipped a beat trying to figure out what to do with it while his body rushed to follow his new train of thought. "Uhm …" He looked up at me as if he were seeking my permission for something.

"Eat while you work," I said, dismissing him with a wave of my hand. "Get me some answers, will you?" I watched him scramble around the wall of the cube and remembered a question I'd wanted to ask him, but a little too late.

I wanted to know what the local PD had done with my mother's body.

But I supposed that could wait.

I scooped up a few more pieces of pizza and headed for my office, taking care to open the door with my wrist instead of rubbing greasy fingers all over it. I stopped in the door and stared at the bonsai still sitting in the middle of my desk, at that unopened envelope waiting in front of it. I cringed, knowing I'd have to read it sooner or later.

I'd have preferred later, but that wasn't the mature response. I set the pizza plate on the desk and circled around to find my chair. I sat down and reached for the envelope, my fingers staining the pure white paper yellow with grease. I slid a finger along the seal and found it already ripped open. Someone had read it and replaced it, apparently. Someone who was perhaps a little more on top of things than I was.

I pulled a small note out and opened it where it was folded in half. Simple words were written inside:

To Sienna Nealon,

I have repaid my debt to you to the best of my ability, given the constraints of time. I look forward to our next encounter, when I will meet you for the first time.

With my deepest condolences,
Shin'ichi Akiyama

I tossed the note lightly on the surface of my desk and listened to the paper slide across it. However he'd intended to help me, whatever I'd done to assist him—or would do—whatever—he'd done one thing, to my knowledge. He'd helped my mom die while killing Weissman. The pizza didn't even taste good anymore. "The best of your ability could have been a whole lot better," I said to the empty room.

Chapter 12

I am ready to help you now, Bjorn said, and I could hear the reluctant sincerity in my head.

I sighed, the sound making a quiet noise in my office as it bounced off the walls. "Thank you, Bjorn." I took it with as much grace as I could, the assistance of a murderer and rapist. It wasn't like I had armies of wholesome people in my head offering me their assistance, so I had to take what I could get, right?

Right.

Don't forget, Bastian's soft voice said quietly, *I'm at your disposal as well.*

"Thank you too, Roberto," I said, nodding as I turned to look out my window across the neatly manicured lawn. The world might be going to hell around us, but our gardeners still worked every day, apparently. I couldn't decide whether that was soothing or galling and eventually decided on the latter. "I can use all the help I can get."

I heard a quiet rustle in the back of my head where Gavrikov and Eve still waited, watching me. I could feel them back there, discontented, their anger with me still fresh on the surface. "What about you, Aleksandr?" I asked.

I think not, his faintly accented words floated up to me. *I do not wish to give you more power which you may hang over my sister's head like a looming danger, an axe or sword ready to fall.*

"That's not me," I whispered, as I felt him retreat to the back of my head. I could nearly taste his bitterness, his suspicion. It fed into all my worst fears about myself, giving me a sense of unease.

What if he was right about me?

I felt another presence, and it caused me to relax just a bit. Bjorn's psyche, as near as I could tell, still held the hard-planted seeds of reluctance and rawness from how I'd treated him. I didn't want to ask, but I suspected he was just being a bigger man. Not literally, but figuratively.

"Thank you," I muttered again.

It is not for your sake, Bjorn said, and I sensed his anger below the surface. *Sovereign deserves to die, horribly, for what he has done to me, and …* I could hear the hints of grudging admiration spiking through his words as he spoke in my head, *… your plan, your ideas … I find them pleasing.*

I frowned then quickly wiped the look off my face, burying my first reaction—distaste—at his approval. I knew he sensed it, but he wisely decided not to comment on it. Our choices were terrible, to either ignore each other, fight each other, or work together. It didn't take anyone with half a brain to realize that those choices were absolute shit to both of us.

But what the hell else was there to do?

"Sienna?" There was a knock at my half-closed door, one that pushed the door open more than the crack it had been at. J.J.'s face appeared in the gap, and I caught a hint of eager eyes behind those huge black-rimmed glasses. "I think I've got something."

"Come in," I said, trying to clear my mind of the distractions imposed by having six people living in the mental space meant for one. I waved him toward the desk and he slipped in, pushing the door nearly shut behind him as he came forward. He dragged one of my chairs a couple inches closer to the front of my desk, scuffing the carpet as he did so and getting an irritated reaction from me, as though I'd heard a single nail briefly scrape a chalkboard.

Ever meet someone and just find yourself repelled by them, as though you'd met your polar opposite? That was J.J. for me. I couldn't exactly explain it (not that I'd put a lot of thought into it), but the guy just annoyed the holy hell out of me. I tried to bury it, since I was his boss and I needed his expertise, but it did not take much effort on his part to set my teeth on edge.

That was probably more on my end than his, honestly. I'm flawed, and one of those flaws is lack of patience. I'd say I was working on it, but that'd be a lie. I was just working on keeping it from ballooning out into murder every time I lost it.

Baby steps.

"I traced the plane," J.J. said, "and you were right." Who doesn't love those words? Music to my ears. And ego. "Looks like it was chartered, and I found a new money trail leading to a shell corporation headquartered in Massachusetts. The Wise Men's Consortium." He glanced up at me. "Heh. Like a play on Weissman—"

"Yes, I got it."

"Right," he said, turning serious and clearing his throat. "And sexist, obviously. Anyway, it's something. Also, the NTSB has traced the plane back to its takeoff point, and they're now on the scene at the hangar, along with the FBI—"

"Oh?" I had a hard time caring.

"They found some stuff," J.J. said, causing me to strike that 'not caring' thing. "Looks like Weissman had been using it as his temporary base, so there was a computer and—"

"Where?" I asked, standing up so fast I nearly overturned my chair.

"At the hangar, still," J.J. said, looking up at me like I was at least a little crazy. "I looked in on the reports filed thus far, from the comm traffic and whatnot. Looks like it's encrypted, so their field guys didn't want to mess with it—"

"What are the odds that Century has something on that computer worth a look?" I asked, thinking it over.

"I don't know?" J.J. said, his voice sounding a little lost. "12.3 percent?"

I frowned. "Where the hell did you get that number from?"

He shrugged. "I made it up. It's not like I know enough about these guys to know what they do with their computers. For all I know, he keeps it because of a Solitaire high score he got three years ago."

"But it probably has *something* on it," I said. "Weissman was a truly nasty piece of work. I can't imagine he'd have brought a laptop to town with him just to game on."

"You never know," J.J. said. "He could've been really into World of Warcraft, and maybe he didn't want to miss raids while he was traveling." I gave him a look. You know the one. "Well, he could," J.J. said, a little reproachful.

"I want a look at that laptop," I said, thumping my hand on the desk. "Can you hack it from here?"

"What?" J.J. said, almost verging on a scowl. "It's turned off, presumably not near a wi-fi hotspot, and about to be checked in to the FBI as evidence." I looked at him blankly until he explained further. "No, I cannot hack it from here. I'd need it to be on and connected to a network that's on the internet, and neither of those things is happening anytime soon."

"So we go to it," I said, straightening my back. I was still standing, like it was some sort of declarative statement. "We go get you a look at it." For me, it kind of was a declarative statement. I'd been reeling from punch after punch from Weissman, Sovereign, and all these Century flunkies.

Now it was time to seize on the first opportunity to come our way in a little while—and go on the offensive.

Chapter 13

That thrill, that feeling of being on the attack, faded as we left the gates of the Agency behind. Sitting in the back seat of an SUV as it headed down the freeway toward the western suburbs of the Twin Cities, I felt a strange, nervous, creeping sensation that tickled my stomach.

It probably didn't help that Kat was sitting next to me. Right next to me. In the middle of the back seat, with J.J. boxing her in on the other side. She smelled faintly sweet, like she'd dabbed on a little perfume that morning.

I tried not to look at her.

Reed was driving and Li was sitting in the passenger seat up front, helping put the kibosh on any conversations that might have taken place. The drive to the 494 Highway loop that encircled Minneapolis and St. Paul was a tense affair, marked mostly by silence and the occasional clearing of a throat.

The sun hung high overhead, shining down through the glass moon roof. It was near noon, probably getting hot outside, and the air conditioner coupled with the car's engine was producing a soothing thrum in the vehicle. I found myself wishing I'd brought some of the pizza along with me for this jaunt, instead of leaving it behind on my desk. By the time I got back, it would be spoiled. Bleh.

I couldn't shake that uneasy feeling, and I couldn't quite attribute it just to the awful silence that was filling the car, either. Part of me wanted to say something to break it, but I really hated talking to Li. And J.J. And Kat, come to think of it—though it was bound to be even more awkward now that I knew killing her was the key to me living a normal life.

You know what? Given that I was surrounded by people I regarded as problems, it suddenly occurred to me, not for the first time, that *I* was probably the problem.

Before I could accept this fact with the humility and grace that was due, however, I saw something black buzz by overhead.

"What was that?" Kat asked, as if she were reading my mind.

"What was what?" Li volleyed back. I was no expert on the FBI agent's state of mind, but he sounded tense. Which was something of an indicator in and of itself, because he was one cool customer most of the time. Li had been in government service for a while, and I got the feeling it had jaded him a little.

It might also have been the fact that he was forced to work with me, a person he considered a murderer and responsible for the death of his buddy and college roommate, but still … jaded. "I saw something, too," I said. "Like something just shot by overhead."

"Like, overflew us?" Reed asked, and I saw him let up on the accelerator a little.

"Maybe," I said. "It went from in front of us to back. Went so quick I didn't really get a good look." I felt that uneasy feeling again. "I hate to sound cheesy, but does anyone else get that sense we're being watched?"

"Yeah, there's this whole 'totalitarian surveillance state' thing going on." Reed waved a hand vaguely at a light post as we passed. "Traffic cameras everywhere to help your commute … and report your whereabouts to Big Brother. You know. The usual."

"You're kind of part of that whole surveillance state thing, you know," J.J. said. "Or weren't you the guy who came running up to me last night asking if I could pull up footage from the cameras around the Como Zoo and Observatory?"

Reed was dusky of complexion, but even I could see him redden. "I am well aware of the boundaries of my various hypocrisies, and I embrace them when it comes to making sure the last surviving member of my family keeps on surviving."

I felt myself suppress a little smile. It wasn't that I didn't know he'd been worried, but it was nice to hear it every now and again. "Awww," I said and meant it. I never mean it. I say it purely for ironic effect. Except for this time.

We settled back into silence as we turned north on 494. After a few minutes, that gnawing, uncomfortable feeling came back, and I was pretty sure it had nothing to do with the fact that I'd said, "Awww" without being ironic. There was something tickling at the back of my mind, and I still couldn't quite land on what was causing it.

I didn't dare close my eyes or speak out loud, but I did the next best thing—I directed a query to someone who understood instinct better than anyone else in the car would.

Wolfe, I said, *what the hell is going on?*

Being watched, Little Doll. It traces faint lines on the mind, runs claws lightly along all your survival instincts.

I looked sharply left, then right, then up. *Where is it coming from?*

Somewhere above, he said. *An eye in the sky, Wolfe thinks.*

"J.J., I said, "is there any drone traffic in the skies above us?"

"Uhm," the geek said, looking like I'd dumped coffee down his pants, "I don't know. Maybe?"

"The totalitarian surveillance state is everywhere," Reed pronounced.

"Hush up," I said, leaning toward J.J. "Would there be any way to tell if we were being watched right now?"

"It may be possible," J.J. said, fumbling for the black shoulder bag he had at his feet. "I mean, if I can use my wireless network card to get online and tap into Air Traffic Control, we should be able to see civilian air traffic and maybe I could…"

I tuned out the next thing he started to say as a white van slid up beside us just outside his window. My instincts growled at the mere sight of it, windowless, matching our speed exactly. I looked behind me and saw an exact duplicate—same model and everything—just outside my window, pacing us perfectly and seeming to drift closer.

Then the sliding doors opened up to reveal men with guns, and the sharp sound of barking gunfire consumed my whole world.

Chapter 14

Rome, Roman Empire
280 A.D.

Marius looked down from Capitoline Hill upon the glory of Rome. In this case, the glory took the form of the Forum, with its columns tipped with statuary and the empty space for the Comitium, where the senate would meet with populace in front of the Curia. Marius had heard the tales in Apiolae, the adults speaking with one another about the workings of the Empire, but to see it in its glory was … well, glorious.

Still, along with the glory came the smells that were anything but glorious. The whole of Rome had an aroma of animals and people that defied those of the barn, even at their worst. Not that the barn had been all that bad; he'd kept it clean, after all. This, though … he'd seen the sewers that took the filth away, but the smell was still pungent. More pungent than Apiolae had been, in any case.

Marius glanced back up at Capitoline Hill as he made his way down the slow, winding road of cobbled stone. He could see the bustling crowds down in the Forum, groups of people talking, making their way to their destinations. He could feel the buzz of activity, the energy of the people below. Arguing, laughing, doing all the things of life, the things he had seen at a distance back home. The things he'd seen people stop doing the moment he walked up.

He made his way down onto the square, up the steps and looked to his left at the Arch of Septimius Severus. It looked new to him, the sheen still upon it, in contrast to the weathered appearance of the Curia behind it.

The summer heat had made its way into the city and the buildings seemed to take in the warmth around him. Marius kept walking, almost furtively looking at the Curia, where the Senate met. It was the place of power; he could feel it. Not as powerfully as the aura from the Emperor's residence on Palatine Hill, but it was still palpable.

Marius stopped in the middle of the Forum, edging toward one of the massive marble columns. He glanced up at the statuary above and it glowered down at him. Marius felt a subtle chill in the hot, dry air. He felt that—and something else.

It was a subtle sensation, the feeling of scrutiny upon him. He knew it well, the sense that someone was watching him, taking in his motions and movements, keeping an eye upon him. It had been a constant at home, whether herding the animals under the eye of the old man or in town in the square, the sensation of eyes following his every move. Waiting for him to expose his madness or harm someone.

And here it was again.

He felt a surge of agitation deep within himself. A journey of weeks to come this far, and he still felt eyes upon him, watching his movement. He made a slow turn, trying to narrow down from whence the scrutiny came. He cast his glance through the arches of the Curia, past the Arch of Septimius Severus, where men in white robes conversed loudly, and finally around to the Temple of Saturn. Someone was lurking within the columns, not bothering to hide their presence.

Marius glanced at them furtively. There were two of them; a man and a woman, both stately in their way, lingering between the columns and looking at him. The white marble shone in the summer sun, causing Marius to squint as he stared back at them. They watched him unapologetically, not even bothering to hide. They seemed to be talking, though they were still at such a distance that he could not hear them speaking to one another.

The man started toward him, slowly. He held his hands out and open, as if to show that he meant no harm. Marius considered running; he was faster than anyone else he had met, and if he put his mind to it, he was certain he could outrun them both.

The woman followed behind the man a few paces, and he caught a hint of sourness on her face. She was striking and regal, though she still looked very young. Her dark hair was bound up at the back of her head, and her robes covered her adequately while revealing a full figure that Marius found … alluring.

The man was closing the distance between them now, and Marius felt a strange calm settle over him. He tried to resist, to remain alert and keep the option to run, but he felt it lull away. *They approach open handed, to show me good intentions. Perhaps they are friends …*

He felt a bolt of alarm shatter the sense of peace that had fallen upon him. *I have no friends.*

He felt the twitch of his muscles, his legs cry out to flee with all speed, but he kept a hand anchored to the column and let his fingers drift over the porous stone, as if he could take some strength from it. The man drifted to a stop only a few feet away—out of arm's reach, Marius noticed. The woman stopped a few steps behind him, the lines that shaped her face moving it into an expression of impatience.

"Greetings," the man said. "Welcome to Rome."

"Thank you," Marius said. He could still feel the call of his body, urging him to run. *Why would I stay to talk to a stranger? This is madness.*

"You only just arrived, is that correct?" The man's voice had a strange accent, a curious lilt that was a little different than what Marius had heard from the Romans he'd listened to since arriving.

"Yes," Marius said. How did this man know that he'd only just arrived?

"I mean you no harm," the man said. "My name is Janus, and this is my sister, Diana."

Marius kept him under close watch as he spoke. He did not reply immediately; he felt almost fearful of giving away his name. But why? It was not as though this Janus could do anything with a mere name. "I am called … Marius."

"It is a very great pleasure to meet you, Marius," Janus said. His beard was thick and full and dark, not a hint of grey in it. His skin was tanned almost to the point of glowing, and as Marius looked at him he saw a sparkle in the man's eyes that spoke of a good humor that Marius had never seen directed at him before. "I sense that you are in the midst of a very difficult transition, having come to Rome for the first time. I take it you are having some difficulty finding your place here?"

"I am not certain I have a place here—or anywhere," Marius said with a little wariness. The woman—Diana—had yet to say a thing to him. Was that cause for suspicion?

"Many have felt just the same," Janus said with a nod. He turned toward Diana as he spoke. "Is this not true, sister mine?"

She gave him a look of severe irritation that was plain even to Marius's unstudied eyes. "This is true." Her voice barely allowed for any emotion. "It is a city where the strong survive and the weak are hunted, flayed and enslaved." There was a flash of anger in her eyes that was unmistakable. "As well you know."

"As well we both know, I think," Janus said, glancing at her. "It seems to me that Marius here is in the midst of Rome for the first time without help or idea of what to do next. We would be very poor hosts to allow him to wander about into the nets of whatever hunters might find him to their tastes."

Diana's eyes narrowed as she looked at Marius, and he felt himself quail before her, feeling as though she would run him down if he tried to flee. He actually flinched beneath her gaze. "He will last less than one more day on his own, that much is true. Jupiter or Alastor will catch up with him swiftly and he'll be done."

"It would seem to me that we should protect the lad," Janus said, and he offered a smile to Marius that felt … oddly warm.

Diana's nostrils flared and Marius only just kept from taking a step back at the hint of anger from the woman. "There is no 'we' in this. If you mean to make it your pet project to take in every spawn of Hades and Persephone out of some misguided effort to recapture what you lost—"

"Diana," Janus said, and it was as though a veil fell over his emotions, "it would seem to me that Zeus has taught us both enough about his appetites and the misfortunes that fall upon those who oppose him. Perhaps we might aid someone—some prey—whom we see staggering toward that waiting trap, yes?"

Her expression became even more murderous, but she fell into a moment of silence. "Perhaps."

Marius caught that same glimmer in Janus's eyes again, as though he had won some hard-fought victory. Marius had felt that feeling himself once or twice, most memorably when he'd gotten the old man to let him stay in his barn. "I will take that perhaps as a yes, for I know it is all I will get from you," Janus said. He looked at Marius and gave him a smile. "I know that things are most likely difficult for you. You left your home behind, afraid because of the secret you carry with you." He pointed to Diana, then to himself. "We have felt much the same at points in our lives. Your burden is great, and I would … offer you assistance, if you would have it."

Marius felt a hint of fear, all the talk of prey and hunters leaving him with a bad sense of what was coming. *No one helps me, not without reason. Why would they? And he says he knows about the secret I carry? How would such a thing be possible?* "Why?" he croaked out.

Janus pursed his lips, and looked once more to Diana, whose face softened and went expressionless. "Because," Janus said, and he smiled, his face becoming warm as he looked back to Marius, "We are like you."

Chapter 15

Sienna
Now

The sound of the first shots striking the metal sides of our SUV was followed an instant later by the squeal of tires as Reed slammed on the brakes. The noise of the rubber ripping at the freeway, trying to keep hold of the asphalt was nearly drowned out by the roaring of the guns to either side of us. I saw the vans pull half a car length ahead of us, the flash of the gun barrels hanging out the open doors casting tongues of flame at each other.

A crunching sound preceded the impact of a vehicle into our rear bumper by only milliseconds. My head jerked as I turned to see a third van slamming into us from behind, the driver's eyes visible out the back window as it shattered.

Time seemed to slow down as my adrenaline kicked in. Shards of safety glass flew around me, twinkling in the light from the moon roof. I heard the engine gun again as Reed floored it, and the SUV struggled to cope with his urgent demand.

There was a moment's silence from the vans in front of us, presumably while the drivers readjusted their aim to cope with the fact that we were no longer directly beside them. I wondered if Reed's sudden slamming of the brakes had caused them to shoot each other. I hoped it had. Fervently.

The smell of smoking rubber filled the SUV, and I coughed once to clear it from my lungs. Grey smoke hung in the air around us. I could hear the whine of the tires against the highway again, even over the sound of crunching metal from behind us.

"MOVE!" I shouted at Reed. He did not bother to acknowledge me. It probably wasn't even necessary, since he was already trying, but I couldn't help but add my command. I could see movement behind the driver of the van that had smashed into us—the movement of men with guns. Their black tactical clothing was visible through the van's broken windshield, and I pulled my pistol, a brand new Sig Sauer P227, from under my coat.

I fired, each stroke of the trigger filling our SUV with thunder that probably would have hurt my eardrums if my system hadn't been flooded with adrenaline. I aimed carefully, painting the driver with a double-tap to the chest, then switching targets to the passenger as our car jerked back into motion. With the strength of Wolfe coursing through me, helping to hold my weapon steady, I could barely even feel the .45's recoil.

I felt our return to acceleration as I was thrust against my seat. I was twisted at the waist to fire backward, and as the sound of my last shot faded, I realized Kat was screaming next to me. I glanced at her, and saw flecks of blood on her face. "J.J.?" I asked, leaning over Kat to get a look at the computer geek.

He was huddled, bent double at the waist, with his arms wrapped around his backpack, head shaking and his eyes clenched shut. It reminded me a little of a child in total fear, because the motion made him look so … small. "J.J!" I yelled again. "Are you all right?"

His right eye cracked open a sliver and he saw me leaning over Kat. "Nothing a fresh change of underwear won't fix."

"Kat!" I shifted my attention to her, grasping her by the shoulders and shaking her once. She blinked. "Are you all right?"

She swallowed visibly. "No." She was more than a little pale.

Klementina … Gavrikov's voice in my head whispered. He would have been more than a little pale and shaking, too, if he'd been corporeal.

"Where are you hit?" I asked, tearing at her jacket, trying to find where the blood splatter had come from.

"Look out!" Reed shouted from the front seat, and I ducked hard, forcing Kat down along with me then reaching over to yank J.J. down as well. I folded all three of us at the waist, knocking J.J.'s backpack out of his lap.

Bullets whipped into the space above us. I hadn't even noticed the side windows shattering, probably in the seconds before the crash. Or during the crash. Hell, it was all a jumble.

I thrust my Sig out the window and fired blindly twice along the direct axis outside our window. The sharp whistling of bullets over my head was unmistakable, a frightening sound even to me. I may have picked up Wolfe's adaptability when I had him front of mind where I could use his power, but it's not like I could think about him all day, every day.

And even if I could, my skin hadn't gotten as tough as his had. Not yet. There were only so many bullet wounds my body could handle before dying. In the case of a head shot, it might only be one. It'd be tough to focus on Wolfe and his power with most of my brain splattered outside my body.

I realized with relief that the side panels of the SUV must have been armor plated. The volume of fire from either side of us was simply astounding, submachine guns roaring at full auto into our vehicle. I didn't dare lift my head to check on Reed's driving (I knew he was doing it blind anyway). The sound of a pistol discharging out the passenger window in front of me told me that Li was still in the fight, too.

I heard something land with a *thunk*, followed by J.J.'s dull proclamation of, "Ow," and I nearly broke Kat's neck clawing for the object I knew had to be in the floorboard beneath one of them. By sheer luck and I tossed the object—an ovoid piece of rippled metal—out the window next to me.

I heard the grenade detonate with a low *WHUMP* half a second after I got it out of the SUV, and the SUV rocked to the left. Reed was struggling for control of the vehicle, driving with his head down as he was, sneaking the occasional glance at the road in front of us from his hunched over position.

It was a formula for one of the gunners in the van to put a bullet in his head any second. A good sniping shot would send us into a certain wreck. It might not kill us all, but it'd probably kill J.J. and Li, and put a desperate hurting on myself, Reed and—

KLEMENTINA!

The voice was like someone sent a bolt of lightning through my head, filled with fear and desperation of a sort I'd only felt a few times in my life.

It was the fear of a man who knew he was seconds away from losing someone he loved.

Help her! Gavrikov said, and his voice was so utterly different from the Aleksandr who had been in my head this last year and a half. I'd heard him proud, whiny, defiant and even indifferent.

Now, he was half a heartbeat from losing his shit.

"I'm kind of limited in what I can do, Aleksandr," I muttered as I fired my pistol out the window over J.J.'s head, thanking the heavens above for the ten-round magazine. I used Kat's back to steady my hands to fire, and she stayed down for it. I painted one of the gunmen with a headshot, and watched him go boneless as he toppled out of the side door of his van. Another replaced him and forced me to duck again as he sprayed the space I'd just been occupying with a hailstorm of lead. "I'm not invincible, you know, and I can't exactly move from this spot. Not with the car roaring down the freeway."

You can fly, Gavrikov said, and as he spoke in my mind I felt a strange tingle run over my scalp at the thought.

"I can't—" I said, but stopped midway through. "I can?"

I give you my power, he said, urgently. *I will help you. Just …* *save my sister, please.*

I blinked, and the hellish chirps of shots passing over my head caused me to duck down lower, involuntarily. "I—"

PLEASE, he begged. *Please*. His voice lowered. *I will help you.*

Please.

I fired my last round blindly out the window over my head at the van just outside then ejected the magazine. I reloaded it with the spare from my holster and jerked the slide as I heard return fire blasting at me from outside. I glanced toward what I could see of the front seat. Reed was hunkered lower than before, and I felt him ease off the gas, and then felt the hard jarring as the van behind us—now presumably under someone else's control—slammed into us again. The sound firing from the van beside us receded slightly as it continued down the freeway, no longer pointed directly at us for the moment it would take their shooters to readjust their aim.

It was now or never.

Taking a deep breath, I ripped at the door handle and pushed. The SUV's door resisted for only a moment, the momentum of the car and the speed of the wind pushing back. I opened it just enough and lunged forward. I saw the pavement blurring beneath me as I hurled myself out of the relative safety of the vehicle and into the open freeway beyond.

And a half an inch before my skin met pavement with deadly force, gravity seemed to just … switch off. I hung there for half a heartbeat until my thoughts caught me and told me to go up, up, up. And I did.

I flew.

Chapter 16

The freeway and the ground raced away as I shot up into the air. It was a weightless sensation, like I'd bounced really high, but without the feeling that the ground was going to come rushing back up to me anytime soon.

I paused for a second above the fray. It was a fray, too, a free-for-all taking up all three lanes of Interstate 494 heading north. Cars were pulling away wildly, hugging the shoulders of the road as the vans spewing bullets out of their open hatches continued on, sliding back into place on either side of the SUV that carried my friends.

I caught my breath for a beat, wondering if anyone had seen my exit from the car. I stared down at the spectacle below and realized I had no time to think about it.

The van on the passenger side of our car was lining up to shoot again, and I doubted my brother would survive another round of it. As if to punctuate that thought for me, I watched as one of the shooters lined up his shot, holding off on opening fire as he aimed his gun barrel into the SUV, the driver easing them across the dots between lanes and closer to our speeding car.

I darted down with a thought, my body flying through the air, wind tearing at my jacket's sleeves. I dove forward and found myself suddenly pacing along with the vans and then catching up to them. I changed my body's position, slinging my legs down, and with a thought I willed gravity to come back to me.

It did.

With a vengeance.

I dropped from ten feet above the van on the right of our SUV and slammed into the roof with all my weight. I felt the metal crumple beneath me as I kicked upon landing, trying to do some damage.

I sunk a good half-foot into the metal of the van's roof, creating a small impact crater that caused the vehicle to swerve to the right. I jumped, wanting to be able to fly again, and it happened with only my will. My feet lifted into the air and I was flying along again, fifty miles per hour over the van's roof.

I glanced to my left and saw the van on the opposite side lining up for a shot. "Reed!" I shouted. "Out your window! Let 'em reap the whirlwind!"

I didn't hear him answer back, and for a second I wondered if he'd heard me over the roar of the highway. Then I saw the hood of the van on the side jerk violently to the left and crash into the concrete divider that separated the lanes of the highway. The van tipped upon impact and crashed onto its side, skidding to a stop as we blew past.

I didn't dare breathe a sigh of relief yet, though. All it would take is one of the two remaining vans getting a good shot at Reed and the whole SUV would come to a sudden, violent stop. The only question at that point would be who would die, because death would be certain for at least one of them.

I arced into the air above the van that was still holding on the right side of our SUV. I was pacing them, just above the dented roof where I'd landed on them. I could see some metal scars where shards of the grenade had exploded. I wondered if it had hit any of their gunmen, and realized that if it had, the evidence was either inside in the form of wounded, or somewhere along the freeway about a mile back in the form of a corpse.

The staccato burst of gunfire from the van's door galvanized me into action at last. I could hear the singing of the bullets bouncing off the metal sides of the SUV. There was almost no paint left on them, the outside surface of the car's exterior a crumpled, shredded mess. Steel girders from the inside structure of the doors were exposed, and from my bird's eye view I could see Li and Kat huddled inside the car. Li's suit was a darker shade at the shoulder than the rest of his ensemble.

He was bleeding.

I flew forward and down, turning in a slow arc so that I could get in front of the van below me. I spun and threw my legs out in front of me and then halted my motion and just hung there. I waited for less than a second, legs extended like I was about to toothpick into water below, arms crossed over my chest, pistol clenched in hand.

When I hit the van's windshield, feet first, it exploded inward like a rain of glass falling sideways. I used my newfound powers of flight to halt me in midair, canceling the fifty plus mile per hour impact of my body against the moving van.

But not before I kicked the living hell out of the first guy to get in my way.

He'd been standing in the middle of the van, probably shooting out at my friends, when I hit him with both feet. I felt all my momentum transfer down my legs and into him as I forced him into motion and halted my own at the same time.

He hit the back doors with his body and sheared one of them off as he spun limply out the back of the van and hit the ground below. He went ragdoll and bounced twice before I lost track of him.

My feet hit the floor of the van and I swept out with a hand, hitting the man nearest me in the neck with a quick chop. His hands went to his throat instinctively and he failed to keep my blow from costing him his balance.

He was nearly under the tires of the van before he even tried to reach out and grab something in the vain hope of hanging on.

Too late. The impact of his body under the rear tire caused the whole van to jump and shake, skidding slightly as it tried to regain traction.

I realized that there was another man in the back with me, one last shooter. His reactions were quicker than the others, and as I sent a kick in his direction, he dodged to the right without losing his footing.

Meta.

Shit.

He had a hand still on his submachine gun, a lovely HK MP5. I'd used one myself from time to time and I knew how much lead they could spray in a short amount of time. They were beyond deadly at close range, and he and I were at point blank.

He made a move to swing the barrel toward me and I slapped it away, toward the back of the van. The gun belched involuntarily but he kept it perfectly level and it cut off after three shots.

If I hadn't already suspected he was a meta, his strength and control of his weapon confirmed it. He went for something on his tactical vest and I would have slapped his hand away, but I had something in my right hand that didn't make it possible.

My gun.

I tried to line up a shot instead, and he jerked his hand away from whatever he was grabbing to slap mine back. He caught me on the wrist with a stinging blow that wrecked my aim a second before I had it pointed at his head.

This guy was good. He was a meta and a fighter. He'd had training, he had experience, and he wasn't some weak-fisted slap fighter, either.

Apparently, as Zollers had tried to warn me, Century *had* been saving the best for last.

I whirled my gun hand 'round again, trying to go low, but he blocked me again. I knocked aside his submachine gun again. No accidental discharge this time (I know how it sounds—but this was potentially much messier) unfortunately, because I'd been hoping to make him fire off stray rounds until he ran out of bullets.

He was fast. Fast enough to keep up with Wolfe-speed, which I was channeling with a vengeance. Most metas can't claim that level of power, and it worried me that I was facing someone of that level in a white-knuckle freeway assassination attempt. It suggested that there might be more trouble waiting for me in the last van.

If I even made it to the last van.

There was a sharp sound of gunfire from out on the freeway, and I realized it was coming from the last van, the one that had boxed us in from behind. They were firing full out, straight into the back of the SUV that had my friends in it. I could barely see Reed's back as he hunkered down, and J.J. was just gone, as if he'd vanished into the floorboard. He had to have been down so low I couldn't see him.

A fist came roaring at me, and I barely dodged it, falling backward and lashing out with my foot at the same time in a bizarre contortion. I managed to knock aside my assailant's submachine gun again as I caught myself with my palms. I arched my back in order to throw myself to my feet, and made it just in time to see my opponent draw a short-bladed knife from his tactical vest. He must have been going for it a moment before when I came at him, and my fall had finally allowed him to get it drawn.

With it in his hand, I was at a distinct disadvantage until I could get my pistol aimed at him. In these close quarters, and with the speed he was displaying, I was not certain I'd even be able to do that.

I need some help here! I shouted in my own mind.

Enjoy the bitter taste of your own blood, Eve spat helpfully at me.

Aleksandr! I called in my own mind as I blocked a knife strike, slapping my assailant's hand down. He altered its momentum by bringing it around in a circular motion that caused him to graze my belly. I felt my shirt rip and a thin slice of pain run across my stomach. *I need fire!*

Can't, he said. *You won't be able to control it without practice, and in your present frame of mind you're more likely to blow up everything in a three-block radius—*

"Not helpful," I muttered as I slapped away my foe's gun again and he slapped away mine—with the knife. I felt the point run over my wrist and gritted my teeth rather than allow the scream of outrage and agony escape my lips. I breathed, hard, my fury lost in the searing feeling running down my arm.

I can help, Bjorn said, and I felt him step to the front of the line. I could see him clearly in my mind's eye, and something came with him, some power that he held which would allow me to—

Oh, God—

It felt like a river of anger ran through my brain, carried on the flapping of crow's wings. I could see the darkness it brought, the pain, the rage, and it all carried forward and out of my skull like it was blasting forth from my eyeballs. I knew it was all a construct of my mind, something that was happening in the inches between my ears, but that made it feel no less real.

It was the Odin-type's War Mind.

I'd been hit with it before, once when I was fighting Bjorn and another time when I'd angered an old woman in a trailer house in northern Minnesota. It was a feeling of leathery wings slipping through your brain, foreign thoughts invading the space of your own—and it was damned distracting.

My opponent flinched under my psychic assault, his arms going slack for just a moment as he mentally batted away the bothersome murder of crows I'd sent swarming at him. He gasped audibly, as though he'd just pulled his head out of the water after a long submergence, his eyes unfocused, staring ten thousand yards past me at enemies I couldn't see.

Neat.

I kicked him in the chest while he was powerless to block me and he slammed into the metal interior side of the van and bounced off into a waiting right cross from yours truly. It caught him in the—again, defenseless—jaw and I heard a crack. He sagged from the power of my blow even as his body pinwheeled from the force of it. I caught his tactical vest with my left hand and spun him once before throwing him out the open van door.

He didn't gather his wits in time to even shield his head before slamming into the SUV right alongside, and I heard and felt him go under the back wheel of the van I was in as well as the SUV. *Th—thump!*

Victory is mine, asshole.

Reed jerked the SUV to the right, and I could see his head peeking up just enough to see the road in front of him now.

That was going to be fatal to him if the enemy fire continued for much longer.

I took two steps to the back of the van and jumped out the rear doors. Gravity left me once more and I flew like a dart, veering hard to the right, into the side panel of the last van with metahuman force. It rocked to the left as if the driver had jerked the wheel in that direction, even though I knew he had done no such thing. It was all me, baby.

I smiled at the thought of how I was dominating them. This was power. The power to—

The pain hit me in the skull like someone had cracked open my gourd and dropped a nuclear weapon inside before sealing it back up. There was a hiccup in my flight and I felt myself drop a full foot. I caught myself just before smacking into the pavement full force, gasping as if someone had just held me underwater for a minute.

I panicked, grabbing hold of the van's side door in a frantic gesture. There was an odd quiet in my head, an empty space where the souls that had been aiding me had been only a moment earlier. I could barely feel Gavrikov, like a voice shouting in the distance.

I felt the power of flight start to drain from me, and realized I'd felt this particular sensation before, only days ago, when a telepath named Claire had paralyzed my body.

Now she was cutting me off from my power.

I hung on to the door of the van, my fingers tight around the steel handle, my feet hitting the side of the vehicle and trying, desperately, to find a foothold.

There wasn't one.

My Sig Sauer fell uselessly from my grasp and I went for the door handle with my right hand as well, trying to cling to it even as the noise of the road and the wind rushing around me nearly deafened me.

I glanced up and saw a face in the rearview mirror of the van. A hearty smile that I'd seen before.

Claire.

She was here.

I saw a glimmer in her eyes, and the smile widened, got crueler. She was trying to kill me.

I barely tightened my hold in time for the next psychic attack. It loosened my grip and my body swayed into the side of the van, hitting the white metal and rattling my teeth. After a moment the pain waned, and I looked up to see her again, the grin all that was visible in the mirror.

Yep. Definitely trying to kill me.

The smell of the tires burning rubber and the thousand tiny pains running across my body came to the fore of my mind as I felt the next attack coming. My fingertips felt attached to the handle only lightly, and as the spear of her attack hit my mind full force, I felt the grip loosen, the last digits falling free of the steel as I dropped toward the freeway—

Without my powers to save me from the painful death that waited below.

Chapter 17

Marius ate with wild abandon, fine foods of a sort he could never have previously imagined arrayed in front of him in amounts that would have seemed absurd to the villagers he'd grown up around. There was cheese and honey and meat—meat!—aplenty, and cooked in succulent ways with spices and flavors the likes of which he'd never even imagined. The smells filled his nose and the heat of them, fresh from the spits and fires and ovens, warmed his hands as he pushed morsel after morsel into his mouth.

"You are hungry, then?" Janus asked, but in a way that left no doubt, even to Marius, that he was not asking. "Have you eaten since you left home?"

"Scarcely," Marius said, pushing more food into his mouth. The flavors were sumptuous, were incredible, were beyond anything he'd ever even considered before. They tasted like a skin of good goat's milk on a hot day after tending the animals, sating him in a way that he couldn't have imagined himself being sated.

"Ah, poor lad," Janus said, and Marius looked up enough to see him ... sympathetic? "Yes," Janus said, as if answering his thoughts, "I do feel more than a bit sorry for you. You

95

have had a difficult life, I would estimate, what with the … additional company … you have in your mind."

Marius halted, letting a clump of meat fall from his outstretched hand onto the wooden table. He stopped chewing, swallowing what he'd eaten with great care. "How do you know … about …"

"About the voice in your head?" Janus asked, and he looked like he was surveying Marius. "I am what they call an empath. I can read the emotional states of people—their sorrow, anger, joy, and so on. You … you have not just the emotional weight of a single person hanging about you. You carry an additional burden, one filled with anger and sorrow and no joy, if I may say. Someone furious at being trapped in your body and being subverted to your will." He looked at Marius carefully. "Who is this person? A brother? Close friend? A girl you knew in your village, perhaps?"

"My mother," Marius said, not taking his eyes off of Janus. "Or at least she says she is." He glanced around, waiting to see if anyone sprang from the shadows of the room. It had grown late, and there were flickering candles casting shadows around the manse. It had looked stately indeed when Janus had brought him here. When the woman named Diana had disappeared after their arrival, Marius had half expected Janus to kill him quietly.

"Goodness," Janus said, stark surprise causing his eyebrows to rise. "And you do not recognize it as the voice of your mother?"

"She died giving birth to me," Marius said slowly. "I never met her, but all the villagers say it is so. That she died in the last moments of labor. That she died from touching me." He raised a hand, palm out, in front of him. "Anyone who touches me will die, they say. Two women tried to nurse me and ended up gravely ill before they determined how to feed me milk through a skin."

"An incubus," Janus said, leaning forward with interest. "And you manifested at birth, no less."

"I do not understand what you are saying," Marius said, leaning back in the chair. He felt the hard wood underneath his back, and realized that he was very tired.

"You are more than human," Janus said, his face now shrouded. "There are many of us, those who have powers beyond those of normal people. You are one of us. We are comparatively few, and our powers tend to manifest, or appear, at around sixteen or seventeen years of age. Yours, which include the ability to drink the souls of those whom you touch, appear to have originated at your birth." He leaned back in his chair, his thumb and forefinger stroking his bearded chin. "Unusual, but not unheard of."

Marius blinked. "But you … you cannot … drain souls? As I can?"

Janus shook his head. "There are many different types of us, with powers of varying kinds. An incubus, as you are, is a fairly unusual power as of now. There are not so many of your kind. They are all of one family, and I can only assume that your father was also an incubus."

"No one knows who my father is," Marius said. "My mother never said."

"It was probably Valerianus," Janus said with an air of distaste. "He has a tendency to float about the countryside having his way with women and leaving them dead in his wake." He looked sickened. "Few of his victims survive, I am sad to say."

"Why would he … do such a thing?" Marius asked, trying to wrap his mind around all he had heard. People with powers, gods walking the countryside? He had had faith, but to hear that it was all true, existing beneath the surface of the cold and cruel world he had witnessed with his own eyes … that was something else entirely.

"Out of desire," Janus said. He sounded like the villagers when they had discussed a murderer who had been caught and killed. "He lets his primal lusts rule him and woe betide any who get in his way." Janus leaned on the table, his eyes connecting with Marius. "I must caution you that there are many of our kind who conduct themselves in this way, treating people as objects to be used for whatever purpose or gain they can find. They view humans around them in much the same way that your hometown likely treated you."

Marius felt a sudden revulsion creep through him. "That is …" He searched for a word.

"Appalling, I know," Janus said. He eyed Marius warily. "Yet I understand the temptation. You will likely feel it yourself, now that you realize your power over others."

Marius swallowed, felt the bile burn down his throat. "I don't … I don't want to hurt anyone."

Janus watched him then nodded once. "That is an excellent place to start, with that intention in mind."

Marius leaned back in his chair again, but now he found no comfort in it. A chair was a luxury he'd never imagined in the barn. There was food before him of the like he had never seen. The house that surrounded him was unlike anything in his village. And yet— "What is to become of me?" he asked.

Janus shifted his weight from his elbow and sat up straight in his chair once more. "An excellent question, and one I would have myself were I sitting in your seat. Now, I think we will have the servants bathe you, and show you to a lovely bed not made of straw, and give you a night to rest before we discuss the paths in front of you." He snapped his fingers and a servant appeared out of the shadows. He gestured for Marius, spreading both arms in such a way as to indicate the nearest door, shadowed under an archway.

Marius drew himself up slowly, his limbs suddenly feeling the weariness of the last few days. He started toward the doorway and halted, looking back at where Janus sat, still deep in thought. "Why are you helping me?" Marius asked.

Janus shifted, turning his head ponderously toward Marius and then smoothing his beard. "Because, my boy, you are, after a fashion, family. And it is good form to take care of one's family."

With that, Janus stood and said no more, as he himself exited the dining hall into the shadow of a doorway in the opposite wall. Marius stood there and watched him disappear before following the servant into the darkness himself.

Chapter 18

GET OUT.

The voice nearly shouted in my head, overcoming the sound of the freeway and the wind. The feeling of weightlessness that had accompanied my flight was gone, replaced by the heady, stomach-dropping sensation of a fall.

My fingers slid across the smooth surface of the white van I'd been holding onto only moments before, hoping I'd find some place to grab onto. The sweat on my fingertips caused them to slip, and I fell in slow motion as I closed my eyes at the sound of the voice resonating in my head.

GET OUT, it repeated again, deep and rich and …

… familiar.

The psychic spear that had been causing my brain to scream in pain only a second earlier was gone, I realize dimly as I slipped past the back wheel of the van. It spun so slowly I could see it turn, faint lines of dust coming off it like mist rising off the low fields around the Agency in the mornings.

I could taste the exhaust from the cars around me, and the ground was rising to greet me. I knew it would hurt, knew that I'd bounce and probably break something. But there was nothing to stop it now—

SIENNA …

The familiar voice called to me. Jarred me out of the reverie of my slow fall to oblivion. I closed my eyes and I could see the speaker in the dark space in my mind where I greeted the souls I'd taken.

Sienna, Dr. Zollers said, his voice urgent. *I've driven her out. Sienna!*

I blinked in my own head, coming back to myself. "Driven her … out?" I felt memory flood back. "Claire," I said, remembering. "Oh, God, she was in my head—"

She was attacking you, he said, quickly. *She didn't get into your mind, just kicked you around a bit. I'm keeping her at bay now. But, Sienna, you're falling—*

My eyes snapped open as I reached within and felt myself clutch hands with Gavrikov somewhere inside. The pavement was inches away—

I lifted off and soared again, matching speed with the white van that lingered behind the battered SUV that Reed was still driving down the highway. I looked and saw it in front of me, looking as if it had been driven straight out of a junkyard and onto the road.

I was flying inches from the ground and I made myself ascend, bring myself up to the side of the van. I caught another look at Claire in the van's rearview.

This time, her eyes were wide. And the smile? All gone.

I swayed to the right and then swooped left, hitting the van in the side and sending it hard against the concrete divider in the middle of the highway. The side door opened as I flew right and prepared for another attack. Instead of slamming into the van again, I flew inside with a spinning, twisting maneuver that knocked both of the gunmen waiting inside the doors right off their feet.

I didn't hesitate, stomping on one while punching the other. Their bones cracked and broke, screams came flying from their lips, and all the while I saw movement ahead with every stolen glance I sent to the front seat. Claire was moving now, her stout form crouched between the two front seats, eyeing me as I finished the two gunmen. Both humans, I was pretty sure.

"Sienna," Claire said, glaring back at me from where she'd perched.

"Claire," I said, twisting a certain enjoyment from seeing her like this. "Fancy meeting you here."

"Well," she said, "you know how I like to harass and annoy you."

"Yeah," I said. "You've followed me from Vegas. It's almost like you're stalking me." I clenched my fist at my side.

"You killed Weissman," she said, and I caught a hint of danger in her eyes. I didn't worry too much about it since I knew she was mentally crippled.

"Did not," I said. "That was my mom. But I did kill the Wolfe brothers and crash the plane. So … there's that." I watched her warily, just savoring the moment. "I talked to your boss last night. He was pretty pissed at Weissman for that whole deal, he said. So I've just gotta ask, between you and me—has he finally wised up to the fact that he doesn't have a chance with me? Because trying to assassinate me and my friends on the freeway like this—"

"Oh, this isn't Sovereign's doing," she said, and I caught a hint of a smile. "And what he doesn't know … will only hurt you."

"You're crossing him?" I almost laughed. "For what?"

"I've got my reasons," she said, and nearly snarled.

"Tell me it's because I broke your leg," I said. "Because if it's to avenge Weissman in some misguided attempt to bring me down, I'm just going to die of laughter."

Her hand emerged from behind her seat, pistol clutched in her chubby fingers. It almost looked like a single-barrel shotgun chopped down to a handgun. "It's for Weissman, yes."

I blinked at her, dully. "Seriously? For that greasy, sorry-ass—"

She fired and it felt like the world exploded around me. I burst out the back doors of the van in a haze of smoke, coughing and feeling the sting of burning pain in the center of my chest. I hit the ground hard and rolled, feeling Wolfe's psyche brushing against mine.

The smell of something burning filled my lungs and my throat even as my arms and legs hit the ground. I rolled and felt my clothes tear, felt my skin give way as my body bounced. I had no will left to summon forth Gavrikov; the pain in my body was everywhere, down every limb and in my torso, too.

After a few moments that stretched into a few years, I felt my body roll to a stop. The sky hung overhead, and I could taste acrid smoke in my mouth. I tried to cough and it hurt. I moved my arm slightly and it screamed at me in such pain that I gave it up.

I heard tires screeching, people screaming, all in the distance, like they were miles away. Sirens sounded, voices called, and I cared about none of them.

I could see the blue sky over me, and faint dots checkered my vision. There were faces around the edges—J.J., I thought, maybe, and Kat. Reed was there, too, and I saw his dark eyes staring at mine from a million miles away. They got darker and darker, and it felt like I fell right into them as I lunged into the blackness of oblivion.

Chapter 19

I awoke without waking, and in the darkness I saw the outline of the construction site take shape once more. I wanted to sigh, but I didn't, instead staring into the hazy night surrounding me and waiting for him to appear. I glanced down and found myself dressed in slacks and a blouse with a leather jacket to cover it all. At least it wasn't pajamas this time.

"All right, come out," I said with that same feeling of weariness. "If you're going to go to the trouble of dragging me here, you could at least show up promptly."

"Just trying to give you a moment to adjust," he said, stepping out of the shadows. He looked much less young this time, furrows in his brow as he stared at me. He seemed taller, too.

"Yeah, well," I said, and ran my fingers over the leather jacket I was wearing, "I don't need that much time to get used to this. It's not like I get a ton of dreamwalk action ... errr ..." I adjusted my jacket to cover the indignity of misspeaking. "Err, I mean I don't really dreamwalk that often, or with many people, or ..." I sighed. "Never mind. What do you want?"

"I wanted to see if you were all r—"

"If I was all right," I said, cutting him off and finishing the sentence for him after he stopped speaking. "If that isn't becoming a familiar refrain ..." I folded my arms in front of me and listened to the leather squeak on my jacket as I did so. Nice detail. "I'm fine, I assume, though I won't be sure until I regain consciousness. You see, I landed on the highway after your friend Claire shot me with a hand cannon and sent me flying out the back of a van doing about sixty on the freeway."

His expression darkened. "I didn't order that."

I rolled my eyes. "Wow. I couldn't have predicted you singing that particular song again. It's almost as familiar as asking me, 'Are you all right?' after your thugs have just attacked me." I let my gaze settle on him. "And just as tiresome."

He pushed his lips together and caused them to subtly turn white from the pressure. "I did not send Claire after you. I ordered her explicitly to stay away from you." He hesitated. "And your friends," he added after a moment.

I looked at him, watched him for a response. I had my own ideas about what had happened here, and he didn't need to know them. "She did mention something of that sort."

He looked as though he wanted to speak but said nothing for a long moment. "I know I don't deserve your trust—"

"You nailed that one," I muttered.

"—and that I've done things you … despise," he said, and his emotions looked closer to the surface than I'd seen from him so far, "and I don't expect you to believe me right now, but I had nothing to do with what just happened to you. I had to hear about it through … other sources." He straightened. "Not from Claire, in this case."

I shrugged. "You're right. I don't believe you." He almost flinched. "But if what you say is true, you've got some serious problems in your organizational structure. You might want to worry about them rather than starting your much-vaunted 'phase two.'"

"I'll think about it," he said. "But you should watch your back just the same."

"Because more of your flunkies are going to come after me?" I asked, twisting the knife a little. "They must have been awfully loyal to Weissman to be so willing to throw their lives away to get back at me."

Sovereign pursed his lips again. "Yeah. They were. He had this whole … inner circle put together before he even came to me. They're the ones who started the ball rolling, who began the recruiting process to build the one hundred that they eventually got to. They believed in his vision long before I bought in, and they were all about carrying it out." He looked suddenly uncomfortable. "Maybe a little too enthusiastically."

I rolled my eyes again. "Let me guess. This is the part of our conversation where you demonstrate how uncomfortable you are with the partners that you've thrown yourself into bed with for this endeavor."

There was a flicker of emotion that tightened every line of his face, and then it fell. "Like I said, I don't expect you to believe me. Or understand."

"But you keep talking anyway."

"And you keep listening," he said, looking at me. "Is it just because you're hoping I'll give something away that will give you a tactical advantage in a fight?"

"Mostly," I said.

His eyes met mine, and I sensed a streak of hope within him. "Just 'mostly'? What's the rest of your reason for listening?"

"I enjoy a good monologue from time to time," I said, and I could feel my palms sweating on the leather of my jacket. Yes, in a dream. I still don't know how that works. "It's not just about you giving something away. It's about you constantly overestimating your chances, showing me how arrogant you really are."

"Maybe I'm just hoping you'll come around," he said softly. Sadly, really.

"Don't bet on it," I said, still staring him down.

He didn't say anything, just stared at me. After a moment, he started to fade again. "Take care, Sienna."

"If I can avoid your thugs," I said, driving the knife home as he disappeared into the shadows of the dreamwalk, "maybe I will." I waited for another moment to see if he would respond, but by then the dreamwalk had started to lose its clarity around me, and I fell into a mercifully quiet sleep.

Chapter 20

I woke with the sour face of Dr. Perugini hovering over me, her dark hair gathered back on her head in a bun. Her lab coat was bright white and went marvelously with the ceiling and her olive skin. She was frowning, as she frequently did in my presence.

As far as wake ups go, I think I preferred Sovereign, actually.

The faint beeping of medical machines and my slow, rhythmic breathing reached my ears a moment later. The place smelled of sterile antiseptics, like Perugini had spilled grain alcohol on the floor and never bothered to mop it up. Smelled like whiskey to me, for some reason. Probably because of a bad night I had with—

Never mind.

"Ah, good, you're awake," she said.

"Now 'get out'?" I asked, helpfully filling in her next words for her.

She did not look amused. "You are still missing quite a bit of skin and have several fractures in the process of healing, so no, I would not advise getting out of bed just yet."

"Gimme a sec," I said, sitting up uncomfortably. I hurt. A lot. She was probably dead on about that skin being missing, because it felt like it had all been scraped off along my arms from my wrists down to my elbows. I moved with nothing less than a full grimace on my face.

"What the hell are you doing?" Her eyes lit up with anger, and she started to reach for me, probably to hold me down.

"I said give me a second." I held up a hand and noticed the bandages stretched along my wrist, along with angry red marks down the back of my hand. I closed my eyes, tried to ignore the pain and failed. Still, I managed to muster enough mental discipline to make a call.

Wolfe.

He came forth when I beckoned, and I heard a gasp from Perugini. I opened my eyes as she recoiled from me. Skin was growing along the red wounds on the back of my hands, and I could feel the pain of regrowth beneath the bandages as well. New skin crawled across the red and ragged mess, eliciting a noise of disgust from Perugini. You'd think, as a doctor, she'd be pleased to see her patients healing, but no, apparently not.

The entire process lasted about ten seconds and it was done. Thin trails of blood marked the points where the regrown skin had met up, soft, crusted lines that dotted my pale flesh. "Well, that ought to do it," I said.

Perugini stared at my newly mended arms and then looked up at me dully before snapping her latex gloves off with a little more gusto. "Well, what do you even need me for?"

"For all that trouble I keep bringing down on others." I threw back the discolored sheet that lay across my abdomen, ignoring the red-brown blood stains that dotted it and put my feet on the cold floor. "You know, that thing you're constantly bitching at me about."

She made a glottal stop noise deep in her throat, a sound of disgust, and then stormed off. She paused only briefly to throw her gloves into the medical waste can before slamming the door to her office.

We had a special relationship, she and I.

I looked down at the hospital style gown that covered my body and made sure to tie the straps in the back before getting out of bed. I wasn't super enthused at the idea of showing my ass to anybody. Literally, not metaphorically. I metaphorically show my ass to people all the time. It's fun and usually takes the form of sarcasm.

I sighed and my eyes swept the nearby area. There was a faint beeping in the corner and I glanced over to see Agent Li with an IV tree, lines running toward him. He was either asleep or faking it, and I didn't want to converse with him badly enough to probe which it was. I saw a bandage on his upper arm and wondered idly how badly he'd been hit. It wasn't immobilized, so I guessed it wasn't bad, but I made a mental note to inquire when next I saw someone who would know.

I didn't see any sign of my clothes, which meant they'd probably been cut off after my rough landing. I wondered if I'd been medically evac'd to the campus and realized it didn't matter. I was here now, and that was all that counted. The last thing I'd needed was to wake up in some hospital in the Minneapolis suburbs where I could make a doctor scream with the display I'd just graced Perugini with. They probably wouldn't have taken it as well as she had, especially when it ended with me disappearing from their care against medical advice.

I felt every cold step on the pads of my feet as I headed toward the door. As I went I pulled the IV out of my arm—I was getting to be a real pro at this by now—and by the time I'd reached the exit the doors whooshed open automatically. I started through and almost ran into a man who was considerably larger than I was. Which is not an accomplishment, really, but he was bigger than even most guys. Tall, dark-skinned, and with eyes that showed no amusement whatsoever. I tried to remember if he'd looked this grim when last I'd seen him, and realized that if I had been dealing with what he'd been dealing with, I'd probably be grimmer, too.

"Hello, Senator," I said, waving my hand.

Chapter 21

I stopped, realizing that the hospital gown had wide sleeves and I had nothing on underneath. I returned my arm to my side and stood there for a moment while Senator Robb Foreman looked at me in that humorless way. "So nice of you to come visit me while I'm under the weather."

He did not even raise an eyebrow in amusement. "When are you not under the weather, Nealon?"

"I've actually been injured very little lately," I said, caught a little off guard. "Comparatively speaking." The number of injuries I'd received needed a bell curve to make the periods of over-achievement look less dramatic. "What brings you out here from Washington?" I frowned. "Or did you come from Tennessee?"

He didn't look like he'd smiled in weeks. "Tennessee? Oh, yes, I remember Tennessee. It's the state where I'm supposed to be living, except I'm not because Washington, D.C., owns me lock, stock and barrel. I haven't been home for more than a night in months."

He looked like he'd maybe put on a couple pounds since last we'd met, but he was so physically imposing it was hard to be sure. "Seems like—"

"Any cracks about my weight are sure to go unappreciated at the moment," he said. Damn, he was good with those empathic powers of his. I was only going to dance lightly around the edge of it, but he'd caught enough sarcasm in my emotional state to figure out the probable angle of attack and preempt me. It reminded me, once again, why formidable was always at the top of my list when I searched for adjectives to describe him. He looked at my hospital gown again. "On your way to get clothes?"

I glanced down at the blue-spotted gown and noticed more than a few bloodstains coloring it as well. "I could walk around like this, but I think it would detract from my professional credibility."

"No, no," he said, and I caught a hint of give in his voice. "The blood adds an element of, 'Do what I say or else.' It's a reputation enhancer."

"The things you learn in Washington," I murmured and stepped through the door to start down the hallway. He fell in beside me. "Since this isn't a social call—"

"I've been getting reports from Li and Ariadne," he said, back to being all business. "And I've read yours as well, when you've bothered to send them. I've also gotten the notices on things like that Century safe house in Henderson, Nevada." He looked sidelong at me and I ignored it. "You could say I'm feeling concerned."

"Glad I'm not the only one," I said as we reached the stairs to the basement and started to descend. My voice took on an echoing quality as we walked, our footsteps bouncing off the walls around us, magnified like every other noise in this confined space. "Century hasn't exactly been pulling their punches."

"You've lost personnel to both death and attrition," he said.

"We're better off without the ones who have left," I said. "And as for the dead—"

"You've left a trail of dead bodies behind you, both in numbers of people you work with who have died in this conflict as well as ones you've killed—" I got the feeling he was going off a list.

"This is war," I said, waving a hand at him. "War with a highly capable adversary that outnumbers my little army by staggering margins. If you want something casualty-free, try the ballet. When you get super-powerful people with ill intentions coming your way, you better be ready for a violent soirée."

"Oh, well, you've certainly provided a violent soirée," Foreman said, and now he was sarcastic, but not in a funny kind of way. "I speak of course of that house full of dead bodies in Nevada. Most were unarmed—"

"Bullshit," I said. "They were metas. We're never unarmed." I paused. "Unless, you know, someone actually chops our arms off—"

"Hilarious," he said in a tone that suggested he found it anything but. "We've got a plane crash down in a swamp south of Bloomington. What if that plane had come down a couple miles north, say in the Mall of America or some neighborhood?"

I wanted to be flippant but honestly, I felt a chill contemplating that scenario. "I didn't crash the plane, okay? I didn't even know I'd done enough damage to cause it to crash until it was already falling out of the sky."

Foreman didn't stop walking and neither did I. He did not look at me. "NTSB is still investigating, but their preliminary reports indicate shrapnel somehow entered the cockpit and injured the pilots so badly they couldn't continue to fly the plane." Now he looked at me. "Was that your doing?"

I blinked. "I don't know. There was a metal door being tossed around, and a lot of heavy hitting between me and the Wolfe brothers, but … no explosions or anything like that. At least not that I can recall."

"And you'd recall explosions?" Foreman gave me a sour look.

"Probably," I said, and now I brought the flippant back, full force. "I'm becoming something of an expert at causing them nowadays."

"So, about this freeway thing—" he said.

"Good grief," I said, aping Charlie Brown. "I'm not even … what? It had to have been less than a day ago—"

"Three hours," he said, terse.

I paused as I opened the tunnel leading from headquarters to the dormitory. Fluorescent lights flickered on ahead of us, filling the air with a hum. "Give me a few minutes to compose myself before you start in on this one, okay?"

"There is no more time for composure," he said. He'd fallen behind me in the tunnel. He grabbed my arm and I twirled instinctively. "The Senate is pulling together an immediate committee to start overseeing metahuman affairs. They're talking about forming an official agency—"

"That's no good," I said with a shake of the head. "I have zero time for Congressional oversight right now." I held up a hand and waved toward the dormitory entrance in the distance. "I mean, I'm straight out of medical care and back to work, all right? Pretty sure that violates some OSHA regulation in and of itself."

"This is a nation of laws," he said gravely. "We've been bending them for a long time and now there's about to be some serious blowback. I'm not the only one reading your Agency's reports, and it's scaring a lot of people who get regular intelligence briefings about Russia's nuclear capacity and how many of their weapons are still pointed at us. This is going to go public in a big way." His face went slightly slack, and he sighed. "Count on it. There are people in Congress and the White House that want to head it off."

"God, why now?" I held a hand up to my face, rubbed my palm against my forehead. "Could they pick a worse possible time? Century is in 'nest of hornets' mode right now, apparently bending against Sovereign's will and trying to kill me."

"That's what the freeway thing was about," Foreman said, and it was like a light went on above him. "You're seeing friction in the organization." His head bobbled as he pondered it for a second. "That's a good sign."

"It's not a good one for me," I said with a low growl. "But I'll grant you that having them fighting amongst themselves provides us with more opportunities for success than having them unified and coming after us with everything they have."

He shuffled back a step and leaned on the concrete wall of the tunnel, shoulder first. "I know this isn't ideal—"

"This is absolutely nightmarish," I said.

"—but it is what it is," Foreman said. "It's not what I would have chosen, but with the run-up to prepare for Sovereign, we've had to break this secret—metahuman existence—to a lot wider group of people than it's ever been exposed to before. We outsourced everything to the Directorate for a damned good reason, but now we're out of options. You're under the federal umbrella, for better or worse, and I'm telling you there are holes in it, so that you're at least a little ready for the rush of cold water that's coming."

"They're really gonna leak it, aren't they?" I said, dim awareness washing over me.

"We think they already have," Foreman said softly. "To at least five major press outlets. Three of them dismissed it as utter rubbish, two are investigating. One of the reporters is … dogged, shall we say." He took in a deep breath and let it out. "We think they have a personal history with a meta-based crime, might have been a witness to something extraordinary." He grimaced. "Word is, the president is talking to the governors as well in the next few days. He's circulating a briefing paper on calling up the National Guard in order to cope with some unspecified internal emergency—

which is really code for whatever Sovereign and Century are planning next." He spread his arms apart. "Word will get out."

"Son of a ..." I pondered the implications of that for a minute. "Can't he just use the Army, keep it federal?"

"It may come to that, but Sovereign and Century are operating in the United States. That makes it subject to the Posse Comitatus Act of—"

"Spare me the legal mumbo jumbo," I said, cutting him off. "Bottom line, metahuman affairs and all this extinction business are about to become front page news." I rubbed my jaw. "I'm going to have to answer to Congress for what we've done in the last few months." I thought about that trail of bodies he'd mentioned. "Aw, shit."

"It gets worse," he said, and I could sense him slumping lower even though I couldn't see him because my head was down.

"Because getting better would be completely unacceptable right now," I muttered. "How?"

"You're not just going to have to answer to Congress," Foreman said. I looked up and saw a ragged weariness on his face that seemed to be all too common in every ally I had lately. "Part of what we think was leaked was a complete profile on our present response to this crisis." His lips formed a thin line as he paused. "Including a full profile of you, naming you the head of Agency operations. So you're not just going to have to answer to Congress when the storm comes." He drew himself up to his full height, and suddenly I felt very small indeed. "You're going to be a household name when this breaks, and that means you're going to be in the full spotlight and scrutiny of every single American watching, in addition to the rest of the world."

Chapter 22

There's a reason the phrase "the shit hits the fan" is such a popular way to express a complete and total mess. Because really, what other image could you conjure up that encapsulates the absolute, disgusting mess you're dealing with when feces hits a dispersal machine like that?

I didn't really know until that moment, but it seemed likely that "Nineteen year old shut-in and murderer has fate of the world handed to her by United States Government" might actually trump "the shit hit the fan."

Foreman had parted ways with me after leaving me with that lovely tidbit. He'd promised to stay around campus for a little longer afterward, which I might have been more enthused about had I not felt like he'd just informed me that someone had dropped a pickup truck from orbit and that it was going to land on me sometime in the next week or two. No, don't worry about it because you can't do anything to stop it. Go perform brain surgery, and try not to think about that inevitable doom that's heading your way. No pressure.

I dressed in silence in my quarters. I cast aside the bloodstained hospital robe and realized I'd been in more of those than most nineteen year olds. When it came to physical wounds, I'd probably had more than most people on the planet. Not that that would matter when the press came calling for me. I kind of had a feeling about how this was all going to play out, and it reminded me of that time I'd been cuffed and perp-walked out of the Minneapolis/St. Paul airport customs area.

Except with a wider circle of judgment this time. Like "everyone on Earth" wider.

Being hated isn't so hard, Little Doll, Wolfe said. *You get used to it after a while.*

"However hated you are, I doubt you've had seven billion people despising you at once, Wolfe," I said.

Perhaps not, he said. *But everyone in the ancient world did hate me at one point.* He let out a soft growl. Wolfe and his brothers were not gentle spirits, and there was so much anger …

The old gods knew the power of vitriol, Bjorn chimed in. *Your lessers will always resent you. That is the curse of power, and it takes a strong person to wield it—*

"It takes someone who has power to wield it," I said, cutting him off as I buttoned my blouse. It felt vaguely silky, and I suspected it was one of the ones Kat had bought for me with a company credit card. At some point I'd had to distract her from Janus's comatose state when he'd been down for all those months and sending her shopping had worked pretty well for a day or two. I'd had to send her back to get bigger sizes after the first trip, but once she'd figured that out, she'd done a decent job. I had stuff in my closet that I'd never even worn.

Which would probably come back to bite me in the ass if they ever held a budgetary hearing, now that I thought about it.

"Wielding power for the sake of it, just to whip it out and swing it around, is the least impressive thing," I said then hesitated, realizing what I'd just said. "You know what I mean. This is the type of thing Century probably sits around and talks about. 'When we're in charge and all-powerful, bwahaha, things will be different.'" I finished buttoning my blouse. "Yeah, congrats, you've got power. Why not try using it responsibly? Why not try using it for actual good instead of running over everyone who disagrees with you?" I shook my head as I started to pull on my slacks. "All these maniacal egos, I swear. It's like being a meta breeds a thirst for power that rivals any Evil Overlord stereotype."

Power is a need in and of itself, Gavrikov said, sounding sullen. *Those who drink from its chalice become intoxicated by its sensation and want more and more. Think about those … what do they call them? Wildfire metas? They commit a crime, then another, and escalate from there as they test their limits. They use their power in ever-increasing ways, asserting it and drinking deeper from the cup.*

It's man's way of making himself a god, Roberto Bastian weighed in. *Think about it. You use your power to shape the world in the direction you want it to go. Like the Russian said, wildfire metas are a great example. They use it for personal enrichment, for robberies, to kill someone who pisses them off. They set themselves up and create their own direction from life, writing over the plan other people have for themselves with force and violence. They play god by taking away the choices of others.*

This is how it has always been, Little Doll, Wolfe said. *Killing is man's way to manifest their own reality by removing the elements they don't care for—by force. This is what the old gods did, bending wills to their aims by threat and coercion, by killing when necessary. They shaped and built their world in the image they desired. This is what power offers you—the ability to bring your vision to life.*

"With force," I said, sliding a boot on over the holster and gun I habitually kept strapped to my ankle. I had lost more guns than I could count at this point. Probably another budgetary hearing for those. "By pushing their will on others through force."

There were democracies back then, weren't there? Zack asked. He'd been quiet up to now.

For a time, Wolfe said, almost shrugging. *Then … empires. Tentacles that grew within them to make them easier to move in one swift motion. Threats around, threats abound, and all the while the strings get tighter and tighter. The unity made it easier for the gods to rule from behind the curtain.* He made a little contented sigh. *It was fun to watch.*

"It doesn't look the U.S. Government means to let Sovereign rule from behind a curtain," I said, staring at myself in the mirror in my room. I slipped on my jacket over the holster I carried. I looked tired, bags under my eyes, which fit well with my assumption that no one around me was getting much sleep at the moment. "Somebody is going to rip the curtain right off."

Don't fret, Little Doll. There's always a way out.

"Oh, yeah?" I considered myself in the mirror, tried to make sure I hadn't missed a button. I may have had meta speed, but I still had to fasten buttons as slowly as a human. "What's that?"

Power, of course, Wolfe said, and I could see his Cheshire grin in the darkness of my head. *The Little Doll is so strong that almost no one could restrain her at this point. No one could catch her, if she didn't want them to.*

I stared at myself in the mirror and realized what was implicit in Wolfe's statement. That if someone tried to hold me accountability for my less-than-legal actions, I could fight back—and probably win. I looked into my own eyes, the blue with the green flecked in them, and realized I hadn't stared into my own eyes in a while.

If they came after me, would I have the nerve to pick up a gun and start shooting at some poor FBI agent who was tasked with apprehending me? Or some soldier lined up with his brothers, M-16 in hand, with orders to have me surrender or take me down? Because it might have to come to that.

I watched my hand, hovering just above the holster on my belt, and I let it drift down to stroke the leather covering my new Sig Sauer. I was faster now. I was stronger. I could take more damage and shrug it off, assuming it wasn't a fatal blow. Put in the same situation Li had forced me into a few months ago, now I might have been able to survive his firing squad if I fought back.

But *would* I?

I felt my palm drift over the rough grip of my pistol, and then jerked my hand away as if I'd been burned, just for considering the idea. Killing people who were sent to apprehend me in the name of the law was ...

It was murder.

It was wrong.

And yet that had never stopped me before.

I let my eyes fall from the mirror, not liking what I saw there, and felt my hand go right back to resting above my holster as I left the room, as naturally as if it were coming home.

Chapter 23

"We got problems," I said as I strode into the conference room. Everybody was assembled and waiting, and no one bothered to get up to meet me as I came in.

"What else is new?" Reed said from his place down the table.

"Well, Li is down with that arm wound," I said, "and most of Century appears to have decided it's now okay to kill me, to hell with Sovereign's wishes to the contrary." I stopped at my place at the head of the table and sunk my knuckles down onto the flat, cool surface. I could hear the air conditioning churning overtime above me, that faint humming noise that I usually didn't even notice. "So, that's new. Oh, and the entire meta world is probably going to get outed in the press in the next few weeks."

"Wait, what?" Scott said, blinking a little. He'd looked so relaxed a moment earlier.

"The president's plans for countering Sovereign include briefing a much wider group of people than has previously been aware of metas," I said. My gaze slid over Ariadne, who looked a little stunned, then to Janus, whose jaw had clenched. "They think it's going to break soon."

"Yay, our secret war is about to get exposed," Reed said without any humor. "Maybe now we can get some soldiers on our side and start fighting it like it's a real one."

122

"The freeway thing felt pretty real to me," Kat said. I glanced at her, sitting next to Janus. She looked pale. Which meant she'd probably used her powers to heal someone. I doubted it was me, since I'd still been a physical wreck missing skin when I'd woken up, so that probably meant she'd triaged and helped someone else. Maybe J.J. "But I haven't been in many wars, I guess."

"This changes things somewhat," Zollers said, staring at me with cool eyes.

"Not really." I shook my head. "I want to find a way to win this war before the word gets out."

"Sure, killing eighty or so more metas, including the most powerful one in the world in the next few days with just us? Easy peasy," Reed said. "And for my next trick, I'm going to make the entire Rocky Mountain range disappear."

"That could work," Scott said with a semi-serious expression. "Get enough pot smoke floating around in Colorado and—"

"Century," I said. "They're going to come at us. We need to flatten them, and do it now."

There was an uncomfortable exchange of looks around the table. "Sienna," Reed said, stepping up to break the news for me. "We don't know what they're planning. We don't know where they're planning to do it. All the hidey-holes we had for them have dried up—"

"Where is Weissman's computer?" I asked, cutting him off. "We were on our way to the airfield to pick it up when we got hit. Where is it now?"

"J.J. has it," Ariadne said. "Li got the FBI to send it over. We found some interesting things too, things that might explain your attack."

"Such as?" I asked.

"Century has a bunch of civilian drones buzzing around here," Reed said with a sour look. "They've been keeping us under surveillance."

I frowned. "Like … Predator drones?"

"Much smaller," Reed said. "I took a few of them out; they're only about the size of a manhole cover, and they sell them on the internet or in retailers. They're supposed to be for fun—" He paused. "Because I can't think of anything more fun than spying on your neighbors."

Scott pursed his lips. "It could be fun, depending on your neighbors."

"Gross," Kat said.

"Try and imagine how it is for those of us who get a full psychic blast of those sort of events, whether we want them or not," Zollers said, giving her a glance full of deep and yucky, yucky, yucky meaning.

Probably in an effort to not think about what he'd just said, I suddenly remembered something I had to ask Dr. Zollers. "When Claire attacked me, you said she didn't read my mind?" I watched him, and he centered his look on me. "Are you sure about that?"

"I'm sure." He gave me a nod, and his placid expression was soothing in its way.

"So what if she had?" Reed asked, frowning at me. "It's not like we've got plans aplenty of how to deal with Century right now. The worst she could have learned was that we were going for Weissman's computer, which they probably already knew since she left it behind when she fled the scene of his death."

"I wouldn't want anyone else in my head, either," Kat said, and I could tell she was trying to be supportive. "I mean, that's a real violation of privacy, the thought that someone might see your most intimate thoughts and moments—"

"Okay, let's just use our ten-foot pole to push away from the shoals that Kat is guiding us toward," I said. "We still need ideas."

"We still need some clue about how they're going to execute this 'phase two,'" Reed said. "I mean, it's not like world domination comes in three easy steps—'Step one, kill all metas, step three, world conquest'!"

"You skipped step two," Kat pointed out helpfully.

Reed slumped in his seat. "That was the point."

"So," Scott glanced around the table, "if you were going to take over the world with your meta powers, how would you do it?"

"I wouldn't," Reed said acidly, "because unless the world's staunchest defenders were windmills and their destruction cowed the human race into instant submission, I wouldn't have a chance. Which brings us to another unknown—how many different kinds of meta powers does Sovereign have access to?"

"More than you would care to count," Janus said, breaking his silence. I looked over at him and felt an immediate sense of discomfort at the look on his face. He was stern. "There are only rumors as to the exact number, but he could have absorbed hundreds or thousands of metas in his life. He could have countless powers at his disposal."

"He can fly," I said, ticking them off, "he's a telepath, can create flame the way Gavrikov can, is nearly invulnerable—"

"He absorbed Wolfe's father," Janus said.

I watched Janus carefully for a moment. "Did you know him?"

Janus shook his head. "I do not know Sovereign." I caught something in his expression that hinted at more.

"What about before he was Sovereign?" I asked, not letting up.

Janus's face was almost impassive. "Before he was Sovereign? Yes, I knew him before he was Sovereign," he said at last, letting it out like a great rush of air.

"What the hell?" Reed slapped the table and leaned forward. "God, you are just determined not to give us an ounce of help unless we drag it from you forcibly, are you?"

"It is more or less irrelevant at this point," Janus said with what amounted to a shrug. "He is not who he once was. He is not the man I knew—when I knew him."

I let the silence hold for a second before breaking it myself, before Reed could do it with an apoplectic rant that would make him seem like the Omega-hating fanatic that he was. "If I'm going to fight him, I need to know everything I can about him." Janus did not stir in his seat. "Do you understand me?"

"There are elements of my involvement with him that I am not proud of," Janus said, glancing up at me. "They are personal and bring me no pride and more than a little shame. I have no desire to root through them so that I may wallow in the particular bit of feces that was my life at the point when I met him."

"You're still keeping secrets," I said, pre-empting Reed again. His dark face was twisted with rage looking for a moment to explode from him, pressure in search of a release valve. "I don't care about your past. The whole world is on the line and the truth needs to come out, right now."

"And yet I sense you are holding more than a few things back yourself," Janus said with a resigned air. It was not accusing at all, just a statement of fact.

It still caught me off guard, and everyone's attention turned to me. "You're speculating."

He raised an eyebrow. "Your response confirms my speculation."

I took a breath and glanced, just for a second at Zollers. He shook his head in the negative. "If I am, I have a good reason for it, I promise." I placed my palms flat on the table. "What's yours?"

"Shame," Janus said, unflinching. "Shame is motivator in this matter. What is yours?"

I didn't dare draw a breath. "Fear." I caught more than a few stray looks at that and ignored them all. "Janus … Sovereign is still at the head of this rodeo they call Century.

He's still a threat to humanity. If there's anything you know about him that you can tell me … please." I actually pleaded, raising my voice to a tone as close to begging as I ever tread. "Please, Janus."

I was expecting another denial. Or quiet resignation. Or anger. Anything, really, but what I got.

Because what I got … was a hard blink of the eyes, and then two tears ran down his cheeks. The lines of his face were so pronounced that I wondered how I forgot on a near-constant basis that he was thousands of years old and had all the attendant pain that life had delivered over that time.

The old man—I couldn't think of him any other way after that—let out a choked noise and spoke once more. "I will tell you … what I know. And afterward … I hope you will all find it in yourselves to forgive me."

Chapter 24

Rome

280 A.D.

"They killed my daughter, you see," Janus said, his voice cracking as Marius listened. "I was a hundred yards away or so when it began, just around a few corners and out of sight. The fire crackled in the hearth and filled the room with a low, smoky aroma and a warmth that Marius found intoxicating, a hint of home that he'd never felt before. Janus's low, soothing voice rolled through him and he listened with interest as the man spun another tale. He'd been telling tales of gods and powers all day long, but this was the first that had caused him to show anything approaching the pain he was showing now.

"I could hear it, the disturbance," Janus went on, low and slowly, his eyes dropping. "I thought nothing of it at first, just some thief stealing. The requisite shouts to that effect were obvious enough, the stall-keeper in a rage that someone had taken from him. These sorts of things were settled quickly, and even had I known it was my daughter who had perpetrated the crime, I would not have been overly alarmed. But I did not know."

Janus reached a hand up and ran his fingers through his dark beard idly. "But she was like you, you see, and that was her undoing. The stall-keeper grabbed hold of her by one arm, another, a friend of his, took her by the other so that she could not escape. They were anchored tightly to her by grip, and even though she struggled she could not get free. She was … six. She had never used her power before, and when it came upon her, draining these two souls—doing what you do—she was unprepared, and it overwhelmed her. She fell to the ground with them and maintained hold of them.

"She was disoriented, I imagine," Janus went on, the strands of his dark beard between his fingers. "Feeling that sick sense of both pleasure and pain that comes after absorbing a soul. She did not even resist them when the mob came upon her. One of them told me later that she looked nearly unconscious, save for the smile on her face."

Janus's face darkened. "And it was that man who ran the knife over her throat, opening it and spilling her precious, precious blood all over the dirt." He paused, and his eyes appeared to sink in his head, becoming pools of shadow that hid a darkness that Marius did not wish to gaze into. "That alone *might* not have killed her. But it was a mob by that point, and they began to beat her—" He cut himself off and turned his face away.

Marius sat there in silence, listening. Waiting. He had been transfixed all the day, listening to the tales of his heritage. They had all been fascinating, but this one struck him in a different way. It was cautionary, a warning of what happened to their kind when they made a misstep. She was like him, she made a mistake, and now she was dead. Dead, and her father mourned her.

In a way my mother would never mourn me should I die. He felt agreement deep within, under the rock where he had placed her with his will.

"I killed them, of course," Janus said, and his face was still turned away. "Slowly, in many cases. Wringing the confession from each of their lips in turn. Right there in the market where it happened. You see, by the time the mob had swung into full action and I heard—truly heard—the disturbance and came to find out what it was … they were …" he paused, "… they were really just beating a lifeless body by that point …" His voice trailed off.

Marius stared at him, this time unable to turn away. Janus did not seem to want him to, in any case. He said nothing for a moment. When he spoke again, his voice was more composed.

"What I did to them was an act of vengeance taken upon fools who had no knowledge of what they had truly done." His fingers moved down and tugged at his robes. "They suffered for what they did and suffered mightily. I was, of course, praised within our own circles. 'You did the right thing,' they said." Janus's face hardened. "Zeus himself commended me for teaching mortals a vital lesson about what would come to them should they trifle with gods. 'It is good for them to be wary,' he said. 'Good for them to live with a healthy amount of fear that we walk among them, and to know that should we be interfered with, the vengeance will be swift and brutal.'" Janus let out a low, cackling laugh, free of mirth. "He said this to me, Zeus did. Jupiter, you would know him as, I think. This man. This beast." His face went slack. "He killed my parents, did you know that? Killed them right in front of me, and he commends me for striking in the name of vengeance because it will 'set a fine example.'" Janus laughed, but it was nearly maniacal and ended in a few seconds with him wheezing in rage.

"I cannot imagine," Marius said into the silence. He looked around the room but there was no sign of the servants who had been there only the night before.

"Of course not, my dear boy." Janus's entire demeanor changed in an instant; he was conciliatory. His expression softened and he nodded at Marius warmly. "I have wandered afield, I think, in my storytelling. I have amused you all day with the tales of our exploits and stories of foibles. You have likely heard all these myths at some point—"

"No, never," Marius said, shaking his head. They had all been so wonderful to hear, even the last. It reminded him of a time when a singer had come to the village, and he had been able to listen from out of the circle near the fire. He hid in the darkness and listened to the songs, the stories told to the music. It had been magic, nothing less.

But he had been at a distance for a reason.

"Your daughter," Marius said slowly, looking up at Janus's shadowed face. "She was like me?"

"A succubus, yes," Janus said with a brief nod. His face lapsed back into darkness for a moment. "She is the reason I sought you out once I sensed you at the Forum. I have tried to … assist others like her, like my former wife, in the days since that happened. I cannot bear the thought of others suffering as the outcasts our society would make them and the martyrs that humanity would make of them." He shook his head. "I do what I can, in my own way, to help."

"And your wife …?" Marius asked, carefully.

Janus looked straight at him and seemed to look right through him. "You need not fear to ask me a question, dear boy. Even when the answer is painful." He straightened in his seat. "She went mad with grief and killed herself. It caused her father—she had been his favorite daughter, you see—to go blind with rage. He lost his mind in the wake of this and the death of his granddaughter and vowed to kill every human." He cleared his throat. "Perhaps you have heard of him. His name was Hades. Or Pluto, now."

Marius nodded. "I have heard of him." He licked his lips, not wanting for the tales to end. There was so much primal emotion bound in them. And a sense of belonging had settled over him, a feeling like he was one of the actors in the tales. "And … Zeus? Jupiter? He still … rules to this day?"

Janus watched him carefully. "Indeed he does."

Marius felt a stir of righteous anger at the thought of that man on a throne. He sounded familiar. Like the countless villagers who had made Marius afraid, made him fear them, lorded over him that he was an outsider and a freak. Stomped him down. Hit him in passing. He glanced up at Janus and met his eyes, and felt the flare of anger reciprocated. Something kindred was there, a pain they shared. Marius nodded. "It seems … unfair … for such a beast of a man to wrong you in that way and to continue to lord it over others." He kept his tone careful, and he looked toward the fire, glancing only once at Janus to see what the man said.

There was a quiet for a moment as the flames danced in the hearth, swirling. Marius could almost picture someone dancing with them, screaming in pain, worthy of suffering. He knew a few that deserved it. He did not dare look at Janus.

"Indeed," Janus said, and Marius could swear it almost sounded like he was smiling as he answered. "It does seem unfair, doesn't it, for those with power to lord it over those who have it not?" There was a long pause. "Perhaps … someday … with the right … help … we might find a way to address these imbalances."

Marius stared into the fire. "Perhaps we may." He listened to it crackle as it consumed a log within its depths, and he found the decision came as easily to him as if he were tossing another log onto it. "I think I should like to help you with that."

Chapter 25

Sienna
Now

I closed the door to my office and leaned against it, what I'd just learned swirling about in my head. The air felt thick with Janus's revelation, like it was a weight on my chest stopping me from taking a breath.

I'd called a halt to the meeting after Janus had laid it all out for us. No one had said anything while he'd spun a tale that was as epic in its scope as that story of warriors and paladins that Scott had tried to get me to read in my off time a few months earlier. Afterward I could tell Reed was still about to blow up, but he kept his cool, thankfully.

Now here I was. The air conditioning in my office couldn't turn up enough to cool the heat that was building under my skin.

Janus, that bastard.

I took a deep breath in through the nose and out through the mouth. Then again. I heard a knock at the door and kept myself from snapping. "Come in," I said finally.

It opened quickly and shut quickly. When I saw it was Reed, I was amazed he hadn't slammed it. "Do you believe this shit?" he asked me.

I stared at him. His face was as flushed as it could probably get, given his dark complexion. His eyes were wide and his teeth were bared. "Yes, I believe this shit," I said and felt my anger leave me. "I totally believe it."

"He didn't tell us," Reed said, and he flung a finger angrily at the door. "If that doesn't infuriate you, I don't know what will. Janus has been holding out on us from day effing one, and you need to boot him immediately—"

"I'm not 'booting' him," I said, "unless by booting you mean kicking him in the ass, because that I would gladly do at least once, and probably twice." I folded my arms. "I can't afford to lose him or Kat right now, and they are probably a package deal. He stays."

"He's a liar," Reed said, and his face darkened even further into a scowl. He took two steps toward me, got close to my face. "He's been lying to us this whole time. He took the young man who was Sovereign, who came into his care, and he twisted him with his powers, with his emotional manipulation, and now we've got a monster to deal with—"

I waved him off. "Maybe Janus moved Sovereign to do … what they did," I said, not being able to quite spell it out in words yet, "and maybe he just showed him the door and let him walk through. I don't know. The guy's had his own crazy mommy in his head since birth; it's entirely possible Janus didn't have to do much compelling to turn him into a vengeful murderer." I sighed. "And it was a long time ago, you have to admit."

"There's a reason there's no statute of limitations on murder," Reed said. I snapped my gaze to him, and his instantly slackened. "Oh, shit, Sienna, I'm sorry. I didn't mean—"

"I know," I said, shaking my head. "I know you didn't."

"Look, this guy," Reed said, "he made the problem we're dealing with."

"Really?" I asked. "Did my mother make me?"

A look of amusement played across his strong features. "In literal terms, yes."

"I meant, did she make me a murderer?" I looked right at him. "She gave me the training. She gave me a purpose—to learn to fight. Did Old Man Winter make me a murderer?"

Reed's eyes were smoky now. "In literal terms, again, yes."

"Not talking about Zack, or Wolfe, or Bjorn, or Gavrikov …" I paused. Man, I'd killed a lot of people. "I'm talking about what I did afterward with those others. Eve and Bastian and Clary and—"

"I know who you're talking about," Reed said, and he turned away as though he were uncomfortable looking at me.

"They didn't make me do what I did there," I said quietly.

"Well, they did a lot more than walk you up to the door and open it for you." I stared at his back as he bowed his head, still not looking at me. "Especially Winter."

"I made my choices, Reed," I said. "I couldn't help what they—what Winter—did to me. But I was in full control of my reactions, and I let Wolfe and the others talk me into bloodlust. *I* did it. I killed them. And whatever Janus did to Sovereign, Sovereign was the one who made it happen when it was go time." I sighed. "And it probably doesn't have much to do with what we're dealing with now, other than some lovely background and a hint that he has powers we haven't seen yet."

Reed's head came up at that. "If Janus lied to us once, he'll lie to us again." He turned back to me, wary. "And he's lied twice in the last couple days."

"Yeah," I said, nodding. "I know."

Reed watched me for a moment, and I could tell he was trying to figure out how to say something. "Was he right about you?" I didn't answer, didn't react. "Are you keeping something from us?"

Remember.

I drew a long, deep breath. "If I was … I promise it's for your own good. For the good of us all."

He nodded sharply and turned on his heel. He paused as he opened the door, and he looked back at me. "You can get away with that because I trust you."

I bit my lip. "I'm letting Janus get away with it because … for some reason I still trust him." I inclined my head slightly. "A little bit longer anyway."

Reed nodded once. "Just as long as you don't expect me to do the same. We can't all go blindly charging over the same cliff, after all." He gave me a knowing look and left, closing the office door behind him.

Chapter 26

I was in my office by myself for all of thirty seconds after Reed left before another knock came at the door. I let out a breath of exasperation and said, "Come in."

Scott opened the door all the way and stood framed in the light of the bullpen. "So …" he said.

"So," I said, not really sure what to say to that. "What?"

"That was really … something." He closed the door behind him. "You all right?"

"I'm fine," I said, placing my hands on my hips. It felt awkward. "We all have our secrets, I guess."

"Not me," he said, taking a step closer to me with what appeared to be reluctance. "I'm an open book."

"Yeah, well," I raised an eyebrow at him, "I'd love to read all about it when this is over with."

He cocked his head at me and gave me a playful smile. "Was that … did you just …?"

I felt a weary smile crack my face. "Yeah, I think I did just say that. I meant it, too. If we get through this, yes, I want to … explore things further." I held up my hands. "Obviously, I'm somewhat limited in my ability to have a relationship, but … I'm open to trying, at least."

He smiled with genuine pleasure. "Cool."

"Cool?" I looked at him with amusement. "I say I'm open to … dating or something and your response is 'cool'?" God help me, I giggled.

"Yeah, I mean, we're nineteen." He laughed lightly. "Shit is crazy grim around here, but every once in a while I remember that we're really not that old. I mean, can you believe this? We'd be a year out of high school if we were normal people, settling into the first job or finishing up freshman year of college. Instead, we get to save the world from some group of crazy super-powered villains who have a mad-on for you."

That took the air out of the conversation, at least on my end. I lapsed into a long silence, wondering what my life would be like if I'd just been born a normal person like Scott suggested. I thought about a red dress I'd bought long, long ago, that had perished in an explosion on a night that had felt like the end of my world. I'd bought it with my first Directorate paycheck because I'd seen it, in all its short hem and sleeveless glory, and thought about what it would feel like to wear it.

It'd feel like I was normal.

"I can't construct much out of 'if only's,'" I said, snapping the door closed on nostalgia. "We're here and we're stuck with the job that we have. That's all there is." I closed my mouth and felt my lips purse. "That and … maybe some possibilities once it's all over."

Scott looked only slightly chastened, but he paused before responding. "So … when the word gets out about us … what do you think is gonna happen?"

"I don't know exactly," I said, shaking my head. "Nothing good. My record gets opened to the public, I imagine it's not going to turn out well for me. Foreman promised me a pardon before this all started, but who knows if he'll be able to deliver once public pressure lands on him." I shrugged.

"But you're still digging in to fight anyway," he said in a tone that sounded slightly awestruck.

"What else am I going to do?" I asked. "Run away? Try and save my own ass?"

"You took out Sovereign's mechanism for hunting metas," Scott said. "Yeah, you could run."

"Hrm," I said with a weak smile. "I may have killed most of his telepaths, but he's still got Claire, who hates me." I frowned. "Or Century still has Claire, anyway, depending on the status of their breakup. Not to mention the fact that he's a pretty powerful telepath himself." I gave him a sad smile. "We may have granted a temporary reprieve to the metas of the U.S. by taking shotguns into that Vegas safe house, but we didn't end Sovereign's ability to kill us all if he's still of a mind to."

Scott let his eyes go a little unfocused, and I could tell something was on his mind. He caught me looking and faked a smile. "Hey, so—"

"What were you thinking just then?" I asked.

"Nothing," he said, and it was so obvious he was lying he might as well have had it stamped on his forehead. He knew I knew, and he hesitated again. "Not a big deal."

"It's something," I said. "Just say it."

He tensed up. "All right, fine. About … Sovereign … and what he wants. Have you thought about …" He stopped, as if he couldn't even complete the sentence.

"Giving him what he wants?" I spread my arms wide. "Offering myself or pretending to do so in order to get him to stop?" I shrugged. "Yeah, I've thought about it."

Scott made a face, and not a sexy one. "I should have guessed that you'd have considered all options."

"It wouldn't work," I said. "He is a telepath, after all, and while Zollers can block him to some extent, I can pretty well guarantee that the old 'Surrender while you pull a fast one on the enemy' trick won't work with him. He's not much of an evil overlord, but he's not a total idiot. Anything I do that sends me lovingly in his direction without real sincerity will provoke enough of his suspicion that he'll use his powers to sniff out my intentions." I clapped my hands together lightly and Scott jumped as though I'd fired a shot at him. "Game over. Because I'll always think of him as a mass murderer first."

Scott nodded slowly. "Nice to know I don't have any competition from him, at least."

I smiled, but weakly. "That's safe to say."

Scott lapsed into thought. "But if he doesn't have any hope of ever winning you over—"

I was fortunate because my phone rang at that exact moment, sparing me from having to go down the path that question would inevitably lead me to. "Yes?" I asked, grateful for the interruption.

"Heyyyyy," J.J. said from the other end. "I think I've got something here."

"As long as it's not a rash, I'm interested," I said, and shrugged at Scott when he gave me a WTF look.

"Well, it looks like our old friends at the Wise Men's Consortium have just made an investment in real estate in the Minneapolis area," J.J. said, ignoring my wisecrack.

I stood there, looking blankly ahead. "I don't … have any friends at that corporation. I don't even know who they are—"

"Sure you do," J.J. said. "They're the ones who rented the Century safe houses around the country. They're the ones who chartered that cargo plane that was taking you out of the city."

Right. I let out a sharp gasp. "And they bought something here?"

"Money transfer just showed up, but it probably happened a few days ago," J.J. said. "I'm kind of a little behind in what I can do, you know, working with a staff of one—"

"You can have whatever staff you want," I said then realized the awkward entendre I'd inadvertently just handed him. "Uhm, or hire people, I mean, if you think it will help you. But about this purchase—"

"Righto," he said. "It's a warehouse in St. Louis Park, about half an hour away—"

"I know where St. Louis Park is," I said, hiding my impatience.

"—just outside Minneapolis, first ring suburb, brushing up against Eden Prairie—"

I rolled my eyes. "Address?"

"Sure, sure," he said, and I scrambled for a pen as he gave it to me. "Now, about this staff thing ... who do I talk to about—"

"You can talk to Ariadne about your staf—" I cut myself off again and just hung up the phone instead of bothering to try and dig myself out of that verbal mess. "We've got something," I said to Scott, holding up the piece of paper with the address scrawled on it.

"What are we going to do?" he asked, and I thought I caught a little excitement in his gaze. "Go in, shotguns-a-blazin'?"

I only had to think about it for a second. "Not quite," I said, and felt myself smile again. "Not this time."

Chapter 27

I stood over a computer console a few hours later, with Foreman next to me, Reed and Scott lurking behind us. Ariadne hovered near the door mostly, I think, because she wanted to observe without getting in the way. I was okay with that.

I was standing over the shoulder of a woman named Harper, who was as serious as anyone I'd ever met. When she'd offered me her hand, she didn't give me the dead fish handshake, she pumped with some strength. Not trying to crush my hand or anything, but enough that I knew she'd shook hands with me. She'd not indicated whether Harper was a first or last name, but I suspected it was last because of her ex-military bearing.

"Man," Scott said from behind me. "That is so cool. You can see everything."

We were all staring at a flatscreen perched in front of Harper. It was big enough to give us a fairly panoramic view. She had two smaller screens on either side, computer monitors we'd had on hand. She was fiddling with the complicated briefcase-based computer she'd brought along, handing us HDMI cables and asking us to sort out where to place them while she set up. I admired her brass; not many people tell the head of a government agency what they need in such brisk terms.

Being a fan of the no-bullshit approach myself, I liked it.

We were staring at the screens, which displayed a top-down view of a building. A warehouse. One of the smaller monitors had a clear-as-day picture, but the one on the main screen was on infrared. We could see five bodies moving around inside the warehouse through the walls, orange masses with human appendages and heads. Harper fiddled with her interface and the picture zoomed closer, focusing on where three of the people stood talking in an office in the corner of the warehouse.

Like Scott said, it was cool.

"How high up is the drone?" I asked Harper.

"That's classified," Harper said neutrally, as if she were telling me the sky was blue.

Reed was standing next to him, just shaking his head. "Like I said, totalitarian surveillance state."

I just shook my head at him. "Yeah, yeah, I'm not arguing with you. But since we live here anyway, I might as well use it to my advantage." Reed rolled his eyes, but I saw the hint of concession within them. What else can you do to keep surveillance on your enemies when they've got a telepath that can pick you up a mile off?

Well, actually, I had an idea for that, too, but it didn't come with real-time, down-looking infrared imagery of the Century facility.

"We've got movement in the southwest quadrant," Harper said flatly. "Town car. MARS ONE is rolling up."

I looked at the left-hand screen and saw what she was talking about after a moment of searching. There actually a lot of cars moving on that screen, given that there were a few major thoroughfares among the surrounding streets. Once I saw the town car, I figured out how she'd picked it out. It was the only vehicle for about six blocks on that particular street. Sharp eyed, this Harper.

"Comms?" I asked, and Harper nodded once before flicking a button on her console. A speaker came on, presumably filtered out of what was going to her headset a moment earlier. Then I realized: she was listening to the car's chatter the whole time, and presumably had been in communication with them. I hadn't even realized it.

"Can they hear me right now?" I asked. Harper gave me a sharp nod. "Janus, are you there?"

Harper gave me an "Are you stupid?" kind of look. "MARS ONE, this is MARS SIX. What is your status, over?" she asked, making me feel like an utter and complete amateur.

"What?" Janus's voice came over the speaker. "Oh, is that us? Oh. MARS SIX, this is … uhm … MARS ONE. We are settling into position and attempting to place the laser on the target." He paused for a good five seconds. "Oh, uhm, over."

"Understood, MARS ONE," Harper said and flipped a switch on her console. I could still hear the fuzzing and fritzing of the speakers, so I assumed she had turned off the microphone on our side.

"Nifty little thing," Scott said. "What's with the speakerphone on the drone controls?"

"We sometimes have to operate in unusual locations," Harper said, not taking her eyes off the screens in front of her. "The communications capability in the system is designed so we can receive orders from units in the field or a commanding officer who's offsite." She shook her head. "This is a new application, I have to admit."

I stared down at her. "Do you have any idea what you're into here, Harper?"

She shook her head, expression moving not a whit. "No, ma'am, and if it's all the same to you, I'd prefer to keep it that way."

I exchanged a look with Scott, who shrugged. "Fair enough," I said.

"Laser is in place," Janus said over the speaker. "Err … oh … I mean, the target is painted. Is that the code phrase? Gods, but I'm rubbish at these communications protocols. Can we not speak plainly?"

Harper sighed audibly and flipped the switch. "Negative, MARS ONE. While the presumption is that these channels are secure, adding an additional layer of communication security is—"

"Pipe down, MARS ONE," I cut her off. "Just do your job."

"Job done," Janus said sourly, and then his voice switched to a stiffer-sounding octave. "Will await further instructions. Over."

"Now that they've painted that warehouse window with the laser," I said, "does that mean we can—"

"Yeah," Harper said, cutting me off again. She flipped another switch on her console and another series of voices came on. They sounded a little farther away, a little tinny, but I could understand every word they were saying.

"—two days," came a female voice with an Asian accent. I couldn't quite place it, but she was speaking English. "We just need to wait until then."

There was a pause, and I spoke. "So this is what's being said right now in that room?" I gestured to the infrared display where the three people were talking in the warehouse room.

"Correct," Harper said, precise. "The laser your people are shining onto that window from a few blocks away is picking up the vibrations of their speech on the glass pane of the window and transmitting them to us via a transceiver in the unit—"

"Nifty," Reed said, again with the sour. "You're just finding more ways to illustrate my point about—"

"Can it," I said, waving a hand at him without looking up from the display.

"How many of them are coming?" a man asked. His voice sounded vaguely European.

"All of them," came the Asian woman's voice again.

"Here?" the guy asked.

"Not here, exactly," she said. "A little further out. Somewhere more isolated, secluded. I—" She paused, and I didn't like the sound of it for some reason.

"Can they detect the laser?" I asked. "Could you see it, a little red beam dancing over the walls?"

"No." Harper shook her head. "It's outside the visual spectrum."

"It's a laser," came the woman's voice, cold and clear.

"What the hell?" Scott asked.

"Shit," Harper said, more than a little chastened. "I have no idea how they would have picked that up." There was a rustling in the room and the sound of a door opening, followed by shouts of alarm in an echoing room I took to be the warehouse proper.

"Janus, get out of there," I said, then looked at Harper. "Can he hear me?"

"Negative," she said, and flipped a switch again. "MARS ONE, are you receiving?"

"—coming right for us!" Janus's voice came through the speaker, more than a little panic edging out of it.

"Whoa," Scott said, and he took a step forward. "They're fast if they got there in seconds—"

"The audio from the warehouse was on a delay while I answered your questions," Harper said, looking pained. She was punching buttons and pulling up visual imagery. I saw the infrared catching five human figures moving swiftly toward the town car, and then a flare of white in the shape of a ball that flew from one of the people at the fore and—

The town car glowed as it hit, and the screen went white.

Chapter 28

Marius could hear the legions in the distance. He stood upon the hill, Janus at his side with others, watching the coming of Proculus the Usurper's army. They were so very, very many, and it made Marius wonder. The fires of war burned around them, thick and smoky. He could almost taste the meat he had become accustomed to in the last months, could nearly taste the flavor of roasted flesh on his tongue from the fires. It was an ill omen in these environs, he reckoned. Even in the summer heat, it sent a chill over his flesh.

"Be not afraid," Janus said quietly from next to him.

"Do you see how many of them there are?" Marius whispered back. "I cannot even count them, they number so many."

This was true. The legions of Proculus outnumbered the Roman ones by factors of ten. Though he had only recently learned about gods and powers, Marius had not been so impressed by the gods Diana and Janus had introduced him to that he could see this sight and remain unconcerned.

"Numbers are not everything," Janus said calmly. "Not when gods are involved." His face darkened. "Though this usurper should not have come anywhere this close to the center of the Empire. It is a dark day, one that shall not be spoken of save for in whispers henceforth."

Marius shut his mouth, holding back his fear. His horse whickered softly beneath him, and Marius responded to it. He brushed a gloved hand against the ear of the creature, letting the dried cow hide that enveloped his fingers run down the back of the horse's neck. He meant to reassure his animal, but he found a strange amount of solace in the gesture for himself. He glanced at Janus and wondered if the man was soothing his emotions. Janus turned to look at him and shook his head.

War horns blew in the distance, filling the valley below. They were outside Rome, Hadrian's Tomb at their backs. An impressive structure, Marius thought, and all the better to try and defend the city from within, at least to his mind. But instead they were out here, in the wide-open spaces beyond the city wall, with a small legion in front of them and a greater legion aligned against them.

The smell of the horse overcame the smell of the fires as the wind shifted directions and came from the west. There were others with them on the hill. Marius knew Diana, of course, who was wearing a white cloak to keep the hot midday sun off her skin. He knew Venus on sight as well, her skin covered but her comely face somewhat visible over the lacy shawl that was pulled up to cover her mouth. He had seen her a few times, and on every one of them had trouble remembering his own name while fighting an impossible battle to keep his eyes off of her. This time seemed easier, though her attentions were on the battle, her eyes not roaming as they had been in every other instance he'd seen her.

He knew one of the others as well. Jupiter.

Colossally built, his broad chest partially exposed, Jupiter sat upon a warhorse that dwarfed Marius's. His long hair was platinum, not white, and his beard matched. His bronzed skin was still youthful, and Marius felt a quiver of fear just being in his presence. Jupiter watched the movement of the armies impassively, but his dark eyes danced about the place that was soon to be a battlefield, and Marius thought they looked hungry for blood and spectacle and were irritable in their absence.

"You see what I see," Janus said with quiet assurance as he looked over. Marius nodded. Jupiter's cruelty was close to the surface, obvious even to his eyes.

Jupiter's wife was at his side, her gaze cooler than her husband's in the way that winter was cooler than summer. She caught Marius's eyes and held them for a moment, watching him. She nodded once then turned away to speak to the man next to her, a physically imposing fellow whom Marius recognized as Neptune. He carried a long spear with three points, and Marius wondered if anyone who saw him riding the streets of Rome would recognize it as the trident.

"So it begins," Janus murmured, and a low hum fell over the gods on the hilltop. Marius paused his examination of their numbers and looked out to the battlefield again. The battle had indeed begun, and he could see the front ranks of the legions engaged with each other, falling blades catching the light of the midday sun, glaring. The Roman Legion was outmatched—it was evident even to Marius's untrained eye. The usurper's forces were pouring into the middle of their lines like a wedge pushing itself into a stump before splitting it.

So it ends, Marius thought, but he held his peace. He caught a glimmer of amusement from Janus and followed his mentor's gaze just past him as a man on a horse clip-clopped up to come to a halt just beside him.

The man was large, like Jupiter. He had flaming red hair that flowed down his shoulders and a flat face with an unyielding nose that barely protruded from it. It looked as though it had been carved out of clay by a lazy sculptor who had cared little for giving the face depth. The eyes were shallow as well, and dark, and they rolled over Marius quickly and on to Janus.

"Janus," the man said in acknowledgment.

"Ares," Janus replied with a courteous nod.

The man called Ares sighed. "I do prefer that name, but all the same, perhaps it is best if you call me Mars now."

Janus chuckled. "Have you met my ward? This is Marius. He is newly in my service."

Mars with the flat face gave Marius another look. "He has little stomach for battle, Janus."

Janus smiled. "Then he should be safe from any accidents should you find yourself slipping in your old age."

Mars let a deep belly laugh out with such force it nearly made Marius jump. "I miss your company since you have become a hermit, Janus. We should sup again soon. It has been so long since the last time."

"You are welcome in my home on any occasion," Janus said solicitously.

"And you in mine," Mars said with a nod of courtesy. He sighed. "I suppose I should get to work."

"It would be greatly appreciated if you could spare Rome from the incompetence of her generals and the far-flung crusades of her emperor," Janus said with a smile that Marius did not quite understand. He glanced back to the battle, which seemed to be going very poorly in his eyes. The usurper's men were now through the Roman legion, had neatly divided it in half. They were swarming back and enveloping them with superior numbers. It was not what Marius thought a victory should look like.

Mars urged his horse forward a few paces with a nudge, putting himself in front of the line of gods atop the hill. Marius kept his eyes on the man—Mars, the God of War. He watched him, and Mars lifted his hands and sighed again, then pushed his hair back over his shoulders.

Mars lifted his hands in the air and held them aloft, eyes closed. He stood, still as a statue, facing the battle below.

Marius heard faint whispering, like voices over the horizon, the maddening sounds of people just beyond his sight but not beyond his ears.

The wind swirled past him in hot tongues, the summer sun heating the air around him. Marius kept his eyes upon Mars, watching him hold there, the whispers raging around them. Marius's eyes broke from the God of War and looked all around for the source of the whispers. The gods were all silent, gazes fixed on Mars, and the hillside around them was devoid of any spectators or speakers.

Marius turned his attention to Janus, ready to break the silence and ask the question, but Janus held a finger up to his lips to quell it before it was even asked. He then took it and pointed it to the battle, and Marius let his gaze fall back upon the site of the rout.

Where the usurper's men were now losing.

It was not even a contest. He watched in the outlying spaces as the men of Proculus's army fell upon their own spears by the dozens, by the hundreds. Even those not taking arms up against themselves were finding the Roman Legion surging through their number with increased ferocity. Marius squinted, his superior eyesight giving him a close view of the fight, as though it were happening right in front of him. The men of the Roman legion were moving with speed beyond that of normal humans, their blades moving up and down in fast, precise motions that sent the blood of their foes through the air in sprays and gushes.

Marius turned back to look at Mars, who was now lowering his hands. The battle was won, the enemy lines dissolved in a frenzy of suicide and panic. Mars let a long sigh of satisfaction and spoke. "Your servant yet lives, Janus. No accidents this time, you see." He wheeled and smiled, his blunt, flat face suffused with a satisfaction that Marius had seen only a few times on the faces of people.

"Indeed, your skill is great, Ares," Janus said with a nod. "I saw one of your children once attempt to influence a battle a tenth of this size." He chortled. "They all killed themselves, to the last man."

Mars's face lost its look of amusement. "What can I say? Sometimes the apple is kicked far from the tree."

"Indeed," Janus said, and his eyes fell upon Marius, favoring him with a smile. "This is true."

Marius turned his attention toward the battlefield below, a bloody mess of corpses and wounded, the screams echoing up to the hilltop. It was an utter display of cruel death, inconceivable defeat pulled from certain victory. Death grabbed whole from the jaws of life.

Marius realized after a moment that the sight of the battle's more grisly elements—the blood, the screams—did not bother him at all. He looked back at Janus and saw the subtle nod. And he returned his mentor's smile.

Chapter 29

Sienna
Now

Reed was already halfway out the door and I was right behind him when Harper yelled out, "Wait!" I glanced back and she tossed me something small, like the size of a shelled peanut. "Ear mic. I'll be able to give you eyes in the sky."

Reed hesitated and she tossed him one as well. He caught it and poked it into his ear, and I saw the look on his face. "We're at least twenty minutes out, if we're lucky. We'll never make it in—"

I surged past him, pushing him out of the way as I headed out into the bullpen. "Maybe *you* won't—"

I didn't bother finishing my statement. I just took off in a flat charge toward the nearest window and called Wolfe to the front of my mind as I leapt through it. No surprise, it hurt a *lot*. Glass doesn't shatter in full windows like it does in cars or in movies. That's called safety glass and it turns into little pebbles that don't tend to do much harm.

This glass shattered into razor sharp slivers, and I felt my clothes and skin suffer dozens of cuts of varying depths as I broke through.

I ignored every single one of them for about two seconds while I felt Wolfe go to work, then I pulled Gavrikov to front of my mind as well and switched off the Earth's gravity.

I shot into the sky like I had a rocket motor latched to my feet, wind rushing into my face. I threw a hand forward like I was Superman ... err ... Superwoman? Whatever. I threw a hand forward as I flew and saw lines of blood running off my newly knitted flesh.

"What the f—" I heard Harper in my ear. "Did she just jump out the window?"

"She did," I said, enjoying the feel of the wind in my face. I surged east, the sky above and the ground blurring past below. "I'm about two minutes out from the site." I followed the freeway east and saw the white line of 494's loop ahead just a few miles. I didn't know exactly how fast I was going, but it had to be in the hundreds of miles per hour. The rush of the wind was probably not helping Harper hear me, I figured.

"Are you in a wind tunnel?" Harper's voice came back. She sounded cautious. "There's no way your ETA is two minutes."

"Status report, MARS SIX," I said.

That seemed to snap Harper out of her state of confusion. "Right," she said with crisp professionalism. "The town car is burning, but we have three friendlies on the ground and moving. Tangos are engaging with them, I'm picking up a lot of heat discharge from one of them, like they have a flamethrower or something, I've never seen anything like it—"

"Understood," I said.

"I am designating you MARS SIX-ACTUAL," Harper said calmly. More calmly than I would have been if I'd been in her situation.

"Neat," I said. "Consider me designated the Goddess of War."

There was a moment's pause, and I figured Harper's brain was crunching away on the other end of the line, trying to come up with an explanation for everything she was experiencing right now. I knew she'd given up when I heard her reply. "Copy that, MARS SIX-ACTUAL."

I streaked through the air, passing the interstate and coming down lower as I got closer to St. Louis Park. I tried to match my geography with the overhead imagery I'd seen from the drone and locked on to Minnesota Highway 7. I skirted toward it and slowed slightly, looking for the turn. My eyes found it a mile ahead and I traced it back to the grid-like latticework of roads. A lone warehouse stood with vacant lots for several blocks on one side, and I knew I'd found it. Even before I saw the flaming car just down the street.

"MARS SIX-ACTUAL …" Harper's voice came into my earpiece. "Is that you flying …?"

"Like a bird, like a plane," I said. "Janus, if you can hear me …" I paused. "Brace yourself."

It was a total furball on the ground, someone scrambling around, someone else—one of my people, I assumed—firing a gun, and someone else throwing fireballs into the air like they were Aleksandr Gavrikov, Jr. Except this one was female. It very much looked like a battle, like a frigging war on a city street, completely with flames and black smoke churning skyward. I couldn't pick out which of the people in front of me were enemies with full certainty, but I caught a glimpse of a guy hanging back from the others, closer to the warehouse than the fight, and I realized he was surveying the scene. And not one of mine.

"Incoming," I muttered and arced sharply downward. I put my feet out and dropped, letting my speed carry me along with the power of gravity. The wind blurred my eyes, and I saw the ground rush up at me in a way that might have scared me yesterday.

I landed feet first on the top of the Century agent's head and slammed him into the ground like I was a sledgehammer and he was a watermelon. His skull exploded when it hit, a cascade of red spraying in a ten-foot cone across the cracked and ragged pavement. It was icky on my nice boots.

And it made a noise, too. Like a *SPLAT.*

Four heads wheeled to look at me, and the gunfire stopped for a moment as the little battlefield caught its collective breath.

I looked at each of them in turns over the next few seconds, caught the stunned looks on their faces as I stood there, one of their people already dead at—or, actually, under—my feet.

"Hi," I said with a little wave and smiled enough to bare my teeth, channeling my best Wolfe impression. "Let's play."

Chapter 30

There were two women and two men remaining, all dressed reasonably well, all of them standing in utter shock at my entrance. I had to say, it was one of the more dramatic ones I'd pulled.

Their shock lasted about another second after my quip, and then the one who had been throwing fireballs tossed a big one at me.

I started to dodge but a voice in my head told me to stop. Gavrikov shouldered his way to the front of my mind. *You may not be able to control the fires within without practice, but this one thing I can teach you to do easily.*

I held out my hand and absorbed the fireball into my skin like a vacuum sucking up a loose plastic bag. Just WHUUUMP! and it was gone like it had never even been there. I turned my palm toward me and there was no sign of burns or blackness, not even a hint of smoke to indicate the passage of the flame from existence. "Well," I said, "how 'bout that."

There was another moment of collective silence and then things erupted. The same woman who'd cast flame at me seconds earlier chucked another ball of it, bigger this time, while a big guy who'd been lingering to my left seemed to grow a couple feet in height. I started toward him, pegging him for a Hercules-type, but Wolfe spoke: *Atlas-type. Similar, Little Doll, but not exactly the same.*

157

"How bad?" I asked as the big guy headed for me. There was another guy lingering back, who looked like he might have been from India, watching me kind of cagily. There was also an Asian woman, probably the one with the commanding voice who'd somehow picked up on the laser.

Bad, Wolfe said. *The bigger they get, the stronger they get.*

Like a Hercules, then.

No, Wolfe said. *Much worse.*

"How does it get worse?" I asked, below my breath.

Ask and ye shall receive.

The Atlas kept growing, his muscles staying in proportion to his body, the way it had been when he'd begun. His clothing started to rip when he reached eight feet of height, and I could see that although he was muscular, he wasn't like a Hercules where it grew to ridiculous, beyond-steroid proportions. He looked like a well-built guy, just ... well ... taller.

And then he grew past ten feet, and I started to worry maybe a little.

I saw something long and black that reminded me of an arrow shooting by, but it sounded like a swarm of bees as it passed. I caught a glimpse of it and had a sense of plague as I watched it, a sense that I realized was coming from Wolfe.

Rudra-type, he said, like that was supposed to mean something to me. *Fires arrows of disease.*

"Lovely," I said, and turned my gaze toward him, letting it drift over the last of the four metas arrayed against me, the Asian woman. "And her?"

While I was watching her, her skin began to glow subtly. It was like nothing I'd ever seen before; when Gavrikov had started to glow, he just caught on fire. In her case it was as though her skin was the sun, and after a second I was forced to look away from the harsh gleam.

Amaterasu, Bjorn supplied. *Japanese Sun Goddess. The real one, I think.*

"Century must have run out of flunkies," I muttered under my breath.

The woman throwing fire, Gavrikov said, drawing my attention to her. She was cold and pale, had a Norwegian look about her. *She is the last of my kind.*

Friend of yours? I asked.

No, he said rather definitely. *Most certainly not.*

The Atlas came at me hard. He was nearly fifteen feet tall now, a giant the likes of which I hadn't faced before. He was reasonably fast, too, operating at a speed which—for most metas—would have been impressive.

I wasn't most metas.

I shot toward his knee with my power of flight, turning myself into position for a side kick as I went. I hit his knee with the force of a speeding Maserati, just at the point between the bones on the side of the kneecap. My foot tore into his flesh and and ripped through, his femur and tibia bowing apart as I blew through.

I landed on the other side and rolled back to my feet, still moving. There was a mighty thump as the Atlas hit the ground, but I was already coming around in a dead run toward my next target, Ms. Gavrikov. I felt a harrumph of annoyance from Aleksandr as I called her that.

"What the hell is going on down there?" I heard Harper mutter over the comm link.

"Something magical," I said as Ms. Gavrikov sent another burst of flame my way. I saw the look in her eyes and it was pure panic. I sensed she'd never had someone go all fire-eater on her before. She'd probably never met anyone she couldn't at least slow down with a timely bit of flame, and it was freaking her out. I saw the whites of her eyes as she froze, deer-like, in my path while I bore down on her. She'd seen what I'd just done to Atlas, after all …

I slammed into her, and freight train doesn't adequately describe my momentum. I led with a front kick this time, and it folded her in half so hard that her face actually hit her feet as they were ripped off the ground. She flew in a straight line, and hit a lamp post with her back. The crack was short and significant, followed by the sound of her arm being ripped from her body at the point of impact—the shoulder—as she and the pole continued their journey another forty feet before they both came to rest. Her arm? I'm not sure where it landed. Poland, maybe.

Krakow, wench.

I saw a blur of light come at me from the right and turned in time to get blinded. It was as though I'd looked directly into the sun, and I wondered if I still had corneas. Based on the scalding feeling in my eyeballs, I would have guessed not. I couldn't tell whether it was tears running down my cheeks or blood. Amaterasu hit me and I could feel the heat. I tried to absorb it with Gavrikov's power but I failed, and the searing pain that hit my arm told me I'd had skin burned off.

No, no! Gavrikov shouted in my head. *It won't work! Different kind of heat energy!*

"Helpful," I gasped out in the midst of the pain. I gritted my teeth. *Very helpful*, I muttered in my head as the agony nearly overwhelmed me. The smell of burning flesh filled my nose, and I realized it was my own.

Something sharp and painful struck me in the back, and I realized I'd forgotten Rude Rod or whatever his name was. All the air rushed out of me at the sharp sensation of the impact, and feverish chills spread out from my flesh at that point. I sagged to my knees, all the strength leaving my legs in a rush like fans at a concert bailing after a no-show.

"Sienna Nealon," Amaterasu said. She sounded eerily calm. Calmer than I would have been if I'd been in her shoes. I had just taken out at least three of her crew. I felt my arm burn and blacken, the flesh burning down to the muscle, and I realized where her confidence was coming from.

I fell to my back, which hurt, surprisingly. Something was happening to it, and it burned in its own way. I rolled slightly and my good hand traced its way up my shirt to find blisters and pustules clustered along my spine. I jerked my hand away at the touch, but not before it caused a howling pain down my back.

I lay on my bad arm—assuming it was still there. I couldn't feel it, except for the pain. My eyes were firmly squinted closed, and though I tried to open them, they failed to respond. I could faintly see a glow, though, and wondered if I was imagining it or if the light of Amaterasu was simply the last thing I would see.

"Should we keep her alive for Claire?" It was a man's voice. It was high and accented and sounded not at all pleasant. *Rudra*, Wolfe told me.

"I think not," Amaterasu answered. I could tell by the sound of her voice that she was above me, and then I felt the soft glow of a sun coming to life. My skin began to burn, and the smell of it filled my nose, even as my body started to quiver in the rising, scorching heat.

Chapter 31

Knowing you're about to die brings a certain amount of clarity. It eliminates the extraneous worries for the most part, the random thoughts, the idle nattering of all those voices in your head telling you to do this, do that, finish your homework, go to school, get a job, do your work, be responsible—

Oh, wait. I never had those voices.

I had one voice in my head (absent those mental hitchhikers that were giving me assistance nowadays). It was my mother's voice, and it only said one thing, ever.

Survive.

I drew upon Aleksandr Gavrikov's power and snapped my speed of flight from zero to maximum in two seconds, heading straight for Amaterasu's voice. I felt myself impact against her, shoulders checking hard against her legs. She registered the pain with a "Hngh!" noise that was followed by her face and upper body smacking the pavement. I could feel the ground beneath my back, less than an inch below as I dragged along blind, then shot skyward to escape the situation.

Wolfe! I called out, the pain clawing at me. I could feel the wind against my face and then my sight began to return. I didn't dwell too hard on whether I'd just regrown my eyes. Instead I focused on regaining my sensation. My jacket was scorched and sleeveless on one side. I watched the flesh return with my newly restored eyesight and struggled to keep my mind on what needed to be focused on—flight and my health. I had a feeling that Gavrikov and Wolfe were giving me a hand with both, because the pain was making it insanely difficult to concentrate.

I halted in midair and looked down. The city looked like a tiny model beneath me, the figure of the Atlas barely, barely visible lying far below. There were clouds, and suddenly I realized that I was having a harder time breathing. "Too … high …" I gasped and let myself drop into a dive again.

The oxygen returned shortly and I felt my head start to clear. My eyes narrowed against the wind and I felt a seething rage. I could still see the Atlas, clawing at the stump of his leg. He was probably out of action for the moment. Probably. Which still left me with the Rudra and Amaterasu.

I could still feel the cold chills that the Rudra had given me with those disease arrows, whatever they were. I flew hard left and took myself out of the center of their sky, hoping they hadn't seen me. I came low, around the corner of the warehouse, and saw them both near the wreckage of the town car. Amaterasu had Janus slung over her shoulder, and I didn't have to wonder very hard where the agents were that I'd sent with him. I could see at least one corpse near the wreckage of the car, blood seeping across the pavement.

Rudra and Amaterasu looked deep in conversation. They were heading back to the warehouse. Amaterasu's clothing was torn and burned where she'd used her powers. She wasn't even bothering to look around; I guess she figured I'd run off after the fight. Which made sense, because she probably thought my recovery time from the injuries she'd dealt was best measured somewhere in hours or days, not seconds.

It was going to be the last mistake she ever made.

I sped sideways, looping around them at top speed. Within seconds I was directly behind them. They were spaced just far enough apart that I couldn't get them both in

163

one, but that was okay. I didn't want it to be all that quick, honestly.

I sent myself to high velocity and flying side kicked Rudra from behind at top speed. I landed the blow at the small of his back and heard the compression from impact break vertebra all the way up the line before he flew forward as if I'd hit him with a semi truck. I didn't know if I'd killed him, but I'd definitely put him out of the fight, and that was enough for the moment.

I spun on Amaterasu and she dropped Janus like he was nothing. Which he wasn't. He was actually either a hostage or an impediment to her fighting, depending on how you looked at it; it seemed her instincts ran to defending herself before thinking to barter with the life of the man I'd come here to rescue. I could respect that.

I mean, I was still going to kill her, but I'd at least try to make it quick.

She started to flare and I interrupted her with a punch to the face that would have put a hole in concrete. I actually felt my knuckles break upon impact, but Wolfe knitted them back together for me as I followed up with an inside elbow to the back of her head. It would have killed a human, but it just knocked her to her knees.

I saw the glow start on her skin again, and I kicked her in the chest hard enough to send her flying a few paces away. It was a sloppy kick on my part, rushed, but it killed the glow for a moment. Mom would definitely not have approved of the technique, but I was all about getting the job done at this point.

"Aldkngh ahhawa—" She said, her jaw moving unnaturally, as she got back to her knees.

"Can't understand you," I said, launching into a kick that hit her in the sternum and sent her flying. That one wasn't sloppy. I could hear her ribs break upon impact. All of them, maybe.

Amaterasu lay flat on her back on the pavement, head hanging half off the curb onto the street. We'd been battling in the dirt of a vacant lot outside the warehouse, but now we were on the street beside it. She was bleeding from a half dozen different places—eyes, nose, mouth, assorted cuts— and her eyes were glazed. I sauntered over to her, trying to be a little cautious and not just cocky. Probably failed at the latter.

"Hey there, bright lady," I said, and grabbed her by the slightly charred remains of her blouse. I lifted her up and was surprised at how light she was. I hadn't noticed how thin she was while she was trying to kill me. Probably because she'd blinded me. "I'd say, 'Let's talk,' but I think your jaw is broken and will be for a while, so why don't you just—"

She went from dazed to focused in less than the space of a second. Her hands leapt up and landed on both sides of my head, clapping me hard. Not hard enough to break anything but hard enough to jostle me. I kept my grip on her, even though I stumbled, and met her gaze. Her eyes were glowing bright, and her skin was already pulsating with a soft light.

"Frckng diiii—" she started to say, blood running down her chin and boiling as it ran. I got the meaning before she finished.

I spun and threw her, as hard as I could, toward the entry door to the warehouse. I was only thirty yards away, and she impacted just inside the threshold. I could see her, still glowing, as her body struck the ground and rolled inside.

I dove for the pavement, burying my face in the half inch of cover below the curb. I doubted it was going to give me much to work with, but I wasn't that big and—

I forced my eyes shut as the glow of a dying sun lit up the warehouse. I wondered if this was what it felt like at ground zero of a nuclear bomb, and I smelled something an awful lot like flesh burning. My face was pressed into the dirt of the gutter, the grains of individual sand burning and scorching my cheek as I lay there. Even through my shut eyes, I felt like

I was staring into a sunny sky, the red cast of the blood running through my eyelids visible as I lay there. I held my breath and felt the hairs in my nose catch fire, the inside of my sinuses feeling like someone had lit a Q-tip and shoved it up there, twirling it as they went.

After painful seconds that flowed like hours, the burning passed, the brightness died away. My throat felt raw, like I'd screamed while gargling acid. I pulled a hand up and felt my face. Cracked and burned skin greeted my touch, and I felt for my long, brown hair. It was gone.

Working on it, Little Doll, Wolfe said calmly.

I felt the flesh pucker under my touch, felt it smooth after another few moments, and felt my breathing return to normal. I opened my eyes and looked up in time to watch strands of newly grown hair fall down in front of me. I brushed them back behind my ears and stood haltingly, like I was taking my first steps.

My clothing was burned all the way around. One of my boots was just gone—the left one, the one closest to the warehouse. I felt something insanely hot still in my other boot and shook out of it. I glanced down to see my backup pistol, my Walther PPK/S, melted into a silvery piece of slag. I sighed and mentally billed the Agency for another.

I stood in my bare feet, glancing down at my body. I had enough clothing still intact—but scorched—to be considered legally decent on most American beaches. But that was about it. It looked like I'd gone incredible Hulk, and all that was left was the tatters, except it was all ashy and scorched. Plus I was pale, pearly white, not green.

The warehouse was no more. There were still some girders half-standing, but they looked slagged in a major way, like they'd been melted down at the top. Some of them were bowed and falling, like wax instead of steel. There was very little fire in the aftermath, just a few places where combustible things had caught, presumably.

I looked over to where I'd left Janus. He'd been a little farther from the explosion than I'd been when last I'd seen him.

He was gone. Utterly gone.

The green weeds that had sprung up in the years of neglect of the vacant lot were completely vaporized, and I saw some of the sand had turned to glass. I cast my gaze to the next nearest thing, the Atlas that had been lying like a wall across the lot where I'd dropped him.

And I wished I hadn't.

He was scorched and shrunken—well, not really shrunken. He looked like a twelve-foot tall mummy that had gotten really burned. The skin was coal black, the hair was gone completely, and if he survived I'd have been so shocked—

Then he moved.

I stood there, gaping. A huge chunk of what had been muscle flaked off his shoulder as the body rolled over, and I realized something was underneath him.

Janus.

I breathed a sigh of relief as the former Omega operative crawled from beneath the giant corpse. He looked badly burned, but alive. Half his face was red and broken.

But he was alive.

I hurried over to him and he waved me off with a hand. "Don't … touch me …" he said. His wire frame glasses were gone, and there was congealed blood running through his grey mustache.

"I need to get you to medical assistance," I said, and started to bend down to him.

"I think I will live," he said, fixing me with a gaze that held just the faintest hint of amusement, "provided you do not rip this piddly remainder of a soul from my body in the next few moments."

I glanced down and remembered that, oh, yeah, I wasn't wearing much in the way of flesh covering for my extremities. And apparently I'd forgotten that my primary power was to drink people like a cold can of Pepsi on a hot day. "Sorry," I said.

He waved a hand, and when he spoke again, he sounded choked. "It is nothing to worry about. It seems I found a use for a Century operative at last."

I chuckled, then again, then felt the inescapable sense of dirge-like mirth flowing from me in fits and starts. I laughed, loud, and long, equal parts sorrow and sickness and gallows humor. And I only got quiet as I heard the sirens of ambulances approaching, growing louder as they came, the heralds reminding me that the crisis was far, far from over.

Chapter 32

"Well, that went well," Reed said through the open window of the town car as he rolled up to the curb at Methodist Hospital in St. Louis Park. Scott was beside him in the passenger seat, and thankfully the backseat was clear. I got in and shut the door, my hospital gown fluttering behind me. I was so sick of these things.

"Yeah, it was great," I said as I gathered my gown behind me. I had left against medical advice, and the one security guard who'd given me a look as I left had been convinced to sit his ass back in his chair with a single glare. I guess he figured it wasn't worth it. "We lost our only lead to what Century's planning in Minneapolis, landed Janus in the hospital, and were responsible for three square blocks worth of destruction to the city." I rubbed my temples. "I'm sure that's going to be another lovely addition to my record when it's made public. Then I'll get to watch the news as they burn my skin off in the not-literal way."

"No other deaths, near as we can tell," Reed said, voice shot through with sympathy. "The warehouse was isolated, the shock wave was powerful but localized. Didn't do much once it got past a block or so of distance, and it looks like the warehouse helped absorb the heat in every direction but the one you were in."

"If only I could have gotten that door closed after I chucked her in," I said, leaning my head back against the leather seat. Amaterasu had been one hell of a tough one. "I have to admit, I didn't see these Century dicks going suicidal in such a big way when they lost."

"Yeah, you must have really pissed her off," Scott said, glancing back at me. He had the puppy dog eyes on, too, which normally I might have found annoying. Now I thought it was kind of acceptable. Kind of.

"Of course I did," I said. I could still smell the ash on my skin. I doubted it was something a shower would immediately cure. "It's me we're talking about, after all. Pissing people off is what I do."

"That and killing them," Reed agreed. "You couldn't have left one of them alive for questioning?"

"I did," I said. "I left several alive. Rudra, I think, barely. The Atlas. And that lady with powers like Gavrikov." I cleared my throat. "Unfortunately, Amaterasu did not share my enthusiasm for taking prisoners." After I'd made sure Janus was okay, I'd walked the area around the incineration site. Lady Gavrikov was still looking bisected where I'd left her, missing an arm and covered in scorched skin. Rudra hadn't looked very structurally sound, either, so I'd nudged him with a toe. He'd flaked into ash. He'd been awfully close to the building when it went up, though.

"What about our agents?" Scott asked.

"Dead," I said simply. I paused for a moment. "What were their names?"

"Baker and Hanlon," Reed replied. Neither of them looked back at me.

I sighed and looked out the window as brick buildings passed on my right. "When this is all over, if I have any sway left, we're going to build a wall—a monument—to all the people who died trying to stop this moronic genocide of Sovereign's."

"I don't even know how much of this you can blame on him at this point," Scott said, shaking his head. "They tried to kill you again, didn't they?"

"They did indeed," I said idly, still staring out the window.

"Seems they're in out-and-out defiance of him now, then," Scott said. He let that sink in for a second. "Maybe you ought to think about talking to him, let him know—"

"I'm sure he knows already," I said. "He's a telepath, and a pretty powerful one. If he doesn't know what happened here, I'd be shocked." I folded my arms over the soft cloth of my robe. "If he wants to denounce what his people are doing, he knows my number."

We lapsed into silence, and I stared out the window again. I didn't want to think too hard about Sovereign right now. What Scott had said was too sensible, made me feel like I'd be weak for even asking him.

And whatever else was happening, I couldn't look weak in front of him. Not now. There was too much at stake to play this in a way that made it seem like I was willing to come to him.

Instead, I settled back in the seat and tried to plan my next move. And blissfully, they were both too courteous to break that silence—all the way back to the Agency.

Chapter 33

We rolled up to the Agency and I had them take me to the dorms. I wasn't going to bother going through the elaborate trouble of working my way there through the basement of headquarters and through the tunnel just so I could expose my nearly naked ass to all the security guys waiting in the lobby of that building at the checkpoint. I needed to maintain some of my dignity, at least.

The dorms had been in lockdown for days. Reed pulled up in the loop outside the building and I hopped out, taking care to keep the back of my gown tightly shut. I might have tried to convince the nurses to let me keep the remainder of my burned ensemble, but it had actually started to deteriorate minutes after I arrived at the hospital, losing structural integrity shortly after they got me to my own room. Too much of it got turned to ash, I guess. The gown was all I had.

I shuffled toward the front entrance, Scott trailing behind me. When I glanced back at him, he smiled. "Sorry," he said, "just admiring the view."

"I invite you to kiss my ass," I said. "Which, thanks to this hospital gown, is easily accessible."

He let a low guffaw which I ignored as I stopped at the biometric scanner next to the door. Heavy metal shutters covered the entire front of the dormitory building. I started to lean down to stick my face into the retinal scanner, but I felt my gown part at the slightest hint of bending over.

"Here, I got it," Scott said, and I felt the tug of a hand clamping the gown shut.

"Thanks," I said, putting my eyes to the scanner. "Trying to hold that and give a palm scan was going to be awkward."

I heard the beep of confirmation as the scanner agreed that I was Sienna Nealon, and the shutters rose over the doors and windows with a series of clanks. I waited until they'd finished and stepped through the glass doors into the dormitory foyer.

It was spacious and well designed but still had lingering scorch marks on the once-white walls, and more bullet holes than I could count. It had been the site of a nasty battle, one which I had won but not without significant cost. I tried to ignore all that as I strode toward the elevator, pausing only to hit the button on the security console to initiate lockdown once more.

"I think I like this place better with the windows open," Scott said as the security shutters dropped and the sunlight disappeared behind the darkened shades.

"I do too," I said as I paused at the elevator. "But I also like that I don't have to worry about getting flanked through it."

Scott was quiet for a minute. "Easier not to worry about those British metas, huh?"

I thought about Karthik and how he had departed with the last of our protectees, a group of metas who couldn't really fight effectively for themselves, for London only days earlier. "It's easier," I said. "Now that they're out of sight and I don't have to worry about protecting them, I can care even less if this building gets violated, security-wise."

"Yeah," Scott said, nodding, his face pursed with a certain amount of evident sarcasm. "Why not, right? We only live here, after all."

I smiled at him. "Yeah, we do. But we're the only ones now—us and Reed and Kat and Janus." And Ariadne and Zollers ... "Maybe I should clear some room on the second floor of headquarters for us to live for the time being. Might be safer."

"Heh." Scott just shook his head. "Honestly, if Sovereign or Century comes gunning for us, do you really think being sixty seconds of run time away is going to save us?"

"It might keep us from mounting a defense effectively," I said and stared at him. "It might be the difference between beating them and having more people die, yeah." My mind was running through the possibilities now. We'd set up to live in the dorms when there had been good cause to—we'd had metas to protect over here and not enough space to house them in headquarters. Now that those other metas were gone, that need was out the window, but we'd failed to revisit it in our recent meetings because … well, let's face it, there was a hell of a lot to think about. "We should do it immediately. Go tell Ariadne."

Scott's face scrunched up. "How do you think she's going to react to being told she's going to lose her private bathroom in favor of the communal showers we've got in the HQ locker rooms?"

"I don't know, why don't you tell me after you see her reaction." I waved him off. "This needs to happen, right now."

He raised an eyebrow at me. "I was escorting you to get your clothes, remember?"

I caught a hint of mischief in his eyes and returned his look with one of faint amusement. Very faint. "As much fun as that would be, saving lives is more important than letting you peep on me getting dressed."

His brows rolled up and he grinned. "You were gonna let me peep? Awesome—"

"Go," I said, shaking my head. I felt my cheeks redden. "You can have a show once this is over with."

"Aw, come on." His face fell. "Why did you have to say that? You practically guaranteed I'm going to die now, because there's no way fate's going to let me collect such a sweet prize."

I felt myself redden more at the phrase, "sweet prize." I started to say, "You'll be fine," but stopped myself. "Worry about it later," I said instead. "Work to do, miles to go, all that. Come on, stay serious. We're in the home stretch now."

He sighed, and raised a hand in surrender. "All right, all right," he said as the elevator dinged and opened in front of me. "I'll head over through the tunnel." A look of childish delight came upon him in the form of a smirk. "Try to stay out of trouble without me."

I frowned. "You dare to jinx me? Ass."

He laughed and disappeared around the corner toward the stairwell to the basement. "Two can play at that game."

I stepped into the elevator and pushed my thumb onto the reader that would take me to the fourth floor. It scanned my print and beeped then started slowly into motion. I liked having a little fun with it, but I didn't take much stock in the whole jinx thing, at least outside of movies.

Still, the thought that Scott—or anyone—might die in the last act of this war was … disquieting. It made my belly rumble.

Death is a fact of life, Little Doll. Death is a fact of war.

War is certain in only one respect, Bjorn said with a rumble. *And death is the only certainty in life.*

"Helpful advice," I said, my tone only mildly sarcastic. If I was a walking violation of the "Thou shalt not be an asshole" commandment, the voices in my head were the fallen angels of that philosophy. "I know death is a possibility, and I'm trying to be prepared for the fact that more of it may be coming. But I can hope that it doesn't." I bit my lip.

Hope has carried people through worse, Zack said. Now that was actually helpful. I smiled.

The elevators dinged and I walked out into the darkened hallway. I headed toward my room and passed the biometrics there with a beep. I'd just downed another five Century operatives, taken them out of the game. Even though there were more coming, according to Amaterasu, it felt like I had a moment to breathe. A moment to take stock, to plan, to come up with a next move.

And then I saw the man standing in my living room, looking at the blank walls, and I knew I'd been such an effing moron.

"Hey," he said, nodding to me as I came in. "This place is kind of ... bland. What's the matter, you don't believe in paintings or posters or ... I dunno, pastels?"

I just stood frozen at the door, staring at him like the unwanted intruder he was. I should have known, in my planning, that it might come down like this. That he might just show up, not in a dream—

"Hello, Sovereign," I said. "I'd say it's nice to see you, but then I'd just be lying."

"That's okay," he said with a casual wave. "I'm an uninvited guest, I know. You don't have to welcome me with false enthusiasm or anything."

"Plus you're already commenting on the décor," I said. "But I have to tell you, if we weren't in lockdown, the sunlight does wonders for the brightness of the place. You know how it is during wartime, though. We all have to make sacrifices."

He got this vaguely pained look and nodded once. "Indeed. We do."

I took a step into the room, eyeing him warily. Just because he hadn't made an offensive move yet didn't mean he wouldn't. "So ... what are you doing here? Got tired of the construction site in our dreams? Because I didn't hear you offer decorating tips there."

"Rebar is hard to accessorize," he deadpanned. "But, yeah, I was tired of meeting in dreams and getting just absolutely brutalized by your sense of righteous indignation and justice."

"So you came to receive them both in person?" I asked, taking another step into the room. "Because I'm not any less likely to lecture you in person. Or hit you," I added. "In fact, that second one is likely to happen at some point, once we're past the niceties."

"You don't have to hit me," he said, and suddenly he looked wary—and weary—himself.

"Pretty sure I do," I said. "What I don't have to do is enjoy it, though I'm pretty sure I'll do that, too."

"Really?" He quirked an eyebrow at me. "Who was it that said that the measure of a society is how they treat their prisoners?"

"Probably a guy serving a long prison term and kind of pissed off about it," I said, my eyes narrowing at him. "But you aren't a prisoner. You're a free-range, genocidal psychopath—"

"Not anymore," he said, and he turned toward me and extended his hands, wrists out. "I hereby surrender to you for the judgment due under the U.S. justice system." He smiled, though it was faint. "You got me. I give up."

I stared at him for a second, regarding him warily, like he was going to spring at me and say, "Fooled ya!" before punching me right in the nose. But a few seconds passed and he didn't, he just stood there with his hands extended like he was waiting for me to cuff him.

"Well, shit," I said.

Chapter 34

"I don't like it," Reed said, staring over my shoulder at where Sovereign sat, in handcuffs, on a chair in the corner of my room.

"What's not to like?" Scott asked, keeping his head down, like not meeting Sovereign's eyes would somehow keep him from reading Scott's mind. "Our number one enemy just broke into our headquarters to surrender. He's only the most powerful meta on the planet, supposedly, and we probably have no way of containing him, or breaking into his mind to figure out for sure it's a trap—"

"It's a trap," Reed and I chorused simultaneously.

"It's a traaaaaaaaap!" Sovereign offered mockingly from his seat by the window. I didn't even bother stationing human guards to watch over him, because what was the point? He could kill them in two seconds flat, even cuffed and shackled as he was. He sighed longingly. "I know it gets a lot of hate among the fanboys, but I still like *Return of the Jedi.*"

"Just another reason I have to despise you," Reed said.

"You know, I can hear your entire conversation," Sovereign said, smiling. "You could just have it over here, make me feel welcome."

"People who start the wheel turning on mass genocide don't get to sit at the dinner table with civilized people,"

Reed said, turning to offer him a nasty look. "Usually, they have the good grace to kill themselves rather than surrender."

"I never killed anyone," Sovereign said, and his smirk was gone, replaced by seriousness. "I don't even know if you could call what I did aiding and abetting, since you'd be hard pressed to find evidence of me helping anyone other than Sienna—you know, with some of her Omega problems."

"Please," Reed said, and turned to face him. "You're going to tell us you didn't have a hand in this atrocity—"

"My hands aren't exactly clean," Sovereign said, his face darkening, "but neither are yours."

Reed looked slightly apoplectic, but he didn't say anything. "Fine," Scott said, and he looked like he was making more than his fair effort at keeping himself under control. His words came out slow and measured. "So you're here to surrender to us. Why? And why now?"

Sovereign moved his head slightly, and he looked a little … upset. "Isn't it obvious?"

I said nothing. Reed, thankfully, kept his mouth shut, still. "No," Scott said at last. "Other than the idea that it's a trap, no, your motives are not obvious."

"I've lost whatever control of Century I might have had," he said, and he seemed just a hint resentful, like things were boiling under the surface that he was keeping a tight lid on. "I thought I was partnering with Weissman on this, that we were going to build a better world together, but it turns out he was playing me the whole time. And now that he's gone, his kids are running amok, trying to kill Sienna."

"Again," I said quietly. "Let's not forget that this isn't the first time Century operatives have tried to kill me.

His weariness returned at that moment, and Sovereign looked like an old man once more. "Yeah. Again. I thought I'd made it clear to the world that you were off limits, but apparently all along I've been fooling myself about who was in charge of this thing."

"'Thing'? This murderous, genocidal operation, you mean," Reed said, regaining his power of speech. "So now you're turning yourself in because this insane, bloody Leviathan you turned loose—with the best of intentions— has decided to disobey you, and thus you're giving up your murderous plans for a better world through the scourging fires of mass killings in order to save the life of one woman."

He looked at me, and I glanced away. "It's a good woman I'm doing it for, but yes. And I was never involved in the killings. That was Weissman's play. I believed in the vision he sold me of a better world, but I was an idiot." I looked back up at him and he was staring into my eyes. "All flip comments aside, I was wrong. You were right. That's why I haven't wanted to argue with you. I may be slow coming to the right conclusion, but I get there eventually. Weissman was a monster. Whatever aid I gave him was a crime of incredible magnitude, and I have to answer for it." He looked from me to Scott to Reed. "And I will, in whatever manner you want me to. If it's prison, I'll go and serve whatever sentence I'm ordered." He straightened in his chair. "If it's death, I'll take the bullet in the back of the head without protest. Maybe I deserve it for whatever help I gave him, I don't know." His lips pulled tight together for a moment. "But if you want help taking them down, I'm willing to do that, too, before I have to pay for my crimes." He held up his hands, the cuffs clinking as he raised them as far as the chains would allow—which was about mid-chest. "I am at your mercy."

"Or lack thereof, I do hope," Reed said, wheeling away from him. "He's too dangerous. Kill him now and get it over with."

"I'm still sitting right here," Sovereign said. "And I just offered to die if you want me to."

"Great, so you won't complain if we just get that out of the way right now," Reed said.

I frowned at him. "You've never been in favor of capital punishment before. We've argued this, remember?"

"My position is evolving on this issue," Reed said. "He's too dangerous. We can't exactly stick him in a glass cell and hope it holds him as he taunts us endlessly while waiting to unfold some diabolical scheme. There's no prison on earth that could keep him in."

"Oh, but there is," Sovereign said.

"Bullshit," Reed said. "And all this 'word is bond' crap is worth as much as wet toilet paper in a tornado. There is no guard and no jail that could contain you."

"Yeah," he said, "there is. Your prison in Arizona could do it, if you had the right guard to keep watch."

"Huh," Scott said. "How thick would the walls have to be in that place?"

"Thick," I replied, realizing that neither of them had tumbled to what he was suggesting yet. "But do you actually think you'll get the guard you're hoping for?"

"I don't know," he said, his features carefully neutral. The corner of his mouth turned up, just slightly, to let me know that he knew I'd caught on. "What do you say? Are you willing to watch me sit in a cell for the rest of my life?" He leaned forward in the chair. "Because as your brother said, if my word isn't good for anything, then you're the only one who could keep me from getting away if I chose to leave."

Chapter 35

"Who do you have guarding him?" Foreman asked, at the opposite head of the conference table. Li sat next to him, arm in a sling and partially immobilized.

"No one," I answered, and watched the expressions change around the table. Reed shot me a "Told you so" look and then he politely averted his eyes by rolling them. Everyone was present except Janus, who was still in the hospital. Kat, Scott, Zollers, Ariadne, Li, Foreman and Reed were all in a rough oval around the conference table, all in varying states of disbelief over what I'd just said. "What's the point?" I asked. "He could kill any human or humans we set out to guard him, or mind-control them with his telepathy, or—"

"So you're just going to let him walk out anytime he wants?" Li asked. His jaw locked into place in a scowl that I suspected had nothing to do with any arm pain he might have been feeling.

"I can't watch him twenty-four-seven, even if we did have a prison that could contain him," I said. "I'm open to other solutions."

"Kill him," Reed singsonged.

I gave him a look like ... well, I don't know what it looked like, honestly. "Your strongly held beliefs about the death penalty vanished awfully swiftly."

"The guy is a walking holocaust if he wants to be," Reed said, his face dark. "We still don't know what phase two is, but you know he's at the core of it, which means he's got the kind of power that could lay the world to waste. To me, this is like … nuclear disarmament. Just be done with it already and make the world a safer place."

I glanced at Foreman, who was studying the table. "I don't hear anything from you on this subject, Senator."

"Me?" Foreman asked. "I'm not here, officially or otherwise."

"Plausible deniability?" Reed snarked. "Wow. I'm totally shocked, given that you're a—"

"This has little to do with politics," Foreman said, and he looked a little put out. "I'm civilian oversight. I can't give you orders even if I was officially here." He nodded in my direction. "You're part of the executive branch, and you have a duly appointed head of agency to answer to."

That provoked another moment of silence, as everyone realized I'd just been handed a live grenade with the pin pulled. "Lucky me," I breathed. "I get to absorb the blame if it all goes horribly wrong."

Foreman shrugged. "That wasn't why I brought you here, but it's a not-unanticipated side-effect of your taking the post. Shit rolls downhill in Washington, and there's a major septic malfunction heading this way. Rapidly, by my reckoning."

"What the hell?" Scott asked, and everything about the way he said it told me he was utterly disgusted. "We've done what you asked. Century has taken some hard knocks, one of their leaders is dead and the other just surrendered. Now you want to prepare Sienna a place under the bus if anything goes wrong?" He made a *pffffft*-ing noise.

"I knew what I was getting into when I took the deal," I said. I was near toneless, because ever since he'd told me that word was going to get out, I knew that bad things were unavoidably washing toward me on the tide. "I've still got a job to do."

"Do you realize what's going to happen if you fail now?" Reed asked, spinning toward me. He was sitting next to Ariadne, and she had her head down, looking at the table. I made note of that for later. "You're gonna get run through by the press."

"Full well aware of it," I said. "But we've still got to survive whatever else Century is coming up with. Because they've still got a meeting in two days, and it sounds like it's going to be a doozy."

"What are the odds it's a referendum on packing up and calling it quits?" Scott asked.

"I wouldn't lay Vegas odds on it," Zollers said, finally weighing in. "I've met with very few Century operatives, but they seem to fall into two camps—deathly scared and carrying out their instructions from on high, or true believers who have bought Weissman's vision, hook, line, and … whatever." He waved a hand. "I would suggest that the ratio of true believers to non is 3 to 1."

"The house always wins," Reed said.

"We need to find this meeting," I said.

"And what?" Reed asked. "Crash it? All ten of us against the … I've lost count. Eighty of them left now? What are we down to?"

"Does it matter?" Kat tossed in. "Seven-to-one and one to nine are just as bad as each other when you're up against this many metas." She looked at me then hesitated. "Is there a chance Sovereign is sincere, that he'd be willing to help us take them down?"

"No way," Reed said.

"Maybe," Scott said. "If he thinks it'll give him a chance to impress Sienna." I didn't look at him, but I felt every head at the table swivel to Scott. He shrugged. "He's not exactly being coy about his intentions. He figures that we won't execute him and that it'll fall to Sienna to guard him because she's the only one who could. He's playing us for that. Give him a chance to impress her and maybe he'll jump at it."

Now everyone looked at me, except for Zollers, who quietly cleared his throat and kept his gaze averted.

"*Could* you play him?" Ariadne said quietly.

"He's a telepath," I said. "Even assuming I could, he'd figure out what was going on because he'd be able to read it on one of you."

"Besides," Reed said, shaking his head, "he's too smart to fall for it. She goes in there and starts talking in a throaty, come-hither sort of way, he's going to know she's playing him for a sucker, big time. She's not exactly subtle when she turns on the charm."

I gave him the daggers. "How would you know?"

"It's true, you're kind of obvious," Kat said, drawing my look of ire. "Because you're nice to a guy when you like him."

"Hey!" I blushed. "I'm … nice." I paused, considering that. "Okay, you got me. But Reed's right, a dramatic change in personality now and he'll know for a fact I'm jerking him along. There's no chance of it working."

Reed settled an inscrutable gaze on me then nodded once. "Which is why I say we call his bluff and kill him."

"Maybe you should ask him about this Century meeting first," Kat suggested.

"He didn't know anything about it," I said. "Or so he claims. He says Claire is now blocking his efforts to try and track Century's movements."

"Do you believe him?" Foreman asked in that deep, compelling voice of his.

"Doesn't matter," I said. "It's a dead end either way."

He nodded once. "I may have a way to track down this meeting for you. Let me rattle some cages."

"He probably means literal cages," Reed said snottily, "where they keep the meta captives."

"What can I say?" Foreman asked coolly, "the U.S. Government hasn't quite embraced the 'kill them all!' philosophy you've suddenly attached your wagon to. At least not yet." He stood, drawing his powerfully built frame all the way up. "Let me make some calls." He departed without another word.

"What about Sovereign?" Zollers said. "Are we just going to let him stew in his own juices in the dormitory?"

"You left him in the dormitory?" Ariadne said with a frown. "All alone?"

"Yeah," I said. "He's probably going through my unmentionables right now, but otherwise it'd be hard for him to do any damage over there. We'll keep him there until we figure out what to do with him, or ..." I let my voice trail off for a moment as I pondered that lone possibility, "... until we get crazy enough or desperate enough to ask him for help taking out whatever else Century is getting ready to lob at us."

Chapter 36

I clicked the door to my quarters shut behind me to find Sovereign still sitting in the chair in the corner, shrouded in shadow. "This still looks like a damned dreamwalk," I muttered.

"Should you be here talking to me?" I could see enough of his face to tell he had a wan smile. Light from the impending sunset was coming through the cracks in the shutters in thin shafts, and the whole place had a dusky red quality.

I thought about flipping a light switch but decided against it. "If I don't do it, who will? I'm supposed to be your jailer, after all."

"Good point." He leaned back in the chair, a freestanding recliner with a footstool that I had thought was tasteful when I ordered it online in the five minutes per day I had back when we were getting the dorms up and running. It was white leather, and I'd fallen asleep in it more than a few times while reading briefings. "So what should we talk about?"

"You're supposed to be playing solitaire, I think."

He held up the cuffs. "Makes it tough to deal."

I walked toward the kitchenette. "Like those could hold you."

"I admit I'm surprised," he said. "There are restraints that actually *could* hold me, but you don't seem like you're even trying."

"They could hold you for a little while," I admitted as I made my way to the fridge. I opened it and found it completely empty save for a bottle of ketchup in the door and I couldn't even vouch for that. How long had it been since I'd been grocery shopping? I couldn't even remember. We'd ordered a lot of takeout and delivery since the cafeteria staff had been furloughed. "But then you'd just jack some poor bastard's mind and have him get you out if you wanted to escape, so why put people in harm's way?"

"Is that why you left me over here by myself?" he asked. "You don't want anyone to get hurt in case I decide to make a break for it?"

"You're the mind reader," I said, shutting the refrigerator door. "You tell me."

"I don't read your mind," he said quietly. "It's a respect thing. For the same reason I haven't gone through your unmentionables." I looked back and caught a slight smile.

"But you don't respect other peoples' minds," I said.

"I have no particular compunction about rummaging through one that's steered by someone who's suggested that you kill an unarmed prisoner without a trial," he said, sounding only a hint defensive in his explanation.

"I'm sure Reed will love hearing that you were going through his thoughts," I said.

"He already wants me dead," Sovereign said with a shrug. "I'm not exactly going to trip over myself trying to change his mind when it's already so dead set against me."

"But you're out to change my mind," I said. "About you."

"I'm not exactly hiding that fact, either," he said. "Unless you're a real slow thinker, like your brother." He paused. "No offense."

"Yeah, you insult my brother, but no offense to me," I said, under my breath. I leaned back on the counter behind me. "I'd have to be a real slow thinker not to believe you might be playing a game on multiple levels here."

"You would," he agreed smoothly. "I hope you're considering all the possibilities. You wouldn't be you if you didn't have a suspicious mind that's always on the lookout for the backstab. You've been betrayed a few too many times to trust lightly, and I understand that. Which is why I came here in good faith. Which is why I'm not resisting. Which is why I'm not doing anything untoward, and why I'm willing to help you however I can." He held up his chained hands again. "You and I are going to live a long time, and I don't think I've made any secret of the fact that you are the reason I was undertaking what I was." He settled his head a little lower. "I realize now that I was wrong. I was affiliated with the wrong people, my aims were just wrong … and I need to make amends for that." He looked up and still I said nothing. "I recognize that it's unlikely you're going to be willing to think of me as anything other than a criminal and murderer for a lifetime."

I felt my jaw settle at that. "But we live longer than a normal lifetime, and you're willing to put in the time proving you're contrite? Is that it?"

"That is it," he said, sounding like he meant it. "I've messed up, and I'll spend however much time I need to convincing you that I'm genuinely sorry for what I've done." He paused and looked down. "If you'll give me the chance."

I studied him, unflinching. He didn't look pathetic, exactly, but he was laying on the contrition with a heavy spoon. I didn't know how good of an actor he was, but he was right about the way my mind worked. I wouldn't have put it past him to be working another angle.

I just didn't know what that angle was.

"All right," I said, neutrally. "Let's say I believe you—which I think we both know I don't—yet. But let's say I did. You have no knowledge of where Century is now, what pieces they're moving, what this meeting is about—or so you claim." I added that last part to needle him, and he took it well. "So how are you going to help me?"

"Well," he said, leaning back against the recliner again, "it's true, I'm on the outs with them. But that doesn't mean I don't know anything. I have lots of information, and I'm willing to share all of it with you."

"Oh, really?" I asked and took a couple steps down into the pit that was my living room. "Okay. Let's start with an easy one. You've talked about phase two, about how you'd put the whole world under Century's boot," I watched as he nodded once, but with some reluctance. I wasn't sure he wanted to part with this one. "How are they going to do it? Take over the world? Beat all the armies and all that?"

"Easier than you think," Sovereign said, and another expression came forward now, causing his lips to twist in something that looked like ... fear? "They have an Ares."

Chapter 37

"What the hell is an Ares?" Scott asked.

"God of War," Reed said as we walked, back down the tunnel to the headquarters building. They'd both fallen in behind me as I walked, churning through the thoughts in my head. "They can take command of anyone whose mind is thinking violent thoughts, force them to fight for them or even kill themselves." I heard his voice change as he directed his next comment to me. "Hera told me they were all dead."

"Apparently not," I said. "Kind of like my uncle the Hades, Century seems to have dug one up somehow."

"As many influential metas as they've recruited—Loki and Amaterasu, for example—they've got thousands of years worth of meta secrets at their disposal," Reed said. "A hell of a lot more knowledge than we've got."

I tapped the side of my head with a single finger. "Speak for yourself. I've got the wisdom of lifetimes."

"Yeah, lifetimes spent murdering and pillaging," Reed said with a snort.

"And that's just Eve," I agreed, taking a little shot at Kappler. She was still circling in the back of my mind, swirling in her own angry juices. I was betting that wouldn't help, but I was beyond caring.

"Seems like there were a lot of meta types that have gone extinct," Scott said.

"It's a downward trend," Reed agreed, "though it's gotten a lot sharper lately."

We fell into a silence. It was a heady feeling, realizing you're part of an endangered species. When I first came to the Directorate and learned about what I was, I'd been told we had somewhere around three thousand metas on the planet. Now we were down to five hundred or so. Three thousand was a low number in a world populated by seven billion people. Five hundred was a rounding error.

"At least they're not hunting the other metas right now," Reed said, snapping us out of that deathly quiet. "So … they've got an Ares. What are they going to do with it?"

"Turn it loose on anyone that has war and violence in mind," I said, repeating what Sovereign had told me. "They think the Ares is strong enough to affect the whole world, and that they'll be able to pretty much kill every soldier and violent criminal and policeman—anyone who's of a mind to do some harm to other people, even in a protective way—to fall on their own sword, metaphorically speaking."

"What if they don't have a sword handy?" Scott asked.

"I don't know," I said with a shake of the head. "Maybe they claw their own throat out, maybe they ram their head against the wall until it breaks open, maybe they decide it's not worth the trouble and sit down to have a cup of tea. I have no idea. I'm not exactly an expert on how these things work."

"I've never even heard of a meta like this," Scott said. "They're not a telepath?"

"This power is kind of like … it's a weird strain of powers, I guess," I said. "Do you remember that girl Athena?"

"The one who died when the Century mercs hit the dorms, right?" Scott frowned. "When Breandan—"

"Yeah," I said, cutting him off. "She was an Athena-type. She had the ability to influence the mind in directions of … I don't know, Janus called it working the 'better angels of our nature.' She could stimulate the brain toward arts and goodness, or something. I don't pretend to understand how it works, but I think Ares types work like that, but in the areas of violence and nastiness."

"So they take out anyone with a will to do violence, and then what?" Reed asked.

"Kill all the sheepdogs and you've got a herd without any defense," Scott said.

"And the world falls right into your grasp, no muss, no fuss," I said. "Without any metas left to oppose them and with everyone who might be willing to take up arms against them impaled on their own swords, Century rules the world and can remake it in their image."

It got quiet for a minute. "That's a lot of dead bodies," Reed said.

"Probably," I said. "But Sovereign's always said it'd be a so-called better world. And it's 'better' because all that tendency to harm each other would be wiped out good and proper. The survivors would get to live with Sovereign's axe hanging over them—step out of line and you catch the blade across the back of your neck."

"You can't tell me people wouldn't fight back," Reed said.

"Maybe," I said. "But if you think about it, he's perfectly positioned to cut them off at the knees every time. All your soldiers and cops are gone, all your civilians who'd fight back are dead. It leaves you with the willingly ruled."

"And this is a better world how?" Scott asked. "You're killing all the people who *might maybe possibly* do harm all at once instead of letting those who *will* do harm do it. That's gotta be like a hundred to one ratio, for all the people who *might* do violence to those who *actually* do violence."

"I don't know, I didn't stick around for the grandiose explanation of the virtues of his final solution to the world's violence problem," I said. "I just know the weapon Century means to use and how it works."

"And as for how we stop it?" Scott asked as we emerged from the tunnel into HQ.

"Well, they are having a meeting of all hands in the next couple days," I said as I made for the staircase. "If we can find that—"

"We can storm in there and get ourselves killed all at once," Reed said sarcastically, "letting the remainder of Century carry out their plans unimpeded by any pesky distractions."

I shook my head wearily. "I'm working on a plan."

I could feel Reed's gaze on the back of my neck as I climbed the stairs. "And how's it going so far?"

"So far it's comprised of 'kill them all' … and that's about it."

"The Wolfe school of tactical engagement," Reed said, voice still laden with irony. He paused, and his tone dropped. "In this case, I actually like it."

We emerged into the fourth floor bullpen and I realized with surprise that the sun was setting. Had it already been another whole day? That was fast. I glanced toward the conference room. "How's Harper doing?"

"She seemed to take it all mostly in stride," Scott said. "As I understand it, she's got the drone over us right now, keeping a watch in case we need it."

"Surveillance state," Reed muttered.

"Hm," I said. "We probably will need it at some point, if we can get a fix on the location of this meeting. Did J.J. manage to scrape anything off Weissman's laptop?"

"Nothing helpful," Reed said. "Seems like this meeting might have been called after he died."

"It's election time in the Evil League of Evil," I quipped. "I wonder who the frontrunner is to be the next Bad Horse?"

"I have no idea what you're talking about," Scott said.

"You look tired," Reed said as we came to a stop outside my office.

"I can't imagine why," I said. "Did we do that freeway battle today or yesterday?"

"Today," Scott said. "I think."

"No," Reed said, "the warehouse explosion was today."

"Nice," I said, and rubbed my eyes. "So my mom died … one or two nights ago?" I honestly couldn't keep track. This was a lot to have going on, wasn't it?

"Yeah," Reed said, voice soft. "I, um … started making the arrangements. I hope you don't mind."

"I don't mind," I said. "Better you handle it than me." Because if I had to handle it right now, I might start to feel dark clouds of emotion descending to fog my brain further. Which would probably be bad. "We need a lead on this meeting. Why don't we gather everybody in the conference room—"

"Why don't you get some sleep," Reed suggested quietly, "and we'll talk about it when you wake up."

"Because we've got two days—" I started.

"And if on the second day you pass out from exhaustion just before the big battle," Scott said, "how's that going to go for your team?"

I shot him a sour look. "I don't know. I can fight better in my sleep than most people can awake."

"Not against these odds," Reed said with a shake of the head. "We need you at your best."

"Not that we're saying that your average isn't good—" Scott added. His voice was full of concern. It was adorable. And annoying.

"I'll be in my office," I said, cutting him off. "I will lie down on my couch, and if sleep comes, I'll embrace it. If it doesn't arrive in the next thirty minutes, I want a meeting in the conference room with all hands, and we're going to sit there and keep mulling this until we crack it." I paused. "Is Janus out of the hospital yet?"

"We're springing him later tonight," Reed said. "Figure he'll be mobile by then. Not everyone shrugs off third-degree burns quite like you, after all."

"And why should they?" I asked, turning to head into my office. I closed the door. "I've had a lot of practice at it."

I let out a long breath and realized that there was no chance I'd make a meeting in thirty minutes. Not a bit of a chance, even. I took a step and my foot dragged. *Using the Wolfe power takes the strength right out, Little Doll.*

Commanding fire exerts a similar tax upon the will, Gavrikov said softly.

"And constantly thinking about how to outwit your enemies when they outnumber you a hundred to one takes a toll of a different kind," I said to the empty room.

It's not a hundred to one anymore, Zack reminded me quietly. I sat back on the couch, felt my head press into the soft cushions, and imagined him leaning over me.

"It's close," I said.

They would follow you to the end, Zack said. *If you let them.*

"I know," I said, my voice echoing in the empty room. "Which is why I can't let them."

Chapter 38

"This will be a very great challenge for you," Janus said quietly. Marius was listening, carefully, watching Janus as best he could reflected in the cloudy glass mirror that stood before him. "The first time you absorb a metahuman, I am told that the battle of wills is fierce."

Marius nodded. "I still have to exert mine with my mother."

Janus made a grunting sound. "As commanding as she is, she is human. Metas have a much stronger will. They will fight back harder, will provide much more of a grapple than you are presently used to. We need to acclimate you by having you take on lesser metas in preparation for the final challenge."

Marius swallowed, felt the dry mouth that always came with nerves. "How will we do that?"

"I am working on it," Janus said with another grunt. "There are metahumans out there who have done terrible things, who travel the land and wreak havoc upon innocents simply to satisfy their own appetites. I intend to find a few of those, to place ourselves in their path, and then cull their abilities to build your strength.

Strength, Marius thought. *What if I could wield such power as Ares over men?* It made him shudder slightly, in fear and … something else. He looked back at Janus, and there was a wary smile on the man's face. "Will I be able to control them?"

"With some effort, I think," Janus said. "It is the act of harnessing their powers in your service that will become the difficult part, I expect. Simply quashing them within your mind is what most incubi and succubi do if they should absorb a meta, and thus never learn the secret to controlling these new abilities that they gain."

"Why do they do that?" Marius asked. The firelight flickered on the walls and cast the room in a dim light. It was still better than going to bed as the sun set and relying on it to wake one up.

"They fear to control these abilities," Janus said. "To draw the powers of other metas freely would be to draw the ire of Jupiter himself upon you. He has forbidden this thing, and now that his brother is dead, no one would stand against him." Janus landed a hand on Marius's covered shoulder. "What we do now, should you wish to proceed, will bring with it some risk. Should we be discovered by the others, they will try everything they can to kill you. Your kind has been hated and feared by the rest of metakind since they discovered what power you have over them. 'Soul stealers,' they call you, and revile your touch. They cast you out of their cities, out of their company, and kill you when they think they can do it unobserved. I have seen this myself and done all I can to ward against it."

Marius felt himself swallow again. "Will they ask about my powers eventually? If I continue to show up in your company?"

"Almost certainly," Janus said, no sense of deception about him. Marius could feel the bracing honesty, the sense of urgency. "Which is why it is of the utmost importance that we acquire for you some power that you can lean on, and as quickly as possible." Janus stood straight again, his face foreboding. "From there, it will be up to you to learn to entice and enthrall that soul, to make it enough your own that its will is broken to yours and its power is in your own hands."

"How do I do that?" Marius asked into the silence that followed. He could feel his own fear building on itself—first at the thought of having no power to show the other gods and goddesses if asked, and second at the thought of failing to bend some mind to his will. Failure in either case would be the same, he thought.

"I am not entirely sure," Janus admitted. "And thus we come to another crucial bend in the plan. I place a burden upon you now that you must decide whether you wish to take up." He sniffed. "Once we meet with Ares—Mars—and I have spoken to him about what must be done, should he agree with my thinking—and I rather suspect he will, based on the emotions I feel from him—then we are committed to action. Your role and abilities must be a secret up until the very second they are needed. This is for your own sake, and ours. You must decide for yourself whether this is a path you wish to undertake. For once we begin down it, it is thorny and walks the edge of a cliff. There will be no leaving it save for down into the abyss below, and be assured that that is the direction we will go should we make even one misstep along the way."

Marius turned to look back in the cloudy glass. He could see himself, barely. He had only seen himself in the reflection of a cold, crisp pond on a still morning before. This was new and different and still very foreign, like the candles and hearths.

But he liked it. He liked it all.

And to fail meant having to leave, to hide, to go back to the shadows once more, taking shelter wherever he might find it.

"I will do it," he said and felt the determination within himself. "Whatever it takes, I will do it. I will bend a will to my own."

He felt the pressure of Janus's hand on his shoulder once more. "I am proud this day, Marius. It is one thing for a man to say he will do something that he fears. It is another to make a true commitment in the face of fear. It would be a simple thing for you to have run. It is quite a bit more complex to face your fears in the way you have chosen." Marius felt the hand leave his shoulder with one more squeeze. "Prepare yourself. Diana will be along shortly, and we should sup together. As a family."

With that, Janus left, but Marius sat there staring at the mirror for a while longer.

Family.

Home.

With one last breath to give himself courage, he turned and walked toward the door. With each step he felt more certain than the last.

Chapter 39

I awoke to a gentle shake, opening my eyes to see Scott kneeling by my side. "You should be more careful waking me up," I said sleepily, "it could get you killed."

"If it means a morning kiss, I might be willing to go out that way," he said.

I ran my tongue over the inside of my mouth. "If you could smell my breath right now, you might change your mind." I shifted my body, rolling it to sit up on the edge of the couch. "What time is it?"

"Just after five," Scott said. "Looks like you needed that sleep."

"Yeah," I said, and smacked my lips together. "What's the word?"

"Foreman's called a meeting in five minutes."

"Good, because we have many important things to discuss and questions to answer." I yawned and stretched, putting my arms over my head. "The first of which is, 'Will there will be coffee'?"

"There's coffee," Scott said. "I heard a rumor he even had breakfast catered in."

"Ooh," I said and headed toward the conference room without bothering to say anything else.

There was breakfast, and it had been catered in by the local bagel chain. I had no complaints as I spread blueberry cream cheese over my bagel. Li was already there, trying to spread his cream cheese with one hand. The plate kept slipping away from him, but he didn't look up to register my amusement, thankfully. A better person than I might have offered to help; I wisely kept my distance, figuring that offering him assistance would be taken as an insult or something.

Kat and Janus wandered in about five minutes later, Janus leaving heavily on his girlfriend. The sight of the two of them together still gave me gut-level heebie-jeebies, and I could tell from Gavrikov's veritable rippling in my head that he was still none too pleased. I got the sense that he and Janus had been more than casual acquaintances, and that he viewed the fact that Janus was sleeping with his sister as something of an insult or treading on his guy territory or something testosterone related. I just viewed it as icky.

Reed and Scott breezed in a few minutes later, followed by Ariadne. She seemed like the odd man out, a little distant as the two of them took their seats. Foreman was the last to arrive; he had Harper and a new guy in his wake. The new guy did not look happy.

He was a touch under six feet, had jet-black hair with a hint of some sort of gel in it to hold the parts in place in a wave over his forehead. He was olive-skinned and serious, but his lips made him look like he'd held onto a taste of something very sour.

Foreman didn't waste moments. He went straight to the head of the table. With a frown, he asked, "Where's Zollers?"

"Sleeping," I answered for him. It was a reasonable guess. "With Sovereign in the building, I've got him on telepathic watch to keep any mental break-ins from happening."

Foreman gave me a grunt of acknowledgment. "And with me and Janus lurking, he won't be needed in the short term."

"Hence the sleep," I said.

"All right, well," Foreman said, and clapped his hands together, "you've already met Ms. Harper. This is Mr. Rocha, from the National Security Agency."

"NSA?" Scott asked as a slight buzz of energy ran through the room. "Okay, I'll bite. Why is the NSA here?"

"Because you need help intercepting and decoding your enemy's transmissions," Rocha said. His voice was thin and light, and he kept whatever displeasure he was feeling out of his voice. "Perhaps you haven't heard, but we have a program or two for that."

"PRISM?" Reed said with a roll of his eyes. "I don't even need to say it again, do I?"

"We're all ignoring you by now," Scott said. "This could be useful."

"Oh, yeah, invading privacy of massive numbers of people is super-useful," Reed said acidly. "To anyone who's actually got control over the data. Those of us whose privacy is being compromised—"

"No one gives a crap about your browser history," Scott said, waving him off. He paused then glanced slightly nervously at Kat. "Although … man, I hope they're not reading our old text messages. And the photos…" He grimaced and Kat gave him a quizzical look.

"I don't understand," I said. "We've had access to PRISM intercepts for a while. What's new?"

Rocha smiled, looking a little pained. "Now you've got me combing through it for you, and I know a lot more about how the system works than your resident tech geek."

I shrugged. "Can't hurt. If nothing else, J.J. will be thrilled to have you on his staff."

Rocha's smile died. "Excuse me?"

Foreman buried his face in a palm while Scott and Reed exchanged a giggle, like the twelve-year-olds they were. "Not what I meant," I corrected. Man, I had to watch out for that one in the future.

Rocha gave me a look that was pure disdain. "If you'll allow me to set up on one of your computers, I can start working immediately."

"Sure," I said. "Scott, set him up, will you? You know, if you're done chortling."

"Man, where the hell was all this help six months ago, when we were stumbling in the dark?" Scott muttered as he headed to the door, Rocha following just slightly after him.

"Where it's always been," Foreman answered, absolutely glacial. "The problem wasn't it, the problem was you—your Agency is deeply classified. Or was," he added, not looking all that happy.

"I'll take it," I said as the door shut behind Rocha and Scott. "At least there's some benefit to us for getting blown out into open. Before when we would ask other agencies for information, they'd end up looking around wondering who the hell just said something."

"Welcome to the federal government," Foreman replied. He was so impassive I wasn't sure how I was supposed to take that.

"So can Mr. Rocha tap us in to Century's communications?" Ariadne asked. "I mean … is it possible that they've just been talking out in the open like this, where anyone could read it?"

"Not just anyone could read it, as I understand," Foreman said. "Something about browser encryptions, and Tor, things that I couldn't explain to you if I had to. However, the NSA does seem to have some experience tracking communications of all varieties, and with your boy J.J.'s help—and the laptop recovered from Weissman—Mr. Rocha seems to think we have an excellent chance to uncover some of Century's back trails."

"Find their trails, maybe find the tip-off for the meeting," I said, tapping the table.

"That's the hope," Foreman said. "But I don't know enough about it to be very optimistic. Still, it's another door."

"Every door we can open at this point is a good one," Janus said wearily. He was leaning on the arm of his chair.

"What about the one with Sovereign behind it?" Reed asked. "Because I'm still not keen on opening that one unless we're going to throw in a few grenades and wait before entering."

"Very concerned about your right to privacy, not so concerned about perforating a man without a trial," Foreman mused aloud. "That's an interesting set of contradicting beliefs you're running around with there, Mr. Treston." Reed flushed but said nothing.

"Acrimony aside," I said and shifted my attention to Harper, "if they find this meeting site, you can provide surveillance, right?"

Harper nodded once, crisply. "I'll have to refuel soon, but that shouldn't take too long."

"Where does that happen?" I asked.

"If need be, we can do it here at the 133rd Air Wing, next to the airport," Harper said. "Preferably I'd send it to Camp Ripley, where the drone wouldn't look quite so out of place coming in for a landing."

"Okay, well, just do it now," I said. "We don't know when we're going to get a break and I'll want something ready urgently."

"With the pull the Senator has, I can get you a few more drones for coverage if need be," Harper said, betraying nothing in the way she said it. "Have them standing off in orbiting patterns and just hand them off to other operators when they need to refuel."

"Whatever it takes and whatever you can give," I agreed. "But once we find these guys, then we have to decide what to do."

"Hit 'em with a missile from the drone," Reed offered, a little viciously. "That's what drones are for, right?" I didn't think he was serious. Exactly.

"We can't do that in U.S. airspace," Harper said with a simple shake of the head.

"Of course not," Reed muttered. "We only—"

"Stuff it, Reed," I shot at him. "So we're back to a ground-based conflict on this one." I looked up at Foreman. "Any other support? Army? Marines?"

He shook his head. "Posse comitatus."

"National Guard?" I asked.

"Not yet," he said. "Get me a clear and present danger and the president might—maybe—move on this sooner."

"Do you have his ear on this?" I asked.

"No," Foreman said with a faint smile. "I'm a junior Senator from the opposing party. He's more likely to listen to a man on the street than me. I'm working through channels with him, but they're not particularly clear ones, if you catch my meaning."

"So we're on our own but at least we have some ancillary support at this point," I said. "I'll take it." It was a hell of a lot better than having nothing. Foreman did not respond other than with a slightly amused raise of an eyebrow.

"So we wait," Janus said. "We wait and hope that this ... technical wonder you have constructed bears some form of fruit?"

"Unless you want to make an effort at questioning Sovereign," I said, staring at him.

His head was bald, his beard gone, and his lined face looked peculiar even in the spots where the flesh had healed from his unfortunate scalding. "I will talk to him if you wish it, but I don't think it will help. We have steered rather clear of each other for a very long time, and with good reason."

"Yeah," I said, harkening back to the story he'd told us, "but do you think talking to him would do any positive good?"

"If you are looking to aggravate him, perhaps," Janus said with a shrug. "Otherwise, I doubt it."

"We'll skip that for now," I said.

"Never underestimate the value of annoying people," Reed said, and I wondered if he knew how much he was living out his own advice at the moment.

"Well, if there's nothing else to discuss …" I said.

"Hold it," Li said from his end of the table. "We still have no actionable plan on what we're going to do when we find this meeting. You're talking about facing down one hundred—"

"Eighty," I said. "Or maybe seventy; I've lost count." I paused, thinking about it for a second.

"You've killed so many people you've lost track of the numbers," Li said, surprisingly calm.

I started to open my mouth to protest out of reflex, and stopped. "Yes," I said, in slightly numb surprise. "I have."

"She's doing her job," Foreman said quickly, not hazarding a look in my direction. "Every member of Century that's removed from their organization makes it more likely that we're going to be able to take them out." He laid his knuckles on the table as he leaned over. "I've heard the basics about this Ares-type they're holding onto, and I have to say—it scares the hell out of me. Watching them come for our people one by one was frightening; knowing they possess the capability to wipe out every last one of our defenders pushes my fear of them up to the next level. They need to be taken out, by any means necessary."

"I am fine with that," Li said, calmly assertive. "But in terms of a plan, even walking in with auto shotguns doesn't seem like it's going to cover all the bases. If we can't just fire a missile and take them out of existence, then that means a fight—"

"No," I said. I felt a slow grin crack my face. "No, it doesn't. We've been looking at this all wrong. If we're at war, and we're up against an army … we need an advantage, right?"

"Right," Foreman said, giving me a cautious look. "But as previously pointed out, we have no advantage to give you. No tanks, no soldiers, no planes—"

"We don't need any of those things," I said, shaking my head. "We just need one thing, and one thing alone—other than the location of their meeting, obviously."

The smile on my face must have been very disquieting, because some cracks of nervousness started to show up in Foreman's facade. "And what would that be?"

I blinked at him demurely. "The same thing any army uses when they want to take out a number of enemies fast and efficiently." I leaned forward. "A bomb."

Chapter 40

I sat in my office after the meeting, the blinds cracked open and the sunlight pouring in. It was blissfully silent, which was a hell of a contrast to how it had been in the meeting after I'd dropped my own particular bomb.

The reaction was predictable, the arguments equally so, and there was a lot of anger and rage. Also predictable. I didn't really care, though, because when you start arguing about killing people, what's the difference whether it's fast or slow? My preference was for fast, obviously, given how much damage these particular people could do if given time to react.

Foreman had been necessarily skeptical, but I thought I'd finally gotten through to him at the end. Maybe. He was a tough guy to read, and I would struggle to guess whether that was because of his meta abilities or his career in politics. Either way, it left me nothing more than the hope that he'd pass my request up the line and get us a bomb we could work with. I'd even talked with him for a minute privately after the meeting to make sure he got the right message. I still couldn't read him, though.

So I sat in my office and waited for the next inevitable knock. Whether it would be Scott and Rocha, hopefully with some news to share, or Ariadne with a budget projection that she knew I'd just sign off on, or someone else wanting to have any number of conversations I didn't necessarily see the value in, it would come as surely as Century's looming meeting.

Though I probably wouldn't have to wait as long.

When the knock came a few minutes later, I didn't even bother to act surprised. "Come in," I said, still leaning back in my chair with my boots up on the desk. Director of a federal agency, and I wear boots every day. Well, when you have to kick as much ass as I do, it's a necessity.

"Hey," Reed said as he eased in.

"Hey, yourself," I replied with all my wit. Well, half my wit. Whatever, I don't deal in percentages. I gave what I had. "What's up?"

"Came to talk to you, of course."

"About my mother?" I asked. "Because I'm still not ready to have that conversation just yet."

"No," he said. "I don't know that I have anything to add in relation to Sierra. Getting to know her these last few months has been a ... different ..." He looked like he'd taken a bite of something he didn't care for, "... experience." He eased over to my desk and sat down on the edge. "No, I'm here because there's something you need to hear."

I cocked an eyebrow at him. "Oh, really?"

"Yes," he said and paused, as if he were drawing a deep breath before bringing the pain. "You're not a mad dog in danger of slipping the chain."

I frowned at him. "What the ...? Is there a 'bitch' joke coming at my expense? Because I'd look dimly on that."

"No," he said. "I wanted to tell you that you're like ... a sheepdog."

Now both my eyes were wide and fixed on him. "I have no idea where you're going with this."

"You're aloof and jaded and have a mile-high fence around you, Sienna," he said. "But you can't hide the fact that you care about people and society. You always talk about the things you've done—killing M-Squad or the Primus of Omega—like it's the start of your psychopath career. But you were willing to die going out against Wolfe back when this whole thing started in order to protect people you'd never even met." He gave me his serious look. "It's why you're doing what you're doing now. This whole 'bomb' idea … I don't want you to feel guilty about it, like it's some reversion to the darker instincts in your soul. You're not a 'kill for a thrill' psycho. You're a woman with a lot of power who's made mistakes. You're a guardian. You're a protector. You're a—"

"Dark knight?" I deadpanned.

"I was going to say sheepdog."

I sighed. "And we're back to bitches again."

"Fine," Reed said. "You're a shield. You stand between the people and harm. It's what you've always done, when you weren't caught up in personal anguish and other …" he harrumphed, "… issues. This bomb idea? It's … it's a good one." He shrugged. "It wouldn't be my first choice because that's not how I'd prefer to fight, but when you're this outnumbered …" He sighed. "You have to do what you have to do."

I looked him in the eyes. "Thank you. I think."

"You're welcome," he snarked. "I think."

I watched him as he left and thought about it. Was it bad that I hadn't even considered wiping out Century with a bomb to be anything less than a moral option? I mean, if they were having a meeting on the fifth floor of one of the big towers downtown, I'd cancel the plan in a heartbeat, but if they did what I suspected they were going to do and held the meet somewhere secluded, like that warehouse?

Boom. I'd have no qualms about reducing them all to cinders. It wasn't like they'd seemed to have any about doing the same to me. They'd started out as a hundred of the most powerful people on the planet, and now they'd revealed themselves to be scheming to take the power away from everyone else and concentrate it in their own hands.

Did it say something bad about me that I was totally fine with just knocking them off and being done with it?

Or maybe it just said that I knew something that Reed didn't.

Remember.

It's all right, Little Doll, Wolfe said. *Nothing wrong with crushing your enemies however you can.*

"Thanks, Wolfe," I said, this time only mildly sarcastic. It didn't worry me until later that I actually *did* find it reassuring.

Chapter 41

Rome
281 A.D.

Marius sat on his haunches on the stone floor, head aching and throbbing, both in concert. He felt as though something full grown was about to spring forth from his skull, a spirit ready to break out of his head and take flight.

"You are fine," Janus said, reassuring. His voice was soothing, a pleasant sound amidst the fire that deluged his mind. "You are just fine. Lay back. Relax. The pain will pass."

"It is … not passing," Marius said with emphasis on every word. This had been going on for years, it felt like.

"It has been two days," Janus said, accurately predicting Marius's thoughts. It was an uncanny ability that the man had, and reassuring in its way. When the pain had not been there, it had seemed more reassuring.

"He is fighting me," Marius said. He could feel the man in his head, ripping about like an angry bull set loose in a town square. It felt as though furious horns were making great rips in his thoughts, shredding their way through him. He could not stand, could not walk.

"He is a strong one," Janus said, "and full of fury. But I can feel him within you. He will tire, his will to fight will falter given time. He already wearies."

"I …" Marius dropped the back of his head to the floor once more. They had gone to a town a day's travel to the south. There they had confronted a man who possessed the power of flight.

Which he had been using to wing away young women from villages for his own ends.

Janus had called the man—Ennias—a monstrosity. Marius had agreed, after they'd spoken with a girl of fifteen who had survived Ennias's attentions and come stumbling home to her village after a week's abduction. The story she'd told had inflamed Marius's rage and even caused his mother's occasional irritable pronouncements to go silent. What Ennias had done had offended him on every level of decency. The girl had reminded Marius of the only villagers who had actually been kind to him, two teenage girls who had offered him bread every now and again.

It had been easy, pressing his hands against Ennias's flesh, when Janus held him there for Marius to touch. A simple arrow from Diana's quiver, shot perfectly by her, dropped him. He had seen Diana's face when she shot. There was a quiet satisfaction there that told him that the village girl's story had made an impression on even her.

So Marius drank his soul.

And now he burned in torment.

"You … will … fail …" Marius muttered.

I will not, came the voice of the murderous beast in his mind. *You watchman, you fiend, you try and capture me—*

"I have … captured you," Marius said. "You are dead. You are kept from crossing the river by my leave only. Your soul belongs to me, not to Pluto."

Never, the voice came. *Never.*

Oh, yes, you will, came another voice, stronger than the weary Ennias.

"Mother?" Marius said, and for but a moment the pain subsided.

214

"Yes," Janus said, quiet, solemn, into the silence. "Yes, this is how …"

Marius closed his eyes and found himself in the darkness. It was nearly complete, a world formless and shapeless, and he stood at the point of a triangle in the dark. A woman stood to his right, and Ennias was to his left, looking haggard, his long hair wild and his eyes drooping like a man about to fall into slumber. It was as real as anything he'd ever felt, this place in the darkness. He knew he could reach out and touch Ennias with a hand, could feel the man's bloodied lip if he held a finger up to it. It was knowledge that came naturally to him, instinctively.

This was his place.

You will fall before the might of my son, his mother said. He had seen her face only in passing, in visions before his waking eyes, and in dreams that were gone when he came back to consciousness. Here, her eyes were fearsome, green as the grass but lit with a hard edge, like an emerald that Janus had once shown him in the firelight. *You will fall before my will as well.*

I will not, Ennias said, but his voice rang with uncertainty. He bled, and not only from his lip. His soul was in pain, was wounded from the struggle. He stood with his hand bent strangely at his side, broken, the way it had been when Janus had held him down.

His mother looked at him, and her emerald eyes flared with light as she did. *You have pushed me down with your will. I have felt the pain you can inflict. You cannot break him on your own, but you could sit upon him as you have me these long years, sit upon him until the end of time yet it will do you no good.*

Marius swallowed. "I don't know what to do," he said in a voice that broke into the darkness, echoing with power that originated in a place far from where he was. "I need what he has. I need it to survive, to do what we …" he hesitated. "What we need to do."

His mother nodded, once. *Then let us face him together. With your will joined to mine, we will make him suffer in such a way as he has never felt pain before. We will make him scream and beg and cry—*

Marius felt the wave of alarm from Ennias even as he turned his gaze back upon the man. The fear was sweet now, easily tasted with the power he felt swelling on his side of the triangle. It was as though there was a cord drawn between him and his mother, something that pulsated with an energy born of will. It was a refreshing sense, like a bite of food when one was starving. It made his head go light, made his pain disappear, replaced with some heady sensation of control.

Of power.

The fear radiated off of Ennias, and he seemed to shrink before Marius's very eyes.

No, Ennias said. *No, I will not—*

"YOU WILL," Marius said, but his voice was deeper and sounded like a chorus to his ears. "YOU WILL BREAK BEFORE US, YOU WILL SUFFER UNTIL YOU DO, AND YOU WILL SCREAM UNTIL YOU YIELD."

An aura of light blazed in the darkness, emitted from Marius's own flesh. His mother was gone—no, not gone. She was there, she was with him, she was the fire under his skin, the light taking away the dark. He swelled in size, growing larger and taller as Ennias shrunk before him. He breathed out and felt fire lick his lips. He reached down and grabbed puny Ennias in his hand, pulled him up to looking him in the eye, and a screaming filled his ears.

Nonononononononononono—

"SILENCE," he commanded in that deep voice, and Ennias was forced to obey. He could feel the pain of the man, could feel his agony. This was a man who thrived on pain, delighted in the infliction of torment on others, on innocents—

The righteous fury caused Marius to burn even hotter, sending the ripples of his anger directly to Ennias's soul. He could feel his mother's rage coupled with his own and it was like a tidal wave crashing upon the shores, destroying all before it. Ennias screamed for hours, for days, and Marius could feel his will simply shatter. For a man who enjoyed the infliction of pain, he had no enjoyment for the weathering of it, and Marius let himself hurt the man a little longer out of sheer spite before pulling his tendrils back, before releasing the husk that was Ennias.

Whaaat … do you want … from me? Ennias asked. He was sobbing gently, face buried in his arm, which was still unnaturally bent.

Marius considered it carefully. "DO YOU WISH TO MAKE THE PAIN STOP?"

The answer was instantaneous. *Yes, yes, please,* Ennias begged. *Yes, I would do anything, anything—*

"SILENCE," Marius commanded, and Ennias obeyed. He felt a smile somewhere deep inside, knew that Ennias would do it, would do *anything* to keep his word, if it meant the pain would stop. "You will … obey me from now forward."

Yes, yes, came the reply, filled with eagerness.

"You will serve me from this day forward," Marius said, his voice returned to normal

Of course, Ennias said. He bowed his head and placed it upon Marius's sandaled feet. *Of course, my master.*

"If you are not with us," Marius said, "YOU ARE AGAINST US." The chorus returned with all force, fearsome in its sound, and the world shook around him with the raw will.

Ennias shuddered and kissed his feet. *I am with you. I assure you, I am with you. In whatever you command.*

Marius looked down at the man. He was pathetic, but he had use. A sob nearly broke free of Ennias, but he cut it off halfway through. "Good," Marius said. "Now … give me your power."

"Marius," came the voice from somewhere outside. Marius felt his eyes close, then he opened them once more.

Janus stood next to him, and they were in the same room where he'd ailed by the fire. Janus wore a broad grin, his teeth wide beneath the cover of his dark beard. "You have done well, my son."

He looked down and realized he stood inches off the floor, his toes hanging in midair as though he were held aloft by an invisible rope. He took a breath and moved left, then right, as easily as if he were walking. Yet not one of his limbs moved. "I have him," Marius breathed. He gave a nod, once, then twice, as he felt that confidence and power return to him here, in this place, as it had when he'd been in that dark space with his mother. "I have it now."

"Oh certainly," Janus said, and he was still grinning. "You do, indeed."

We have it, his mother whispered in his thoughts.

Marius stared at Janus, and Janus nodded once more before clapping him on the shoulder. "I will let you rest. Tomorrow … we continue by taking the next step." He paused at the door to give Marius one more reassuring smile. "You have truly done a wondrous thing here today. I feel certain you have a bright future before you, one that will change the very world." He shut the heavy door behind him, leaving Marius alone.

Yes, my boy, came his mother's voice again. *You have a very bright future ahead of you. Why, together, we could rule all of Rome.*

Chapter 42

Sienna
Now

"We've got it," Scott said without preamble, as he poked his head into my office. I sat up in my chair, waiting for him to elaborate, but instead he gestured for me to follow, and I was after him in a hot second.

"Where is it?" I asked as I followed behind him at a jog. He was hustling—human style, not in meta terms. Meta-style hustling would have forced people to dive out the way in fear for their lives.

We were passing cubicles, whipping through the half-occupied bullpen "Gables, Minnesota," he said. "There's a resort up there called Terramara. I've already had J.J. verify, and it looks like this is usually its off-season, all low occupancy and whatnot. But it's fully booked for the next few days. Private party." His eyes gleamed.

"How'd you find it?" I asked as we entered conference room. Reed was already there, sitting over Rocha's shoulder as the man worked on a laptop that was hooked to a projector.

"Because I'm extremely good at what I do," Rocha said simply, and I got the feeling that arrogance ran over him full-force. It gave his voice a quiver of pride.

"We traced cell phone signals in proximity of the jail attack in Arizona," Scott said with a hint of his own pride. "Managed to trace them back to the source, then Rocha used NSA resources to hack their communication—"

"It wasn't hacking," Rocha said with a little irritation.

"Yeah, when you do it, it's considered government compliance, right?" Reed shot at him. Rocha didn't even bother to look at my brother.

"Useful," I said, hoping to end any argument before it started. "What did you find? Text messages?"

"Everything," Rocha said, a little more muted now. "Once we knew what smartphones your targets had, it wasn't too difficult to pull the data through our system. We have emails, web histories, calls made, and yes," he glanced at Scott, "text messages."

Reed looked at Scott and mouthed, "Text messages," at him. Scott looked a little flushed for a moment after that. I tried to pretend I didn't see it.

"It was the emails that gave it all away," Scott said, his expression returning to normal as he got back on track. "Apparently Claire and the rest of Century have been very, very bad at internet security."

"Why be so good at kicking our asses and eluding us but fail so hard on something so damned trivial?" I asked.

"You're not thinking like them," Zollers said, and I realized he'd snuck into the room behind us. "I told you before, they're on an offensive footing. In addition, they are the powers of their day. Gods and monsters dating to before recorded history." His eyes gleamed. "In other words, they're not exactly tech-savvy. I doubt any of their number have been born in the last century."

"We're up against people who don't realize their emails are being read?" Reed asked, shaking his head in disbelief. "How tuned out do you have to be to not notice basic bits of news like that?"

"The world changed slowly up until recently," Janus said, entering the conversation from where he'd been standing in the shadows. I hadn't even noticed him, sitting in a chair next to Kat and Li in the corner. "You could go away for a hundred years, come back and things were more or less the same. Technology such as this has only been around for a flicker of a candle's flame to our kind. Be amazed that they even know how to use a cellular telephone."

"Could this be a trap?" I asked.

"Anything could be a trap," Janus said, a little wary. "But I doubt it."

"Remember," Zollers said, "they weren't expecting your move in Vegas, either. They think they have the initiative, and they're still moving as though they're the aggressor and they have nothing to defend against. They're failing to react to the fact that you have additional resources moving into position. Possibly because they don't know it, or possibly because they just don't have the strategic thinking necessary to operate in a world of high-tech warfare."

"They're like Khan," Reed said, "thinking in two dimensions while we hit them from above."

I pondered that for a moment. "Well," I said, noticing that it seemed like everyone was waiting for me to finish my thought after I spoke, "we can't hit them from above," and I let the smile take over my face, "but we can sure as hell watch them from above ..."

Chapter 43

It was a three-hour drive to the town of Gables, into what Minnesotans called "the northwoods." Outside Minneapolis the forests grew heavy, broken by fields for farms and the occasional lake. It wasn't like southern Minnesota with its flat lands and forever corn fields. It got hilly in places, and the highway rolled along.

We followed the interstate for a while, north out of the cities, and when we left it, we got on a state highway that had probably seen better days. It was the middle of the week, thankfully, and whatever traffic there might have been up here in cabin country was clearly not out in force, though we did see quite a few more cars than I would have expected in a county of only twenty thousand people.

I rode in an SUV with Scott, Reed and Zollers. Janus, Kat, Foreman and two agents were in the van behind us. I'd considered bringing more of our security, but frankly, this wasn't their fight. So instead they were all standing around in the lobby of the Agency, behind barricades, guns pointed at the door in case this was an elaborate bait set up for my benefit.

I doubted it was, but I lost zero points for being too cautious.

Besides, I had an ace in the hole in the van behind us.

"Approaches to the resort are clear," Harper said in my ear. I could hear her as if she were speaking right to me, though I knew everyone was hearing what I was.

"I've got the schematics pulled up," Rocha said.

"Hacking," Reed muttered.

"I've overlaid them with what Harper has on the infrared," Rocha said, either not hearing or ignoring Reed's comment. "Looks like there's a big meeting going on in a conference room."

"Hard to tell," Harper said, "but I'd guess seventy or so people in attendance there."

"The rest of Century, I presume." I muttered, and sighed. The SUV's air conditioner blew cold air into my face.

"We've got guards on perimeter duty sporting assault rifles and submachine guns," Harper went on. "Probably twenty or so hanging around the grounds, another cluster in the main lobby."

"Any civilians?" Scott asked. I looked over at him in the driver's seat and he blushed. "I know, I shouldn't be so soft—"

"No, it's fine," I said under my breath. I raised my voice and said, "We get the civilians out first. We'll assault the main building and do everything we can to ensure that employees of the resort don't get caught in the crossfire."

"Hey guys," J.J. rang in. "I've hacked the payroll system and found the resort work schedule for today. Looks like one person on duty in the front desk, fifteen in the kitchen, and eight maids to clean the rooms."

"Century needs its hot, catered meals, you know," I said. "Harper, we need likely positions on those people."

"I've got about twenty-five in the kitchen," Harper said tonelessly. "Some gun carriers among them, so they must be keeping watch on the exit there. I've also got eyes on the maids, they're spread throughout the building."

"Guys, I just sent the blueprints to your phones, and I have the most recent positions of enemies marked on the map," J.J. said.

I heard a sequence of dings from everyone in the car, and then one instance of someone's phone going off and playing Pharell's "Happy," as a ringtone. I glanced back at Reed in the backseat and he muted it. "What?" he asked me accusingly. "It's a great song."

I looked down at my phone. The blueprints showed a building that looked like half a jack—three long wings jutting out from a central building where I assumed the lobby was. Guards were stationed at the end point of each wing—two per door, by the count of them, and I saw markings to indicate approximately where the maids were.

There was also a big, hand-drawn arrow that led to lettering indicating, "KITCHEN" and "AUDITORIUM." I figured out the lobby all on my own.

"Yikes," Reed muttered. "This looks like a hostage crisis."

"Then we brought the right backup," I said.

We rolled up to the entry to the resort's driveway. I knew from the preliminary briefing that we had two miles to the main buildings, and Harper's eye in the sky told us the nearest sentries were no more than two hundred yards from the resort. So it was clear sailing up until that last bit.

Woods shrouded the entry, flanking the driveway on either side. I slammed the door to my car, cringing and wishing I'd done it more gently. "Let's look the blueprints over one more time together and prep the assault." There was the soft sound of crickets from all around us, and then I heard doors start to close more quietly on the other vehicles in our little procession.

I glanced back at Reed as he stepped out of the back seat of the SUV. He had a slightly low look as he met my gaze, one that evaporated as Scott joined us.

"What did I miss?" Scott asked.

"A meaningful look," I said, not bothering to lie.

"Oh, yeah?" he asked, glancing between the two of us. "What was the meaning behind it?"

Reed shrugged and kept his stoic silence. Then he feigned a smile and shuffled away, back toward the chase car that held Janus and the others.

Scott and I watched him go. "No, seriously," Scott said, "what was that about?"

"We're about to go into the last battle," I said, tightly, as I watched my brother slouch up to Janus and say something. Janus turned in slight surprise and nodded then the two of them shook hands. "I think it meant that whatever happens … not all of us may be coming back alive."

Chapter 44

I crept through the woods, Reed, Kat and Scott at my back. Janus was a hundred feet away with Foreman, Zollers and one of our two agents. Stevens, I think I'd heard him called. He was carrying a European-style bullpup assault rifle. Though it would hardly be silent if shots were fired, the suppressor would hopefully limit the sound carry.

Awww, who was I kidding? If there was even one meta in the group of guards—and there should be, if anyone in Century had any damned sense at all—the moment we opened fire, it was game on.

My job was to make sure that we didn't open fire until absolutely necessary. If at all.

"Van, report," I said in a whisper. I had eyes on the nearest guard patrol, three guys in black tactical gear loitering near a sand volleyball court in a really shitty guard formation. Two of them were smoking, which told me that their level of preparedness was lower than low.

Either this was a heavily baited trap, or they weren't expecting us. I leaned toward the former in my planning but hoped for the latter. Better prepared than not, right?

"Janus," I whispered. I heard his group coming up behind me.

"I can distract them whenever you are ready," he said, "but if anyone is paying the slightest bit of telepathic attention, it will be obvious quickly."

"Those two over there," Zollers said, nodding toward a pair of guards patrolling closer to the building. They were clearly visible against the grey concrete surfaces of the resort. Actually, the resort looked like a seventies-era fallout shelter or something, it was so drab. Three levels of concrete edifices separated by a series of glass windows on each floor. There was wood to dress the whole thing out, a dark cedar color so blah that I looked away quickly. "They have an ongoing bit of tension. I think they've fought recently. Should be easy to start that fire again."

"Interesting," Janus said.

"Want some help?" Foreman asked. He wasn't wearing his usual suit and tie; he was in jeans and tactical vest and had a pistol hanging from his belt. It looked natural on him, and I had a feeling he hadn't just carried a gun to photo ops with the sportsmen in his state; he knew how to use it.

"The less of a signature we leave," Janus said, shaking his head, "the harder it will be for someone like Claire to detect us right now." He sniffed, rubbing hands over his smooth, bald head. He looked funny with all his hair burned off. "I can do this easily."

I waited and kept an eye on the two guys sauntering near the wall. It didn't take long for whatever Janus did to have an effect. One of them halted in his tracks and then jerked his head around to look at the other. He reached out, pulling a hand off his rifle and gave the guy a quick shove. The recipient of the push staggered back a step, then leaned into returning the shove himself. A loud exclamation reached our ears like a gunshot, and the two guys were all over each other, pushing, then throwing punches, rolling around in the grass like schoolboys, but more vicious.

The smokers near the volleyball court saw it happening and broke formation. They ran for the guys who were fighting, just tossed their cigarettes aside and kicked it into a run. They had a half a football field to go to reach them, but I estimated it wouldn't take long.

"What have we got, Harper?"

"No other patrols on that side of the building," Harper replied. "You have a spotter on the third floor balcony on overwatch. He's looking in the other direction at the moment, though."

"FOX ONE," I muttered, "take the shooter."

I heard the faint noise of a suppressed rifle go off somewhere to my left. It was a bark that echoed only a second, and then I saw movement on a third floor balcony as one of Century's mercs dropped behind the solid balcony rail.

"Tango down," came the reply through my earpiece.

"Game on," I said and leapt into the air. I felt in my mind for Gavrikov and switched off the gravity as I did. My leap became an upward jump of superhuman proportions that carried me skyward three hundred yards. I let myself reach an apex and paused there, for just a second, while I checked my targets.

All five of the mercs in my sight were right there, huddled together, two of them holding back their fellows. The other looked like he was playing mediator, and it was as good a point to interrupt them as I'd get.

I shot down out of the sky at top speed, banking hard and feeling the grass blades run across my face as I almost blew the turn. I made it, though, and spun around to come at them in a blur of speed, inches off the ground.

I hit one of the guys holding back a fighter first, and my kick landed on the back of his knee. He lost his footing in a big way, and my momentum carried me through the next guy, the one he was holding back from fighting. He got his legs kicked out from under him, too.

I was going so fast I wasn't sure if I was even visible to the guys I was attacking; I hoped not, for my sake. I swept past the mediator and swung an arm out to knock him over. I could hear the cartilage in his knee rip as I took him down.

I crashed feet-first into the last two. They were in a similar posture to the first two, with one of them holding the other back from fighting, except this time they were facing me. I went for knees, but by this point I was out of control. I'd already slammed into two guys, but only the first was a well-placed kick. The second was just collateral damage from my impact into the first.

I spun and slammed into the last two, only one foot making contact with one of them, solidly in his femur. It broke, which was something I'd never pulled off before (the femur is a damned strong bone) and he started to scream. I tumbled into him, knocking him and the other guy backward in a jumble from which I was the first to recover. I realized I was lying atop them both and quickly jabbed out with a hand that crushed the windpipe of the guy on top.

He made a choked noise, and then I pushed his head to the side and delivered another blow just like it to the second guy. I knew I'd hit him right when I crushed his throat. There was not much chance of mistaking that sickening sound.

I rolled to the side to disentangle myself from those two and saw the mediator going for the walkie-talkie at his hip. He had gotten to all fours, so I rolled toward him, coming to my knees and planting an elbow right in the back of his neck. It snapped, and he dropped. Three down.

Of the last two, I saw movement, one trying to shove the other off of him. One had managed to get a scream out, and it was loud enough that I was sorry I hadn't cruised into his neck first. I'd never make that mistake again. I sprang up and leapt in a giant, belly-flop style move like something out of pro wrestling and came down on the back of the top guy. I heard his spine snap near the waist, heard him issue a muffled cry of pain.

That was all the time I could spare for him, though, and I threw his body to the side in order to deal with the last of them.

I needn't have bothered.

This guy was already near death, panicked out of his mind. Looking down, I saw the answer in a half-second. When I'd smashed into him, I'd hit him so hard that his tibia and fibula (never can remember which is which) had shredded his calves. That had opened up both arteries in his legs, and he was bleeding to death, flailing around in a hot panic, but his breath was already going shallow as his mind caught up to what his body was telling it and started to put him into shock.

I wasn't much for slow death, so I just reached down and broke his neck in one motion. I felt bad for it in that space of a second.

"Clear," I uttered as I pulled back from the corpse I had just made. I stared down at the man, his eyes glassy, looking into my face.

"No, you're not, Sienna!" Reed's voice came back. "Get the guy with—"

He didn't get a chance to finish his sentence. Another voice broke in, strong, scared, near panicked, and I turned to see the guy whose back I had just broken lying flat on the grass, his walkie-talkie in his hand. "Perimeter breach!" he shouted. "We're—"

I kicked him in the head so hard it killed him, but it was too late. I could hear movement in the distance, the sound of men springing into action. The guard force preparing for our arrival.

And somewhere behind them, I knew, were the remnants of a group of one hundred metahumans who wanted me dead.

Chapter 45

It was a hell of a throne room for not being a throne room. They may have been far from Palatine Hill, but this place was palatial nonetheless, all the glory of a winter or summer palace for the Emperor, all the splendor. Grandiosity was on full display and in full measure.

And even the dramatic fight taking place in the middle of it all could not take away from the glory of it.

"Go!" Janus shouted at Marius, who had heard and was already in motion. It had not been difficult to convince his body to move, averse as he was by instinct to the lightning that was being hurled between the columns at the moment.

They were columns of marble. Just as Marius dodged behind one, it exploded with the force of a blast above his head, showering him with dust and fragments. He ran on, seeking cover behind the next column, only to have it explode above him as well.

Marius hesitated as chunks of marble rained down on him. The fine dust of caused him to cough. It settled in grains in his mouth and he nearly choked on it. His eyes were squinted tight, and a thick white powder hung all around him in the air. *This is not exactly how we planned it.*

They had planned the attack to be a surprise. To be a subtle assault on Jupiter, one in which he would not realize the peril he was in until Marius had him firmly by the hand and Janus had his guards lulled into a sense of absolute security.

That plan had ended before they had even finished walking through the door. It had ended on the tip of the spear that the phalanx of soldiers lying in ambush had applied to Janus's servant Tullius, who had led the way into the room.

And now we fight against innumerable odds, all pointed against us.

Marius ran for the next column, sticking his head out only briefly to catch a glimpse of the center of the room beyond the column he was skirting. There was another series of columns holding up the other side of the room, and both helped support the massive center of the building, which rose up higher than either side. He caught a glimpse of the figure before the throne, but only a glimpse before a shock of blue lightning flew at him and he ducked back behind the ruined marble.

The impact of the bolt roared in his ears and another cloud of dust exploded around him. Marius kept his head down, eyes nearly closed, waiting only a second before jumping out and sprinting to his left. He crouched behind the next column, the blood rushing in his ears helping to lessen the sound of a full-fledged battle raging at the rear of the room.

"You think I am so doddering as to fail to notice treason under my very nose!" Jupiter's deep voice filled the hall. "You think me so decayed that you would try to push me off the throne as though I were already a corpse?"

Marius ran to another column. Two more to go until he was at the far edge of the room, only a simple rush from the throne and the figure in front of it. He cringed, considering his options at that point. *My power takes the better part of a minute to work. His lightning comes in the better part of a second.* He was no mathematics student, but his calculations did not give him hope.

"I think you have lost your mind!" Janus's voice came from the fray at the back of the chamber. "You have killed good people—decent people—whose only crime was to disagree with your selfish whims!"

"You are a fool, Janus," Jupiter said, "and I was a fool to let you and your sister live after destroying your parents. I thought you could fill their roles, see the wisdom and know your own places in our order. But you don't know power when you see it, boy, and you're far too ignorant to be allowed to live now."

Marius ran again, finding himself covered behind the next column. Jupiter was focused on the battle at the back of the room now, and Marius heard the lightning roar in that direction. "You think that you can gather your weakling allies against me? Against *me*?" The rage in the god's voice shook the room. "I, who put asunder Cronus and took his place? I, who united our people in these lands long before you were even thought of? I, who am worshipped, who directs Emperors and tells gods in other lands what to do and when to do it?" Thunder roared once more. Screams followed, and Marius wondered who had succumbed.

"Discordia. Venus. Vulcan. I see you slithering alongside Janus. Diana! Fool, to follow in your brother's wake, to share his idiocy in this challenge!" Jupiter was bellowing now. Peeking briefly out from behind his column, Marius could see him striding about the throne room. "And your little stableboy, who you send at me with nothing more than the strength of a weakling in his hands and naught but the power to fly." Jupiter's voice turned his way. "Fly away, little servant. Or fly to me and I will show you what my dominion of the skies feels like."

Marius held his position, listening, and almost missed the soft crunch of boots just behind him—

Lucretius had him by the throat. He knew the man mainly by reputation and only little experience. Lucretius was bestial, practically feral, his teeth showing. Marius felt his body dragged from behind the column, Lucretius's hand firmly wrapped around his neck as tightly as if a serpent had coiled around it. His feet only brushed the ground and he was pulled, without fight, from his hiding place.

"You send an alliance of sucklings and babes against gods and monsters," Jupiter said. Marius could see his face now as Lucretius pulled him along. It was undignified, certainly. "You know the tale of Lucretius, boy? His sons are the three-headed dog that guarded Hades himself." Jupiter laughed, his back turned to Marius. The pressure, though, around his neck, was incredible. He sensed that he was only a bare moment's thought away from death.

"You are a fool, Jupiter," Janus said from the back of the room. Jupiter now stood in the middle of the chamber, Lucretius just behind him. Marius could barely see Janus and the others, faces barely showing above a pile of rubble that had been carved out of the back wall of the chamber. Black scorch marks darkened the marble walls, and Marius wondered at the force of the lightning that had taken whole blocks out of the palace wall. "You rule over people with power, and you do so by abusing your own to create fear."

"Fear keeps you in your place," Jupiter said without any emotion. "Fear lets you know who is in charge of you. You, better than anyone, should know the value of fear. When your daughter was killed, you showed the humans responsible who they should fear more than anyone. Fear keeps the order. Fear of Rome maintains the Empire. Fear of us keeps the Emperor from straying. And fear of me keeps you fools from exposing yourselves so you don't end up dead like that idiot of a girl of yours."

Janus did not dignify that with an answer, though Marius knew the man must surely be boiling inside. Marius could feel the burn in his neck and knew that it was not from Lucretius's grip on his throat. *Seconds more. Seconds more.*

Lucretius jerked a moment later, his grip slackening. His legs buckled, just slightly, but enough for Marius to get to his feet. He slapped a hand upon Lucretius's mouth and pushed him down. The man's strength was fading with his life, and he made to scream just as Jupiter sent another frenzy of lightning across the chamber. The noise drowned out Lucretius's cry, and Marius stuffed his hand farther down into the beastly man's throat. He felt strong teeth and jaws bite hard against his hand and ignored them.

Yes, take the pain and shut it away, his mother's voice came, intertwined with Ennias's, and the voices of all the others whom he had taken in the last year and made his own. They spoke in a chorus, as he did when he was joined with them. One will, one mind, wedded to his own in an unstoppable force.

He felt Lucretius sucked free from his body and thrown into the depths with the others. He sensed the fear, the abject terror in the man at the separation from his own body.

YOU WILL BE OURS, Marius said, his voice joined with those of the others. YOU WILL BE ONE WITH US.

I will not, Lucretius said. *I will not!*

The screaming lasted only seconds, the howls of an animal as it was picked apart by a pack of wild things. Marius's fury was that of the ten people he carried with him, all their rage and anger and fear and pain collected over their lifetimes and their imprisonment with him, all his to command. He turned it loose upon Lucretius and the man broke in mere seconds.

YOUR POWER IS MINE, Marius said, Lucretius's voice added to his chorus.

My power ... is yours ... came Lucretius's voice for the last time as it dissolved into his own.

There was a flash of light around him as Marius came back to his senses in the throne room. Lucretius's body lay beneath him, one of his hands still anchored on the man's cheek, the other buried to the wrist in his throat. He pulled the hand free from the mouth as Lucretius's eyes stared up at him, empty yet somehow accusing. And Marius stood.

"Your power is mine," he murmured and felt the essence of Lucretius come to the fore with the rest of his subjects. His slaves.

His souls.

He flew at Jupiter, his broad back partially covered by robes. He slammed into it hands first, grabbing hold of him at the neck and smashing his face into the ground. He dimly felt the first shock, but it was weak and Lucretius's power made it hurt not at all after a moment. He felt the flesh pull together where it had burned into his skin as he stared down at the back of Jupiter's white hair as he ground the God of Thunder's face into the floor.

"You have always misjudged weakness and strength," Janus said, and he appeared from behind the pile of rubble. "You have always glazed over courage, over friendship, over the value of care and concern for others. You think decency is base and stupid, gratitude and loyalty the things of animals." He limped across the throne room, and Marius could hear the screams of Jupiter begin in his head.

"You ... cannot ..." Jupiter muttered, his face against the marble floor.

"I remember thinking something similar as you sent your power against the flesh of my parents over and over," Janus said. "How many enemies do you think you have made over the years in just such a manner as that?"

"A ... Alastor ..." Jupiter said weakly. Marius could feel the man's soul, and it was a great, struggling beast. His will was fearsome, larger than any other he had touched in his time.

"He will not come to you," Janus said quietly. He stood only feet away now. "He is with us, you see, and is helping

Ares to maintain control of the Empire as we make this … transition."

"N … Nep …" Jupiter's voice flagged. "Po … seidon …"

"He is gone," Janus said. "On a tour of the Empire you so lovingly control from behind the scenes with his aid. It is a shame that you did not do what he has done; then you might have been indispensable."

"He … ra …" Jupiter said, and Marius felt the last of him begin to slip free of the bonds. There was a stir of electricity that hummed at the god's fingertips as he grunted.

"She has betrayed you," Janus said, and in this Marius heard the cold satisfaction at last. "She knows you for the fool that you are, for the detriment to our continued authority that you are."

"You cannot do this … I am …" Jupiter said, voice cracking, "… the alpha!"

"And we are your omega," Janus said quietly.

With a cry, Marius felt Jupiter's soul slip free of him, screaming into the depths. He felt the power of the man, the sheer weight of his will, and held fast, kept him at a distance. Marius's breathing was intense, heavy, and his head felt light with both the joy of an absorption and the terror of the man he now kept inside.

"Are you all right?" Janus asked, keeping his distance.

"He is dead," Marius said, shaking his head. "But I can feel him. Absorbing him may be a challenge."

"I am certain you are up to it," Janus said, but he said it quickly, and his eyes left Marius as soon as he'd said it. He turned away, sandals making a noise like a scuff upon the cracked marble floor. "My friends … we have work to do."

"You have done it, Janus." This came from Vulcan, his scarred face visible in the knot of people in the rear of the room.

"We have done it, you mean," Janus said, his back to Marius. "We have deposed a madman. We must now secure our empire."

Whose empire? The voice in his head came, in a twisting, nearly whining, chorus. Marius thought he could hear his own voice in there, somewhere.

"The Emperor," came another voice—this one Diana's. "Probus. He feared Jupiter," she said, her long hair unknotted, hanging limply around her shoulders and frizzed as though a stray bolt had hit close to her. "How will we control him now?"

"In much the same way," Janus said. And now he looked to Marius, and smiled. "For while I am certain that Jupiter was wrong about a great many things—rule over us foremost among them—he was right about one thing. Fear … is an excellent motivator."

Marius felt a little shudder as he sat there, and Janus turned away from him again. Then he swept from the room with the others, discussing in rapid exchanges their next movements. It sounded very far away to Marius's ears as he felt the strength of that soul unsubdued suddenly cease its push against him. Jupiter stopped fighting like a wild animal straining against the edges of its pen, and he felt him turn, ever so quietly, and join the wills entwined against him, holding him back.

Whose empire? The tenor of the voice in his head changed just a little, but Marius could still hear his own within it, and it put him at ease.

Chapter 46

Sienna
Now

We hit the lobby with the crash of gunfire all around us, rifles thundering from the FBI Hostage Rescue team snipers hiding in the woods behind us covering both sides and from the mercenaries Century had hired who were returning fire and trying to get in a few shots at us from where they were being systematically chopped down by the FBI's superior sniper ability. It was a free-for-all before we even hit the lobby, and after we burst through the doors, well—

Well, it was like a ballet of frickin' death, that's all.

The lobby was glass on the front and done up in a sweeping lodge style with a ton of rustic décor combined with concrete. It was a natural extension of the architectural scheme we'd seen outside, something somebody in the seventies had thought was a really good idea. LSD was big in the seventies, right?

Now it looked like the northwoods version of the Matrix lobby scene. Bullets were already flying at us as I came in the front door. There were a series of planters leading up to a three-story waterfall that cascaded down behind the registration desk in the middle of the massive lobby.

The glass panes that lined the front of the room shattered within seconds of me leading the way into the building, my team a few dozen steps behind me. I'd meant to draw the mercenaries' fire to me, and wow, boy, did I succeed in a big way.

I rolled behind a concrete planter and heard a hundred rounds lodge in the cover I'd chosen. I'd heard about auditory exclusion, a temporary loss of hearing caused by an excess of adrenaline, but it obviously hadn't kicked in for me. My adrenaline was in overdrive, but I could hear a hell of a lot of gunshots, and they were *loud*.

I edged my gun just slightly around the side of the planter and fired in the direction of the nearest shots. I had no hope of hitting anything, but the gunfire tapered slightly as I did so, which was my main goal. I didn't know how many assault rifle rounds it would take to bust through two sides of a concrete planter and the three feet of dirt in the middle of it, but I was guessing a hundred rounds per second would eventually do the job.

Fortunately, the FBI's Hostage Rescue Team had given me an app for that.

I tossed the flashbangs that had been hanging off my belt and curled into a ball. I heard Reed in my ear as I did it. "Stacked up just outside!" he called.

"Two seconds!" I replied, and there was a blast of light as blinding as Amaterasu even behind the planter and a thunderous noise that sounded like the bass roar of grenades exploding around me.

I heard the chatter of guns firing from where I'd entered the building and saw Reed, Kat and Scott making their way into the building with their guns ablazin'. I knew Zollers, Janus and Foreman would be somewhere outside, coordinating their powers to throw a damper on the area as much as they could.

I came up shooting, pegging three guys in less than three seconds, headshots all. Tangos down and all that jazz. Yippy-ki-yay.

I saw the flare of a gun blind fired from behind the registration desk in the middle of the lobby and realized that all the holdouts had cover by this point, because anyone out in the open when those flashbangs went off had been shredded by Reed and company's entry. Reed was lurking behind a planter a row up from mine, and Scott was next to him. Kat was behind the planter opposite mine on the right side. She was reloading, I saw, and I threaded my way forward along the side of the lobby while firing a couple shots at the front desk. I hoped there was no clerk hiding behind the desk, but there wasn't much I could do about it at this stage if there was.

The steady chatter of an AK-47 answered me, aimed at approximately my last position. It hosed the tree above me with a good ten rounds before it ceased.

"Harper," I said, "call it out."

"You've got three, say again—zero three—tangos behind the planters in front of you. At least two are definitely still in play, and the third is either wounded or playing a real good game of possum. You have three more tangos behind the registration desk along with a possible civilian. Civilian has their head down and is curled up, left hand side. Tangos are on your right."

"And the rest of Century?" I asked as I reloaded, sticking a fresh mag into my Sig.

"Acting cautious. They're all clustered in the labyrinth of hallways behind the lobby, moving real slow."

"Roger that," I said. "First things first, the tangos behind the planters—"

"Got 'em," Kat whispered, then I heard something truly horrific.

The trees in every one of the planters came to life simultaneously, with the sound of branches cracking and whipping through the air. I poked my head up in time to see a man jerked from the ground with a broken branch impaled through his shoulder. He screamed as the tree jerked him to his feet, and I shot him in the head out of mercy as he was ripped in two by the strength of the branch heaving through his chest.

I heard another call from across the lobby and watched a guy get hit by a stray branch like it was clubbing him. It came down on him once and he staggered. It landed on his head the second time and flat-out crushed it like a boot on a grapefruit. He dropped and didn't move, and the slow ooze of red across the floor signaled to me that his resistance was done.

There was the heavy sound of branches whumping against something on the ground from behind the third tree, the one nearest the registration desk, and I cautiously looked out to see it flailing against the ground. There was no noise from behind the planter, and I thought about what Harper had said about the last tango being either dead or playing possum. I figured there was no doubt which it was now.

"Front desk," I muttered. "Three on the right—"

"Got 'em," Scott said, and there was a rumbling from the waterfall above.

I had an inkling what was coming before it happened, but that made it no less spectacular when the stone fixture three stories up burst with a sudden explosion of excess liquid. It came like a flood had just blown over the edge and when it landed, it took on a life of its own. It formed a circular ball of solid water, like an aquarium filling before our eyes, and the cascade of water joining it from above continued to fill it as it held there, without glass to hem it in, only the will of Scott Byerly to keep it in control.

I could see the three mercs trapped inside as the invisible aquarium continued to fill. It seemed to stop and then I saw the men caught within kick and thrash in a frenzy as the water kept pouring in but the space it occupied grew no larger.

It took me until the first man began to bleed into the liquid to realize that Scott was compressing the mercenaries inside the aquatic prison. He wasn't just drowning them—he was crushing them under the weight of all that water in a confined space. It took only another moment before the water just went red, too red to even see anything in, and I started to wonder why he was keeping it in that shape.

Then Century's first metas burst out of the hallway to the right of the registration desk, and he let it all go in that direction.

It blew out in focused pulses no bigger in diameter than my wrist, shooting in streams a foot or two feet in length. It hit the first meta and he lost his head from the force of it. The second guy caught it in the midsection and when the flush cleared, I could see the shirt of the girl behind him through the hole it had made in him as he toppled.

The water drained quickly, Scott directing it into blast after blast at our enemies, sending them scrambling for cover in the hallway. A lot of people were too slow to dodge, and the hall cleared within seconds, leaving a half dozen corpses and a few moaning survivors behind when the water finally finished rushing out.

"Let's go," I called and advanced behind the registration desk. "Harper, status report."

"You've got a damned mess," she said, "that's the status."

"Not quite what I was looking for," I muttered as I sunk behind the desk. There was a bloody mess behind it, whatever Scott had left of the mercs he'd trapped glistening in a puddle on the floor. But there was also a woman, shuddering and breathing heavily, all curled up in a ball. "Miss?" I said, and shook her. "Get up, out of here."

"What?" She looked at me sideways, still in the fetal position. "What?"

"Get up, get out of here," I repeated. "Out the front door, now!"

I must have put enough command in my voice to make her hear it, because she did move, quickly uncurling and standing, her bare legs covered with spots of blood where the skirt she wore hadn't protected her from the mess made by Scott's maneuver. She moved, though, moved like her life depended on it.

"Kat," I said and nodded at her. "Get her out. Harper? The other civilians?"

"Kitchen crew is out," Harper said. "HRT has got all but one of the maids and they're moving now. Probably ten seconds to intercept with the last maid. The package is moving up the driveway—"

"Understood," I said and looked back over the top of the desk at Scott and Reed, who were waiting behind the last of the planters. "Boys, be ready to move."

"Yes, ma'am," Reed said with a tight almost-smile.

"Oh, and Reed?" I said, catching his attention. "Let 'em reap the whirlwind."

"Yes, ma'am," he said again, this time with a grin. He stepped from behind the planter and aimed down the hallway with his hands, thrusting them out from his chest like he was throwing a snake from his upper body. It made a roar as the air around us was sucked into a vortex that rushed down the hallway to the right of the desk. It was loud and looked like a tornado, a wall of grey winds rushing through the confined space. I saw bodies and limbs poke out of the wall of air at various points, and even heard a scream or two over the sound.

"Harper?" I asked.

"Last maid is on the move," she said. "Kitchen staff is clear, HRT is disengaged, moving back to the treeline for rendezvous and extraction. Black Hawks will be landing in zero-three minutes on the south lawn."

"Roger that," I said. "Move out!"

I flung a hand at Reed and Scott and saw them motor, running through the lobby. Just outside I could see a van rolling across the parking lot. I stayed in cover by the registration desk, watching the right-hand hallway as I waited. Scott and Reed dodged out through the broken glass at the front of the lobby as I heard the engine of the van roar just outside.

It crashed through the metal framework that had held the doors just as the last of Reed's tornado was dying down in the hallway. I could see movement down there, motion as I covered with my pistol. I grabbed one of the bullpup rifles from the floor and held it up, looking through broken optics. I frowned and ripped the sights loose and tossed them aside. I was a meta; I didn't need fancy sights.

I glanced back to see the agent shaking his head in the van, which was now parked squarely in the middle of the lobby. "Go!" I shouted to him and saw him nod. He opened the van door and bailed, tearing off out the hole he'd just created in the lobby.

I heard movement behind me and raised the rifle in time to splash a lady who came around a corner. I pegged her right in the brain and she dropped in her tracks. I fired again for good measure, just to discourage anyone from coming from that direction. I didn't need much more time, just enough for the agent to get far enough away that the others could cover him and I could—

I heard the footsteps only a millisecond before I got leveled. The hit to the back of the head was catastrophic, all but scrambling my brain. I brought Wolfe to the front of my consciousness but the next hit was so devastating, landing against the side of my skull, that I forgot everything—that there was a plan, that I was supposed to be doing something, what my name was—everything.

I came to on the floor, staring up at a face that I didn't recognize, but one that was filled with purest fury and a seething rage. Then I saw another, and another, and another. Men, women, creatures I barely recognized as human. My head was swimming, I was dazed beyond belief—but even still, I recognized the danger.

All metas.

The moment of peace lasted only another second, and then they fell upon me in a frenzy of kicks and punches that drove me gladly into the realm of unconsciousness.

Chapter 47

I opened my eyes to find myself facing a room full of people, and I sighed through bruised and battered ribs. "Ugh," I managed to get out. "*You* people." At least I thought it sounded like that. *Wolfe*, I said in my mind, and felt him stir to come forth.

"Us people," Claire said with mild amusement. She was right there, front and center, and I remembered without having to work very hard that I truly despised her. "Us people, who have categorically devastated you."

I felt my swollen lips subside a bit and the pain began to disappear. I pulled Wolfe back from healing me. I needed to be functional, but having them see me go from wounded and beaten to flawless in seconds would probably tip them off that some things were seriously amiss. Then I remembered that Claire had seen me fly, and I realized she probably had at least an inkling of what I was capable of at this point. Clearly not a full understanding, or I'd already be dead.

I could work with that.

"I wouldn't go so far as 'devastated,'" I said, a little cocky, putting a slur into it. "But you certainly did just outnumber me and deliver a beating. Oh, yes, you're all very impressive at a hundred-to-one."

"We don't have a hundred anymore," Claire said, and she sounded snippy. There were a lot of angry faces behind her. "You saw to that."

"Mmmhmmm," I said. I walked back the cockiness a little bit on this one. I could have said so much worse; admire my restraint.

A guy came down into the room, which was a sort of big conference room, like something you'd see in the United Nations if they held UN meetings in a seventies-era resort in the Midwest. He had a couple people following him and wore a battered suit that looked like it had been through at least twelve ringers. He paused just in front of Claire, and she looked at him.

"S—s—stop it," he said. "I don't like when you r—r—read my mind!" he said.

"You must be Griswold," I said, staring him down. He looked up at me in surprise.

"How did you know that?" Claire asked, remarkably composed, though I could tell there were hints of fury peeking through her expression.

"R—r—read her mind," Griswold said, stepping closer to me.

"I can't," Claire said, turning away from me. "Zollers is blocking everything."

"But he's gone," Griswold said, shaking his head, eyes tracing her path as she took a short—and I mean short—walk across the room in front of me. She paced in front of her minions. "The Agency chopper t—took off without her, and with the whole staff—"

"I guess you guys will have to make do without turndown service," I cracked.

Claire looked back at me, and her annoyance turned to a poisonous smile. "Just so you're not left thinking wise-assing us will get you something ... it won't. We disarmed your bomb already." She held her palms up. "Ooooh. Planning to blow us all up?" Her expression went flat. "I believe the kids call that 'epic fail' nowadays."

"That's so yesterday," I shot back, sounding like the teenager I still was. "But I wouldn't expect anything less from you."

"Fine, yesterday, uh huh," she said, taking pains to cover her annoyance. I could see it anyway, just creeping out at the corners of her eyes. "Let me tell you what's today—I don't need you alive for very long."

"Then kill me," I said.

"Not yet." There was a gleam of triumph in the eyes as she said it. "And before you get any ideas about escaping using those Wolfe-powers of yours, be aware that we outnumber you so badly that you'll have your brains dashed out quicker than you can summon the will to stitch your skull back together. And believe me, plenty of us here would be glad to do that."

"So I'm bait?" I asked. I glanced around the room, took the temperature. They were angry. "For what?"

She laughed like I was an idiot. "Sovereign, of course. We just have to wait for him to come save you."

I blinked. "You want to lure him here? Why?" My head swiveled, looking for some explanation in the crowd's faces. There wasn't one, but I caught some self-satisfaction breaking through the fury. "There are easier ways to commit suicide."

"Let's just say we're ready for him," Claire said with a certain amount of satisfaction.

"He's otherwise occupied right now," I said, and tested my bonds. That only took a second, and I was satisfied that strength alone was not going to get me out of this.

"Because he surrendered and you have him bound up in chains?" Claire rolled her eyes. "Please. If he's not already roaring his way here, he'll be along as soon as your crew of merry morons informs your headquarters that your plan went sour. He can't possibly resist the opportunity to ingratiate himself to you by saving you when you're in distress."

I felt my skin crawl at that one, and I'm pretty sure I made a face. "Ugh."

Claire smiled at me. "What's the matter? Still resisting your inevitable fate? You could do worse."

"Yeah, like Weissman," I said, playing a hunch. Her face went dark immediately, fury descending on her as though a curtain were closed over her expression. "Ooh, looks like I hit a soft spot. And this time I don't even have a broken leg to play with—"

She took two steps forward and smacked me one right across the face. I'd be lying if I said it didn't hurt, but I'd been hit worse. I smiled a bloody smile at her and she hit me again, a little harder this time. I stopped the smile because I was just pissed now, and I gave her the full venom of my eyes as I rolled my head back around.

"You can look at me like that all you want," she said, voice low. "You look because you're impotent to act."

"I'm not technically capable of impotence," I said.

"You talk the best game," she said, smarmy and vicious at the same time, "but you are constantly in over your head. You pick fights you can't win, and when luck comes to your rescue, you add a notch to your belt and think you're the best." She snorted. "You're nothing, little girl. Your luck is gone. And your boyfriend—when he comes to rescue you, which should be soon—he's gonna die."

"You call Sovereign my boyfriend again, I'll kill you." I let that loose with all my anger. All of it. People in the front row took a step back and everything. I've got a good resting bitch face, that's no secret. But when I put my game face on, even people who have never met me before apparently take notice.

"You're going to kill me?" Claire said, and shook her head, letting out a little laugh that let her show just how pitiful she thought I was. "Sweetie, you are tied up to the point you can't move. Your friends just ran—just left you behind, and you're surrounded by the most powerful people in the world." She leaned down, just a little, to look me in the eye. "So … why don't you tell me, short of Sovereign coming and trying to save you, little princess—how you're gonna … kill me?" She let that little snorting laugh again. "Poor little girl, all alone." She turned her back on me.

"Hey, Claire," I said, and I could hear my voice change. A thrum of nervousness ran through the crowd. "A girl like me doesn't wait for some boy to come save her. And for the record—I was gonna kill you even if you didn't call Sovereign my boyfriend again. Harper?"

Claire turned slowly to me. "Who the hell is Harper?"

"The chopper has reached minimum safe distance," Harper replied in my ear. "You are good to go."

Claire straightened. "I heard that. Minimum safe distance applies to a bomb, sweetie. We broke your bomb." She smiled, and I knew it was a taunt. "It got vaporized into atoms, just to be sure. Stupid move, and we saw it coming. It's not like you could beat us in a fair fight, yourself, so—" She shrugged. "It was predictable. I can't believe you thought we'd fall for it."

"Oh, but you did," I said, and I giggled. "You did fall for it, you lecturing, bloviating, fatass evil overlord wannabe. You fell for it like it was an all-you-can-eat buffet table wheeled right into the middle of your jerk-off circle." My skin felt hot, and suddenly the chains that had bound me so tight melted away under the heat of flame. "You're a fucking moron, Claire." I reached out and grabbed her by the neck, ripping her off her feet and pulling her over to look me straight in the eyes. "I didn't need to sneak a bomb into the middle of your meeting. Because," I chortled again, looking at the sea of horror in the eyes surrounding me, and my voice dropped low as I whispered to her, looking her in the eyes—

"I *am* the bomb."

I exploded with the force of Aleksandr Gavrikov, and I watched Claire's horrified expression melt as a wave of flame swept off my skin and consumed the world around me.

Chapter 48

I coughed and realized I was naked, lying in a hole in the earth. I reached out and felt the ground around me, smooth as glass under my fingertips. My eyes rolled right, then left, assessing the crater I was in. It was a few feet deep, and a cloud of smoke hung over me, turning the sky a grey darker than any thunder clouds I'd ever seen.

Things had gotten hazy after the explosion, which was not exactly a surprise. "Are you there, Aleksandr?" I asked.

Still here, he came back. *And it was a very fine display of my abilities, I must say.*

"Thank you," I said, coughing. The air hung with an acrid smell. "I think we got 'em."

"You got 'em," came a voice from above me. I looked up to see Sovereign part the clouds as he came through, appearing out of the fog like a ship coming into view on a dark night. He still wore chains around his hands, and his body was shrouded with a little white dust that looked like he'd probably gone through the roof of my quarters in the Agency dorm. "I did a quick sweep once the explosion died down, and it's …" He shook his head. "You killed 'em."

"How far out did the explosion travel?" I asked, staring at him.

He kept his eyes off mine and, indeed, off me altogether. I realized again, rather sharply, that I was naked and scrambled against the glassy ground like I could find some sand to cover up with. That didn't work, though. "Not too far," he said, voice higher than usual as he stared out into the cloud. "A couple miles, maybe more."

"Good," I said, nodding as I struggled to cover myself with just my hands. "Uhm … could you maybe make yourself useful and find me some clothes?" I hated to ask, but I hated to be naked in front of him even more.

"Right. Sure," he said and disappeared into the smoke without another word. He did glance back, though, and I caught him doing it. He looked a little embarrassed before he vanished into the haze.

I sighed and lay back down on the glassy ground. I suspected I could stand and walk, but I'd be exposing my naked ass in order to keep everything else covered and I really didn't feel like I had the body of a swimsuit model, able to pull off a pose like that, so I just stayed hunkered down until he came back a few minutes later.

"Here you go," he said, and tossed a cloth bundle to me before turning away to avert his eyes. "Found it on a clothesline a few miles from here."

"Nice," I said, and got to a crouch. It was a dress, a long one, not low-cut, thankfully, a size or two too large and meant for a woman much taller than me. I still put it on, slipping into it as quickly as I could. I stood, felt it billow in the shoulders and adjusted it as best I could. It still dragged against the glassed crater. "Thank you," I said, a little grudgingly as I stood.

"No problem," he said, and I heard the rattle of his chains as he turned back around. "I, uh … guess you didn't need my help after all."

I kept my eyes off of him as I started to climb my way out of the crater. I didn't want to fly because—well, I was standing on a glassy, reflective surface and I had no underwear on beneath my dress. I'd heard of upskirt videos, and so I kept my legs very, very close together as I took small steps up to the lip of the crater.

The ground was blackened all the way to the tree line. Only hints of the Terramara resort remained, a few walls here and there, the tallest of which reached to five feet, maybe. The forest's edge sported trees that were still burning, any hint of leaves or greenery gone. "Damn," I whispered.

"Really something, isn't it?" Sovereign said, shaking his head. He was hanging in the air just a little above me. "Having the power of flame like that at your fingertips? I've never used mine quite that way, but …" He let out a sharp exhalation. "It's like hell on earth."

Remember.

I stared out on the burnt ground in front of me and remembered I was in a different place, a different time. I stood at the edge of the crater and stared out at the wasteland I'd created beyond.

Sovereign whistled. "Man. As I was flying up here I was thinking how nice it was to be back in the land of ten thousand lakes."

I glanced back at the crater. "Ten thousand and one, next time it rains."

"Hm?" He looked down at me. "Oh, yeah." He shook his head, and something flitted over his expression. "I guess … it's good I didn't have to face them again."

"Because you didn't want to kill them?" I asked, still staring out at the devastation.

"I don't want to kill anyone," he said, and delivered it with enough conviction I almost believed he meant it.

"I know how that feels," I said under my breath.

There was a faint sound of helicopter blades and I looked up. I could see a Black Hawk circling in the distance, coming closer to the scorched field in which I stood. The acrid smell of smoke remained strong even though most of the dark clouds had cleared by now. The trees in the distance burned quietly, and I knew that they'd need a lot of fire departments working in concert to put out the blaze I'd started there.

"You want me to ride with you or just meet you back at the Agency?" he asked me, drifting down to stand next to me on the ground. The chains rattled as he did so, and I noticed that they were broken neatly in the middle.

"Just meet us there," I said.

"Sorry about your roof," he said, and he floated skyward again.

"I don't suppose you have powers to spackle it shut again?" I asked, not even looking at him.

"Sorry," he said with genuine contrition, and then he shot skyward in an arc that carried him back into the sky, over the smoking trees and south. I heard him break the sound barrier as the sonic boom cracked through the air.

The Black Hawk settled onto the flat, empty ground before me and I ran up to the side, sliding in where Reed held the door open for me. His leather jacket whipped under the rotors, and he didn't even bother to hide his concern. "Was that Sovereign?" he shouted over the wash of the blades.

"Yeah," I said as I jumped in, sliding into the seat between him and Scott. Foreman, Janus and Zollers sat across from me, and Kat was on the bench behind me with the two agents. "Harper said all the civilians got out okay?"

"Yeah," Scott said into the headset as I put it on. The roar of the helicopter became duller when I did, and Scott's voice had that electronic radio sound to it. "We dropped our load off in the middle of Gables; the FBI guys did the same and are headed back to Minneapolis." He frowned at me. "What happened to the earpiece?"

"Same thing that happened to my clothes," I said, looking away from him. "It burned in the explosion."

"Nice dress," Scott commented. "I don't think I've seen you in one before. Where'd you get it?"

"Sovereign stole it for me," I said.

"Did you let him go?" Reed asked.

"Told him to meet us back at the Agency," I said, settling into my seat and fumbling to fasten the belts as we lifted into the air.

There was a pause, and Foreman spoke. "And you think he'll just do that?"

"Yes," I said. "Did you call in fire and rescue down there yet?"

Foreman dropped his head and looked at me with a pretty incredulous look. "Yes. Did you not think about discussing it before letting him go?"

"I didn't let him go," I said. "He broke out of the room we were holding him in in order to come rescue me. He said he'd go back, and he will."

"And you believe this *why*?" Reed asked me. I got the feeling he'd been holding it back for a while.

"Because I'm what he wants," I said and glanced out the door to see the black smoke of the fires I'd started as we circled once around the crater that I'd made. I tore my eyes from the scene of the carnage and looked around the helicopter. "And that means he has nowhere else to go."

Chapter 49

Rome
282 A.D.

"There's nowhere else I'd care to be," Marius said to the empty room. He shook as he paced the floor, hands vibrating unconsciously as he struggled to keep them steady. "This is my home now. It has been since—"

"I know this, dear boy," Janus said, "but you have to understand … you make the others nervous."

"Maybe they should be nervous," Marius said, his voice quivering just a little.

Janus sighed and lifted a hand to his head. "Good lad, you have been allowed to absorb a great many souls that have caused us immense trouble." He hesitated. "Far be it from me to suggest that you might have had enough, but—"

"They're scared," Marius said. "They're scared because I have power that they don't. Power they'll never have."

Janus looked at him flatly. "Yes. But these are not people who you want to scare, Marius. Neptune himself has convened councils to discuss—"

"The problem with me," Marius said, spinning on his heel to look away from Janus. He sniffed the air, catching a hint of the fire in the next chamber. "Well? You were there. What have they decided?"

"They have decided nothing," Janus said. "I have argued in your favor, but of late you are more distant and temperamental in your dealings with the others. I cannot read you anymore, Marius, and that is concerning—"

"That's all right," Marius said with cold precision. "I can read everyone else."

Janus clicked his tongue. "So it is true. You have absorbed the powers of a telepath."

Marius spun around to him and gave him a slow smile. "Among others, yes."

Janus appeared to consider things for a moment before speaking. "You should be careful in gathering the sort of power you are. It does not come without some cost."

"Cost?" Marius laughed. "You are a peculiar one to lecture me about costs of power. Was it not you who manipulated me into helping you kill Jupiter?"

"To establish a safer course for our people and a better path for this Empire, yes," Janus said, and he sounded unapologetic. "For—"

"Revenge," Marius cut him off.

Janus did not even blink. "It was a consideration."

Marius nodded once then again. "I can't say I haven't taken a little revenge myself."

Janus hesitated. "I suspected it was you who burned your old village to the ground. The others thought perhaps an earthquake, or an incursion through Gaul." Janus shifted and folded his arms. "Tensions are high right now. There are too many outside considerations with usurpers causing uprisings. Neptune does not want fractiousness. He wants a united front, a safe haven. The Emperor is already nervous enough. Ares—I mean Mars," he said, shaking his head, "is handling more than he can deal with, trying to reach to the edge of the empire to handle this foolish man's requests for territory."

Marius blinked. "Perhaps he should tell them no. Let them fight their own battles for a while."

"They likely could for a time," Janus said, shaking his head. "But we hold this empire together." He clutched a hand tight in front of his face. "They exist because of us. The rule of law, the peace for the citizens, it comes from us. Men cannot handle holding together what gods have made."

"Maybe gods should rule it, then," Marius said, unflinching.

Janus did not blink. "What you suggest runs in the opposite direction of what Neptune is proposing. He wishes us to distance ourselves further, to let ourselves fade into the background of the empire, exercise the power needed to keep it running and no more. Keep the enemies at bay and grow powerful through other means."

Marius stared back at him. "Why would we fear to stand before them and declare ourselves? They fear us. They worship us. We are fit to rule them. Indeed, we are the only ones who are."

Janus looked at him carefully. "That sounds ... much like Jupiter speaking."

Marius turned away. "Jupiter is dead."

"Is he?" Janus asked. "Or is he in there somewhere, in you? Whispering words in your ear about who you are, what you can do? Does he tell you that you can be emperor? Does he define for you what you are capable of, what your ambitions are?" Marius heard Janus's steps just behind him. "Is he telling you to strike me down right now, merely for speaking these words to you?"

Marius whirled and thrust a finger in Janus's face. Janus did not react but to glance at it. "I am the most powerful man in Rome."

"Indeed," Janus said, looking him straight in the eyes. "And who points the finger of the most powerful man in Rome?"

"I do," Marius said, the pride burning in his chest.

"Then why is your finger dancing with lightning?" Janus said and looked down.

Marius stared at his hand, and it shook. Blue electricity crackled over the flesh, and Marius took a step back, staring at it in horror.

"He has been whispering to you all this while," Janus said. "I could tell, before you took steps to block your thoughts from me. I did not wish to say anything because, let us face it—you do not trust me anymore. You think I have used you and cast you aside. I could assure you all day that it was untrue, but it would be pointless. You see now the truth of what inhabits your mind."

Marius fell to the floor, felt the cold smack of the stones against his palm as he hit the ground and began to skitter backwards, as though he could back away from the truth as easily as Janus. "I ... I ..."

"The others would kill you if they knew," Janus said. "I would suggest you not give them opportunity to find out." He turned his back on Marius and started to leave.

"You wanted him in me," Marius said, and his voice cracked. "You put him in my head."

Janus paused, standing in the middle of the room, and then his shoulders slumped slightly. "I did. I thought it was the only way to kill him, and I took it."

"Now you are done with me," Marius said, staring at his hands. "You expect me to—what? Go into exile?"

Janus glanced back. "It is either that, or you will eventually be killed by the others. Perhaps I have used you. Perhaps I have given you more power than I should have. But it is your power now, and your responsibility. You can listen to the voice in your head, and you could force the issue with Neptune. You could become the next Caesar, great and terrible as any who have ever lived. You could take control, kill each of us one by one, assert yourself over the kingdoms of man until you ruled the whole of the earth."

Marius heard him, heard the words he spoke, and a jealous pleasure rushed through him at the thought. "And why would I not?"

Janus held out his hands. "Because then you would be no better than the people who ground you under their feet in your village. Back when they had all the power and you had none."

Marius felt the spear of truth stab into him and he drew a sharp breath. It felt like something had hit him in the chest, and he blinked. The voice that had whispered so long in his thoughts, louder than the other voices in the chorus, it spoke. *You* are *greater. You deserve to*—

"No," Marius whispered. "I am not … one of them. I am not … *like* that."

You could do it more subtly. You could make them suffer, make them pay, make things right—

"No," Marius breathed. "No, not that …"

"You see the truth of it now," Janus said. "You see the truth of the man in your head. He ruled by force. What he could not use to control the empire, he crushed. We expanded in all directions under his rule and direction, but those who opposed all died. In order to do what you wish to do, you would have to be prepared to extend your grasp over the whole of the empire, and direct your military commanders to break them all if they moved out of line so much as an inch." Janus stepped toward him. "Are you ready to slaughter whole villages, whole cities?"

"I am a killer now," Marius whispered.

"Are you a murderer of the innocent?" Janus asked. He did not sound anything other than curious at the answer.

You can do it. One step, one easy step—one death, one man— Neptune, and you can be the head of the council. And then, from there, the Caesar—

"No," Marius whispered and felt all the grand plans he'd imagined in the last year slip from him in an instant. "No. This I will not do."

Janus nodded. "I thought not." With that, he turned and began the slow walk back to the exit of the chamber.

"I will go into exile," Marius said as his mentor—his father—his friend, had nearly walked out on him. "But know this: I want nothing to do with your empire, or with the world of gods, with the affairs of your kind, or with your manipulations of men. I will leave this day and not come back, and if you so much as send a messenger to seek me, I will send him back to you in pieces."

Janus paused then nodded his head once. "So it is, then. Good journey, Marius. I wish you fair travels." He disappeared behind the arch.

Marius felt a hot blush on his cheeks. "And I wish you an empire of ash to sit your ass upon."

Chapter 50

Sienna
Now

"So what are we going to do about Sovereign?" Reed asked, breaking the silence that hung over the conference room.

We were all sitting around. It should have been a victory party, but it wasn't. Too much else on the mind, I guess. Or maybe the fact that our glorious plan had ended with something that looked like a nuclear bomb going off in the northwoods of Minnesota was putting a damper on things. I didn't pay much attention to the news, but I'd seen a few people watching live feeds of footage from Gables, and I knew it was not a pretty bit of optics, as the political class might say.

"I think you're well on record as being in favor of killing him," Scott said.

"It's expedient, if nothing else," Reed said.

"Yes," Scott agreed. "It's certainly not merciful, decent or humane."

"I have a hard time weeping over him given what he's done," Reed said with a shrug. "But it's not my decision."

"He came to help Sienna," Kat said. "Shouldn't that count for something? I mean, he broke out of his non-prison imprisonment and came to save her." She smiled sheepishly.

"It was kind of sweet. And now he's back in chains that don't actually do anything to hold him."

"Yeah, it's really cool how he's willing to just sit there like that," Reed said acidly. "Except we don't know that he actually is. He could be dodging out to Taco Bell for a Loco Taco and hanging out at the local bar, dropping back in whenever he feels like it. Imprisonment for murder shouldn't involve a furlough."

"Agreed," Foreman said. "If he's to be imprisoned, it needs to start happening for real, and now."

"No courts to rule on the matter," Scott said, shaking his head. "No evidence to prove what he did, even though we all know what he did."

"Do we?" Kat asked. "Do we really?"

"I watched him burn Old Man Winter to death," I said, breaking my silence. "Plus those other two Omega stooges."

Kat's eyes seemed to race, like she was trying to craft an excuse. "But, really, is that so bad?"

I didn't blink at her, but only through long practice. "Yes. I know it sounds funny coming from me, but yes, murder is bad."

"Now she comes to this conclusion," Li muttered.

"What should we do, Senator?" Reed asked, turning to look at Foreman. "Or are you still not here?"

"I am most definitely not here for this," Foreman said, shaking his head. "Not for Gables, not for the aftermath, and certainly not if Sovereign loses his head." He frowned, deep furrows appearing in his brow. "What was his name? Before Sovereign?" He directed this to Janus.

"Marius," Janus said, barely looking up. "Though that was so long ago I can barely recall."

"He left Rome because he was mad at you after you guys conspired to kill Zeus, right?" Reed asked.

Janus shifted his gaze to look at my brother. "There was a little more to it than that, but yes."

"What more was there?" Scott asked.

Janus sighed. "When we took over for Zeus—who was by then known as Jupiter—we were faced with an Empire that had already reached a point of disbelief in the gods. The rise of Christianity coupled with events within our hierarchy caused a fall from grace that led to exile from the Empire for us and the fall of said Empire a few centuries later."

"That sounds like the Cliff's Notes version," Reed said, narrowing his eyes. "What aren't you telling us?"

Janus blew air through his lips noiselessly. "Quite a bit, actually, because we are talking about centuries of events, after all. Zeus had pushed the Emperors too far, kept them in too much fear. When Poseidon took up his role, with Hera at his side and the rest of us advising him, he ended up with a string of noncompliant Emperors who culminated in Constantine the Great—so called—defying us entirely and embracing Christianity. That, coupled with the fact that we no longer had the power to defend Rome from usurpers and internal threats caused him to tell us to 'get out' in no uncertain terms. This led us to go underground at Poseidon's behest." He spread his hands. "Does that satisfy you?"

"No," Reed said.

"Why couldn't you defend Rome?" This came from Li. "Strong group of metas like you, it seems like you'd be able to raise enough hell to scare the Visigoths, Vandals and Gauls away."

"How to put this nicely?" Janus said, rhetorically. "We were not fighters by that point. Certainly none of us were willing to go out on the battlefield—"

"And why should you, when it was easier to sit back and pull the strings?" Reed said.

"Exactly," Janus said with a thick layer of resentment. "Can you imagine the effect of seeing a god on the battlefield against you? Then try to imagine the effect of seeing one felled by the enemy. Our presence in armies did almost as much ill as good, and we had long before devised a strategy to protect Rome that did not put any of us in a position to be killed and thus demoralize an army and destroy the power of our mythology." He thumped a palm lightly against the table. "However, once our strategy did fall apart, some of us returned to the battlefield on occasion, never in an obvious way—"

"How did your strategy fail?" Li asked, cutting right to the heart of the matter.

Janus sighed again. "Because Ares—Mars, the God of War—was killed on the frontier while trying to aid the legions in modern-day France. He was our primary defense. Without him to destroy enemy armies before they could pose a threat, our power in the Empire was much reduced."

Reed started to speak. "How did he—"

A loud beeping cut him off, and Foreman froze for a second before reaching into his pocket. He did not even speak before a voice came on the other end and blazed loudly for almost thirty seconds before hanging up without bothering to say goodbye.

Foreman pulled the phone away from his ear and stared at it dully then let it fall to the table where it landed with a clatter that sounded almost explosive in the small conference room.

"What?" Reed asked, looking alarmed, which was probably how we all were looking at the moment.

"Three of the biggest national newspapers are set to blow the whistle on metahumans and the extinction tomorrow morning." Foreman swallowed visibly. "They've got sources in the government, multiple agencies, and probably congressional staffs corroborating. Probably some foreign sources as well. And ..." He paused and shook his head like he could make what he just said disappear. "... Cable news is already running with it, at least the basics." His eyes met mine, and I could read the consternation without even having to try. "The word is out."

Chapter 51

"Do they know about us?" Reed asked, cutting into the silence again.

"I don't know," Foreman said. "Until they hit news stands, it'll be impossible to know unless one of the networks breaks it." His phone buzzed and he stared at the screen for a second before turning it back over again. "All the major networks have broken into afternoon programming to tell the basics of what they know." He let out a painful exhalation. "This is it."

"Do they know about Sienna?" Scott asked. I glanced at him and he gave me a smile of support.

"I don't know for sure," Foreman said. "But almost certainly, yes. If there are leakers in the government, they likely have her entire file. It could have been disseminated to the entire White House Press Corps, for all I know."

"Why?" Reed asked, his voice a low rumble.

"Because of Gables," I said, and every eye in the place turned to me. I spoke calmly and in a low voice. "Because metahuman incidents like what we just did—what *I* just did—need an explanation. Especially with the truth coming out, there have to be some consequences in order to make people feel safe—"

"You're talking about a sacrificial lamb," Reed said. "You're talking about someone who's going to go under the bus for this. For the extinction, for the failures to respond until it was damned near upon us, for everything we've been trying to fight single-handed all this time—"

"They need someone to blame," Kat said, her voice almost a whisper.

"A multiple murderer in charge of the U.S. Government response is a more convenient target than any other," Li said, more neutrally than I would have expected given the circumstances.

"Though one might just question how a multiple murderer got into that position," Reed said acidly to the FBI agent, who shrugged it off. "Maybe blame the government who put her there."

"I put her there," Foreman said softly, "and I'm sure the White House will be more than happy to assign that blame my way."

"What about the pardons you promised?" Scott asked.

Foreman looked unmoved. "Most of you don't need pardons."

Scott shot a look my way, and now he was alarmed as well. "But Sienna does. What about her?"

Foreman leaned a cheek against his hand. "There was an agreement with the White House for that—"

"The same White House that might well be throwing her under the bus very shortly," Reed said, and I could hear the anger rising in his voice.

"The very same," Foreman said, almost in a whisper. "Look, this thing was supposed to stay quiet. Even if it went loud, it was supposed to be covered on our side as a 'terrorist incident,' not as the unveiling of a government conspiracy to keep secret that there was a whole 'nother race of humans with powers beyond our understanding. Terrorists are easily explained." He leaned harder on his hand, covering one eye. "A girl who can fly and explode with the force of a bomb requires something else entirely. And if the truth about her past comes out …" He just stopped speaking, dead in the middle of a sentence, and when he spoke again he sounded like death. "Try and imagine the president explaining his way out of giving her a pardon after the truth about her actions with M-Squad comes out. Think through the political fallout following an admission that Sienna, acting as a government agent, damned near nuked a resort." He fell back in his chair. "Yeah. It's like that."

"You made a deal," Reed said, and I could see his face darken. The winds in the room started to change, like the air conditioner had swept on suddenly. "You made a promise to her—"

"Which I would keep, were it in my power," Foreman said, looking at him limply, like he'd had all the energy drained out of him. "Even knowing the consequences. But unfortunately it is not in my power, nor anywhere near my power, because now the press isn't going to be actively looking the other way anymore. There is no cover for this. There is no hiding, if it all makes its way out. This is the sort of shitstorm that blows even the brick house down, and the only thing the little pigs can do is run and hide."

Run and hide, Little Pigs, Wolfe said, like he couldn't even control himself. *Wolfe will blow your house down*. I felt my face pucker at that one, but I said nothing.

"I'm sorry," Foreman said, looking directly at me. "There's nothing I can do. I wish there was, but there's not."

I didn't say anything, just stared straight ahead.

"What do we do?" Scott asked, and I heard a slight crack in the way he said it.

"If I were you?" Foreman said, and he looked weary down to the bones. "And, I'm gonna guess, I probably will be counted as one of you …" He looked up, and there was nothing but bitterness in the way he said it. "I'd run."

Chapter 52

That broke up the meeting in a hurry, at least in its official capacity. Foreman left, saying nothing except he wanted to be with his family. He gave me one last look of absolute contrition before he closed the door. I tried to convey my sincere regrets, but I doubt he noticed in his haste to leave.

Li jetted to his office, probably not wanting to be involved in anything else that could get him charged as an accessory. As funny as I would have thought it could be to see him turn tail and run, I couldn't blame him a bit. In truth, he'd done everything he could to aid our mission. A few minutes later, I watched him through the window as he crossed the bullpen with a box under his good arm, and I silently wished him well. But, you know, silently, in my own head, not where he might hear it.

Because I suspected that if he came back, it'd be with a warrant to arrest me. He was all about the law, after all.

Ariadne slipped back into the conference room a few minutes later to find us all sitting in silence, staring at the walls and ceiling. I noticed movement in the bullpen as people started to clear out. "I initiated a furlough for all the rest of the workers who haven't taken off," she said. "Since we don't really have anything for them to do here."

"Good call," Reed said. "No point in letting whoever comes here to start arresting people have an easy job of it."

I glanced out the window and caught a glimpse of Harper leaving with her giant suitcase. Rocha walked next to her, gracing her with a smile that didn't look forced. It was an odd spectacle, watching them walk and talk. Like almost everything else in my life, it was me watching from the outside once more.

"Sienna?" Reed asked.

"Hm?" I glanced at my brother.

"We've got some decisions to make," Scott said.

"Did you send security home as well?" I asked.

"Yes," Ariadne said. "Except for a skeleton crew. Didn't see much point in keeping them around since we're not even guarding Sovereign and there's no other source of attack." She paused, and her eyes flitted to me. "Right?"

"They wouldn't even make a dent in Sovereign and they'd die trying," I said. "It was the right call."

"What about all those Century mercs?" Reed asked.

"We're bailing out anyway," Scott said, "so who cares if they burn down the installation of the government that's about to turn on us like we're dogs?" He sounded thoroughly disgusted. "Let them torch the place. Again."

"It is never pleasant when a government turns against you," Janus said, shaking his head. "Having seen this before several times, I would recommend picking a good non-extradition treaty country and offering your services if necessary."

"And now we're fugitives," Scott said, shaking his head. "We just went to the fricking wall to save the world from the greatest threat ever—"

"Not ever," Janus clarified.

"—in modern times," Scott amended.

"Not really," Janus said. "There was—"

"Whatever, it was a big damned threat!" Scott said, smacking the table with his palm. "I didn't see anyone else stepping up to do battle with a hundred of the nastiest metas on the planet, and we got the job done! These guys killed all of Omega, all of Alpha, changed the course of the meta world." He slumped in his chair, rage spent. "If there were bigger threats than this, I don't even want to know about them."

"It is best you don't," Janus agreed, "if you ever wish to sleep at night again."

"He's right, though," Reed said, shaking his head, almost scoffing. "This is a ton of bullshit. We do the work, and now we're going to be the pariahs who get all the blame. 'Oh, what a piece of work is man.' Shakespeare nailed it."

"What are you going to do, Sienna?" Ariadne asked me.

"I've still got Sovereign to deal with," I said.

"Oh, screw this," Reed said to me. "Let's just go. Pick a place, somewhere without an extradition treaty, like Janus said, and let's just run for it."

"Preferably somewhere with a beach," Scott said.

"I know several governments around the world who would gladly make accommodations for metas of our power," Janus said to me, and it held the air of an invitation.

"I'll think about it," I said quietly.

"You cannot be serious," Reed said, looking at me in disbelief. "Sienna, you do not deserve what's about to happen to you—"

"Deserve?" There was some bitterness in my voice. "I hear a lot of talk about people 'deserving' this or that, or not deserving some dire fate that befalls them." I let out a scoffing noise. "Well, so what? Does the cute, fluffy bunny deserve to live?" I smacked my hand against the table, causing all of them to jump. "It doesn't matter, because when the hawk swoops down, he becomes dinner. So tell me, please, what I deserve." I leaned back in my chair and straightened the dress I still wore.

There was a moment's silence and then Reed spoke. "You saw that YouTube video of the bunny getting snuffed after that family released it, huh?"

I stared back at him. "It hurt my soul, I'll admit. But it's a good lesson. 'Deserve' is irrelevant when we're talking about what happens to us." I let out my breath slowly. "But I think there's a reasonable debate that could be had over whether I deserve punishment for all the people I've killed."

Reed looked like he'd been hit in the face. "No. No. You don't."

"Reed," I said. "It's okay."

"Sienna ..." Scott said warningly and then stopped.

"I've got Sovereign to attend to," I said and stood up. I pushed my chair back as I did. "You all should get out of here. I hope you all saved your money over the years, because it's looking like a Rainy Day Fund could come in really handy about now."

"I'm not leaving without you," Reed said, and he stood too.

"There's nothing left for you to do but go to jail," I said gently. I turned to Scott. "You, too."

"Maybe we should all go together," Scott said, and he stood as well. "Make a stand. Tell our story."

"One voice or seven is not going to make a difference." I shook my head. "I think you all know that. And with the exception of Kat, us going to prison together wouldn't do anything."

Kat frowned, her pretty face crumpling. "Why would me going to jail with you make a difference?"

I stared back at her. "Because you'd be my bitch," I said with a smirk. I saw her eyes widen and hastened to add, "Kidding, kidding." I looked around the table and my eyes settled on Zollers. "There's only one duty left to fulfill. I'm going to go to Sovereign and figure out what the next step is. The rest of you need to get scarce." I lowered my voice. "If any of you end up taking a fall for this after I dragged you in, well ..." I swallowed. "... I don't need any more guilt on my conscience, okay? Leave. For me."

In the empty silence of the conference room, Kat was the first to move. She came over to me and brushed my shoulder. "You're always so brave, Sienna. No one else could have done this." She pulled me in for a hug and I let her. She smelled faintly sweet, and I started to say something about how I wished all along I could have been more like her, but I stopped myself.

She would never have believed it coming from me.

Janus was next. "If you change your mind," he said. He kept his distance but offered his hand. I shook it quickly. "Please, change your mind."

"I can't," I said, and I smiled faintly. "One last duty to attend to."

He nodded, paused, and then leaned toward me. "What are you going to do to Sov … Marius?"

"I don't know yet," I said. "Whatever I have to in order to make sure the world is safe."

Janus looked faintly stricken. "I feel responsible at least in part for this, and I have tried to make amends all along. I apologize for not doing more to aid you in your fight."

"You did all you could, didn't you?" I asked.

He looked down. "I could have told you things sooner. Things I was forbidden to mention by others. Things I should have let go of long before I did—"

"It's all right," I said and made a faint gesture with my hand. "I absolve you."

He stared at me, and his eyes were full. "You truly were the bravest. After Adelaide …" He stopped. "I never wanted any of these things to happen because you … and she before you … you reminded me so much of my own—" He stopped abruptly then pulled me in for a hug that nearly strained my ribs. When he broke from it a moment later, he could not meet my gaze. "Fare well, Sienna Nealon." He left with Kat on his arm.

"This is not goodbye," Quinton Zollers said, making his way over to me, "this is merely 'til we meet again, as surely we shall."

"Don't get elaborate with me now, Doc," I said. "I've got a job to do."

"And you'll do it well, whatever you decide it is," Zollers said. "Be assured that whatever happens, I will always support you."

"I know," I said, nodding and drew him in for a hug as well. His arms were warm and heavy, wrapped around me. I felt a glistening in my eyes and held it back. "Be careful."

He pulled back from me. "You know I will." With a last smile, he too headed for the door, leaving me alone with Scott, Reed and Ariadne.

Ariadne looked at us, hesitated, and then shuffled forward. "I guess I'm next, then."

"I hope you're going to Bora Bora," I said, staring her down.

"Or somewhere," she agreed. "I don't really fancy the thought of being your bitch in jail, assuming they even housed you with the normal inmates."

"Fair enough." I hesitated. "I know I've said it before, but—"

"I know," she said, dismissing me. She hugged me lightly. "I know." She pulled back and I saw in her eyes that she meant it, but there was still pain there, though not as fresh as it once was. "Safe journey, Sienna." She paused at the door and drew back. "You've come a long way from the girl I first met in the Directorate interrogation room."

I stared at the four walls of the conference room around me. "Not so far some days, I think. Pretty soon I suppose I'll be just as confined as I was then."

"You're still different," Ariadne said. "The environs may not be all that different, but you're worlds apart from who you used to be. Nothing can take that away." She said it, and she was gone. I watched her red hair retreat slowly outside the window.

"Reed—" I started to say, turning back. I ran into some resistance when he enfolded me in a hug that lifted me off the ground. I felt it, which is to say he was really damned strong.

"You don't have to do this, dammit," Reed said, and he set me down. "We go in there, we get Sovereign to turn around, we put a bullet in his head, boom. Job done. Then we exit, stage right, and head for wherever Janus calls rendezvous."

"I don't think it'd be quite that simple," I said. "Assuming he did voluntarily turn around, which is kind of unlikely."

"You walk in naked, get him to face away from the door, I follow in and boom, done," Reed said.

"I don't like this plan," Scott offered. "Except for the naked part."

"No," I said gently. "No to the naked part, no to the idea of shooting him in the back of the head." I was a little more forceful on one of those parts than the other.

"What are you going to do, Sienna?" Scott asked. "If you're not going to kill him?"

"Maybe I'll just guard him until the feds come," I said. "Maybe we'll have a conversation. Maybe I'll turn him loose and run to catch up with you guys." I felt my face harden. "Or maybe I will kill him and then come join you."

"I'm all in favor of killing him," Reed said, "but I'm not a huge fan of sending you in there alone."

"I'm the only one that can face him," I said.

"No," Scott agreed, "you shouldn't be alone in this."

"Get past your egos, boys," I said. "As much as I love you both, when it comes to a dance between me and Sovereign, you're hostages or splatters and that's it. This is my job, the one I signed on for, and I'm going to do it myself." I looked at each of them in turn. "I won't have you in the way, because if you hamper me and get yourselves killed in the process, even if I beat him, it would kill me inside." I made them feel it, both of them, with a hard-edged look that made them each break eye contact in turn. "Do you want to put that on me?"

"No," Reed said first.

"No," Scott said a moment later.

"Then this is where we part," I said, and opened my arms. They both hugged me, tightly and as long as they could get away with it. When I pulled away, I could sense Scott wanting to stay a moment longer. I shook my head at him. "I'll see you again. Or you'll see me at least, I think."

"Don't get yourself killed, Sienna," Reed said. "If he's willing to lay down the sword, let him do it. Just be done. You don't have to do this anymore."

"I never did," I said. "That's what makes me … me." I smiled, but it was totally fake and they both knew it. "Take care of yourselves."

Reed gave me a cursory salute and left before I could see him tearing up. Scott waited just a moment more, like he was going to say just one more thing, but I shook my head and he ducked out. I watched the two of them leave and knew that once again I was all alone.

Chapter 53

Once upon a time, Wolfe had held the city of Minneapolis hostage for my surrender. I'd gone out and faced him, knowing I would suffer and be tortured and die, because I couldn't bear the thought of anyone else dying in my place.

I don't know exactly what it was about walking down the empty corridor of the dormitory that reminded me of that moment, but the feelings came flooding back to me as I went down the hall toward my room.

The campus was empty. I'd seen to that. I could feel it in the echoes of the footsteps I was taking toward my door. The smell of drywall dust was in the air, a smell that reminded me of new construction and new destruction at the same time. I saw the dust drifting in the sunbeams, lazily falling out of the air. It had probably been prompted by Sovereign's exit to come to Terramara earlier, though this particular building had never really lost its new construction smell for me.

I thought about knocking, but it was my room so I just went in. The biometrics that had once secured the door were offline, another pointless precaution to keep Sovereign from trying to mind-control someone who could access them. He was the least kept prisoner ever, I figured, and I suspected he knew it.

"Hey," he said, rising to greet me as I came in. His dark eyes looked worried. "Are you okay?"

"As much as I can be," I said. "Why?"

"Well, I picked up on some things—"

"You sensed a great disturbance in the force, huh?" I sat down on the bed and faced toward the seat he'd been occupying only a moment before. He slowly lowered himself back into it, the remainder of the chains clanking as he did so. "Here, let's get rid of these." I gestured for him to come to me, and he did.

"Why now?" he asked as I unlocked the cuffs around his ankles. They were all broken anyway, and his limbs were able to move freely.

"What's the point?" I asked. "You're here of your own free will."

"I'm supposed to be detained by you, remember?" He smiled, and it was full of irony as per usual. "I'm your big career-making capture."

"I don't have a career," I said with a shrug. "The press has figured out about metahumans and the government is leaking like a sieve. All these years of closely holding the secret and now it's busted loose in less time than it takes Shia La-whatshisname to unspool."

He stared at me, and it felt like dawning comprehension came over him all at once. "You think you're about to take the blame for … what? The explosion up north?" I nodded. "The extinction? Century?"

"Everything," I said. "I figure I'll catch everything that needs to be caught."

He folded his hands in his lap, and I couldn't read his expression for a moment. "They're going to turn on you."

I shrugged again. It was my expression of choice for the current state of events. "So it would seem."

He looked deeply contemplative for a moment. "I wish I could say I didn't see this coming …"

"Oh, please," I said. "You didn't see this coming." I waved at him. "It's obvious on your face."

He frowned. "I … I think I've deceived a person or two in my time."

"You haven't needed to deceive anyone," I said, dismissing him. "And why would you? Even when you were pretending to be Joshua Harding, you were practically begging for me to realize that there was more to you than I was seeing on the surface."

I saw a gleam in his eye. "Maybe I just wanted *you* to realize there was more to me. Not everybody."

"Still trying to impress me, huh?" I said, and it came out wary.

"Trying," he said. "I don't know how well it's working, but I'm trying. Surrendering myself, aiding you in taking down Century even though you know I believed in the idea of what a better world could bring to us—" I rolled my eyes, just a little, before I could stop myself. "All right, well, you know, maybe we should just avoid that topic of conversation for a millennium or two."

I put a hand over my face. "Won't that be around the time you reach the end of your lifespan?"

"Could be," he said. "Time starts to lose meaning for you after a while. We live a long time, our kind. Incubi and succubi have that going for them. Of course the downside is that even our own people hate us for our powers. I mean, metahuman vampirism isn't as sexy as the movies make it look—"

"You're rambling," I said, and pulled the hand down from my eyes.

"I'm rambling," he agreed, and I watched him rest both hands on his knees. "So … the campus is feeling pretty empty."

"It should be totally empty."

His eyes shifted left then up. "It is. You sent them all away."

"Yep."

"Alone at last." He stared at me. "So … are you planning to shoot me?"

I stared back at him. "Not right now."

He cracked a smile. "It's a start. I'll take it."

I shrugged. "Would you even hold still if I told you I was going to shoot you?"

I could see the tension on his face in the form of his jaw halting partway open. He met my eyes and I could see the surrender. "Well, since you just told me I'm a horrible liar—"

"You proved it a second ago, incidentally, when you started to answer and froze up."

"—no, I wouldn't hold still and let you kill me." He gave me a light shrug of his own. "I'll submit to punishment for what I've done, but I'm not likely to sit still for the death penalty."

"Well, then there we are," I said. "I couldn't shoot you if I wanted to. And I think we've already established it wouldn't do any good anyway." I glanced down. I was down to one pistol now anyhow, thanks to having to grab something in a hurry from the armory to replace the weapons I'd lost in the explosion.

"So why are you here?" he asked. "Now that everyone else is gone?"

"Because I have to deal with you," I said.

"Even your friends left?"

"I sent them away," I said. "And let's get back to talking about you."

"You want to talk about me?" He stared at me. "Why?"

"Because I'm secretly in love with you."

He blinked in surprise. "Really?"

"No, not really," I said and gave him a frown. "It's because you've been a huge pain in my ass and the focal point for all my problems for the last year and a half, even when I didn't know it. Wolfe and all the other Omega stooges came at me because they needed a succubus to try and bribe you with. Century came at me because you had

Weissman steering them toward me. Winter turned on me because he was petrified you were going to kill him."

"Which I did."

"No points from me," I said. "Indirectly, you're the reason I had to leave my house for the first time a year and a half ago."

He nodded. "I know."

"How?" I asked. "Did you read someone's mind?"

"No, I was there," he said, never looking away from my eyes. If you've ever seen creepy stalker eyes, that was the vibe I was getting right then. "I was there in the parking lot of the supermarket when Wolfe grabbed you. Weissman and I jumped out to help. He touched my skin—"

"And you partially drained him," I said and felt my stomach turn in disgust that I hoped was well hidden. "I should have known that a dart wouldn't do squat to him." I pictured the first time I'd seen Sovereign as Joshua Harding. "No wonder you looked so familiar."

"I've been watching out for you since the beginning," he said, leaning toward me. The stalker eyes were just a little self-aware, just a little more cunning than I would have hoped for. "I've done everything I could to try and organize things right, but I've made serious mistakes even so. Siding with Weissman was disastrous. Going with his plan was horrible. Reprehensible. I wanted the world to be a better, brighter place, somewhere that someone like you didn't get abused by the people who were supposed to protect you." He paused. "See, I know how it feels when a parent torments you. How it is when the person who is supposed to love and care for you turns on you, the harm it can do—"

"Yeah, I heard about your mom in your head," I said, cutting him off. I was keeping myself as cold and aloof as I could manage. And I could manage a lot.

"She couldn't hurt me physically," he said, never looking away from me, "but she did everything she could to break me mentally."

I looked at him without looking him in the eyes. It's not like I was afraid I'd fall into him or something, metaphorically speaking. I just didn't want to look him in the eye. "I can't imagine what that would be like."

"Probably like having Wolfe in your head," he said with some humor. "Maybe a touch less horrific." He paused. "Except in the teenage years. That was awkward."

I couldn't help but give him the disgusted look for the overshare. I tried to rein it in, but there are limits to how much yuck I could take. "Ugh," I said.

"I'm sorry," he said and dropped from the chair to his knees in front of me. I looked up at him and must have had another WTF look on my face, because he held out both hands. "Relax, I'm not about to propose marriage or anything."

"Good, because the answer would be 'no' followed by a punch to the face for you." That came out reflexively.

"I know you don't know me," he said. "And … if I'm right … you probably still don't want to know me. But I'm also guessing you see the weight of what's chasing you right now and you're more than a little afraid."

I stared back at him, not saying anything.

"That's okay," he said. "I'd be scared, too. You poured your life into stopping me, into stopping all the bad guys that crossed your path, and you've done a damned fine job of it. I mean, you killed the top one hundred strongest metas still alive. That's … that's pretty big. And you did it in service of a government that's … uh … well, they're turning on you. No easy way to say it."

I kept looking at him, waiting to see if he'd get to the point.

"I don't think you want to suffer for your crimes," he said flatly. "Do you?"

"What I want doesn't matter," I said. My voice sounded weak to my ears, filled with the tiredness that had settled in on me in the last hour or so. Maybe it even went back further than that, to the explosion. I felt it, though, and a kind of weariness that reminded me of what I'd heard about runners in mile twenty of a marathon—the mile where most of them quit because all the hope was gone.

"You don't want to suffer for this," he said, voice tinged with sorrow. "Your friends are leaving, getting away because you wanted them to. You wanted them to be safe, to not suffer like this. Why didn't you go with them?"

"Because," I said, almost whispering, "I have to deal with you."

There was a flicker of emotion behind his eyes. "Fair enough. You have to deal with me." He spread his arms. "Here I am. I am your prisoner. But do you really think they'll let you watch over me if you're in jail?"

I shook my head slowly. The logic was obvious in that one.

"Sienna," he said quietly. "They wouldn't be able to stop me. Only *you* can stop me. I won't stand still for them. I will for you, because I care about you, because I want to be able to spend the time with you that it takes for you to see who I am. I won't do that for anybody else, and if they take you away, I will not be a prisoner anymore." Each word came flatly, and there was a menace hanging with them. "I will not submit myself to any man or government. That's not who I am. I surrendered to you because I trust you."

"I can't let you hurt anyone else," I said and lowered my head into my hands.

"Then I have a perfect solution for you," he said, and his voice was strong, commanding. "Your friends have already left. Why don't you come away with me? We can go somewhere safe, somewhere like they did—and you can keep an eye on me for the rest of my life if you want, as my jailer—and you'll never have to worry about me hurting anyone else again."

Chapter 54

The car rattled along, tires slipping on the turns as they drove away from the supermarket. Marius—though he hadn't been called that in so many years he barely thought of himself in that way—could still feel the ice sliding down the collar of his shirt from where Wolfe had manhandled him.

"Urk," Weissman said in some sort of complaint from the driver's seat, "I haven't been hit like that since grade school."

Marius cocked an eyebrow at him. "Someone as strong as Wolfe beat the holy hell out of you in grade school?"

Weissman flushed, his skin going nearly purple under his greasy bangs. "No, I just meant that I hadn't gotten my ass kicked like that in a long time."

Marius stared Weissman, who had turned back to focus on the road ahead. It was coated intermittently with ice, heavy snow piled high on the median and both sides. A thick layer of grey clouds lay overhead, something he knew not unusual here in the Midwest. *I bet she's never seen the sun*, he thought to himself.

SHE IS A CHILD, came the voice from within, a flexing, moving thing in his head. It had so many voices now, and he could barely hear his own among them any longer.

But Mother's was still in there.

He looked over at Weissman once more and called forth the power of the telepath he'd absorbed so long ago. He tunneled into Weissman's mind without effort, tasting the fresh stock of pain and horror there. He found a memory with little effort, a juicy one, of a child in grade school taking painful hits to the face, the chest. Blood ran down his face and coated the inside of his mouth, and the screaming that filled his ears was his own. One word stood out from it all, one word repeated over and over—

Daddy.

Marius shook the horror from his mind, wanting to spit it out as though it were something foul he'd taken a bite of. "That explains a lot," he muttered.

"What's that?" Weissman asked.

"Nothing," Marius said, and looked back out the window. "The girl—"

"I've got a guy already in at the Directorate," Weissman said. "He was one of the first I put in place. Him and a few others with the big powers. Eyes on the big meta farms in China and India—they need to be our first targets. Anyway, this guy can keep an eye on the girl for you." Weissman spoke in a staccato rhythm, his excitement inflecting his tone.

"All right." Marius frowned. "Her mother was stubborn. We may need to play some games with her if we're going to pull this off."

"What kind of games?" Weissman asked.

"Manipulation," Marius said casually. "I can't be the bad guy to her. She's young, probably prone to fits of idealism. I don't want to be the villain. I have to be the natural choice, the solution to her problems and not the scary guy who's destroying the whole world." He paused "Unless she's so cut up inside she's into that, in which case I'll swoop in as soon as possible."

Weissman shrugged. "Women want power. You get enough of it, she'll come around."

"Maybe," Marius said. "But in any case, for our purposes, in this endeavor, you'll be the stick and I'll be the carrot. If I have to deal with someone, they need to die."

"I have no problems being the enforcer," Weissman said, and took his hands off the steering wheel to crack his knuckles. He smiled. "It's gonna work."

Marius shook his head. "This plan of yours ..."

"I'm telling you, it's brilliant," Weissman said. "And its success is its simplicity. We just have to eliminate the threats, right? The metas, the armies? Once we break their will, we're in charge, and with your powers, we just ... hold back the tide. Make it obvious that certain things are not acceptable, that this plague of people being complete and total shits to each other is going to end."

Marius stared at him. "What you're outlining is impossible in conventional terms."

Weissman shook his head. "Not with a meta army."

Marius put his head back against the headrest. "Yes, even with a meta army it's still impossible."

Weissman broke into a grin that did not look pleasant at all. "I found a Hades."

Marius felt a mild surprise run through him. "Did you? That's interesting. That line was supposed to be wiped out." *Or at least that's what Janus told me, the liar.* "Still," he said, carefully turning his expression back to neutral, "that's not going to be enough. A Hades can kill a lot of people, but we're talking about a need for a two-stage plan here."

"Oh?" Weissman sounded more than a little snotty as he said it. "How would you do it, then?" A challenge.

Marius thought about it for only a second before answering. "First, you kill the metas. Quietly, behind the scenes. You kill them first because no one is going to notice or care that they're gone, and once they are, you can't exactly resurrect them to fight for you. Second, you kill the armies of the world, the police—anyone who would raise a weapon to do harm to us."

Weissman's eyes were large, hiding behind those greasy bangs. "That was a fast answer. But I'm detecting a mighty big flaw in your plan."

"Oh?" Marius waited for it. "What's that?"

"Uh, namely that we don't have a way to wipe out every single army and violent person in the world." There was a snippy self-satisfaction in the way Weissman said it.

It was Marius's turn to smile. "Actually, I do."

Weissman's eyes narrowed in suspicion. "Oh, you just do? Just like that? A simple method by which to snap your fingers and BAM! There goes all the opposition in the world." He leaned slightly. "If you have this, why haven't you used it until now?"

"I've thought about it," Marius said, and he drummed his fingers along the armrest built into the door, pleather thumping with each touch of his fingertips. "In truth, I've thought about it every day for the last two thousand years." He sighed. "But I never had a coherent reason to until now. No plan. And, as you know, I've just been content to stay the hell away from humanity as a whole and run my own life apart from them." He pictured her again, the girl he'd just seen. *Sienna Nealon.* "Now you've given me a reason."

"All right," Weissman said grudgingly. "So what's this way of destroying all opposition you've got? Does it have a name?"

"It does indeed," Marius said. And he felt something shift inside him, a voice in the throng in his brain. *I am ready to assist you,* it said, only faintly resembling the fearsome man he had met on the hilltop outside Rome all those years ago. "I think you would know him as … Ares."

Chapter 55

Sienna
Now

I stared at Sovereign and he stared back at me. He had warm eyes, somewhere under the crazy stalker ones. Or at least he was trying to present that aura. I could still taste the drywall dust floating in the air, and though the sun had started to sink lower in the sky, light shone through the cracks between the mechanical armored shutters. He waited for my answer and I could see the hope on his face.

And then I crushed it.

"Just exactly how stupid do you think I am?" I asked.

"Wh–what do you mean?" His whole demeanor changed, caught completely off guard.

I put aside the weariness I was feeling, dragging Wolfe to the forefront. A predator urge shot through me, along with adrenaline. "You killed and absorbed Ares back in Gaul."

"Wha …" He shook his head, shut his eyes for a second and they shot back open wider than ever. "What does … I don't know what you mean—"

"You are a terrible liar," I said, shaking my head. "Thanks for confirming it." He looked at me dead on. "I suspected it," I said, "after Janus mentioned how he died all mysteriously, knowing that the threat we were waiting to get

289

hit with was a long-hidden Ares type. But I didn't know until you answered it for me just now."

"Ohhh," he said, and he looked first annoyed then resigned. He knew he'd been had. "Come with me."

"I think you know I'm not going away with you—"

"Not away," he said, and stood up, taking a couple steps back. "Just a little ways. Back. Back to the beginning." He flew up, out through the hole in the roof.

And me? I was after him in a heartbeat.

I did have that final duty, after all.

He was already close to sonic speed when I cleared the hole in the roof. I angled after him and took off, racing to catch up. He poured on the speed once he knew I was following him, and I heard him break the sound barrier. I followed, feeling the cold air race over my body, causing the dress I was wearing to flutter in annoying ways. This is why I don't wear dresses. Well, it's one of the reasons, anyway.

We shot over the 494 loop. Houses passed in a blur underneath me. He slowed and started to descend moments later. He clearly wasn't hotdogging it, so I followed slow, making sure he wasn't setting a trap for me.

He wasn't.

I recognized the street when he came down. The trees lined either side, the late summer heat shining on us from above. I was about a hundred yards behind him as he set down under one of the giant maples that shrouded the house in front of us. He disappeared under the cover of it and I took my time coming down, finally landing in the middle of the street. I had to use my hands to keep my dress from billowing up like a parachute as I descended. What a pain in the ass.

I saw him waiting at the front door, and he cracked the knob and stopped there. "Like I said, back to the beginning." And then he disappeared inside.

Great. I stared at the house, low annoyance thrumming through me.

It was *my* house.

I crossed the yard, halting by the front door to peek in. "I'm not waiting in ambush," his voice came from somewhere deeper inside. "I'll be in the basement if you want to change first."

I couldn't argue with that idea.

I slipped inside and found he wasn't visible at all. I walked through the living room and stopped by the glass coffee table. "Where are you?" I called, cautious. The place smelled like it always had, minus the aroma of bad cooking that I was pretty sure hadn't been here before mom and I moved in.

"I told you, in the basement," his voice came back, and I could tell he was exactly where he'd said he was. I took a breath and headed toward my room, shutting the door behind me.

I dressed quickly, pulling on jeans and a t-shirt and grabbing a spare holster out of my closet to change over to. I'd been wearing an ankle holster before and, with the length of the dress I was wearing, could just about get away with it. The gun didn't quite fit, being a little smaller than one you'd normally wear at the hip, but I wasn't in a mood to be picky.

I exited my room, thinking briefly back to the day I'd left it, and kept going out the front door. It hadn't been that long ago, really, but it felt like forever.

I walked toward the basement, remembering a very different day. Of all the times I'd had to fear the basement, the one I would always remember most was the day I faced Wolfe down there, sure that it was going to be the end of me.

Something about that memory gave me a spark of confidence. Because that day had not been the end of me.

It had been the end of Wolfe.

Not the end, Little Doll.

"You're non-corporeal now, so it was kind of an end."

"Did you say something?" Sovereign's voice came from behind the door to the basement stairs.

291

"Not to you," I replied as I opened the door.

Each step caused a clumping noise on the wooden stairs. I wore heavy-tread boots, laced tightly because the steel toe did wonders for the damage of my kicks. Aesthetically, they were a nightmare, and I'd be the first to admit that. But aesthetics were never my primary concern.

Sovereign was waiting, and he watched me as I took the turn at the L of the stairs. I paused on the wooden landing and looked at him, lurking in the dark close to what had once been the bane of my existence.

The box.

It was metal, stood about six feet tall, and looked like nothing so much as an overlarge gravestone hiding in the shadows behind Sovereign. He gestured to it in a very Vanna-White-esque way, like it was something I'd never seen before.

"Are you going to monologue now?" I asked, leaving a hand resting on the wooden rail next to me. "Because if so, I can come back later."

"Come on," he said, inviting me down into my own basement. "You've figured it out, and credit where it's due— I thought I had outwitted you on the Ares thing, but hey, it's not so bad."

"You're planning to destroy every soldier in the whole world, every police officer," I said and took my hand off the railing to fold my arms in front of me. "It's pretty bad."

Any amusement in his expression vanished. "Well, plans can change."

I let out a fake laugh that actually made him take a step back. "You're still a terrible liar. You've been running a scam on me all along. There wasn't an inch of daylight between you and Weissman at any point after Andromeda."

His mouth warped and his eye twitched. "What gave it away?"

"The plane he put me on," I said. "The flight plan said it was bound for Tulsa."

He shook his head like it didn't matter, but I could see the lie written on his face. "So?"

"So you were going to have him put me in storage," I said. "In a stasis unit."

His lips pursed with fury. "Maybe that was Weissman's plan, but—"

I drove a fist through the railing and splinters exploded from it. Sovereign took an abrupt step back. "No more lies," I said.

"Okay. Fine," he said. The shock in his voice had been replaced with a menace I doubt he even realized was there. "I just wanted you to see the real me."

"I've seen the real you," I said. "I've probably seen more of the real you than you have."

"You don't know me," he said quickly, with a flare of indignation.

"I know what you've done," I said. "What you planned to do."

"No, you don't know, you don't know *anything*." He shook his head and now he just looked furious and disgusted. "I can't believe you figured—" He let out a grunt that sounded primordial. "I was just trying to show you the way. We were fixing the world. Imagine a world without violence. Without cruelty. Without people trying to hurt and kill each other. A place where—"

"Where if you step out of line, the power of a vengeful god descends upon you, prepared to smite you for your wrongs," I said. "That's what you were planning to be: the hammer of righteousness."

"I was—I *am* going to be the one who makes sure that if someone steps too far over the line, they get what's coming to them." He was breathing a little harder now, staring me down. "What if someone had done that for you when your mother was sticking you in here?" He flung a hand out to indicate the box. "What if you had been raised in a world where the threat of violence didn't hang over you?"

"Except the violence you would do if I stepped out of line," I said. "You've got aspirations to be a petty tyrant. To run an Empire like Janus and the others did. And you'll rule from on high, making sure the peasants and slaves don't step out of line."

"That's not how it would be," he said, but he sounded like he was becoming more progressively unhinged. "I want to help people—"

"Provided they've survived your genocide and are appropriately loyal to your new regime."

"It's not like that!" he shouted, crossing into maniac territory. I could tell I'd succeeded in getting not only his goat but his whole herd. He'd been got. "I wanted to make it a better world! Free from war, crime, poverty—"

"Free from humans making choices," I said. "A utopia ruled by the iron fist of—"

"If you say 'a god' again, so help me—"

"You'll what?" I asked, staring at him from the landing. "You'll make me the first to fall?" I took a step down and then another until I stood on the concrete, staring at him, breathing hard, his face reddening. "You know what you want to do? You want to lock the whole human race in a box of their own. Take away all their freedom and choices and power—"

He made this kind of squeaking noise of fury, and I had to steel myself to keep from stepping back. "You see this the way you've seen your life play out up until now." He sounded strangled, like he was barely hanging on. "Everything that's happened to you is coloring your perceptions of this future. It could be grand—and bright —"

"I've seen your future," I said. "There's nothing bright about it."

He cocked his head at me. "What are you talking about?" His eyes narrowed. "What do you know?" He looked at me, face straining, eyes trying to see into my soul. "He's blocking me. How the hell is he blocking me?"

"Dr. Zollers?" I asked. "You wouldn't know this, but he's been blocking you all along." I took another step forward. "He's been blocking you since I got back from your attempted abduction."

"Why?" Sovereign sounded furious, but just a hint of weakness had crept into his voice. "How would you know——"

He shot through the air without much in the way of warning, and he was upon me, inches away. His hand flew to my throat and jerked me from the ground, fingers clutching around my windpipe. He lifted me off the concrete, and I could feel my vision darken, the sensation of being choked, of having the blood to my brain stopped. "You know what?" he asked. "It doesn't matter anyway. Because I am not going to take this shit from you. Not from you. All my work, all my efforts, none of them mean a damned thing without you, and I will not lose you. Not this close to——"

Chapter 56

The darkness closed around the edges of my vision, and sensation disappeared. My head drifted to a place I had been only a few days earlier, a place full of life and sensation, a place as far from a dark and dingy basement as could possibly be imagined.

It was a forest.

The sounds of living woods were all around me. I could hear the chirp of birds, the thrum of insects. The smell of fresh greenery had been in the air. The lovely warmth of the sun shone down upon my pale skin, and I lifted my face to it where it streamed through the canopy above.

I'd come here in my mind when I'd been in the box, on the plane. And ever since, it had been a memory that played in my head over and over, always at the surface.

And it was the thing I could not let Sovereign see.

Yet.

"Hello, Sienna Nealon," came the voice of the girl standing across from me. "I have been waiting for this moment. I have been waiting here in the darkness.

"For you."

"Adelaide," I said and looked up into the sunlight. "It's a pretty nice darkness you have here."

"This is but a memory," she said, and I saw the faint echoes of the girl who had once been Adelaide change, shift like an illusion wavering in the summer heat. "You are still in the darkness of your captivity."

"I am," I said, knowing it was true. "The Wolfe brothers … they're going to—"

"Shhh," she said, and her finger was upon my lips. "They are nothing. A worry for another time. I can teach you to make them as irrelevant to you as they are to the world at large. But there is a greater consideration that you need to be made aware of."

"Sovereign," I said.

"Sovereign," she agreed and took a few steps back from me.

"You can teach me how to use my powers?" I asked. "Really? Truly?"

"I can teach you," she said, nodding with that sense of peace I'd always associated with her. "But first I must impart to you something else. Something of vital importance."

"All right," I said. "Hit me."

"I can feel your spirit flagging," she intoned. "I can feel your strength waning. You are the last one who is able to fight, Sienna. You are the last to be able to take up this challenge. Omega fed me full of souls so that I could be ready to accept the mantle." She lowered her head. "It was all against my will, of course. They made me a weapon and were to make me a bride sacrifice. I was told to follow whoever opened my tank, to become indebted and bonded to them. They meant to give me over to him if it came to it, and if he would not accept me, I was to fight and kill him."

I swallowed. "But you didn't."

"Because you freed me," she said, and she took my hands once more. "Because you saved me—"

"I led you to death," I said, and closed my eyes. "I got you killed."

"You let me see the sun once more," she said. "You let me make my choices. I was not a pet, but they made me one. They took away my will, subordinated it to their own, and kept me in captivity where I could do nothing but witness the world roll by around me." She turned her eyes to me. They found mine, and something like a fire roared inside them. "I know what comes," she whispered.

The forest faded around us, and was replaced by something else entirely. Something ... horrifying.

Black skies were clouded with a dense fog. The skeletons of buildings stretched around me in every direction. Girders and broken concrete were all that remained, like a tableau straight out of any post-apocalyptic CGI-fest you can imagine. It looked as though the whole world had been washed away by fire and destruction, and all that remained was ashes and bones of the civilization that had once been.

"What the hell is this?" I asked, staring at the horizon for any sign of life, of movement. There was no breeze and the air stunk of death and fire.

"This is the world as it will be if you fail," she said. "This is what will remain if Sovereign has his way." She stretched out a hand to encompass everything around us. "This is his legacy, what he will forge should you surrender."

"My God, this is ..." I looked at the nearest building, a structure where nothing remained but a half-foot wall with the occasional burnt wooden stud to mark what it had been. A massive maple had been turned utterly black in the yard beyond, and it took me a moment to realize what I was looking at. "This is my house."

"And so will be the rest of the world," Adelaide said, sounding like some sort of oracle. "I have seen it, and now I give it to you to be its keeper. Remember this moment each time you wish to give up. Remember in darkest night. I said to you once before that I would be waiting for you in the darkness. This is the darkness in which I have dwelled. This is the vision that Adelaide—not Andromeda—lived to pass along to you." She took my hands in hers, and they felt warm. "Andromeda was a broken creature of men." There was a subtle shift in her appearance, and I saw a faint hint of a mohawk replacing her long hair. "Adelaide fought to the last in hopes of finding a kindred soul to carry on with what she saw, with what she knew." The British accent came full-on, damned near Cockney to my ears.

"I won't forget," I said, taking it all in once more. "I can't … forget."

"*Remember*," she said, and it was a word that reverberated through my soul, soaking up all the sensation—the charred smell, the hot, dead air, the feeling of my flesh prickling—and filling the word with its essence. "Remember, and ready yourself for the moment when you will need it. He is the most base and deceitful of liars, and he thinks his world will be bright and glowing, not filled with ash and death borne of his fury and impatience and wrath."

"I don't think he'll believe it," I said. "But I'll … keep it to myself."

"Until the moment you need it," Adelaide said. "No man wants to know they've unmade the world while they're trying to build it anew in their own vision."

"I won't let him see it," I said. "I promise. And I will … remember." The word send a stir through me, a sickening, rushing feeling that this was on me, that there was no one standing between the world I saw and the one I'd left outside the box before Frederick and Grihm had shut the door on me. "I won't stop. Whatever it takes. I swear it."

"Then I have but one final thing to teach you, Sienna Nealon," Adelaide said, with a ghost of a smile. "One last thing to show you, and then you must go back into the darkness, then take your light out into the world that awaits …"

Chapter 57

Sovereign's hand was around my throat and I didn't care for it. I punched him in his, hard enough that he noticed it, then smacked his arm with enough strength to deaden the nerves for the second it took me to slip free. I landed and kicked him in the chest with a boot, flinging him into the concrete block wall, which shattered, sending dust into the basement air.

"Don't touch me," I said simply. I could feel the fury reverberate inside, though.

"Still don't know … how you knew," Sovereign grunted as he got back to his feet, dusting himself off. "No one knew but … Weissman and Claire and me … and I had her scooping out those memories whenever he had even a chance of running into a telepath without her …"

"I knew because a girl named Adelaide knew," I said.

"Who?" He shook his head, partly in rage, partly in disbelief, partly in sheer frustration and WTF.

"She was a succubus," I said, "who had a Cassandra-type shoved in her brain along with a ton of other metas so she could either be your bride or your worst enemy." I sneered at him. "Care to guess which she turned out to be?"

"Ohhh," he said, and the rage just pooled off of him. "You look so cocky, so smug, standing there. Like you have a chance. Like this isn't going to be the fight you can't win." He snorted. "You think you're done already."

"Going by the numbers, I'd say I'm about ninety-nine percent done." I cracked my knuckles. "One to go."

"Well, that last percentage point is gonna be murder," he said, and there was no trace of Joshua Harding in his features now. He was scorned, plain and simple, and his rage had taken over. "I'm going to—"

He came at me again, full on, and I kicked his ass right through the ceiling.

The floorboards shattered as he changed course radically upward. I lost track of his progress as splinters and shards of wood showered down on me and I was forced to duck to cover my eyes. When I looked up again, I could see the blue sky above.

I shot straight upward, using the power of Gavrikov's flight to take me after him.

I kept going past the point where I suspected he'd stalled and started scanning the horizon with my eyes. I didn't see him before I heard him coming, and he slammed into me around the midsection, howling his rage as he did so. He tried for a punch and I blocked it, but he kept coming for another one and I let him carry us with his momentum as I sped up into a frenzy of blocks to counter his maniacally fast strikes. He was untrained but operating on pure rage, while I was in a weaker position but relying on my training.

Without ground to use for leverage, I knew I'd have a harder time getting him off of me. So I kicked the gravity back on and let myself fall, his speed still shooting us forward in a graceful arc. It took him a second to realize what I'd done as I started to slip away from him. He tried to use his legs to anchor himself to me but failed, and as I slipped out of his reach I turned the flight power back on and did an abrupt in-air flip that culminated in a kick to his groin.

I heard the wind leave him in an "Oof!" and righted myself midair. He sailed on a little farther with the extra momentum my hit gave him. He started to come around slowly, and I shot at him, leading with a foot.

I caught him in the face and the impact smashed him into a two-story brick building. Right through the wall, pieces of brick falling down around him. It was almost like in the cartoons when someone leaves a silhouette going through a wall, except his was really more just a gaping hole.

He popped his head out a moment later, looking not quite fresh as a daisy, but close. There was still a rage in his eyes, but some caution had taken over. There was some blood, but I could tell he'd used Wolfe's father's power to heal up quickly. "Why?" he asked.

"Because the building was there and I figured if it didn't break open your thick skull it would at least make a decent backstop for your sorry ass." I smiled meanly at him and could tell he took no amusement in my joke. "Why what?"

"Why do you fight so hard for this?" He made a grandiose gesture with his arms, the wannabe dictator taking in the unworthy world around him. "Abuse, murder, violence, war, starvation—why would you fight so hard for a world that's been so cold to you? That has such things in it? That let these things happen to you?"

"Because I'm a shield," I said. "I'm *the* shield."

"You know what a shield is? It's a tool. You're a tool of other people!" he taunted me.

I just sat there, hovering, defensive, waiting for him to make his next move. "One of us is a tool, that's for sure."

I watched him clench his jaw, baring his teeth inadvertently as he did so. "I thought you were the one."

"And I knew all along that I could do better than a maniac who set out to destroy our entire species." I pointed at him. "Helpful hint—women actually do like nice guys. Or maybe a guy who's confident, and only slightly dickish—not someone who got rejected as a villain from a James Bond movie."

"We could have done something great together," he said.

"I would never have signed on to be your Eva Braun," I spat at him before I lunged forward and kicked him right back into the hole in the wall.

The building was set up as a studio office of some sort, and I saw as I kicked him that everyone had cleared out of the middle of the floor. Which was lucky, because there wasn't much chance I could have stopped before hitting him.

He blasted through furniture and out the other side of the building. I was after him in a flash, and just as he started to come down, I caught him and punched him in the face, sending him aloft again. I could see downtown ahead of us, looming a lot closer than I would have preferred. Beyond the damage I'd just done, this had the potential to get a lot worse for the city of Minneapolis.

I caught him on the low arc again and hit him with an uppercut that mustered everything I had. He shot up into the air, propelled by the strength of my attack, and I followed after him. He made a grunting sound as I caught him and yanked him forward into a punch, grabbed him by the front of his shirt and punched him again, caught him by the back of his neck before he got away and slammed my elbow into his nose.

He flipped through the air and righted himself, floating. I watched as his face went from deformed to normal in a matter of seconds. "Anything you can do, I can do better," he said, and it came out as a spiteful gloat.

"Try having a menstrual cycle," I said and launched myself into his chest with another boot. He tried to dodge but he was a little too slow. I caught him on the arm and heard it snap as he flipped away from the impact.

He stopped a short distance away, watching me with those heavily lidded eyes, breathing heavy. "I don't understand you."

"Clearly."

He started to ramble on, but I tuned him out. *Little Doll, this isn't working.*

Tell me something I don't know.

He beat me, Wolfe said. *He can beat you if you hold back and let him. If you play his game.*

He is fast, Bjorn said.

I'm as fast or faster.

He can heal from your every attack, Wolfe said.

I flung a blast of flame straight from the core of Gavrikov's power at him and he stopped monologuing long enough to throw up a hand and absorb it. "You can't beat me," he said, eyes flaring.

"Beat you? I just wanted to shut you up for a minute. Can't even hear myself think over your yammering—"

He came at me with a roar of anger and I rolled at the last second. I got the feeling he wasn't used to dealing with someone who operated at his speed and, like anyone who's been sitting at the top of the food chain for too long, it had made him weak. He grazed my jaw and I laid into his. The impact of the traded blows threw us a good thirty feet apart, staring at each other across open sky, the city of Minneapolis's skyline hanging behind him in the distance.

"You can't stop me," he said. "You know why I was trying to lock you up in the stasis chamber?" He sounded tired, almost defeated. "Because I was going to use my Ares power to destroy every army in the world."

"But you didn't," I shot back at him. "And you can't just crate me up like a dog because you want a servile bride—"

"I wasn't doing it because of that," he said. His weariness made way for a slow smile. "Do you know why we were killing the metas first?" I waited, waited for this maniac to just spit it out already. He was drunk on the sound of his own voice, clearly. "Because the power of an Ares doesn't work unless you're carrying an instrument of war—and most metas don't." His smile made way for a grin. "Tell me, Sienna … are you carrying a gun?"

I felt something take over my body, something run through my mind like I'd lost control over all my muscles.

Whatever Zollers had done to block him from entering my mind was completely useless against this power. My hand went to my hip and drew my pistol. I felt it rise in my own grip, my arm unable to stop moving, to fight against it, to do anything—

The barrel of the pistol pushed tight against my skull, and I knew not even the power of Wolfe would be able to stop the bullet from sending my brains out the other side of my head. With a last breath, I just held on against my will and felt my finger start to pull the trigger.

Chapter 58

Nyet! Gavrikov's voice rang in my ear, and suddenly the air grew hot around me. I felt something in my hand burn, dimly, like the first hints of a sunburn on a clear day.

"No!" Sovereign yelled, and my head started to clear. I looked toward the pistol and saw the weapon melting to slag before my eyes. My hand was on fire and I tossed the remains of the weapon clear. It fell down, down below me toward a pond in a park.

I lunged at him and he was a hair too slow to react, his eyes still following the downward path of the gun I'd just tossed. I bloodied his lip with the first punch, opened it with the second, smashed his teeth out with the third—

He threw me off with a counterpunch that rocked my head back and sent me flying. My t-shirt was partially burned through on the right shoulder and I heard it tear as I twisted from the hit. I managed to come around and ready myself for a counterblow, but he was just standing off from me again.

"It shouldn't have been like this," he said, almost like he was talking to himself. The frustration was rising with every syllable. "I've waited ... for thousands of years for you. I planned everything ... *everything!*" he screamed.

"I've been manipulated by the best," I said. "Compared to Winter and Omega, you're an amateur. Probably that whole 'apart from mankind' thing. It's hard to get good at pulling peoples' strings when you're not around people—"

"You're just sitting there mocking me," he said, and turned hateful eyes toward me. No gentleness, no puppy dog, no googly, not even stalker eyes. This was just raw fury, the breath of hell.

I'd seen worse.

"You open yourself up to it," I said. "Or to coin a popular phrase ... 'you were asking for it.'" I let that sizzle on him for a minute.

He screamed and came at me again, bull on a charge. This time I didn't bother to veer off, I came right back at him. I hit him so hard I heard his jaw break, teeth crack, nose shatter, face smash—he flew at the earth and cratered it like he'd dug his own grave.

And a few seconds later, he rose right back out, face rearranged and back to normal.

"Son of a bitch," I breathed.

Not working, Little Doll.

"That's a real talent for news flashes you've got there, Wolfe. You could have a wonderful career in broadcast journalism."

"I'm not going to stop," Sovereign said, coming back toward me slowly. His eyes were glowing with malice. "I'm gonna break you, little girl, break your will, and then I'm going to fix this world—"

"First of all, it's not your world to fix," I said. "Again, with the living apart from humanity, you lose the right to make changes in people when you don't like what they're doing. Second, you said it yourself—my mother used to lock me in a metal casket until ... do you know when she'd let me out?" I waited to see if he'd answer, but he just hung there, all malevolence and anger. "Until my will to resist her broke. Except it never did," I spat at him. "Not really, anyway. I just learned to do and say whatever it took to get out." I glared down at him, resolute. "So if you think you can break me, good luck, jackass. Because I stayed behind to beat you when I could have run. I'm here to knock your ass flat, and I walked into that room knowing that was my task at hand. Whatever it takes, no matter what. That's my motto."

"You could live for thousands of years," he said in a low rumble laced with fury. "As near to forever as your nineteen year-old mind can imagine. In a perfect world, free from all the sins of humanity that plague us."

"I'd rather die right now than listen to you go on and on and on—" I said, shaking my head and rolling my eyes at him. "God, do you even listen to yourself? You've gone round the bend, dumbass. You're so drunk on your own damned glory you probably can't hear how crazy you sound."

"It's not crazy if I can make it happen," he said in a low grunt. "It's not crazy when we have the power to do it."

"And all for the low, low price of annihilating the whole world," I said. "Zollers, you can stop now." I looked down at Sovereign. "Take a glimpse into my mind. See what Adelaide showed me. It's your future, if you live and get your way. Take a look at your perfect world—"

He shook his head, left to right, so rapidly that I thought he'd been afflicted with some sort of nerve malady at first. "You're a liar. She's a liar. You're trying to trick me, you deceitful—" He shuddered, full body.

"Don't go all Gollum on me," I said. "You really do it. You bring about the end of the world if you keep trying to go down this road." I figured by this point he was beyond reason, but since I was skeptical that just beating his ass was going to produce the desired result, I gave it a try anyway.

"SHE'S A DECEIVER." His voice had changed, grown fuller, like someone had taken over behind the eyes. He looked a little wild, too, and I got the feeling not for the first time that Sovereign was a man whose engine had thrown a piston a long time ago. Or whatever it means in car talk when someone loses their shit. Breaks a belt? Something like that.

He threw a bolt of lightning at me and I barely dodged it. I tossed a blast of fire back at him as large as a boulder and he stopped tossing lightning long enough to absorb it and throw it back. I caught it and pulled it in with one palm, dragging it behind me as I drank it back in. Lightning lanced after me again, and I sped away at full tilt, remembering Janus's cautionary tale about how his parents had been immolated by Zeus's lightning.

This running away thing was not going to work, either, and I knew it.

Lost his mind, he has, Wolfe said.

"Keen observation, Yoda," I said. Downtown loomed in front of me, and I tried to think about what I could do. I shot upward, not stopping for a thousand feet or more. The city shrank beneath me, but I could still see him back there.

I paused in flight and held fast. Sovereign thundered at me, flying full force.

I waited until he closed and pulled Bjorn to the front of my mind. I hit him with the War Mind, and it looked like he'd had to shrug off a punch to the face. That lasted about a second, and then he had to contend with an actual punch to the face from me. His right hand glowed blue and I knocked it aside with my left, which was covered in flame. I wondered if he could channel two powers down the same arm and a moment later my question was answered as he absorbed the fire and then shot electricity into the sky above.

"Did you know a slow-bled pig produces the most succulent meat?" His voice gave him away as full-on crazycakes, just in case the words themselves hadn't gotten it across.

"That's good to know," I said. "But there's not going to be anything slow about how I bleed you, pig." I kicked him in the chest, once, our grips with each other anchoring him to me. He took it with a grunt of fury, and I kicked him again. His sternum and ribs broke and he screamed in pain and rage. "You've been talking all along like I'm some kind of object that's yours for the taking." I kicked him again, faster than he could heal, and he really did squeal like a pig. "Like I'm a puppet that you can control. Like I'm something that's *yours*." I reeled him in close as he continued to make that pitiful noise. "This should go without saying, but you're crazy as hell, so let me make this clear—I'm a person." I punched him in the jaw. "I make my own decisions." I smashed him in the side of the head. "I do what I want." I twisted his arm behind his back and broke it as I faced him away from me, pushing hard to dislodge it through his skin. "And I am not beholden to you or anyone else."

With that, I kicked him in the back and heard it break. He plummeted toward the earth, screaming as he fell. I sighed and watched him drop, breathing heavily as he went.

Of course he stopped himself a few hundred feet down and healed, and I wondered exactly how much damage I was going to have to do to him to kill him.

He came back at me again, because apparently that wasn't enough. I just watched him get closer.

He will keep coming, Wolfe said.

He will not stop, Bjorn said.

He is unmerciful, Gavrikov said.

He is unstoppable, Bastian said.

"So am I," I said.

"You can't beat me," Sovereign crowed as he came back up. He looked like hell, true, but he was alive. "You've tried. You've tried again. It ain't happening." He sounded like he was off the edge a little. Maybe he'd gotten a grip on his sanity, if such a thing existed.

"You're an idiot," I said.

He laughed, further driving home that certainty that he was cuckoo crazypants. "You can't beat me, I told you. I am unbeatable."

"Are you sure? Because I've beaten you quite a bit."

"Aren't you tired of it?" He shook his head. "Tired of fighting? We're made for each other."

"You abso–frigging–moronic knucklehead," I said. "I'm made for my own damned self, not for you."

"Just give in," he said, opening his arms. He was still laughing, crazily, but laughing. "You can't win."

"Gavrikov just called you unmerciful," I said.

"He knows me," Sovereign said with a smile, voice as smooth as poured honey. "You can't. You won't."

I just rolled my eyes. "All my life I've been told I can't. Had walls put up. Doors closed. Funny thing about that is that after you've gone through a few head on, you start ignoring them."

"You can't ignore me," he said.

"I can't stop you either, sadly," I said, and shook my head.

"Glad you finally realized it." He was smirking now, basking in his impending victory, probably.

Then I pulled the rug out from under him. "You don't understand. See ... a hero would just stop you. I'm going to have to kill you."

He rolled his eyes right back. "You can't do that, either."

"I told you I would, no matter what," I said. "That willingness is the gift my mother gave me. You haven't seen the 'no matter what' part yet. But you're about to."

Now he had that faint crackle of amusement. "This should be good. Bluster is always worth a laugh. Though I'd thought you were finally caving to reason."

"You left reason behind a long time ago," I said.

"You. Are. Outmatched," he said. "Just give up and surrender to reality. It's going to happen. You can't beat me. You can't kill me. You can't—"

"There go those words again," I said, and I knew my expression was darkening. It was a little colder up here in the air. I felt a revulsion fill my stomach at the realization of what I was going to have to do. "All my choices, light and dark, have led me to this moment."

He stared back at me. "Now who's monologuing?"

"I'm sick of you," I said, and the righteous anger was really getting rolling now. "Sick of your smug face, sick of your psychological games, sick of your bullshit inevitability gimmick, trying to beat me down and make me think I'm defeated without ever finishing the job." I could feel the air humming around me as it seemed to crackle with electricity. I didn't care. "This is a fight, and you haven't won yet. This is a fight, and I'm not your girl. This is a fight, and you are my damned enemy, and I will KILL. YOU."

"We're the same!" He called out to me. "This is pointless! Don't make me kill you for no reason—"

I pulled out the last stops and summoned Bastion, Wolfe, Gavrikov and Bjorn front and center.

I hit him with the War Mind again and he blanched like I'd smacked him with a metal girder, hanging there like a big sack of meat dangling in midair.

Use me as well, came Eve Kappler's soft voice.

I summoned her forth and blasted him with a net of light that wrapped him up like the pig he was. He looked shocked as it curled around him, pinning his arms to his sides. I could feel the invulnerability of Wolfe and his speed coupled with Gavrikov's flight as I slammed into Sovereign. I hit him again and again, crying out with inarticulate rage as I broke every bone I could find.

"WE ARE … NOTHING … ALIKE!" I screamed into the wind.

"We … are …" he said through bloodied lips. "And you'll realize that … given time …"

"Your time just ran out." I could feel the change in my body as I drew forth the power of Roberto Bastian. I could feel his embarrassment at the ability he so rarely used, but I had no similar reticence holding me back. My clothes ripped and tore as I drew forth the power of the Quetzlcoatl-type, my arms turning into wings and my legs flattening and smoothing out. I could see scales on the parts of my body that grew beneath me, and I elongated like a snake until I was the size of a four-story building.

Sovereign hung there, staring at me, still bound in the net of light, his mouth agape.

And then I burst into flames.

"Wait," he said as I hovered over him, a dragon on fire with rage and power. "You can't—I'm the last—if not with me then you'll never —" He took a breath and sounded calm. "You'll never be able to touch him."

"This is as close as I'd ever let you get to touching me," I said, in a voice I didn't even recognize. "You picked the wrong fucking girl, jackass."

I went at him full out and he didn't even have a chance to move. My jaws were around him in an instant, ripping and shredding him faster than he could heal himself. Pieces dropped out of my mouth, and it felt horrifyingly natural, this deep, predatory need to destroy. I could hear him screaming, but whether it was from the grinding of his bones or the fire burning around my jaw, I did not know.

I spat him out a little piece at a time, in small enough segments that I knew Humpty Dumpty wouldn't ever get put back together again. I moved as I did so, and the last bit came out as I drew closer to the ground.

I blinked as I caught sight of a house below that looked different from the others. There was a mammoth, gaping hole in its roof, and I knew it immediately.

Home.

I felt the power flee my limbs and my body shifted back to its normal shape. I was still wreathed in flames, and the power of flight stayed with me as Eve, Bastian and Bjorn withdrew to the back of my mind.

My body was filled with fatigue, my limbs aching, my mind taxed. I dipped as I came down, intent on the house with the hole in the roof. My vision grew cloudy, and I knew I was seconds from passing out.

Well done, Sienna, Wolfe said. *You did very well.*

Marvelous, Gavrikov said.

Not bad, Eve conceded.

Tactically impressive, Bastian said.

You did the impossible, Bjorn added.

I hit the grass and rolled, the flames snuffed upon impact. My naked body fell back, staring up into the blue sky, and the sun shone down upon me.

You're safe now, Zack said. *I'm proud of you.*

"I'm proud of me, too," I murmured and caught a glimpse of the house somewhere off to the side. I realized I could just barely see the window I used to peer out of to look at this very spot. "Thanks, Mom," I muttered.

And then I passed out.

Chapter 59

When I woke up, I was outside my house, in the backyard, and the sun was shining down on me. And after a moment, I realized I was naked.

I rolled to my feet and hurried to the back door, breaking the lock and slipping inside before anyone could see me through the cracks in the fence. There was a giant, gaping hole in the middle of the living room floor and it had that whole deconstructed scent that I'd become so familiar with at the Agency. I frowned as I looked up through the hole in the roof at the same sky I had seen from the backyard. Then I sighed and went into my room, put on some clothes, and sat on my bed for about thirty seconds before I heard tires squealing outside.

I scrambled for a weapon, but I'd lost my last spare when Gavrikov had saved my life by burning it out of my hands. My eyes searched my bedroom and fell on a pair of eskrima sticks by the door. I grabbed them. Not that I necessarily needed them to beat the living shit out of someone, as I'd just proven, but it never hurt to have a weapon at your disposal.

Unless you were fighting an Ares, I guess.

The front door opened with a thump, and I heard heavy footfalls just inside the threshold. I paused next to the doorframe and held my breath, listening for what came next.

"Sienna!" Reed shouted, and I let out a breath.

"Are you here?" Scott called.

"Holy hell, it looks like she was here," Reed said. "Look at that hole in the … well, ceiling and floor. That's gonna cost a few bucks to remodel."

I took a breath and let it out then slid out into the open door. I stared across the sunlit living room at the two of them, and saw the relief flood their faces.

"Sienna," Scott said. "You're safe."

Reed elbowed him. "Start with, 'you're alive' and work down next time."

"Is she here?" Kat's voice came from behind them, and I saw her blond head peek out from behind Scott. "Oh, good," she said with a sigh of relief.

"Kat?" I stared at her. "I would have expected these two, but you?"

"We're all here," she said, like it was the most natural thing in the world. "We saw you on the news and came running."

"The … news?" I felt a little chill.

Reed broke into a smile first, folding his arms. "The president went on and made a speech. It was … pretty effective," he said, like he was conceding something painful.

"He talked about you being the head of the response team battling against this threat to national security," Scott said, with a slight smile of his own. "Named you as head of the agency. Midway through, he gets interrupted with footage from local stations showing your battle over Minneapolis—"

"And they tagged you right away," Reed broke in, grinning. "'Sienna Nealon fights Sovereign,' like it was a friggin' newsreel out of a comic, complete with supervillain."

I felt the eskrima sticks I'd forgotten I was holding fall right out of my hands. "You … you saw that?"

"Pretty much all of it, Dragon Lady," Reed said with that same grin. I saw Scott wince a little. "Though we only heard about that part from Ariadne. We were kind of busy rushing to try and get to wherever you were to offer our limited brand of support." His face darkened. "Then we heard you fell out of the sky …"

"That was a pretty dramatic moment, even on the radio," Scott said. His face looked a little closer to sick. "Glad you're all right."

I shook my head. "I'm fine. Sovereign isn't. We're all good here."

"Better than good, actually." Reed was smiling from ear to ear. "You're like … famous. Your fight with Sovereign got broadcast on every channel, and just after the president of the United States told everyone that *you* were the official U.S. Government response. You're golden, sister of mine. Absolutely golden."

I felt my eyes shift left and right as I weighed what he just said. "Because if he just built me up in front of the world—"

"He can't tear you down and make you the villain now," Scott said with a nod. "And—"

There was a sound of screeching tires outside and a horn honking before car doors started slamming. I could hear chatter, then Reed's phone went off and he answered it. "Yeah? Got it. We'll move." He clicked it off and looked straight at me. "That was Ariadne. We gotta get back."

"Back?" I felt dazed, like I'd woken from some perverse dream where the world had flipped upside down.

"Back to the Agency," Reed said, still smiling. "The press are here, and we're supposed to control your exposure. Or at least that's the official order from both the Executive Branch and Senator Foreman. There's going to be a press briefing at some point soon, and they don't want you talking before they have a chance to control the spin." He kind of rolled his eyes. "Or something like that. Politics, you know."

"No," I said, shaking my head. "I really don't."

"Come on, Sienna," Kat said, urging me across the room. "The press is here. They're congregating. If we don't leave now, we're going to have a hell of a time getting away."

"Okay," I said, and like I was still living in that dream of an upside-down world, I threaded my way around the giant hole in my living room floor to make my way toward the door.

"You look good," Scott said, smiling at me as I reached him.

"Thanks," I said, and smiled back. "I feel good."

Reed thumped him on the shoulder. "Lead with that next time, actually." He touched me on the shoulder, too. "Let's go."

I followed them out, the three of them acting as my bodyguards. There were cameras already on the lawn, reporters with microphones, and I heard the shutters snap as I walked out the door. Blinding flashes went off even though it was midday, and a flurry of questions hit me as I made my way down the path.

"Miss Nealon—"

"Sienna—!"

"Could you—"

"How does it feel—"

"What were you thinking when—"

It all blurred together in one loud jumble of noise, and my three protectors gently pushed through for me. I followed them numbly, probably looking around into the spotlights flashing at me, stunned. We reached the curb and I realized that among the news vans and reporters' cars, there were two black town cars waiting.

Kurt Hannegan was waiting at one of them for me, door held open. A reporter got too close and he made a menacing move that drove them back a step. "Right this way, Miss Nealon," he said.

"Thank you, Kurt," I said, blinking at him in surprise. I glanced back at the house, remembering when he'd last been here and remembered the feelings associated with it. I looked up at the blue sky, so different from the grey days of the past, and slid into the back seat.

"Miss Nealon!" came the voice of one of the reporters over all the others. "How does it feel to be a hero?"

Kurt slammed the door of the car before I could even answer. Reed walked around and got in the front, and Scott slid in next to me. Hannegan slipped into the driver's seat, and I turned my head to see Janus in the car behind me, sitting next to Zollers. I nodded silent thanks to Dr. Zollers. He nodded back with a graceful smile, and I could hear his words in my head.

You're welcome.

"So," Scott said, and he smiled at me from where he sat in the seat next to me. "Miss Nealon, how *does* it feel to be a hero?"

I looked up at Reed and saw a great big grin on his face as he stared straight ahead. The reporters were clearing the way, a little at a time, and Kurt was easing the car forward. I couldn't be sure, but I caught sight of the big man's eyes in the mirror and even he looked a little happy.

I looked at Scott and I smiled, and it felt ... right. For the first time in a while. Not a faux smile, not a mean one, just a real, genuine smile born of some happiness I had springing up deep inside like the sun beams poking out from behind dark clouds.

"It feels ... good," I said and meant it, every word. I looked down, and I could still feel them all there. I spared one last look for the house where I'd been raised, the house that had sheltered me for all the years of my childhood, a place of such acute pain and loneliness that had prepared me for everything I'd just faced. "It feels good."

And I could hear my own voice in my head as we drove away:

It feels like I'm not alone.

Epilogue

They were sitting around the TV, just watching it all unfold. It was a helluva thing to see, just crazy as all get out. Flaming dragons, girls falling from the sky, and the president—the damned president!—talking about metahumans and extinctions and all manner of such that one couldn't have imagined seeing on the TV news just a day earlier.

There was a smell of the last of dinner still simmering on the stove. It was probably long past burnt now because they were anchored to the couch, all three of them, and Momma wasn't doing anything to get them moving. She was feeling a little too riveted to what was going on herself to make 'em move toward supper.

"What do you think?" It was the boy that asked, just taking it all in. He was a clever one, like his daddy. Always calculating some angle or another.

"He said something about her once, didn't he?" The girl was asking now, pointing at the TV screen. The little bar with the name said, "Sienna Nealon," and it was under a video of a dark-haired lady walking out of a house flanked by two men and a skinny little blond-haired stick of a girl.

"I b'lieve he did," Momma weighed in at last. "Mentioned her by name." She kept staring at the TV screen. "Seems a mite peculiar, don't it?"

The boy pondered it, and Momma waited for him to think it through. "You think she's the one?"

Momma gave him a nod, a vigorous one, trying to leave him without a doubt. "If she is, I reckon we better find out."

"Then what?" This from the girl. She had them beady eyes, just staring with pools of black.

Momma gave her the look, the one that almost made her flinch back without a word. "Then we kill her." Like it was the most natural thing in the world.

London, England

He wasn't the sort who was usually glued to the telly, but in this case he gladly made an exception. He had his teacup close by with his window shades still open to the dark night, the sounds of London echoing in around him through the panes of glass. He scarcely paid them any notice, though, riveted as he was by what was transpiring on his screen.

They had been outed, of course. Gloriously outed, yet outed nonetheless. The grand secret, one preserved and kept since Poseidon's decree some two thousand years earlier, was now as obvious as the Emperor's utter lack of clothes.

His tea had gone cold long ago. This information was something quite interesting, something that could change the very shape of the world in which he lived and operated.

For the dozenth time since this drama had caught his attention, he picked up his teacup and saucer, recalled they were cold, had a passing thought about brewing another, and then set them down again untouched. For now there was a girl upon the screen.

The girl.

He studied her pale face and rounded features as she was escorted out of a house by three bodyguards. It was an impressive spectacle, really, to see her protected by these three as though she hadn't just turned into a flaming dragon and shredded a man in her jaws.

His hand fell to his chin and he stroked it, the natural posture of consideration for him. Yes, this had possibilities. Many, many possibilities. Now all he had to do was find the appropriate course of action to take advantage of them ...

Florence, Italy

The two men sat out on the overlook, not noticing the view. It was a villa, one of the finest in Firenze—Florence to foreigners—and the entire town was lit up below them.

Instead they were utterly focused on the television in front of them, tuned to American news via the satellite dish on the side of the house.

"Capo," the junior one said, breaking his silence. "This changes things. Their eyes are opened."

The older one stared at the screen, thinking it over. The young man next to him was no fool, but he was young. "It means nothing," he said after a moment, "save that they should fear us more now that they know what our kind can do."

Edinburgh, Scotland

Alistair McKinney was dying, and he knew it, and he damned well hated it. But what could he do?

He was lying flat on his back, feeling the life running out of him in the last. It came and went in bits and bytes, like he was copying a file, except his bits and bytes were his life, and they were running out.

There was someone with him who seemed to be having a much grander time of it than Alistair was. He could hear the voice, faintly, as he lay there, just lay there, unable to move, unable to think. There was a fly buzzing around him, like it could tell he was nearly dead and unable to fend it off.

"… the American president announced …"

Alistair's ears heard a little of that as he tried to move. The TV was on, wasn't it? God, it seemed so far away.

"… named Sienna Nealon managed the agency response to the crisis …"

He felt the abrupt pain again, this time so searing he knew it was the end, but he couldnae find it in himself to scream. Instead, he heard something that sounded to his ears like a cross between a whistle and a choke, and it stayed with him until the pain faded and left him with almost nothing.

Except a view of the figure who had killed him, watching, unable to look away from the TV, even as Alistair died.

Location Unknown

The flare of the television in the dark fell on the face of the watcher. He stared at it in the blackness, watched it flicker as it told its story in silence. He needed no sound, no words, to know what it said. He saw the girl—the woman—with her dark hair and pale skin, and he knew her face. All too well, he knew her face.

The watcher had waited in the dark for some time and would wait here for a while longer. He was tasked with a duty to keep his charge, and to make sure they were kept safe. His eyes slid to the corner of the room, to that which he watched over, and he felt the assurance of a job done.

His eyes fell back to the television, to the flickering, to the girl. Sienna Nealon. He knew her.

He knew her all too well.

She was the reason he was here, in the dark.

And when the day came that he left it for the last time, she would die just as surely as the sun lit the sky.

Sienna Nealon will return in

LIMITLESS
Out of the Box
Book One

Coming November 4th, 2014!

A Final Note From the Author

('Final' for like five minutes, anyway, until Out of the Box starts.)

First off, if you want to know when future books become available, take sixty seconds and sign up for my NEW RELEASE EMAIL ALERTS by CLICKING HERE. Don't let the caps lock scare you; I don't sell your information and I only send out emails when I have a new book out. The reason you should sign up for this is because while I have actually set a release date for Out of the Box #1, it is not something I usually do, and even if you're following me on Facebook (robertJcrane (Author)) or Twitter (@robertJcrane), it's easy to miss my book announcements because…well, because social media is an imprecise thing.

Now that the PSA is out of the way…

Well, that was a hell of a thing.

Alone: The Girl in the Box, Book 1 was released on April 11, 2012 and here we are, approximately two years and four months later, and it's done. Ten books in less than two and a half years. (Plus I released another six books in other series during that time, and some of them were REALLY long…hey, what's that tooting sound? My own horn? Oh. I'll stop, then.) Girl in the Box was always meant to be an origin story, the tale of a girl who's stunted emotionally by the things her mother has done to her in the name of protecting her, about her journey out into the world to become an isolated and yet self-sacrificing protector of society. I wanted to show her grow up, suffer betrayals and grow stronger than she would ever have imagined possible.

Also, I wanted cool fight scenes. Because really, cool fight scenes make the world go 'round.

Sienna has become part of my world, and I have had an absolute blast telling her origin story. I've laughed with her, cried with her, and I hope you have, too. I dedicated this book to the fans because without you showing your support by buying the books, this series would have died uncompleted, like so many other authors' series' have.

So, thank you. I appreciate you more than you know. Especially if you've stuck with Sienna from the beginning until now.

That said, this is an *origin* story. That means it's just the beginning. The problem with having as much fun as I have with Sienna is that ideas just keep coming to me...I'm now up to twenty five books plotted for Out of the Box. (If that sounds intimidating to you, imagine how intimidating it is for me! I have to write all those damned things...) Out of the Box will follow a much less rigorous story structure than Girl in the Box, with story arcs lasting only about three books at a time at most. Well...mostly. Of course there's a larger, overarching story I'll get to, but it's much subtler than this time around. Still, it's there, and I can almost guarantee Sienna fans will find plenty of things to enjoy about the new series.

So here's my promise to you – as long as I'm having fun with this world and these characters, I'll keep writing them. It's probably a good sign that I honestly had the most fun I've ever had with a Sienna book while I was writing book 10, isn't it?

Come join the Girl in the Box discussion on my website: http://www.robertjcrane.com !

Cheers,
Robert J. Crane

Acknowledgments

Once upon a time, I was deep in the telling of a fantasy story about a warrior and a paladin. It was a very different sort of story than the one you've just read, and although I thoroughly enjoyed the telling of it, I was worried that it would not have the broad-based appeal to allow me to make a living as an author.

In a really long conversation with my friend Kari Phillips, I told her my idea for another series I'd tentatively sketched out about a girl confined to her home, mysteriously trapped by her mother until the day mom doesn't come home and she wakes up to find two men in her house. "You should write that," she told me. "I think that would do well."

And so it has.

Thanks to Kari for helping Sienna get out of the box.

There were others, of course, almost too many to count. Robin McDermott, Julia Corrigan, Erin Kane, Damarra Atkins, Calvin Sams, Paul Madsen, Kea Grace – all these people reviewed preliminary manuscripts at some point in the series and provided guidance to either help me feel like I didn't suck or helped me fix genuine errors in the books. They were fixers and reassurers, people who helped keep the car on the road, and I appreciate every one of them for it.

Thanks especially to Jo Evans, Jessica Kelishes and Nicolette Solomita, who each worked on this particular book to help it be the best it could be.

In April 2013, I traveled to London, England to write Enemies (Book #7). While I was there, I tried to coordinate a meet-up at a local pub, figuring it would be a good chance to chat with fans on a one-on-one basis. There seemed to be serious interest, and I was excited to be able to interact with some people who enjoyed my work.

I sat in the bar by myself until half an hour after the start time, feeling like a complete and utter arse. I selling very well at the time, and according to Facebook, London was my biggest city for social media traffic. And yet, there I was, Guinness in hand, face red with embarrassment, by myself in a pub in a lonely city.

Thankfully, Carien Keevey walked in and completely saved the day (and my fragile ego). It was a very lovely evening, and I owe her my thanks for that in addition to joining the proofreading team to help make the books better.

Annie Sullivan gave Sienna a voice for the audiobooks, worked tirelessly to give her heart and emotion, and deserves all the credit for how wonderful they turned out.

Karri Klawiter has provided the covers for every single Girl in the Box book except for #1, and done a stunningly magnificent job every time. Kudos to her for making the books look très magnifique (or however you say it in French).

Sarah Barbour has been the tireless editor for the vast majority of the Girl in the Box, and she's done fantabulous at it, going so far as to research everything from Roman town names to the proper spelling of Black Hawk helicopters. Where the Chicago Manual of Style fails, Sarah doesn't, always coming up with an answer for everything.

When I was first starting out as an indie author, I had so much help from Nicholas Ambrose that I can't even enumerate it all. He edited the early volumes, formatted them, and designed the cover for book #1. In short, as I said in the dedication to book #9, he made being an indie author seem so very, very easy until I was in far too deep to even think about bailing out.

Finally, my thanks to three ladies who helped get this show on the road. Heather Rodefer, Debra Wesley and Shannon Campbell were my first readers back when the series first started, and you could not find a more enthusiastic group of cheerleaders than the three of them. This series would not exist without them helping me so very, very much in the early stages.

My wife. My kids. My parents. These are the people who make it possible, and who I do this for. Gracias.

About the Author

Robert J. Crane is kind of an a-hole. What, you don't remember how he killed Zack? ZOMG NEVER FORGET!11!!!!1

Website: http://www.robertjcrane.com
Facebook Page: robertJcrane (Author)
Twitter: @robertJcrane
Email: cyrusdavidon@gmail.com

Other Works by Robert J. Crane

The Sanctuary Series
Epic Fantasy

Defender: The Sanctuary Series, Volume One
Avenger: The Sanctuary Series, Volume Two
Champion: The Sanctuary Series, Volume Three
Crusader: The Sanctuary Series, Volume Four
Sanctuary Tales, Volume One - A Short Story Collection
Thy Father's Shadow: The Sanctuary Series, Volume 4.5
Master: The Sanctuary Series, Volume Five* (Coming Fall
    2014!)

The Girl in the Box
and
Out of the Box
Contemporary Urban Fantasy

Alone: The Girl in the Box, Book 1
Untouched: The Girl in the Box, Book 2
Soulless: The Girl in the Box, Book 3
Family: The Girl in the Box, Book 4
Omega: The Girl in the Box, Book 5
Broken: The Girl in the Box, Book 6
Enemies: The Girl in the Box, Book 7
Legacy: The Girl in the Box, Book 8
Destiny: The Girl in the Box, Book 9
Power: The Girl in the Box, Book 10

Limitless: Out of the Box, Book 1* (Coming November 4th, 2014!)

In the Wind: Out of the Box, Book 2* (Coming Late 2014!)

Ruthless: Out of the Box, Book 3* (Coming Early 2015!)

Southern Watch
Contemporary Urban Fantasy

Called: Southern Watch, Book 1

Depths: Southern Watch, Book 2

Corrupted: Southern Watch, Book 3* (Coming Fall 2014!)

Unearthed: Southern Watch, Book 4* (Coming Late 2014/Early 2015!)

*Forthcoming

Made in the USA
Coppell, TX
23 March 2020